W9-AAX-645

THE FIRST GARDENER

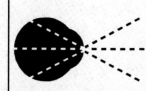

This Large Print Book carries the
Seal of Approval of N.A.V.H.

DISCARD

THE FIRST GARDENER

DENISE HILDRETH JONES

THORNDIKE PRESS
A part of Gale, Cengage Learning

Mason County District Library
217 E. Ludington Ave.
P.O. Box 549
Ludington, MI 49431
231-843-8465

GALE
CENGAGE Learning·

Detroit • New York • San Francisco • New Haven, Conn • Waterville, Maine • London

GALE
CENGAGE Learning®

Copyright © 2011 by Denise Hildreth Jones.
Thorndike Press, a part of Gale, Cengage Learning.

ALL RIGHTS RESERVED
This novel is a work of fiction. Names, characters, places, and incidents either are the product of the author's imagination or are used fictitiously. Any resemblance to actual events, locales, organizations, or persons, living or dead, is entirely coincidental and beyond the intent of either the author or the publisher.
Thorndike Press® Large Print Christian Fiction.
The text of this Large Print edition is unabridged.
Other aspects of the book may vary from the original edition.
Set in 16 pt. Plantin.

LIBRARY OF CONGRESS CATALOGING-IN-PUBLICATION DATA

Jones, Denise Hildreth, 1969–
   The first gardener / by Denise Hildreth Jones.
     p. cm. — (Thorndike Press large print Christian fiction)
   ISBN-13: 978-1-4104-4373-1 (hardcover)
   ISBN-10: 1-4104-4373-6 (hardcover)
   1. Governors' spouses—Fiction. 2. Children—Death—Fiction. 3. Grief—Fiction. 4. Nashville (Tenn.)—Fiction. 5. Large type books. I. Title.
PS3610.O6243F57 2012
813'.6—dc23   2011036264

Published in 2012 by arrangement with Tyndale House Publishers, Inc.

Printed in Mexico
1 2 3 4 5 6 7 16 15 14 13 12

*To those who have ever needed
a friend to walk through life's
tough places with them . . .
and to the friends who have.*

A NOTE FROM THE AUTHOR

As a citizen of Franklin, Tennessee, I'm aware that the current occupant of the governor's mansion in Nashville is not named Gray London. I've borrowed his house and some of the many challenges faced by him and his predecessors and adapted them for the sake of my story. However, much of what you read here about the Nashville area and the governor's mansion is absolutely true — the charm of downtown Franklin, the beautiful (and environmentally sensitive) renovations completed during Governor Phil Bredesen's administration, the controversy over Conservation Hall, and Minnie Pearl's former residence next door to the governor. Sadly, the devastating flood of 2010 was also a reality — but so was the amazing neighbor-helping-neighbor spirit that emerged in its aftermath. That spirit of service was part of the inspiration for this book. I may have messed with the mansion a bit for the sake of my story, but I have never been prouder to be a part of the Volunteer State.

Jeremiah

The sides a my bologna gone and curled up in that cast-iron skillet when a pop a grease splattered out. Landed smack-dab on the mornin' paper I done set on the counter.

Didn't much care to look at that paper anyhow. It been totin' nothin' but hurt all week — and we all 'bout had our fill a hurtin' 'round here. I think I cried me more tears them past seven days than I cried since my Shirley died summer 'fore last. And Shirley and me, we was married fifty-seven years.

Miz Mackenzie done cried with me back then.

Now it be my turn to cry with her.

I seen her picture on the front a that paper, tryin' to hide herself behind a big ol' black hat. But can't hide that kind a pain. Photographer gone and caught her with her Kleenex held up against her li'l nose. Ever'one else leanin' in close like she gon' fall over any minute. And that chil' lookin' up at her with an eyeful a questions. 'Bout near break my heart, I'm tellin' you.

They let me stay back yesterday 'til the last limo pulled away. Two young'uns come up and stood over that open hole in the earth. They pulled up the straps and rolled away that fake green turf and put away the contraption that helped lower the casket down. Then I watched them two boys go for a backhoe. But seemed my heart would break right there if I didn't step in.

I held up my hand. "Y'all mind if I take care a that?"

They faces was drippin' from the stiflin' heat this ol' Tennessee August thrown at us, but they was polite. "This be our job, sir."

I ain't cared one lick 'bout they protestin'. I flung off that black suit coat I borrowed and throwed it 'cross the limb a this big ol' live oak standin' over to the side. Seemed that tree stuck its arms right out, like it beggin' to hold my coat. Like it tryin' to share my load.

"Fellas, it be my job the last three years to tend the garden a this family. So I'm wonderin' if y'all could give an old man some grace today. It's purty important I tend this one. Now, one a y'all go fetch me a shovel."

Them two strappin' boys look at me. I

10

knowed they could lose they jobs if they left. They knowed it too. I could see the debate played 'tween they faces, though they didn't say nothin'.

"Just go get me a shovel; then you boys just sit right there and watch me. That way you won't get in no trouble, and you can make sure I don't do nothin' foolish. Shoot, they watchin' me too." I pointed to the two police cruisers still sittin' by the gates.

Them boys laughed 'em some nervous laugh. "You sure you be wantin' to do this, mister? 'Cause we young and got a back-hoe, and you . . ."

I chuckled and pulled my handkerchief from my back pocket. "And I be as old as this dirt I'm 'bout to throw on top a this here casket. But I move dirt 'round ever'day, boys. And I be needin' to do this. So if you just step aside . . ."

They shrugged they shoulders good and hard and went to fetch me a shovel. I took it in my hands and let it fall in the ruts a my calluses. It knowed right where it belonged. And me and that shovel, we went 'bout our work while them boys sat almost reverentlike on the ground.

After I tamped down that last shovelful a dirt, I laid the shovel down and swiped my forehead, the white shirt stuck to my back

11

like sweat on a glass a summer lemonade. One a the boys act like he gon' do sump'n, but I raise my hand again. Not through yet. He sat back down without sayin' a word.

I put back the sod they done stacked in big square pieces over to the side — laid it down nice and smooth over the dirt and pressed it down so the roots could take hold. "You boys be sure and water it good the next few weeks, y'hear?"

Then I walked over and took the big ol' blanket a white roses that laid on top a the casket and put it 'cross the top a the grave. I stood back and studied all the other wreaths and bouquets that sat there waitin'. And like the gardener I am, I 'ranged them flowers as beautiful as the life that laid 'neath 'em.

I took the last one and let my eyes, best as they still could, take in the banner that draped 'cross it. When I poked its three metal prongs in the sod, the li'l Tennessee flag tucked up in that banner done dropped down at my feet. I gone and picked it up and brushed at the dirt that clung to it. That dirt held on for dear life. Then it come to me — that be what I really tryin' to do. Hold on just a li'l longer.

When I done patted it clean, I put it back in the droop a that banner, and it seemed like that banner gone and swaddled it in with them red baby roses.

I took my jacket back from the tree and felt like I should show that tree some gratitude or sump'n. But I just flung my jacket 'cross the top a my shoulder. I looked back at the two young men. They watched me as curious as folks probably watched crazy ol' Noah.

I gave 'em a nod. Then I gave a nod to that mound a sod and flowers. I walked toward the car in a blur a tears and a burden a prayer.

CHAPTER 1

Ten Days Earlier

The heat of the stone bathroom floor warmed Mackenzie London's entire body as she took her first steps of the day. Beauty surrounded her. Every fixture, fabric, element in this home had been redone to perfection by the previous occupant. The day she moved in, she had determined that she would appreciate every moment she spent in this exquisite place — because she knew those moments were numbered.

There might not be much certain in this world. But in Mackenzie's world this much was certain: she would not live here forever. She had known that when she moved in. And her Italian-Irish heritage pushed her to embrace every facet of life passionately, wildly, and completely. She was determined not to waste one moment of this opportunity she had been given.

Today, however, the mansion was the last

thing on her mind.

"My, my, that's a good-looking man standing in front of that mirror." She leaned against her side of the brown marble countertop and gave her husband a sad smile.

Gray London leaned over his sink, electric razor in one hand. The other hand tugged at the base of his neck, where salt-and-pepper stubble clung. His blue eyes met hers, and she saw their delight in her arrival. "How's my girl?"

"Heartbroken." She scooted up behind him, wrapping her arms around his waist and resting her hands against the top of the towel tied around his hips. She laid her head against his bare back and listened as the buzz of the razor evaporated. Her heart felt heavy inside her chest.

He laid the razor down and placed his hands on top of hers. "It's a new stage of life, huh?"

She moved her cheek up and down against his back.

He laughed and turned so he could face her. His six-foot frame towered over her five-foot-four. He wrapped one arm around her, lifted her chin, and wiped at a tear that had left its wet trail down the side of her cheek.

"I know it's silly." She dabbed a tissue at

her nose. She had one in virtually every pocket she owned. "It's just kindergarten. But maybe we should have waited until she was six. You know, five is still really young."

"She's an old five, Mack."

She leaned her head against his chest. "She was an old two."

He laughed. "Yeah, she was. But we talked about this, and she wants to go. I know it's going to be hard. It will be for me too, but it doesn't happen until tomorrow. So let's enjoy today and deal with tomorrow, tomorrow."

She raised her head and batted her eyes. The tears fell freely. She knew he was right, but it didn't change the way she felt. Natural childbirth had been less painful.

He leaned down and pressed his lips against her face, then moved his mouth to her ear as one hand grazed her stomach. "Plus, who knows? You might have another baby here in about nine months."

"I pray so."

He leaned back. "So you want me to give you your shot before you get in the shower?"

She moved her hands up to the soft curve in her hips, a smile fighting with the tears. "You just want to look at my booty."

"Prettiest one I've ever seen."

The smile won. She reached for another

tissue and swiped at her eyes, then walked back over to her side of the bathroom. The Pregnyl stayed in prominent sight in her top drawer.

It had taken her and Gray almost ten years to conceive their Maddie — ten years plus four miscarriages and thousands of dollars. But when Maddie came along, Mackenzie finally had the one thing she felt her life was missing — a child. And now, five years later, she was desperate for another. Wanted it like an ache in the soul wants a healing balm.

The latest round of fertility treatments had begun again almost a year ago. They'd bypassed the Clomid altogether this time and gone straight to the injections. To date, the only thing they had to show for it was her sore behind.

Mackenzie let her robe fall to the marble floor. The matching lingerie set in black was all that remained. She saw Gray's expression change. "Just the shot, mister. You might get action this afternoon, but right now, just the shot."

He had been a good partner in this journey. Though she knew he sometimes wearied of the routine, still he was at every doctor's appointment, shared each piece of heartbreaking news, and was a pretty good nurse. He'd even become fairly handy with a needle. As she leaned against the cabinet, she suddenly got the giggles.

He moved the needle back. "You've got to be still, or this is liable to end up in your side. What's so funny anyway?"

She could hardly talk now. The laughter had all but taken over. "Wonder what Tennesseans would think if they knew that their governor was putting shots in his wife's booty this morning. That would make a front-page picture."

"I'll tell you what they would think. They'd think, 'Man, I knew that governor could do anything. What a specimen.'"

She turned her head toward him, and that was it. She threw her head back and laughed until she was wiping a different set of tears. He crossed his arms, the syringe still between his fingers. But it would take another five minutes before the governor was able to take care of his first order of duty on this beautiful Sunday morning in Tennessee.

The twenty-minute drive from the governor's mansion in Nashville to downtown Franklin, where Mackenzie had grown up, encompassed almost everything she loved about middle Tennessee. America's perception of the area seemed to be limited to country music, rednecks, and the term *NashVegas*. But natives like Mackenzie knew there was so much more. A straight shot down Franklin Road took her from her present house to her childhood home. And along the thirteen-mile stretch, she passed twenty-one churches, acres of gently rolling farmland with grazing cattle and horses, golf courses, schools, antebellum homes, and dozens of "meat and three" restaurants offering sweet tea and chocolate pie that were so good you'd want to slap your mama.

Of course, Mackenzie could never slap her mother. Her mother would declare that none of it was even capable of being as good as hers. Mackenzie couldn't argue because her mother was one of the best Southern cooks she knew. And Sunday afternoon dinners with Eugenia Quinn were as much a ritual as Friday night football in the fall.

The screen door of the recently remodeled Victorian home slammed against the white wood casing, the noise potentially heard two blocks over on Main Street. "Are y'all still taking my granddaughter to that church where the preacher says 'crap' in the pulpit?" Mackenzie's mother asked.

The same words had greeted them every Sunday afternoon since they had taken Eugenia to their church. It just so happened

19

their preacher used a word she disapproved of that Sunday. She had never let them forget it.

Eugenia was carrying a big bouquet of zinnias and daisies from her garden, but she still managed to reach down and scoop her granddaughter up in her arms.

Gray gave her a kiss on the cheek. "What? You don't do that, Mom?"

Eugenia turned her pink, powdered cheek away from him in mock disgust and returned her affection to Maddie, kissing her multiple times on the face. Maddie giggled beneath the kisses. When Eugenia leaned back, a smile spread wide across her pink-painted lips.

Mackenzie chuckled and shook her head at the exuberant display. Eugenia had been almost as desperate for Maddie as she had been. Since Mackenzie was an only child, Eugenia's hope for grandchildren rested solely on her. A load she rarely forgot.

Maddie wrapped her arms around her grandmother's neck. "Gigi, I learned about midgets today!"

Eugenia raised expressive eyebrows above her crystal-blue eyes and turned her head, her coiffed bleached-blonde bob moving as a unit. Beauty shop day was every Monday. Tomorrow she would get it redone to look just like it looked today. "Of course you did," she answered Maddie, looking straight at Mackenzie. "Your pastor says the *c* word, darling. Why wouldn't they teach you about midgets?"

She put Maddie down, handed her the bouquet to hold, and led the way through the house to the kitchen, her silver pumps clicking on the refurbished pine floor. When the door of the oven opened, the fragrance of heaven flooded out. The faithful metal pan that held their Sunday afternoon feast was placed on the counter, the aluminum foil piled up in a mound.

Mackenzie knew what was underneath that silver dome. Paradise. The aroma had already leaked into every pore of her skin.

She walked over to the cabinet and pulled out the glasses. "Smells amazing, Mama."

"We're almost ready." Eugenia took the flowers from Maddie and started arranging them in the cut-glass vase that sat on the kitchen table. "I went out and cut these right before you got here. Look as good as flowers from the governor's —"

The back door opened. Mackenzie looked up to see her mom tug at the bottom of her baby-blue linen suit jacket. She still hadn't changed from church herself. Eugenia had attended Southeast Baptist Church since before Mackenzie was born, and at Southeast Baptist they dressed up for Sunday service — another thing she often pointed out to Mackenzie.

Eugenia reached up to pouf her hair just as Burt Taylor's voice boomed through the kitchen. "Well, good afternoon, everybody."

Gray walked over and extended his hand. "Good afternoon, Burt."

Eugenia, fussing with the flowers, spoke to Burt as if he were a last-minute invite. "Hello, Burt. Glad you could join us. Now, dinner will be ready in a few minutes."

Mackenzie stifled her smile. She hadn't seen her mom this nervous in a long time. Eugenia had always been a symbol of strength to Mackenzie, who had seen her cry only once — when Mackenzie's father died ten years earlier. Once the funeral was over, Mackenzie had never witnessed another tear, and she'd only heard Eugenia weeping a few times behind a closed bedroom door.

Eugenia was tough, a rock. Mackenzie envied that about her. If anything happened to Gray, she couldn't imagine surviving.

"Hey, Burtie!" Maddie squealed and took a leap into Burt's arms. He let out a half chuckle, half groan.

"Easy, Maddie," Gray said.

"I love it," Burt responded, leaning down and planting a kiss on Maddie's cheek. "I don't get to see my grandbabies much now that they have all moved away, so it's mighty nice having a little one in my arms." The edges of Burt's plaid suit jacket crinkled beneath her weight.

"Maddie," Gray said, "let's go sit outside with Mr. Burt while Gigi and your mom get dinner ready. You can tell him what you learned in Sunday school about midgets." His laughter erupted as he turned toward Eugenia.

She fluttered her hands at them. "That's a great idea. Y'all shoo on out of my kitchen."

Maddie jumped from Burt's arms, and the three of them walked out onto the front porch. "I think the midget's name was Zach something. . . ." Maddie's words faded as the screen door slammed behind her.

Mackenzie started to put ice in the glasses. "Burt has been coming over a lot lately, huh?"

Eugenia didn't even look up. "He's old. He's hungry. And I'm a good cook."

"That you are. But you and your friends are a pretty wild bunch."

Her mother huffed as she pulled the chuck roast from beneath the foil and laid it on a white platter. "I'm not wild, Mackenzie

London. I hang out with old women who get winded playing Skip-Bo and think Starbucks is a newly discovered planet. Trust me. I'm boring."

Of all the adjectives Mackenzie would use to describe her mother, she was certain *boring* had never been one. She was a quintessential lady, a master gardener, a lover of beauty, but she would just as soon cuss you as look at you — though she would *never* do it in church. She kept her husband's 12-gauge under her bed and would shoot you first and ask who you were later. She was opinionated and her tongue could be downright withering, but she was also loyal — fiercely loyal.

And if the world ever fell apart, Mackenzie was certain that Eugenia Madeline Pruitt Quinn alone could put it all back together.

As usual, Maddie was the first one to burst through the door of the governor's mansion when they finally made it home late that afternoon. Mackenzie heard her pounding up the stairs to the family quarters as she and Gray walked through the front door.

Following Maddie up the stairs, she was greeted first by her daughter's skirt, draped carelessly from one tread to the next. Her eyes moved up the stairwell at the trail of clothing Maddie had deposited on her way to her room. Gray had been the first to use the word *poop* for what Maddie often did with her stuff. Mackenzie had thought the term was gross, but Maddie was five — she loved it. So it had stuck. And in less than two minutes flat, Maddie had "pooped" her skirt, then her sweater, her shoes, and her socks, leaving a trail of clothing up the stairs.

Mackenzie sighed. When Maddie was three, this habit had been cute. Now, not so much. And though they had been working with her on this for the past year, in moments like these, Mackenzie wasn't sure what all the effort had been for.

"Maddie." Her voice traveled down the hall as she picked up the skirt.

The tiny voice came from what she assumed was Maddie's bedroom. "Yes, Mommy?"

"Want to go outside and play?"

"I'm getting ready to."

"Well, why don't you come here first and see how quickly that is going to happen."

She heard little feet patter in the hallway. Maddie stood at the top of the steps, blue jean shorts already buttoned, yet still topless. She looked down and giggled. "Oops."

Mackenzie held out the skirt. "Yes, oops."

Maddie snatched up her skirt and the rest

of her clothes and raced back up the stairs. "Maddie went poop," she announced as she made her way down the hall, filling it with laughter.

Mackenzie had to smile. She was way too lenient with Maddie, she knew. Gray reminded her of that often enough, and so did her mother. But she couldn't help it. Maddie was her miracle baby. And there hadn't been children in the governor's mansion since the Lamar Alexander years. Mackenzie was grateful she and Gray had been able to bring this kind of life back into this magnificent house.

Restored by the former first lady in a massive renovation project, the mansion displayed all the beauty that a governor's residence should. But there was something about children in a home. They brought fingerprints to the artwork and syrup-covered hands to the marble side tables. They brought cartwheels to the foyer and a slight irreverence to what could be an often-stuffy environment. Formal dinners could be interrupted with bedtime stories, and hallways lined with pictures of former governors could turn into dance studios for little ballerinas. Best of all, Maddie and her friends brought a contagious laughter that the entire staff loved.

More footsteps pounded, and a camouflage streak left the smell of sweaty little boy in its wake. "Hey, Oliver," Mackenzie said as their seven-year-old next-door neighbor ran past her on the stairs. She glanced at her watch. "We've only been home a full five minutes."

"I know. I was watching ya from my driveway. Headed up to see Maddie — okay, Mrs. London?" The boy's disheveled curls bounced on his head as he took the steps two by two.

Mackenzie laughed. "Have at it, buddy." The fact that he had just entered the governor's mansion without so much as knocking was lost on Oliver. But Mackenzie didn't care. She liked having him around.

Oliver and Maddie had become bosom buddies last summer when his family moved into Minnie Pearl's old house next door. His mother, Lacy, had tried to keep him away, but Mackenzie had assured her that Maddie loved him. And he had pretty much become as permanent a fixture around here as Eugenia. The security and house staff knew to let him come and go. Maddie adored him and he her. And Gray declared that marriage was in their future.

Mackenzie reached the top of the steps and walked into the family quarters just as

27

Mason County District Library

Maddie and Oliver rounded the corner. "Mommy! Mommy!" Maddie said. "Oliver has a new French word."

Oliver's family had lived in France for two years, and he did know a little French, but for the most part he simply spoke words with a French accent. But to Maddie, who was American and Southern through and through, he might as well be a French interpreter.

"Oh, you do?" Mackenzie said. "What is your new word?"

Maddie chimed in, "He can say *lightbulb*."

"Oh my." Mackenzie tried not to smile. "Go ahead, Oliver. Let me hear it."

He shook his head as if all of it was silly, but his expression gave his delight away. He squared his shoulders like a French gentleman. *"Leetboolb."*

Mackenzie nodded, her lips pressed firmly together to keep from cracking up. "That is wonderful, Oliver. Keep teaching those to Maddie, and before you know it, she'll be speaking French too."

The two smiled. Maddie threw her hand up, yelled "Bye, Mommy," and the pounding footsteps resumed, this time headed to the backyard. Mackenzie walked to the palladium windows in the family quarters living room. The two flashes darted across thick grass and headed straight for the trampoline. Their energy could bust through brick and mortar.

Mackenzie smiled as she sank into the deep, plush sofa and picked up her pink- and white-striped folder from the glass top of an iron side table. Her assistant, Jessica, always prepared her weekly schedule on Sunday afternoons and left it here for her. She thumbed through her responsibilities for the coming week. Tomorrow she was slated to speak to state educators at a luncheon meeting about volunteerism in elementary schools.

It was a subject dear to Mackenzie's heart, a cherished part of her heritage as a native of the Volunteer State. The term went back to the War of 1812, when General Andrew Jackson mustered thousands of citizen volunteers to fight the British in the South. It had been reinforced during the Mexican-American War, when then Tennessee governor Aaron Brown requested 2,800 men and 30,000 showed up. And it still applied in Tennessee today, at least as far as Mackenzie was concerned.

Convinced that the initiative of volunteerism needed to begin early, she had helped devise an elementary school curriculum to help even the youngest see not only the importance of volunteerism but the endless opportunities as well. She was a firm believer that if you reminded people of what they were created for, they would rise up to meet the challenge — and the earlier it happened, the better.

Her own experience as a young volunteer had started over a bowl of fried okra, which Eugenia had set in front of her at a Sunday lunch. Mackenzie, who normally loved fried foods, had popped one of the cornmeal-encrusted balls in her mouth — and hated it. Hated it. That first complaint had resulted in a trip downtown to feed the homeless and hungry. "Next time you whine about okra that I picked from my own garden and fried with my own hands," Eugenia had told her, "you need to think about people who don't have food and would love some of your mama's okra."

That one experience didn't change Mackenzie's opinion of okra, but it did change her life in significant ways. Helping at the soup kitchen so touched her heart that she began to refuse food just so she could go again. Eugenia caught on after the third showdown, and they started volunteering regularly at the Nashville Rescue Mission.

Mackenzie had gone on to major in social work at the University of Tennessee and later worked as an advocate for children in crisis. Now she had the opportunity to help children themselves recognize the needs around them. That was one of the benefits of her role as first lady. She could be a mouthpiece for the issues most important to her.

Mackenzie scribbled down a reminder to review her notes before bedtime and checked to see what else her calendar held. It was going to be a full week, especially with Maddie's first day of kindergarten and the big soiree on Wednesday night honoring the volunteers and heroes of a string of natural disasters that had hit the area the past few years.

It had all begun with the horrific flood a few years back — an unprecedented disaster for Tennessee. For the first two days in May, some areas of Tennessee had received a record-breaking nineteen inches of rain. There had been twenty-one deaths and more than 1.5 billion dollars in damages. The devastation included some of Nashville's most precious landmarks — the Grand Ole Opry, the Ryman Auditorium, and the Opryland Hotel and Convention Center. And because few outside the state even knew about the floods — they coincided with an oil spill in the Gulf of

Mexico and an attempted car bombing in New York City — Nashvillians had mostly been left to fend for themselves.

But Tennesseans had done what Tennesseans do. They hadn't complained. They hadn't blamed. They'd just dug in their heels and served . . . each other.

Mackenzie had been right in the middle of those efforts — and similar efforts in the wake of a massive tornado in northwest Tennessee and an ice storm that crippled two-thirds of the state for a full week. Each time, she had recognized the spirit that made her state special.

That was the reason for Wednesday's dinner. Mackenzie was determined to honor those local heroes she had come in contact with day after day, those heroes the national media or *People* magazine would never interview. She had been involved in every detail of the celebration, and she couldn't wait for it to get here.

"What're you doing, babe?"

She looked up. Gray was in his running shorts and red Nike T-shirt. Sweat clung to his face and glistened as the light hit it. He paced around the room, trying to cool off.

"Seeing what the week holds. Good run?"

"Felt great." He leaned down and kissed her lightly on the lips.

She closed her folder and set it down. "Getting hungry?"

He was back to pacing. "Yeah. Have time to shower?"

"Sure. Maddie's out with Oliver. She'll enjoy not being rushed."

He wiped the top of his head with the sleeve of his shirt. "Maddie figured out what kind of pizza she wants tonight?"

Sunday nights at the governor's mansion were pizza nights. Maddie's favorite. The child could smell a pepperoni six streets over. She spotted pizza deliverymen quicker than Mackenzie spotted a nice pair of shoes.

"She's not branching out this week, if that's what you're thinking."

He laughed. "I guess after almost three years of the same meal every Sunday night, I should quit hoping. But what's life without a little hope, huh?"

She smiled. "A little hope got us a long way, didn't it?"

"That's what I'm saying."

The phone rang on the side table by Mackenzie. She picked it up. In a few moments she said, "Sure, Joseph, send him up."

Gray looked at her. "For me?"

She nodded, certain the disappointment showed. "Yep." She had hoped for an entire day to themselves without an interruption.

He looked at his watch. "Well, we made it almost twenty-four hours. Unfortunately not all of those were in the same day."

The buzzer sounded at the entrance to the mansion's family quarters. Mackenzie watched as Gray walked down the long, carpeted hallway.

This was a piece of the sacrifice — the only piece that really got to her. The capitol hill bickering she tried to ignore. The picketing of events outside the mansion she saw as people's rights to their opinions. The media's interest in Gray's breakfast choices she simply found silly. But the constant interruptions to their life and the heavy demands on their time challenged her on her best days.

Gray opened the door to Kurt Green, his frazzled-looking chief of staff. Kurt's white polo shirt hung loosely over his khaki shorts as he hurried through the door. He had been in a rush since Mackenzie had met him. And except for his bald head, he looked virtually the same as when he and Gray were Kappa Alphas at the University of Tennessee.

Gray closed the door and moved past Kurt. "What happened to your phone? It's Sunday. You should be doing something. Family something."

Kurt's flip-flops beat against his heels as he followed Gray across the thick damask carpet and into the living room. "Okay, sure. I'll call next time." He extended a folder from his hand. "But today we've got a lawsuit on our hands."

Gray reached out and took the file from his friend's hand. "I know. The lawsuit from that victims' advocacy group over the prisoner release." He raised an eyebrow at Kurt. "The lawsuit we agreed to look over next week."

"That was before the press got wind of it and decided it would make a great Monday morning headline." Kurt ran his hands across his hairless skull — a bad habit Gray jokingly claimed had led to his present state. "Stuff like this is what completely destroys reelections." Kurt had been thinking about the reelection since the day Gray took the oath of office. Maybe even before.

Gray scanned the file. "A reelection campaign won't prevent me from doing what needs to be done, Kurt."

Kurt shook his head. "Well, that's fine, Gray, but we've got to respond to this *now*. There are Democrats and Republicans alike who want you out."

"And there are Democrats and Republicans who will change their minds tomorrow. It's those same Democrats and Republicans who have left this state with no choice but cutbacks. I would prefer to not release prisoners either. But it's nonviolent offenders only, and it's better than firing schoolteachers." Gray closed the folder and handed it back to Kurt. "Though I still haven't ruled out shutting down the government and letting everybody go a couple of months without paychecks."

Kurt looked at the file in his hands, then back at Gray, his expression utterly dumbfounded. "We are just a little over a year away from an election, Gray. We have made huge progress in this state in spite of all the budget issues we've faced, and there's so much more we need to do. We can't let something like this lawsuit prevent the voters from seeing the real impact you've made here. Remember, voters have short memories."

Gray's sigh was heavy in the room. Mackenzie felt her shoulders sag. She knew he was going to work now. "I'll give you two hours," he told Kurt.

The veins in the front of Kurt's head stopped bulging. "I'll call Fletcher. He can come over and help us draft a statement."

"You can call him from my office." He motioned toward the stairs, but Kurt was already there. Gray walked over to Mackenzie, gave her another small kiss, and ran his hand through her soft black hair. "Sorry, babe. Save me some pizza."

She puckered her lips. "Yep, I'm sorry too. And no one likes your pizza, remember?"

He laughed. He was sensitive to dairy, so his pizza never had cheese. Maddie declared it gross. Oliver found it intriguing. "Good thing, then, huh?"

"Two hours only, right? It *is* Sunday. Even the governor deserves some rest."

She watched his brow furrow, and he opened his mouth to speak.

"I know. I know," she interrupted. "We knew this part when we took the job."

"I'll be done as soon as I can."

She watched him as he too headed downstairs toward the office he kept there. And sighed. Over the last three years, it seemed, she had seen more of him going than coming.

CHAPTER 2

"Berlyn, give me a break. I don't have a shred of desire for that man. Seriously, you and Dimples need to get you a life." Eugenia snatched up the Skip-Bo cards scattered across her glass-topped breakfast table and plopped the deck in front of Sandra.

She'd known the women gathered around her table since grade school. Their mamas had been friends, and so the progression of their friendship had felt natural, even though Eugenia was the youngest of the bunch. They called themselves the last four remaining Franklin natives, since most everyone else in the city was a transplant. And even though she knew she could never live without them, they had the ability to make her madder than a hornet.

Dimples, the oldest of the bunch at seventy-four, picked up one of Eugenia's good cloth napkins and coughed right into it. Eugenia tried to give her the eye. But poor Dimples only had one good eye. The other was so cockeyed she had to tilt her head just to look at you straight. So Eugenia was pretty certain she never really saw her looks of disapproval. If she had, she would've quit hacking into Eugenia's napkins forty years ago.

Berlyn stood up from the table and tugged at the low-cut blouse she had tried to cram her double-Fs into. The resulting floral explosion only enhanced how big they were. Berlyn was a year older than Eugenia — seventy-one — but still had her grandchildren telling people she was thirty-nine. Eugenia was pretty sure Berlyn had convinced even herself it was true.

Berlyn picked up her glass Coke bottle — the only way she'd have a Coke — and headed toward the trash can. "Say what you will, Eugenia Quinn, but everyone knows you and Burt Taylor got the eyes for each other. Ever since that wife of his died from heatstroke trying to beat you for the best hydrangeas in Franklin, he's been after you."

Eugenia huffed. "You sound like you're twelve, Berlyn. Mary Parker Taylor did not die trying to beat me at anything. She died from pneumonia in the wintertime and was a beautiful lady who was never in competition with me like you are."

Berlyn huffed back, but Eugenia went on. "Besides, I have had eyes for one man and that is all."

Sandra got up from her side of the table and picked up her empty iced tea glass. Her gnawed lemon lay at the bottom of the glass as if a piranha had spent the afternoon with it.

Sandra was actually only two months older than Eugenia but had always acted just plain old. She was the most prim, most proper, and according to Berlyn, the most prudish. She didn't know how to not dress up, and most of the time the collars of her clothes looked like they had a stranglehold on her neck. Even her short-sleeved blouses had ruffled collars.

"He is such a sharp man, Eugenia," she said. "So dapper and refined. There would be nothing wrong if you two went out on a date. But I do agree that Berlyn's characterization of it is simply tawdry."

Berlyn grabbed a toothpick and jammed it in her mouth — something Sandra swore ladies never did. "You read too many bad Southern novels, Sandra. Get out of books and into the land of the living. No one has said *tawdry* since Scarlett O'Hara."

Dimples rose, leaning slightly to the right as if she were trying to follow Sandra with her good eye. "I think he's hot," she announced.

Eugenia about swallowed her teeth — and she and Berlyn were the only ones in the room who actually still had theirs. Sandra would deny that to her grave, but Dimples would just pull hers right out of her mouth to clean them whenever she needed to.

"Dimples Bass, what in the world do you know about someone being hot?" Eugenia asked.

Dimples came into the kitchen and scratched at her head, her blue curls moving beneath her hand as she did. "I know my fifteen-year-old great-granddaughter says that about that boy who sings those songs about pop."

Berlyn sidled up next to her and leaned down toward her ear. "You mean, sings pop songs."

"Yeah, sings them pop songs. Says he is h-o-t, hot. And I've seen Burt Taylor, and —" she leaned against the side of the granite countertop, more to hold herself up than anything else — "well, he *is* hot!"

That was it. Eugenia swatted them out of her house and bolted the door. As she returned to the kitchen, she dropped her clothes along the way and walked through the house plumb naked, just because she could. She poured herself some sweet tea, grabbed her iPod, climbed into the tub, and clicked on her new Kenny Chesney album.

Who cared if she had borrowed the CD from the kid up the street? Mackenzie might call it stealing. And Eugenia's late husband, Lorenzo, a circuit court judge, would probably agree.

But after a night like tonight, Eugenia just called it therapy.

CHAPTER 3

Gray stepped out into the early morning and stretched hard, letting loose a loud grunt as he did. He heard Jeremiah chuckle. If not for the laughter, he would never have seen the lanky figure striding up the driveway with all of Gray's morning newspapers tucked under his arm.

"Greetin' the mornin', Gov'nor?"

"Yep." Gray put his hands on the waistband of his khaki slacks. "Thought I might beat you out here this morning, Jeremiah."

"Gov'nor, you should know one thing 'bout me. I always gon' be here right at five thirty so I can get the boys started. And I always gon' be *leavin'* right at five thirty too. Been that way these twenty-five years, and I ain't thinkin' it gon' change much 'til I up and retire. Besides, these is the best hours for a gardener." He extended the bundle of papers toward Gray with another chuckle. "I ain't knowed we was racin' anyways."

"I'm joking. I wanted to say hello. When you leave the papers in the kitchen, I get caught up and forget to come say hey. How's your morning so far?"

"Got me a real green valley today." Gray saw the white flash of Jeremiah's teeth in the darkness. "And we can congregate out here if you want."

"I just like talking to you, is all."

"Well, now, I appreciate that. I like talkin' to you too. Be a honor."

Gray had enjoyed Jeremiah's company from the time his family moved into the governor's mansion. Gray could almost always find his head gardener nearby, pruning something or weeding something or working in his greenhouse. And after his first several reality checks as governor, when he learned the job was even harder than he expected, Gray had found a welcoming ear in this kind old man.

Not that Jeremiah couldn't be ornery. In fact, he could be downright stubborn. Gray knew Jeremiah's story. He also knew he held the authority to give Jeremiah a better life. But Jeremiah wouldn't let him. Said what he had was what he had. Gray had honored an old man's wishes. But that didn't stop him from seeking Jeremiah's company.

"Actually," Gray said, "I wanted to ask

you a question. You know we've had prisoners out here keeping up the grounds of the Tennessee governor's mansion for years. And with you overseeing them all this time, I wanted your thoughts on something."

"Don't know much, Gov'nor. But I always been good at listenin'."

Gray curled the papers under his arm. "You've been listening to me for the last three years, haven't you?"

"Appreciated ever' day of it."

"How do you feel about this prisoner release that we've done?"

Jeremiah shook his head with a slow sway. "Way I see it, if somebody gone and give you rotten lemons, you ain't gon' get no lemonade worth drinkin'. And there ain't nothin' 'bout life the way it s'posed to be anyways. Wish I could be tendin' me the Garden of Eden, but it ain't here no more. So we do the best with what we got."

"I did the best I knew, Jeremiah. My other options were worse."

Jeremiah reached over and touched his shoulder. Gray felt the boniness of the old man's hand through his starched white dress shirt. "Ain't got no doubt, Gov'nor. Ain't got no doubt."

"Thanks. I appreciate it."

"Y'know, one time when I be real down

'bout the way my life turned out, my Shirley say to me, 'Jeremiah Williams, you got two choices. Either you stick with what you know to be true, or you gon' do sump'n you regret. And ain't nothin' worse than a life full a regrets.' "

"I agree with Mrs. Shirley." Gray tapped the newspapers. "Well, I'd better start reading these, huh?"

Jeremiah expelled a puff of air. "Better you than me. Now, I'm gon' go talk to some flowers. Bet my garden smell lot better'n yours."

Gray laughed. "Yeah, but what I got in my garden is the only thing that will make yours grow."

"Hee-hee. Ain't gon' tell no politicians the gov'nor just gone and called 'em manure." Jeremiah chuckled and disappeared around the corner.

Gray closed the door to the north entrance, pulled out the Memphis paper, and turned it over to read the headline. " 'Victims' Rights Group Sues over Prisoner Release'?" He shook his head and stuffed the paper underneath his arm again.

The press wanted a governor relegated to sound bites. Tennesseans wanted a governor who knew their names and responded to their needs. And Gray aspired passionately to be the latter. He failed at times. He knew he did. Weariness alone could do that to anybody. But he did his very best to make a real difference to the people of his state. He would never trade his precious family time for anything less.

He stacked the newspapers on the edge of the kitchen island — the *Tennessean,* the *Knoxville News Sentinel,* the *Chattanooga Times Free Press,* and Memphis's *Daily News.* He had already consumed the *New York Times* and the *Washington Post* during his run on the treadmill. And he'd used his time lifting weights to focus his heart, unclutter his mind, and talk with a Creator far more capable of taking care of Tennessee than he was.

The lawsuit was front-page news for each paper. The response from the governor's office was sixth-page news. "Hello, Monday." Gray rubbed his hands together and placed his elbows on the island. "Rosa, today I think I'll have Belgian waffles with Devonshire cream, sugared blueberries, and warm maple syrup."

Rosa shook her head. "*Absolutamente,* Señor London."

He took a long sip of orange juice, the pulp thick as it went down. Rosa set his plate down before his glass made it back to its place. In front of him was a spinach, mushroom, tomato, and bell pepper omelet.

He studied the plate, then looked at Rosa. Her black eyes didn't budge from his stare until that wide grin fell across his face. *"Perfecto."*

She smacked him with a damp towel that she had laid across her shoulder. Yesterday the request had been chocolate-chip pancakes with chocolate drizzle, and he had gotten it. But in order to stay as fit as he could for the office of governor and for chasing after a five-year-old, he gave himself grace for ridiculously unhealthy food only on the weekends. So Rosa knew that, no matter what he asked for Monday through Friday, he always got an omelet.

Before he left, he gave Rosa a peck on the cheek, reddening her olive complexion, and took his second glass of orange juice and the papers down the hall to the office he kept in the residence. He could put in almost two hours there before Mack's eyes even opened.

The office was rich and warm, with paneled walls and floor-to-ceiling bookcases that housed most of his books from his previous life as a lawyer, plus the autobiographies he loved to consume. He sank into the cool leather of his chair and leaned back, setting his glass of juice on the coaster in front of him. It was one Mack had given him at Christmas, decorated with a family picture.

Compared to most governors he was pretty young. He had been sworn into office at age thirty-nine and now, at forty-two, plans for his reelection were already well under way. But being governor hadn't been a lifelong plan. Far from it. Even now, there were moments when he shook his head over the direction his life had taken.

There had actually been a brief time in college when he wondered if he should go into ministry. He had been president of his Fellowship of Christian Athletes chapter at the University of Tennessee, where he had enjoyed a pretty good run as quarterback. But he was no Peyton Manning, so professional ball had not been on his radar. Nor had politics, just people. Gray London had always loved people. And he had finally settled on law as a good way of serving them.

Then came a trial where an obviously innocent man went to jail because of a questionable judge and horrible antics by both prosecution and defense. Gray saw it all firsthand, from the trenches, and he believed his state was getting a disservice. He had become a lawyer to defend people, to protect them — to provide a voice for people who didn't even know they had one or who couldn't afford one. But maybe that wasn't enough. Maybe he needed to work to change the system. That's when he started on the political path that had led to the governor's mansion.

But politics could be brutal, as he'd quickly learned. And there were a lot of complicating factors, such as the need for reelection. As soon as you took office, it seemed, you had to start thinking about getting reelected. Kurt had long ago organized a campaign committee and laid the groundwork for the upcoming campaign. But Gray had sworn he wouldn't get personally involved in the process until the year of the election, and that no decision he made as governor would be influenced by the desire for reelection. It would be made solely on what was right for his state, whether Democrats, Republicans, his fellow Independents, or even his own staff agreed.

So far he had stuck to his guns on that promise, and he thought he had done a lot of good. But a few issues were a constant challenge — like the state budget. Gray's years in office had coincided with a dismal national economy. The string of natural disasters in Tennessee had made things even worse, especially on the jobs front. Every year falling revenues had necessitated deep cuts. And the situation wasn't helped much by Gray's fellow politicians, who typically agreed that tough measures were needed — *except* when they affected their personal constituencies.

And Gray had to admit he'd made some poor decisions in the beginning. He had approached his first year of the whole budget process with an ax instead of a pruner, generating anger instead of a healthy team spirit in the General Assembly. He'd learned quickly that Robin Hood wouldn't accomplish his goal of being a unifier. He had spent the last two years working closely with his colleagues in the legislature. But the impression he'd made that first year still haunted him, especially when it came to the media.

He looked at the stack of papers on his desk and picked up the folder that held his weekly agenda. His phone beeped.

"Good morning, Governor." The familiar voice sounded tired.

"Morning, Fletch. Tell me that you and Kurt slept."

"What's sleep?" Fletcher Perry was Gray's communications director and another friend

51

from college days. "Anyway," he added, "we've got the special session meeting today with the Education Oversight committee and the TEA members before we go to final vote. Anything you need me to have a heads-up about before we meet? Any announcement you want to make?"

Gray leaned back in his chair. "No, I think we're good. We'll make an announcement after we have the vote. A few committee members still feel wishy-washy to me. I don't want to play anything until we know it is solid."

"Sounds good. You headed this way?"

"A little later. It's Maddie's big day."

"Oh yeah. Forgot about that. Well, I'll see you when you get Mack put back together."

Gray laughed. "You won't want to wait that long, I assure you." Gray hung up and looked at his watch. His girls should be up by now. And he knew exactly what they would be doing.

CHAPTER 4

If heaven had a backyard, it would look like this.

Mackenzie stood on the mansion's back veranda, breathing in the dampness of the already-sticky day and enjoying the breathtaking beauty before her. This home had been named "Far Hills" when it was built in 1929 because of the spectacular view. A large fountain and a reflecting pool adorned the middle of the grounds, the splashing water circled by stonework that seemed to hold the fountain in the palm of its hands. From there, immaculate manicured gardens spread out. Boasting some of the South's most beautiful flowers and trees and at least thirty varieties of roses, they were tended by trustees from the Tennessee prison system under the careful supervision of Jeremiah Williams. In charge of these grounds for the last twenty-five years, Jeremiah ran as tight a ship as few she'd ever met and was as kind as few she'd ever known.

Mackenzie looked at the playhouse that sat next to the swing set and the trampoline. It was just one of the reasons she treasured Jeremiah. Their first week in the mansion she'd been so busy setting up their home that she'd had little time to focus on Maddie. Eugenia was away on a long-planned cruise with her girlfriends, so Mackenzie hired a babysitter.

But Maddie was far more intrigued with Jeremiah, who seemed to know exactly what an almost-three-year-old needed. He made sure her swing set was set up their first day in the house. And when Maddie got bored with swinging, he took the time to show her *and* the babysitter around the garden.

By the end of that week, Maddie knew the Tennessee state flower was a purple iris and could name quite a few other plants. And by the end of the second week, Jeremiah had built her the most beautiful playhouse, fully equipped with a little bench and a tiny flower garden out front.

Mackenzie had looked at that playhouse and burst out crying. Her emotion had startled him.

"Ain't mean to do nothin' wrong, ma'am."

"You didn't, Jeremiah. It's just . . . well, my dad made me one just like that when I was a little girl."

He nodded. "I knowed your dad. Good man, Judge Quinn."

She looked into Jeremiah's black eyes and saw compassion. "You knew my father?"

"Yep, met him a time or two. And he always do what's right. Ain't ever heard one bad thing 'bout that man." He chuckled. " 'Cept from folks he done put in jail."

She laughed too. "Thank you. My dad would have loved Maddie's playhouse."

"Ain't nothin'. Just think little girls need playhouses; that's all."

She had leaned over and kissed his freck-led cheek, startling him once again. "You just gave me a piece of my daddy, Jeremiah." And from that day on, a friendship had developed between the two of them, one that ran to deep places, strong enough to bridge the gap between an elderly African American gardener and a much younger governor's wife.

Mackenzie hugged herself, her fingers rubbing the smooth silk of her baby-blue Christian Dior robe. She came out here nearly every morning to greet the day. But today her heart was in her throat, and she was exhausted. She had stayed up until two getting everything ready. Now every crease of Maddie's little skirt was perfect. The white collar of her polo shirt lay as if it had just come from the store. Her little backpack contained supplies and a few secret treats.

Madeline London was ready for kindergarten. Whether her mother was ready — that was another question.

"I'm here, Mommy." Maddie's little hand tugged at her mom's side. The other rubbed at the sleep in her eyes while still managing to hold on to her doll, Lola.

Mackenzie looked down into those endless blue eyes and took Maddie's hand for their morning ritual. It had been Mackenzie's alone for years, but since Maddie had learned how to talk, she'd decided it would be hers too. And as if she had some internal alarm, Maddie always showed up right on time.

Mackenzie glanced at the tiny fingers interlaced with her own, fingers that barely made it past her knuckles, and thought, *This is the best moment of the day.* Nothing else in her life — not the twenty countries she had visited or the hundreds of events she attended or the soirees she herself arranged — meant as much as these sweet moments with her baby girl.

"Would you like to start, Maddie?"

"Sure!" Her voice rang out, saturated with the sweetness only a child could have. "Our

Father who art in heaven . . ."

Mackenzie tried to join in, but the lump was too hard and thick in her throat. She finally got out a whisper, and in unison, they welcomed the day. Mackenzie was certain it welcomed them back.

"Great job." Mackenzie knelt down and pulled Maddie into a bear hug. Maddie flung both arms around her in response. Unfortunately, one hand still held Lola. "Ow!" Mackenzie laughed as the doll crashed against her back.

Maddie leaned back and stared at Mackenzie with that thirty-year-old look that came over her sometimes. "It's a really big day, Mommy."

"Yes, I know. Really big."

She slid her hands up Mackenzie's arms. "I'm a big girl now."

A soft burst of laughter stopped the tears. "Yes, this is what big girls do."

"Big girls go to school and have teachers and take their lunch." Maddie's black bob bounced slightly as she patted Mackenzie's arms. It was the "big girl" haircut she had asked for this summer.

Mackenzie leaned over and kissed the soft olive skin of her little one's face. "How about we just start with breakfast?"

Maddie clapped her hands. "Chocolate

gravy and biscuits!"

The little girl had returned, and Mackenzie was grateful. "On a Monday?"

Maddie's hands moved to her tiny hips and pressed her pink satin nightgown to her waist. "It's not every day you start school, you know."

Mackenzie shook her head and grabbed Maddie's hand. "You're right. What was I thinking?"

Maddie raised the doll in her hand. "For Lola too."

"Of course. This is a big day for Lola too."

Mackenzie let the hand of her little one swing with hers as they stepped forward into their new life as kindergartner and kindergartner's mother.

CHAPTER 5

Gray caught Mack coming down the stairs, her sweater over her arm and a pair of Maddie's socks in her hand. He could only imagine where she'd found those, probably on top of the breakfast table. He waited at the bottom for her, his blue eyes taking her in. Even after sixteen years of marriage, he never got tired of looking at his wife.

And she looked wonderful today, even though her eyes were a little puffy. He loved her in red, and this dress was one of his favorites. It was sleeveless, so it showed that hint of a dip in the top of her bicep, proof that even if she gave in to temptation and overdosed on sweet tea, the girl still could tear up a Boot Camp class.

"You are one beautiful first lady." He leaned in to kiss her.

"Thank you. You look pretty good yourself." She laid the socks and sweater across the banister and straightened his yellow-

and blue-striped tie, though it was already perfectly straight. Straightening his tie was just part of her morning routine. And this woman loved routine.

"Our baby girl still in the kitchen?"

"In the kitchen, about to be led to the bathroom."

"You headed to get her?"

"Yep."

"And how's my other baby girl?"

He could tell she was fighting hard against the tears, but they welled up before she could retrieve them. She bit her lower lip and shook her head. He pulled her toward him, his mouth resting against her ear. "She's going to love it, babe. By the end of the week, she's going to be begging us to take her."

She rested her head on his shoulder, and he felt the surge of tears as he held her body close to his. "That's what I'm afraid of," she whispered.

He let her stay there until she was ready to let go. Finally she pulled away and dabbed a tissue at her running mascara. "Probably should have just gone in my sweats with no makeup, huh?"

Gray laughed and took her by the hand, leading her into the kitchen. "How's my Maddie lady today?" He pulled his daughter from her barstool and wrapped her, sticky fingers and all, in his arms.

Mack grabbed a damp towel to wipe off his jacket. "You're either going to have to change or spend your day feeling like a booth at a waffle house."

"Who cares about a little syrup." He kissed Maddie's face and set her down again.

"Yeah, who cares about a little syrup, Mommy," Maddie echoed.

"Well," Mackenzie answered, moving from Gray's jacket to Maddie's fingers, "it's time to get that face washed and some clothes on that body. And don't forget Lola," she added as Maddie jumped down from the stool and started for the door.

"Lulu can stay here with me." Gray smiled as Maddie turned, pressing her small hand against the curve in her hip and cocking her leg out the way Mack had done a thousand times. Mack pressed her lips together to hide her amusement. Rosa turned back toward the griddle, her shoulders shaking.

"Her name's not Lulu, Daddy. Her name is Lola." Indignation flashed in her blue eyes. They were complete replicas of his own — as far as he could tell, his only contribution to Maddie. Otherwise she was Mack made over, from her tiny frame to her anything-but-tiny personality. And she was growing up so fast.

He put his hand over his mouth. "Oh my goodness. I'm so sorry. I forgot." He extended his hand toward the doll, who was still flopped on the island near Maddie's plate. "Lola, please forgive me."

"You say that to her every day," Maddie reminded, hand still firmly planted.

"I know. But sometimes I need to be forgiven a little every day. Plus, Daddy's getting old. My memory's not what it used to be."

Maddie walked over to Gray's barstool. He leaned down to look at her, and she ran a hand through his hair. "You'll never be old to me, Daddy."

And of course Gray melted. He might be governor of Tennessee, but he was no match for this particular five-year-old. "You hit my soft spot, Maddie lady."

She giggled. "I know."

Mack smiled and grabbed Maddie's hand. "Come on. We've got to get you ready for school, or you're going to be late on your first day."

Gray picked up Lola and handed her over. "Go get spiffy, Maddie lady."

He smiled and took a sip of coffee as he listened to her bouncing through the halls.

"I'm ready, Daddy!" Maddie pranced out the back door and ran to the open door of Gray's black Escalade. But Mack gave him that look and shook her head slightly, her eyes pleading.

"Maddie lady, how about we take Mommy's car today since school is just right up the street." He said it loudly enough for his staff and the highway patrol officers who served as security at the mansion to know what his plans were. As long as his whereabouts were known and he could be reached immediately, it was okay if he went without a driver.

"But why?" Maddie's whine added extra syllables to her words.

"Because Mommy and I want this to be our day. Just us."

"And Lola," she reminded.

"Of course. Lulu."

"Daddy!"

He laughed and took her hand as they headed into the garage. "I mean Lola is welcome."

Mack was already in the passenger seat of her white Volvo SUV when he got in. "Thank you," she whispered.

He reached across the middle console and took her hand. She pulled his hand up to her lips, kissed it lightly, and looked back at Maddie, who was perched on her booster seat. "Hook your seat belt."

Maddie protested. "Mommy, I don't want to wrinkle my new outfit."

"Well, I'm sorry, but that isn't an option. We always wear our seat belts. It's the law."

"Uh-uh. You sometimes don't when you don't want to wrinkle *your* outfit."

Gray gave Mack a sideways glance. He knew she had done it, and she knew he knew. But she wasn't about to let Maddie have this one. "Well, if Mommy has done that —" she emphasized the *has* — "then she was very bad. And she won't do it anymore. So hook your seat belt."

A deep and loud sigh came from the backseat as he started the car.

Maddie's new school was only a mile down the road from the mansion — the neighborhood elementary. Gray had wanted to send Maddie to a public school as a sign of his faith in public education, and Mackenzie had agreed once she had checked this one out thoroughly. And thorough she had been. She'd come home with details on everything from the teachers' training to the lunch offerings to the school uniforms.

Today all that would become part of Maddie's daily life. Gray had all the confidence in the world that she would do fine, but he still had to swallow hard as she climbed down from the SUV, clutching Lola in a tight little fist.

Mack knelt beside her, the back door still open. "Baby girl, Lola is going to have to spend the day with Mommy."

A look of utter disbelief swept across Maddie's face about the time her bottom lip started to quiver. "Hey, hey now." Mack took her arms. "This is *your* big day, remember. You're a big girl now, and Lola isn't quite big enough yet to go to school with you. But Mommy will take good care of her, and when she gets to be a big girl like you, then we'll think about taking her to school too."

The pool of tears had already settled in the bottom of Maddie's eyes. "You'll take her everywhere?" Her voice quivered.

Mack nodded solemnly. "I'll take her everywhere." If he knew Mack, by nightfall there would be a full report on the adventures of Lola.

"She gets hungry for cookies after lunch."

Tears now welled in Mack's eyes too — or so Gray thought. But it was hard to tell because his own vision was a little blurry.

"Cookies after lunch for sure." Mack held out her hand and waited patiently until Lola was in it. Then she put the doll in the car and closed the door. "I'll take perfect care of her." And with that they headed into the schoolhouse.

When Gray finally went to pull Mack from the classroom, he found Maddie engaged in dialogue with two little girls, oblivious to the fact her parents were even still there. He watched her for a long minute, then took Mack's hand and headed back to the car. When he opened the door to let Mack inside, Lola sat staring at them.

Mack and Lola cried all the way home. Gray had to change his suit when they returned to the house. Syrup it could handle. Mascara not so much.

CHAPTER 6

Mackenzie didn't think of herself as a covetous person. But the five miles of gorgeous chocolate leg swinging under the hem of Jessica Ryan's khaki pencil skirt made her reconsider. She would pay her for just two inches of those legs. She had even told Gray that if plastic surgeons ever offered leg stretching, that was the surgery she'd pay for. She figured if she could have a greater area of distribution, then all the sweet tea she liked to drink wouldn't be an issue and she wouldn't have had to switch to unsweetened.

Her mother told her she was buying into Hollywood voodoo by believing sugar wasn't good for you. She would pat her thighs and say, "Your daddy loved these. And it was sugar and Crisco that got them here. Worked out pretty good for me, then, wouldn't you say?"

How could you argue with that? But Mackenzie still coveted those legs.

"We've had a change in the schedule for today, Mrs. London." Jessica placed the pink and white folder next to Mackenzie's place on the kitchen island.

This was what they did every morning. Jessica reminded Mackenzie of all her commitments, and Mackenzie fulfilled them. Enjoyed most of them. Tolerated a few of them. And almost always looked forward to the end of the day and having dinner with her family. Whenever Gray's schedule allowed, it would be all three of them. But even when Gray couldn't be there, she and Maddie would eat together, then curl up on the sofa to read a book and dip Rosa's oatmeal raisin cookies into a glass of milk.

Right now, though, it was a long time until dinner. And Jessica meant nothing but business.

"Want some chocolate gravy and biscuits?" Mackenzie asked her assistant, slowly putting another forkful in her mouth and watching Jessica's reaction.

Jessica's lip turned up slightly. "No. No thank you. I ate already."

Mackenzie looked at Rosa and gave her a wink. Rosa turned away as a smile swept across her face. If it wasn't made of some kind of leaf, Jessica wouldn't eat it. Rosa had patted her own plump frame one morning and speculated in her broken English that Jessica juiced spinach for breakfast. That had really cracked Mackenzie up.

Not that she didn't appreciate healthy. In fact, she had drastically changed her family's eating habits in recent years, stressing organic foods and trying to phase out simple carbs and saturated fats, much to Rosa's frustration. But she was still left at a disadvantage with a half-Italian father, a Southern mother, a cook from Mexico, and a child who thought macaroni and cheese was a vegetable.

Mackenzie opened the folder and looked over the schedule change. She had known about the luncheon with the educators and the meeting with the chef for Wednesday night's dinner. But she hadn't planned on the meeting with the Child Advocacy Coalition of Tennessee, for which she was the spokesperson. "Ooh, busy day."

"Yes, ma'am. We've got a lot to accomplish today. And Chandra needs a word with you today or tomorrow about the children's volunteer curriculum." Jessica stood stiffly beside Mackenzie's barstool, obviously anxious for her to finish eating.

Mackenzie had three people on her office staff, which operated independently of the household staff. Susan ran her office — answering phones, screening e-mails, handling all the nitpicky details and paper shuffling. Chandra handled all the initiatives Mackenzie was a part of. Jessica was her executive assistant, traveling companion, and the only person besides Eugenia officially authorized to tell Mackenzie what to do.

Not that she always listened. "Why don't you sit down, Jessica? Sure you don't want something?"

Jessica pulled out another barstool and sat. Her simple gold bracelet clanked against the white marble countertop as she did, and she drummed her fingers without even knowing it.

Jessica didn't do well with waiting. She tended to be uptight and a little hyper — the perfect balance, Gray said, to Mackenzie's schedule-challenged attitude. Mackenzie could spend an hour or more chatting with people after an event, even when she had a back-to-back schedule. But she couldn't help it. She'd never liked living in a hurry. She loved a plan. She just didn't want to rush while doing it.

"A real Southerner isn't in a hurry," she'd tell Gray when he complained about her tardiness. She was just like her mother in that regard, and it had driven her father crazy too. A native New Yorker with a passionate Italian mother and expressive Irish father, Lorenzo Quinn had fallen in love with Eugenia during her brief freshman semester at New York's Fashion Institute of Technology. He'd been a senior at Columbia at the time. He'd stayed on for three years of law school while she moved back home to Franklin and worked at a flower shop. But as soon as his schooling was complete, he had moved to Tennessee to marry the chronically late, slightly ornery, *very Southern* girl who had stolen his heart. Southerners had driven him crazy until the day he died, but he'd been willing to endure them for Eugenia's sake.

Mackenzie knew she pretty much drove Jessica crazy too, and it had nothing to do with being Southern. Jessica had been born and raised in Nashville. She was just naturally tense — and seemingly oblivious to Mackenzie's efforts to lighten her up. Mackenzie had tried pretty much every tactic in her arsenal, from changing the schedule at the last minute to jumping out from behind doors to scare her. But all these efforts just seemed to make Jessica's edginess worse, and Mackenzie had practically given up. With her tight bun of black hair, her tortoiseshell glasses, and her two-stranded pearl necklace, Jessica had probably made about all the progress she was going to make.

Mackenzie wiped her mouth and set her napkin down beside her plate. She ran her hands through what was left of her attempt at curling her hair, but the humidity had collapsed the curls into limp waves. Come to think of it, she should probably adopt Jessica's strategy and plaster it all back. But no, she chose to torture herself. She pushed her barstool back and picked up her red cotton argyle sweater, letting it hang loosely from her left hand.

"Breakfast was absolutely perfect, Rosa. Just like my mom would make, but don't tell her I said that." She winked and turned to Jessica. "Okay, let's do it."

They left the kitchen and headed for her office. But then Mackenzie caught sight of a familiar figure through the windows. "Be right back, Jessica." She didn't wait for the protest. "Jeremiah!" she called out to the figure standing over a bed of hydrangeas that formed a sea of pom-poms at his feet.

Jeremiah Williams turned as she came out on the veranda and stood smiling as she descended the stone staircase.

"You late today, Miz Mackenzie," he said softly.

She leaned in and kissed him on his freckled cheek. "My life has officially changed, Jeremiah. My baby just walked out of my house with a book bag and lunch money, and I don't quite know what to do with myself."

He reached out one hand and took hers, his calluses hard against her soft palm. The other hand extended the most perfect thorn-free red rosebud. "Well, it still be Monday."

"This is the most beautiful one yet, Jeremiah."

He pulled a blue handkerchief from his back pocket and wiped the beaded sweat from his high forehead. "You say that every Monday. But I sure 'nough think it be the purtiest one we findin' today."

She removed her hand from his and pointed at the hydrangeas. "Do you mind cutting me some of these for our dinner Wednesday night?"

"Thought that there florist gon' do your flowers for that dinner."

"She is; she is. But ours are beautiful and I'd like to use them." She smiled mischievously. "I'll let Jessica tell her."

"You let me know how many you be

needin', and we'll be gettin' you some."

"I'll have Jessica give you a count."

He shook his head. "She all wound up, Miz Mackenzie, and now you gon' go on and wound her up some more."

Mackenzie laughed. Jeremiah missed nothing — probably knew more about what went on in the house than she did. "Jessica's good at her job," she said.

He shook his head in that sweet manner he had, as if he would have to trust her on that one. "How'd our Maddie do today?"

The emotion came hard. "It was even tougher than I thought. For us, that is. But she didn't even notice we were gone. What did she say to you this morning?"

"She gone and ax me to go with her."

Mackenzie laughed. "I'm sure she did. She would have dragged you around there like you were a kindergartner too."

"My baby girl, she do the same thing her first day a kin'ergarten. Don't know what it is 'bout little girls and schools. My boys, they run fast as they could 'side that school-house and forget they gots a mama and daddy soon's they feet hit that concrete. But not my girl. My girl wanted me in the whole way. And they love 'em some purty outfits too, don't they."

"They sure do."

"Maddie Mae showed me that outfit a hers."

"I saw her swinging around for you."

He patted her arm and spoke, his cadence soft and slow. "She gots to grow up, Miz Mackenzie, even though it be hard on her mama." He chuckled. "Way I figure it, though, that girl gon' be principal a that school by the time her first week's all used up."

Mackenzie laughed, grateful that it pushed the tears back to their place. "You're probably right about that." She looked down at her flower. "Well, I've got a packed day. Thank you for my flower today, Jeremiah."

He nodded and turned back to work his magic. He made these grounds come to life in a way that rivaled the Garden of Eden.

If God was the very first Gardener, Mackenzie was certain he had taught Jeremiah Williams everything he knew.

"No heart is bigger than a child's. And at no time is a heart more moldable than in childhood. So our job is to offer children the opportunity to see where the needs in their community lie. And I am confident that when they see the need, they will have a desire to help meet that need. All we have to do is lead them. I'm willing. Are you?"

Mackenzie let the silence linger. Then she walked from the stage back to her chair. Lola sat in the chair beside hers. Picking up the doll, Mackenzie hurried from the auditorium into the bathroom. She pulled a thermometer from her purse and took her temperature. The baby-making hour was upon her. And she had two more appointments before it was time to pick up Maddie. She returned the thermometer to her yellow leather handbag and exited the bathroom.

She couldn't skip the after-luncheon conversations, but she moved more quickly through them than usual. When the door of her car finally closed, she set Lola between her and Jessica, noting the stickiness in Lola's wiry blonde hair and wondering how many layers of syrup were actually in there.

"I need to make a change on our itinerary today," she said, knowing the mere mention of a scheduling blip would make her assistant squirm. But she'd warned Jessica when she and Gray started their new round of fertility drugs that on certain days the schedule would just have to bend. Thankfully, Jessica hadn't asked a lot of questions and, for the most part, had handled it well. She twitched a little more, but Mackenzie could deal with that.

Now Jessica tugged at her skirt as if that would fix what she was about to have to undo. "Are we talking change everything or just an appointment?"

"Well, what's Gray's schedule today?"

Jessica reached into her portfolio and pulled out a piece of paper. "He's just finishing up his Monday afternoon lunch briefing. And he has a two o'clock meeting with the joint Education Oversight committee and the TEA."

Mackenzie glanced at her watch. It was one fifteen, and Gray's office was only a ten-minute drive away. That gave them thirty minutes before Gray had to leave for his meeting.

"Perfect," she said. "Let's head to the capitol. Move my meeting with the Child Advocacy Coalition to another day this week if they can. Let them know I'm really sorry, but this is something that can't be avoided. Ask Chandra if we can talk first thing tomorrow. Then we can move the meeting with Chef Robert to after I pick Maddie up, and all will be well."

By the sound of Jessica's voice as she began her conversation with their one thirty, she guessed that all was not quite as well with Jessica.

■ ■ ■ ■

As many times as Mackenzie had visited the Tennessee state capitol building, she always felt a little twinge of pride when she approached it. Finished in 1859, the white limestone Greek Revival building — one of only eleven state capitols without a dome — had served as a fortress during the Civil War and still struck a dignified presence amid the bustle of downtown Nashville.

Their car pulled into the underground entrance. Mackenzie had already made Gray aware that she was coming and that her intentions were completely sordid. He had laughed out loud — and told her that was exactly what he had wanted to add to his day. Though he sometimes wearied of the demands the fertility treatments made on their life, he never objected to impromptu visits like this.

She made her way straight to his office, having encouraged Jessica to take a thirty-minute break. She knew her assistant was incapable of taking time off, however, so she supposed Jessica would find a place to work. Mackenzie had considered forcing the woman to take a vacation, but she feared a complete emotional breakdown would ensue.

"Good afternoon, Mrs. London." The senators from Memphis and Clarksville greeted her as she hurried up the elegant hallway.

"Good afternoon, Stan, John. Looking forward to seeing you Wednesday night. Tell Jane and Meredith I can't wait to see them either." She took two more strides toward Gray's office, then turned. "John, how did Carlton do in his cross-country meet? I forgot to ask Meredith."

The senator's eyes registered surprise. "He was in the top ten."

"Tell him great job."

"I'll do it."

The thickness of the navy carpet stopped the noise of her heels as she entered the governor's offices. Gray stood in the doorway to his private office, leaning against the doorframe, smiling. His executive assistant, Sarah Hughes, was behind her desk, glasses perched atop her nose, fingers moving like woodpeckers across the keys of her computer.

A young law clerk looked up from the small desk by the hall doorway. "Hello, Mrs. London."

"Hey, Troy, studying hard?"

"Yes, ma'am." He turned and looked at Gray. She smiled. It was evident he wanted the governor to know he was a hard worker.

The announcement caused Sarah to raise her head. A smile swept across her face. "Hello, Mackenzie. Our governor here has been expecting you."

Sarah and Mackenzie had known each other since Mackenzie was a little girl, and Sarah's daughter, Anna, was still Mackenzie's best friend. Sarah had worked for Gray's law office for ten years before she made the move with him to the capitol. There was very little she didn't know about Gray, including what an afternoon visit from Mackenzie usually meant.

She had to know for it all to work. But knowing that Sarah knew still made Mackenzie's face flush.

Gray's smile was wide as he backed into his office, white shirtsleeves rolled up, tie loosened around his neck. He closed the door behind them. Sarah would make sure they were not disturbed.

"Baby-making time?" Gray bent down to kiss her.

She ran her hand down the side of his head, his hair soft beneath her fingers. She loved the way he wore it — short, neat, with just a hint of distinguished gray at the temples. "You only have a few minutes."

He looked at her and smiled. "You've been checking my schedule?"

She crinkled her nose. "Yeah."

He took her hand and led her across the yellow-and-blue Tennessee seal rug that virtually filled his entire office. He opened the door to the quaint study off his main office and let her go inside, pressing his hand against the small of her back to guide her. This was where he read his briefs, made his phone calls, and — sometimes — made love to his wife.

He closed the door behind them. Mackenzie was already facing him, reaching for his tie. "We only have about twenty minutes. I know you don't need all of —"

He pulled her hands from his tie and pushed her back slightly.

She giggled. "But you can take *all* twenty minutes if you want to."

He reached up and slid her jacket from her shoulders. "Thank you. I think I will."

"Wonder what your constituents would think if they —"

He kissed the side of her neck, his words brushing against her ear. "I'd prefer not to think about my constituents right now, if you don't mind."

Mackenzie laughed again. She didn't

mind one little bit.

Mackenzie wrapped the tie back around Gray's neck. She knew him so well. She remembered those early days of dating when she began to learn his history and then his quirks. And, Lord have mercy, he did have his quirks.

The one that always got her the most tickled was how the covers on their bed had to be just so at night. The top sheet had to be neatly folded over the coverlet before he could actually go to sleep. But she liked her covers stuck up underneath her chin. After their first year of marriage, he had finally given up on her side.

He also had to sleep with a box fan in the room, turned on him just so. Every night before he climbed in, he would situate it precisely so it would blow on his face. Before she married him, Mackenzie had never liked noise at night. She wanted it completely quiet and totally dark. But now she had gotten used to the sound of the fan.

Oh, and he didn't like to be touched when he was ready to go to sleep. He wanted Mackenzie on her side and he on his. But that was where she drew the line. She couldn't help it. If it was with nothing more than her big toe, she was going to touch him. And he either had gotten used to that or was just tired of complaining about it.

Thinking about each of his quirks made her smile.

"Thank you, baby," she whispered as he buttoned the final button of his shirt.

He leaned down and kissed her softly on her lips. "Mack, you don't ever have to thank me for making love to you."

"I know. Just thank you for always making me welcome." She finished knotting his tie and pushed it up closer to his neck. She knew Sarah was well aware of what was happening, but she still didn't want it to be too obvious.

"You are always welcome."

She leaned her head against his chest. "I love you, Gray London."

"I love you too, babe."

"Let's pray this worked."

His lips moved against her forehead. "Even if it doesn't, I like it when you visit me like this."

She leaned her head back, laughing. "You like this wild woman, huh?"

"Love it."

She moved toward the door and turned the gold doorknob. "I'll see you at home."

"Call me when you pick up Maddie," he

said. "I can't wait to hear how her day went."

"How 'bout if I have her call you."

He was slipping his feet into his shoes. "That'd be perfect. Love you, Mack."

"Love you too." She turned back toward him, then grinned. "Oh, hey — your zipper."

"What?" He reached down and felt his exposure. "That wouldn't give anything away, would it?"

"Might give away more than you intended." She laughed.

He zipped his slacks as she walked across his office and out the door. She prayed silently that this one was it. That this afternoon encounter would result in the baby boy they both desired and they both deserved.

CHAPTER 7

Gray struggled to get his mind back on work. It was difficult because Mack's visit had taken over all of his senses and co-opted his thoughts.

The truth was this whole baby-making process left him badly torn.

He certainly didn't mind the afternoon trysts with his wife. And it was true that he wanted another child — especially a boy. He wouldn't trade Maddie for the world, but there were still days when his heart ached for a son. He wanted so much of what a father and son could share, what he and his own dad had shared.

Yet Mack's body wouldn't cooperate. And the reality of another round of fertility treatments was beginning to wear on him. He was tired of the mood swings the medication caused in Mack, tired of having to order his entire love life around thermometers and calendars, tired of worrying about the whole thing. It wasn't like he didn't have anything else on his plate. He was the governor of Tennessee, for goodness' sake!

Of course he could never tell Mackenzie any of this. She had her heart set on another baby, and she had suffered so much trying to have children. They both had. The last thing he wanted was to pressure her.

He sighed. No point in worrying about what he couldn't control. Better to focus on what was. Mack. Maddie. And his work, which was —

The chirping phone interrupted his thoughts. "Yes?"

Sarah was on the other end. "Gray, I've got Green Hills Nursing Center on line two."

His sigh was heavy. For a moment he'd forgotten about that particular worry.

"Thanks." He pushed the button. "This is Gray London."

"Governor, this is Harriet Purvis." Harriet was the nurse who oversaw his father's care at the Alzheimer's unit in the Green Hills nursing facility. There was almost no chance that she was calling with good news.

"Your father had him a bad spell today. He's been yelling at some of the other patients, calling them some names I'd rather not repeat — you know, like he would have called the North Koreans. And then, well . . ."

She paused, and Gray steeled himself. "Go ahead, tell me. Is he dropping his pants again?"

Silence on the phone. Then, "We found him in bed with another patient. A female patient. And he put up quite a fight when we tried to move him. Said she was his . . . war bride. We barely got him out of the room before the poor woman's husband showed up."

The laugh almost slipped out before Gray could stifle it. He knew the situation wasn't funny. But sometimes, well, you just had to laugh. Like the time when Dad was still living at the governor's mansion, escaped his nurses, and mooned an entire busload of tourists. . . .

"Governor, I have to tell you, we're getting complaints. He seems increasingly agitated, and the doctor is wanting to change some of his meds."

The laughter subsided. He knew what she was saying. "What do you think, Harriet? You know I trust you." And he did. The last five years of overseeing his father's care through his slow decline, even before they put him in the nursing home, had earned her that confidence.

"I think it's time to up the meds."

Gray sighed. "Okay, I'll talk to the doc about it. And I'll come by tonight to see Dad."

"He'd like that."

He hung up the phone and took the back exit out of his office. He wasn't exactly embarrassed by his tryst with Mack, but he'd just as soon not look Sarah in the eye before he left for his meeting with the Joint Select Committee on Education Oversight.

The meeting room was bustling with activity when Gray arrived. The high-backed tan leather chairs sat at attention around the mahogany tables as if aware that what went on within these four walls was important. Democrats and Republicans from both houses were there, along with three members of the Tennessee Education Association. The Speaker of the house was in one corner talking to Fletcher while Kurt poured what Gray was sure was his tenth cup of coffee. Assistants buzzed around the walls like bees waiting to swarm. The committee members offered their hellos and took their seats around the table when Gray entered.

Gray tried hard to be a leader who led by example. He didn't ask his staff to do anything that he wasn't willing to do himself. When he asked them to cut their budgets, he cut his. When he asked them to stay late, he stayed late too. When he asked them tough questions, they could be assured he had already asked those questions of himself. That style of leadership had gradually earned him a level of respect from both parties. Respect was what had them here today, in a month when the General Assembly wasn't usually in session.

The economy had plagued him since his arrival. Every item on the state budget, from schools to highways, seemed to be hemorrhaging money, and Gray had been forced to get drastic in his measures — such as the controversial release of nonviolent prisoners — to stop the flow. More still had to be done — and done now. Despite small signs that the economy was improving, a government shutdown was still a possibility. Schools were also having to tighten the belt strap — the reason for this week's emergency session.

Gray had to give the committee members credit when it came to the reform bill that was coming up for a special vote on Wednesday. They had all worked diligently to avoid hindering teachers' ability to actually teach. But it had taken months to get everyone here and remotely happy.

"Mr. Governor," Speaker Norm Johnson began, his white hair a measure of his tenure and his Southern drawl a measure of his roots, "there are some teachers who are furious about this here legislation."

Gray shook his head. He had read each of the hundreds of letters he had received about the bill — pro, con, and in between.

"Plenty of 'em love it as well." Ted Lamont, the house majority leader, tugged at the back of his toupee as he spoke, a nervous habit that indicated he didn't like the way a conversation was headed.

The three TEA members sat across from him, taking in the beginning dialogue without offering any words of their own. They had submitted their thoughts in writing months ago, and today was more about formalities. It was a final consensus meeting before the bill came up for a vote in the General Assembly.

Speaker Johnson continued. "We do believe, however, that this is the best thing for our state."

"I'm glad to hear that," Gray acknowledged.

"And I'm proud to say we have enough house votes to pass it."

Gray sat back in his chair. "Marcus, what about the senate?"

"We're good, Governor." Marcus Newman's polished voice matched his twelve-hundred-dollar suit. One of the new faces at the capitol, Newman came from a long line of Memphis legislators. He was clearly an ambitious man, and being assigned to this committee showed he was moving ahead fast, but so far he had operated as a team player. "Both sides agree that something has to be done, and we believe both sides have been fairly represented."

The crisis in education had left them little choice. With the cutbacks about to hit the schools, Gray had to offer the public something to make them see public education was worth investing in. So they had changed the graduation standards as well as the teacher evaluation guidelines. Both teachers and students were getting extra scrutiny in hopes of giving the public a school system they'd be willing to send their kids to. He had made his own contribution when he took Maddie to school this morning.

Gray's chair swiveled beneath him as he placed his arms on the table. "So we're saying all the bantering is over?"

"We'll vote tomorrow in our special committee meeting. It will have to be by proxy, of course. There's a limit to how many folks we can get back in town this time of year, even with the special circumstances of this budget." Speaker Johnson coughed and then reached for his water. He had been the Speaker for the past twelve years and a senator for thirty. Gray believed it was time for him to go, but he figured the man would die with his gavel in his hand — or die beating his opponent over the head with it. Either way, Johnson wouldn't be letting go of the gavel as long as he had any fight left in him.

Gray looked at Fletcher. His friend's red-and blue-striped bow tie tilted at his neck, and his thick head of brown hair looked rumpled. "Set up a public signing for Thursday morning," Gray told him.

"Will do."

"Well, gentlemen, I am off to see which paper I can get to write about me tomorrow." He laughed. The rest of the room did too, proving they had all read the morning paper as well. Gray stood, grateful the meeting had gone well. He shook hands and headed back to his office. Fletcher was right behind him, with Kurt on their heels.

"They may pull a last-minute stunt." Kurt ran to catch up. "I don't trust Newman. He's too . . . too . . . *pretty.*"

"They'll sign it," Gray assured.

"They've got too much to lose if they

don't," Fletcher added.

Kurt wasn't appeased. "They're looking for a reason to get rid of you."

"You read way too many newspapers."

Fletcher laughed. "No, he's just been in politics too long."

Gray chuckled too. Kurt didn't. "Y'all laugh. But don't be surprised if they throw you a curveball before Thursday morning. And I need us to sit down and go over this lawsuit from the Victims' Rights Association of Tennessee."

Gray looked at his watch. Almost three o'clock. Maddie would be getting home soon, and he didn't want to miss that call. "I'll give you thirty minutes. But when Maddie calls, you're finished."

Kurt huffed. "When Maddie calls, I'll give you a break, and then we can finish."

Fletcher patted Gray on the back. "You hired him."

There was nothing like deep friendships, and these ran the deepest. The three of them had played baseball and football together. They had gone on dates together and won Gray the student body president election together. And they had vowed that wherever the road took them, they would go together. So far they had done just that.

"Yep, I did, didn't I? Stupid college promise."

Kurt rolled his eyes. Fletcher and Gray laughed. It had been that way since college. Gray was grateful it hadn't changed.

CHAPTER 8

Mackenzie drove through the six-foot scrolled-iron gates, then peered in her rearview mirror to see them creep toward each other like old lovers. Beyond them, she caught a glimpse of the stately mansion. It still amazed her this was home.

She made the short mile drive to Maddie's school and pulled into one of the pickup lanes. She had never been in a pickup lane. For so many years she had longed for this day, the day she'd get to be like every other mother and pick up her baby from kindergarten.

She remembered all those years driving by schools, desperate for a child of her own, until she'd finally vowed never to go by a school at that time of the afternoon. It was just too painful a reminder of what she lacked. There had been so many of those reminders: kids' clothing stores, Mother's Day at church, diaper commercials, babies on playgrounds, jogging mothers pushing their babies in strollers — all of them feeling like slaps in the face.

And the questions — those were the worst. "When are you going to have children? What are you and Gray waiting on? Don't you want children? Don't you know the risks of pregnancy over thirty-five?" She had promised herself she would never ask anyone those questions. If people didn't have children, there was a reason — and she never wanted to add to their pain by pressing the issue.

The ten years of trying to conceive Maddie had been so deeply painful. But something inside of her had held on to faith — faith that she would have a child, a child who looked like a piece of her and a piece of Gray. And it had finally happened. The day Maddie was born, she and Gray had cried tears from wells so deep she hadn't known such depth could exist in the human soul. And when the nurse placed Maddie in her arms, she'd known what every pill, every shot, and every vial of blood had been for.

It had all been for the miracle of this little girl. She reached over and straightened Lola in the passenger seat. "Now you tell her what good care I took of you today, okay?" Mackenzie reminded. "Tell her about all the people you met at the luncheon and how we drove Jessica crazy. But it would be nice to assume some discretion and keep my little rendezvous with her daddy just between the two of us." She looked down and gave Lola a wink. Lola's painted-on smile assured her she would. Mackenzie's phone vibrated in the console between her seat and Lola's.

"Mrs. London?" Jessica's voice sounded tight. Anything else would have surprised her more.

"Yes, Jessica."

"Chandra told me the mission just called. They've had a father come in with his wife and eight children. They got evicted and need a place to stay until the mission can make room for them at the shelter."

Mackenzie shook her head. The economy had wrecked the lives of so many hardworking people in her state. She had never seen it like it was now.

She didn't hesitate. "Tell them yes. And tell her I'd do it at the mansion, but with the big dinner Wednesday night, I don't think that would be a good idea. Too much commotion for those children."

"That's good to hear." Jessica hated it when she let families come stay at the mansion. She said you never knew who you were letting in and it wasn't wise. Mackenzie had informed Jessica that the mansion belonged to the people of this state, and if they needed a place to lay their heads in an emergency, it was available. In the nearly three years she and Gray had lived there, almost a dozen different families had taken temporary residence there.

"Have Chandra call one of those residence hotels that has the sitting rooms and the refrigerators and stovetops. Get as many rooms as they need and put it on my personal credit card. Tell Mary at the mission that we'll pay for a week, and if she needs more time, to let us know. And be sure —"

Just then Mackenzie spotted a dark head bobbing above the front end of another car in the lane nearest the curb. Maddie's blue eyes popped up long enough to see her mother.

"Never mind. I'm going to go now because I see my baby girl." Mackenzie hung up the phone.

One of the teachers was helping a pack of tiny people, book bags hanging like sacks of bricks on their backs, cross into the second lane of cars and crawl into the safety of their parents' arms. Mackenzie was craning her neck for another glimpse of Maddie when the back door opened. Maddie tossed her backpack on the floor with a thud, then pulled her little legs up into the car and bounced into the backseat, her feet swinging wildly. "Oh, Mommy, what a day!" She threw her head back dramatically against the black leather seat.

Mackenzie laughed. "That good, huh?"

Maddie jumped up and leaned against the console between the driver's and passenger's seats.

"Maddie, you know you're supposed to immediately buckle your seat belt."

"I know." She climbed into her booster seat with a heavy sigh. "I just wanted to be close to your face to tell you about my day."

Mackenzie searched for Maddie's eyes in the rearview mirror. "Okay, here's my face. Tell me all about it."

"Where's Lola?"

Mackenzie passed the doll back to Maddie and watched as Maddie cradled her baby.

"Did my mommy take good care of you?"

"Lola and I had a very adventurous day. But we want to hear all about yours first. Did you eat your lunch? Did you remember to go to the bathroom? What did you do?"

"It was great, Mommy. We sat in a circle and said the Pledge of 'legiance. And I already knew it 'cause Daddy always makes me say it. And we got to pick out our desks, and she signed them to us and everything."

Mackenzie smiled. "You mean assigned?"

"No, she signed them to us. She wrote our name on a piece of paper and put it on top of the desk."

Mackenzie laughed. "I stand corrected."

The remainder of the drive home, Maddie talked nonstop. As the iron gates began to part for their arrival home, Mackenzie's cell phone rang. It was Gray. He couldn't wait. Mackenzie pushed the speakerphone button so Maddie could talk.

"Hey, Daddy!" Maddie hollered from the backseat.

"Hey, Maddie lady. How did it go? I know you were such a big girl today."

"I was, Daddy! I get to be the helper for the whole first week of school!"

"You do? Well, I'm so proud of you. How about you let Daddy take you and Mommy out for a really nice dinner, okay?"

"To celebrate?" Maddie responded with her infectious excitement.

"Yes, to celebrate. That okay with you, Mack?"

"Sure. You need to work late tonight?"

"Not tonight."

"I want Rotier's!" Maddie declared.

Rotier's was the place where Gray and

Mackenzie ate the night they knew they loved each other. Neither of them had expressed it until the next day, during halftime of a University of Tennessee and Vanderbilt football game, but they knew. Maddie loved that story as much as she loved Rotier's famous cheeseburgers on French bread, which had garnered them eleven straight years of being named the best burgers in Nashville. Their shakes and Reuben sandwiches were just as good. Though "really nice" it wasn't.

Gray's voice filtered through the car. "Rotier's, huh?"

"Or Chuck E. Cheese's?" Maddie offered.

Gray's laugh echoed. "That was going to be my second choice. How about we go with Rotier's. I may just fall in love with your mother all over again."

"Sounds good to me," Mackenzie said.

"Me too," Maddie echoed.

"Well, I've got to check on Dad first. They're wanting to change some meds, and I want to talk with the doctor."

"Do you need me to go?"

"No, I've got it this time. So I'll pick up my two best girls a little after six for some cheeseburgers."

"Three girls!" Maddie hollered, raising Lola by one arm and shaking her as if Gray could see her.

He answered as if he did. "Oh, right. Lulu's coming too, huh?"

"Daddy!"

Mackenzie's car pulled into the garage. "We'll see you later." And in that moment all was perfect with her world.

JEREMIAH

Maddie Mae done bust out that door like her britches on fire. I chuckled to myself today ever' time I thought 'bout that li'l spitfire takin' over that schoolhouse with her spirited self and that mouth that don't close 'less it's full up with some kind a ice cream cone or sump'n. That chil' can carry her an entire conversation with them big ol' blue eyes and thick eyebrows. She raise 'em, roll 'em, squint 'em, and purty soon she gone and tol' you 'bout the whole day without ever openin' her mouth.

"Jeremiah!"

Lord knows I love to hear that chil' call my name. Took her a while 'fore she able to say it where you had a clue what she was sayin'.

"Maddie Mae!" I knelt down 'cause I knowed what be comin'. The mud on my overalls was still kinda wet as I planted my ol' creaky knees down on the cushy grass.

"How your valley be today?"

She throwed her li'l frame up against me 'til she 'bout knocked me backward. "Green!" she squealed.

Make my belly shake ever' time. Hers too. She laugh that li'l giggle that make me glad God thought 'nough 'bout this ol' earth to make chil'rens. Ever' time I see her, I think 'bout my own granchil'ren. On days like today, I get to wonderin' what they like. How they smell. How they voices sound. I ain't never seen any a them kids. Life gone and messed that up good. But when my ache to hold 'em or know 'em floods over me, I thank God he give me this chil' to love.

I finally let go and put her back on her own two feet.

"Jeremiah, it was awesome!" Them bony li'l fingers still planted top a my shoulders like she the teacher and I'm her pupil. That girl love tellin' anyone what to do.

"Awesome, huh? That's a big ol' word."

She let go my shoulders and throwed her body down in that grass we just cut and then laid on her back like she could drink in the world. "My teacher loved me, you know."

I plopped my own self down on that furry grass and stared at the eighth wonder a this ever-spinnin' world. "I ain't got no doubt."

She popped up, pushed her palms behind her like she seen some big girl do. "You didn't? You mean, when I left this morning, you thought my teacher was going to love me?"

"Yep, sure 'nough did."

She crossed her ankles. "How'd you get so smart, Jeremiah?"

I stuck a piece a grass 'tween my teeth. "Just come out that way, I guess."

She wrinkled her nose and pushed her lips up, then grabbed her a piece a grass too. "She said I can be her helper this entire week."

"Well, ain't no better helper in this whole universe."

She nodded her head while she chewed as if she agreed. "Wish I could do it all year."

"Well, you gots to give those other chil'rens chances too."

"That's what Mommy says. She says I've got to share."

"Yep, sharin' always be a good thing. Way I see it, you keep your hands open . . ."

She fell back in the grass like she do, starin' up there at that big ol' blue sky, and finished my sentence. ". . . and God can get more in. But if you keep 'em closed, all you got be all you get."

Couldn't help but chuckle at that. "Guess I done said that a coupla times."

She lifted her hands up to the sky and twirled her fingers. "Trillions."

That's when I gone and spied with my li'l eye sump'n big and ornery — Miz Eugenia comin' down them stairs all decked out in some yeller outfit. I knowed she gon' be carryin' on like the canary she look like. She act like she live here. Drop in whenever she want and ain't got the sense to keep her opinions to herself. She think all creation need to know her thoughts. I know God don't make no mistakes, but with Eugenia . . . well, he mighta come close.

Shoulda knowed she be showin' up on the first day a school. She kinda hobbled down them stairs — been walkin' like that since she got that new knee. Look to me like she mighta got some used parts.

"Madeline Quinn London, how was my favorite grandchild's first day of school?" The voice comin' out a that red painted-up mouth ain't sounded near as pleasant as any canary I done heard. But Maddie, she jump up and smile at her grandma like there ain't no happier chil' in this here world. Provin' to me, kids'll love 'bout near anything.

"Gigi!" Maddie gone and wrapped her tiny arms 'round that cushy middle section a her grandma. 'Bout near melted into her. I thought for one second I might need to go in and snatch her out. "It was awesome!"

Miz Eugenia raised her eyebrows and looked at me. I just nodded. Safest response I knowed. Learned that the hardest of ways.

"Awesome, huh?" she said.

"Yeah! Sit, Gigi. Sit." Maddie plopped herself back down in the grass and patted the ground beside her like Gigi be a new puppy.

I was wonderin' if Miz Eugenia actually gon' do what Maddie want her to 'cause that woman be pretty picky 'bout her fancy outfits. She looked at herself, and I knowed she be figurin' if she could sit in that green grass and rise up just as yeller. But she done shocked me and plopped herself right down there next to Maddie Mae.

Don't know why I be so surprised, though. Miz Mackenzie bein' Miz Eugenia's only chil' and all, and she and the gov'nor havin' trouble makin' 'nother baby — all that make Eugenia plumb near crazy over Maddie Mae. 'Bout took all I had, but I grabbed hold a her hand and helped her down. Her hand felt smooth as silk 'gainst my ol' ruts.

Li'l one never knowed that sittin' in the grass probably be one a the sweetest things her Gigi ever done for her. 'Cause she went right back to jabberin' and carryin' on.

"There's going to be a school play this year and a field trip and I can take my lunch to school if I want, but I don't know why I'd want to do that because they have tables and tables of food and you can just pick whatever you want. It's kind of like Sunday dinner at your house, Gigi."

If anyone else in the entire city a Nashville gone and compared Eugenia Quinn's Sunday eatin's to a school lunch, they be tarred and feathered and it'd be 'nounced in her church bulletin. But when Maddie say it, Miz Eugenia take it for the sheer compliment it be.

"Well, baby girl, sounds like you are going to have the best year ever. Now take that grass out of your mouth. You look like a boy."

Maddie Mae pressed her lips together as if she be thinkin'. Eugenia eyed her. Li'l one just as stubborn. But she finally spit it out. The neighbor boy done saved us from any showdown. "Maddie!" he screamed.

Her legs automatically pushed her up off the ground. "Oliver! I went to school!"

"I know, silly. I saw ya there."

I studied that boy's wild curls. If he and Maddie grow up and get married, I sure hope she make that baby brush his hair.

"Wanna hear my campfire song?"

Chil' ain't never been without a campfire song.

"Sing it! Sing it!" Maddie squealed.

And off he went. All that chil' need is an audience, and Maddie always give him one. His campfire songs, he just make 'em up right there on the spot. Chil' got more 'magination than most people out there in Hollywood. Somebody needs to find this chil' and make him famous.

"I was sitting on a log eating hair,
And then my grandpa came with a chair.
He chewed that up and hit me,
Then he went to see a movie.
It was Shrek T-h-r-e-e.
Then he went to Subway
And bought a pack of Lay's.
He chewed that up and hit me,
Then he went to see a mo—"

Miz Eugenia cut him smack-dab off. "Seriously, darling, does your grandpa have to hit you in your new song?"

"It's just a song, Gigi," Maddie 'nounced.

"I've got one about my grandma. Want to hear that one?"

Gigi shook her head. "Why don't you two run along and play. Looks like you both have a lot of energy that needs to be exerted."

I ain't sure either a 'em chil'rens knowed what *'xerted* mean, but ain't no grass growed 'neath they feet neither 'cause they took off like streaks. Only problem, they done left me with Eugenia.

"They have the attention spans of gnats at that age, don't they, Jeremiah?" She put her red-painted nails in that there grass and tried to push herself off. Didn't work. She just kinda plopped right back there in place.

I got my own self up and reached down to help her. Lord knows I done filled up my quota for good deeds in one day. "Yes, ma'am, I reckon they do. Maddie Mae been talkin' 'bout her day and bouncin' so many directions, alls I could do is nod my head."

She laughed. "I've no doubt." Then she gone and said it. See, Miz Eugenia owned a flower shop 'fore Miz Mackenzie was born, so she convinced it be her Christian duty to tell me how to take care a my flowers. But she always start out complimentin'.

"The gardens look beautiful, Jeremiah."

But there always be sump'n up under Miz Eugenia's compliments. She never give one that ain't followed up with a *but*.

"Aw, thank you, ma'am." I dabbed at the top a my head with my ol' blue handkerchief. I done started sweatin' the minute I seen her lemon self come through that back door.

Then it come. Like it always do. Wrapped up in syrupy sweetness that would make a honeybee sick. "But you need to pay a little closer attention to your peonies over by the steps. You're drowning them."

"I'll check on 'em, ma'am. I'll check on 'em."

"I know you've been doing this for a long time, Jeremiah, but I've tended gardens a long time too and have multiple awards to prove it."

"Yes'm, you done tol' me." She tol' me that so many times it be up inside my head 'fore it come moseyin' out a her mouth.

"My friends Dimples and Berlyn have been saying that my gardens could be featured in *Southern Living*."

Good Lord amercy. That Dimples woman, half–cross-eyed, has to tilt her head just so she can make out somebody's face. And that Berlyn. Last time I seen that woman, she had more flowers on her dress than in my 'tire garden — even with half her bosoms hangin' outside it. If them two be tellin' Miz Eugenia she needs to be featured in *Southern Livin's,* she sure 'nough hurtin' for some compliments.

"Bet you could, ma'am."

She smiled like she glad I 'greed. "Well, good, then. I guess you've got everything under control here."

"Done my best for the last twenty-five years, ma'am. Ain't always got it right, but I come pretty close most a the time."

She gave me that same look she always give me, like she thought I was up to sump'n. "Well, have a good evening, Jeremiah."

"You too, ma'am." Soon as she take flight, I'd be right back to havin' me a good evenin'.

Right 'fore it was time for me to leave, Maddie come dancin' through my garden. "Our Hairy Toad Lilies are back, Jeremiah!"

"Yep," I said. "Be that time a year."

She shook her finger at me like she the teacher or sump'n. "Well, we got to get some fertilizer and stuff for 'em."

I reached down, pattin' that silky black hair. "We'll take good care a 'em, me and you."

She slipped her li'l hand inside my ol' gnarly one when I started back to the house. She giggled. "I love that name, you know."

I laughed. "Oh, yes'm, I sure 'nough know."

Her mama done called out for her then.

But 'fore she go, she tugged me down and gave me one a her soft kisses, smack-dab on my cheek. Then, 'fore I knowed it, she take wings and fly. She done reminded me a the words to that song my Shirley loved so much, from that movie where Julie Andrews had all them chil'rens. There be this line that say, "How do you catch a cloud and pin it down?"

Ever' time I see that li'l thing come scootin' through my garden, I hear them words. I know the answer too: you can't. Ain't no way to pin down no cloud.

I come to 'nother 'clusion too.

You simply ought not be tryin'.

CHAPTER 9

Gray gathered Maddie in his arms. She hung there like a rag doll. "Guess kindergarten can wear a little girl out."

Mack set the book they had been reading on the side table and clicked off the terracotta lamp. "I was sure the chocolate shake would keep her up all night."

He laughed. "She drank the whole thing, didn't she?"

Mack laughed too as she followed him toward Maddie's room. "Informed me I needed to get my own."

Mack pulled back the pink toile coverlet from the twin bed. Gray laid Maddie's sleeping body down and got her favorite Snow White nightgown from her top drawer. Scanning the Disney princess's often-washed, fading face, he remembered how he had always wanted to marry her. He liked to tell Maddie that he had — that Mack was just like Snow White. Looked like her, was sweet like her. That's why the Snow White nightgown was Maddie's favorite.

He sat on the edge of the bed and studied the tiny feet of his baby. Everything about her was so delicate and petite — just like Mack. Her fingers were dainty; her toes were dainty; her thick lashes were sweeping and fine. His heart ached, looking at her. Realizing that one day some man could come and pretend he was all that. And she would believe it, and off they would ride into dark and looming clouds on some redneck Harley. . . .

He shook his head like a dog after a bath to rid himself of the runaway thought. But life had been like that for Gray ever since Maddie came along. Things that he never thought about before now mattered tremendously. Having this little girl to love had even affected the way he governed. Most everything he did was determined by the fact that the decisions he made would affect her future. And he wanted her to have a good one.

She was still decked out in her school uniform. She hadn't wanted to take it off when she got home. So he slipped it from her body now and pulled the nightgown over her head without her even knowing the world was moving around her.

Mack sat on the other side of the bed, and he felt her studying him as he laid Maddie back down, her head on the pillow. "What?" he asked.

She smiled. "Nothing."

"With you it is never nothing."

She snickered. "It's nothing. I promise; this time it's nothing."

He pulled up the coverlet and turned his face to Mack. "You're lying."

"I love watching you with her, Gray. Whenever I see you with her, something inside me loves you more. I can't explain it. It's like this love I have for you just bores deeper into my innards."

"Now that's a visual." He smirked. "I bore into your innards."

He leaned down and kissed Maddie on her head. Mack kissed her too. He took Maddie's tiny palm in his own hand and studied it resting there as if his could consume it in a moment.

He reached over for Mack's and prayed. "Lord, thank you for the sweet day you gave us with our Maddie lady. Thank you for the new friend she made, for the teacher she loves, and thank you especially that she didn't get kicked out of school for telling the cafeteria lady the chicken nuggets don't taste like chicken."

He heard Mack giggle.

"And, Father, thank you for the gift she is to us. For giving us exactly what our hearts so longed for. Protect her heart. Don't ever let her give it away to anything but what you desire. And we trust that you know when it will be time to add another child, though you know how much we want one. Keep us safe tonight. Give us wisdom in our duties, and —" he glanced at his wife — "deepen the love in our innards."

Mack punched him.

"Amen."

"You're not supposed to joke when you pray."

He stood. "You don't think God laughs at my jokes?"

She walked toward the door. "I didn't say that. I just said when you're praying."

He draped an arm around her shoulder and pulled her close as they walked down the hall. "Good answer."

When they got to their bedroom, Mack slipped away from him and stepped into the bathroom to start her nightly routine.

"How much stuff do you have in there?" He peered into her drawer full of creams and cleansers as he reached for his toothbrush.

"As much as I need, thank you very

much." She patted the washcloth on her face.

He wiped his mouth. "I'm going to run downstairs and look over a few things real quick."

She turned quickly. "Gray, no. Honestly, every night last week you said that, and you didn't get to bed until past midnight. I'm tired of us not going to bed together. And the longer you're in office, the worse it gets."

He hated this argument. He glanced out at his nightstand. The marriage book *Love & War* was staring back at him, a reminder of the fine line between the two in a relationship. "I promised Kurt I'd read through this lawsuit before I went to the office tomorrow."

"Some days it's like you're married to Kurt," she snapped. "And what do your clerks do anyway?"

"Whatever I tell them to do. Right now we have more on our agenda than we've ever had, and it isn't even a legislative session. I just need a little grace."

"Gray, you know I give you grace. I hardly ever say anything about this. Last week when you were working late, I didn't say a single thing. When phone calls interrupt dinner, I rarely say anything. When Sunday afternoons are interrupted, I do my best to let you do what you need to do. But you don't always look ahead. And right now, do you know what I see ahead of us? In just a few months the reelection campaign will start in earnest. Now that Maddie is in school, we can't take her with us when you campaign. And I'm not leaving her. So I'm going to be here, and you're going to be traveling all the time. And that means the time we have together now is that much more valuable."

"Mack, you know I value our time."

She turned back toward the mirror, picked up a skinny tube, and started dotting some sort of fragrant cream beneath her eyes. But even if she smelled like a garden by the time she came to bed, that temper of hers could make her as thorny as a rose. "I wasn't saying you don't value our time. I was saying that when we do have the opportunity to be together, we need to do it. But if you really need to read that lawsuit, then go. I'm a big girl. I can tuck myself in."

He walked forward and gave her a kiss. "I promise I won't be long. You'll still be watching the Food Network by the time I get back." Though he knew she wouldn't. She could fall asleep more quickly than anyone he knew.

"Yeah, yeah." She left the bathroom and

disappeared into the closet.

He headed down the hallway toward the stairwell. She was right. The longer he had been here in the governor's mansion, the more consuming he had let the job become. Now time together was a rare commodity for them. They even had tour groups walking through their home on a regular basis. Virtually their only haven was inside the four walls of their bedroom. And Mackenzie did grant him a lot of grace. He shouldn't have said that. But the tug of his responsibilities could be so strong.

He turned the light on in his office and immediately caught sight of a huge stack of papers on his desk. The tug gripped his chest. He stood in the doorway for a moment, trying to resist. But the pressure wouldn't leave. He really needed to make some headway on that stack.

He clicked the light off, tiptoed upstairs again, and opened their bedroom door. The light of the television filled the bed and illuminated Mack's sleeping face.

He walked to her side, leaned down, and kissed her cheek. "Sorry, babe," he whispered.

It would be one o'clock before he came back to bed.

CHAPTER 10

Nashville's Ryman Auditorium was already considered the mother church of country music when a Californian evangelist named Charles Fuller held a revival there in 1953. After each night's service he would walk back to his hotel, and on these nightly walks he'd come across the homeless men of Nashville. Most people called them bums back then. Some asked for money, others for a handout. And with each request, another piece of Dr. Fuller's heart went out to them. When the final offering had been taken up for his revival meetings, he returned all of it to the people of Nashville, asking only that they use it to take care of the homeless men of the city.

That was the beginning of the Nashville Rescue Mission — an organization that had occupied a special place in Mackenzie's heart from her first visit as a little girl. By the time she got to high school, she was a regular volunteer. She'd chosen her social work major in college on the basis of her work there and had become one of its most vocal advocates while working for the state. And though she'd quit her social work job after Maddie came along, she'd never quit coming to the mission. She just brought Maddie with her.

"Baby girl, wait on Mommy."

Maddie had jumped out with her two Dollar General bags the minute their car stopped outside the mission's newly renovated Family Life Center on Rosa Parks Boulevard.

"I know; it's not always safe." Maddie's words came out with that exasperated tone as if she had heard this warning a hundred times.

"Yes, that's exactly right. Let me get your critters." Mackenzie reached into the trunk and pulled out a sack of stuffed animals. After spending a recent day playing with kids at the shelter, Maddie had decided she wanted to donate some of her toys.

Mackenzie closed the trunk, and Maddie's feet danced their way to the front door. The metal doors of the celery-green stucco building opened, and Maddie pranced through the metal detector, throwing her hand up to the glass window as if she did this every day. Mackenzie signed them in, then proceeded through the metal detector herself. They walked together into a green-painted hall filled with vibrant activity.

"Hello, Maddie," one of the young workers called out.

Maddie held up her bags. "I gotcha something, Vanessa."

"You got me something for my goody room?" Vanessa's smooth brown hand patted Maddie's shoulder.

"Yep, coloring books and crayons." She dug her hand through one bag as if she were on a treasure hunt, then looked up quickly. "And stuffed animals too!"

"Oh my goodness, you have outdone yourself." Vanessa held out her hand. "Do you want me to take it and put it in the Bright Spaces room?"

Mackenzie watched indecision play across her daughter's face. She had enjoyed buying the art materials and picking out which toys to bring, but she wasn't ready to hand them over. Vanessa noticed too. "I know. How about me and you take it to the room, and you can decide where we should put it."

Maddie nodded as if that was the best idea she had heard all day. Mackenzie watched as she and Vanessa headed toward the room

123

where children could play during the day when their mothers were in the dayroom, or at night, while their mothers were making arrangements for a warm place to rest their heads. The Family Life Center served women and children. The men's shelter was at the Rescue Mission headquarters two miles south. This was the primary reason the shelter had called her earlier about the family who had been evicted — because they didn't want to have to separate a family.

Today, for the most part, things were pretty quiet. It was a beautiful August day, so very few women were settled in the dayroom, where many retreated on cold or rainy days in winter or on especially hot summer ones. During daytime hours, women were allowed only in that room, in one of the classrooms, or in the cafeteria to work. They had to vacate the beds in the mornings and couldn't return until four o'clock, when dinner was served. And they had to attend evening chapel if they wanted a bed, because though the mission fed people, clothed them, and gave them a place to sleep, its primary purpose was to lead them to a personal relationship with Jesus Christ.

"Hey, you got here quicker than I

thought." Mackenzie's best friend Anna breezed through the metal detector, her long blonde hair swinging. Her pink T-shirt was creased by the weight of the taupe leather purse slung across her shoulder.

"Yeah," Mackenzie said, "we came straight from school."

"So how's the first week going?"

Mackenzie made a face. "For Maddie, wonderful. For Mommy — well, I'm surviving."

Anna put an arm around her. "I'm proud of you."

"What, because I haven't forced the teacher to let me sit in the classroom all day?"

Anna's round blue eyes sparkled as she laughed. "For that, yes, and for being a big girl. I cried all week. Gray said you've only cried for two days."

"It's only *been* two days."

Her friend gave her a wink.

They were interrupted by Maddie's feet pounding down the hall. "Nana!" she yelled as she launched herself at Anna. She hadn't been able to pronounce Anna's name when she was little, so *Nana* had stuck.

Anna knelt down and wrapped Maddie in her arms. "Are you ready to go feed some hungry people?" Anna asked.

"Yep. I brought 'em some toys and colors, and now I'm ready to go deliver their trays."

The three of them walked toward the elevator, and Maddie pushed the button to take them to the second-floor cafeteria, the hub of the center's activity. Almost six hundred meals were served there daily. And the current economic climate meant need for such help was growing.

In 2009, for the first time in the mission's history, more men were in the mission's life-recovery programs because of losing jobs and homes than because of drug or alcohol abuse. Women came to the mission for many of the same reasons, plus the fact that domestic violence increased in difficult times. No hungry person was ever turned away. And for those willing to walk through the life-recovery programs, the mission had a 70 percent success rate in getting them back on their feet and living independently.

That was a statistic Mackenzie loved to roll out when she recruited volunteers for the mission — and she was a passionate recruiter. In fact, some of her oldest friends were volunteers. She had convinced them to volunteer with her every Tuesday night, and they brought their children to help. From four to five thirty, they would offer each woman and child a meal to feed the body and a smile or a word or a touch that would hopefully feed the soul. Maddie and other young volunteers delivered trays to the women, especially those who had little ones. At last count there were fifty children staying at the shelter.

The smells of dinner were thick inside the cafeteria, which was crowded with round white tables and school cafeteria–type metal chairs with royal-blue backs and seats. Maddie ran to the stockroom and returned with plastic caps for their heads and plastic aprons. Once dressed for the evening, they went to work.

"Cleo, you look beautiful," Mackenzie said as she scooped some mashed potatoes for a young woman.

"Thank you, Miz Mackenzie." Cleo looked out through the stringy red hair that fell over her eyes.

"Maddie is going to want to play with your little one for a while tonight before we leave. Is that all right?"

Cleo kept her head down, but she smiled softly. "It's fine."

"Wonderful! I can't have her here long because she just started kindergarten. But I know she won't want to rush home."

Cleo moved down the line with a quick nod of her head.

For the next hour and a half, women filtered through the cafeteria. Mackenzie made conversation while she dished out the mashed potatoes. Maddie kept busy delivering trays and talking to babies. When the last woman had been served, they helped a little with cleanup, then turned in their hats and aprons and prepared to leave.

They ran into their friend Harrison Wheeler at the elevator as they were leaving. "Maddie, how cute do you look tonight?"

"Harry!" Maddie's hands shot up.

The young man shifted his bulky duffel bag and gave her a fist bump. "I bet you were a big help in the dining room tonight."

"I put out twenty trays."

"Twenty trays? Oh my goodness, that is amazing. I should bring you back in the kitchen to cook next time. Whoops, here's our elevator."

Harrison had been volunteering in the center's kitchen for about a year now. His mother had gone through a life-recovery program a few years back and now worked in the mission's corporate office. Her son was serving the place that had saved his mother's life.

On the ride down, Mackenzie heard a noise coming from Harrison's duffel bag. Maddie obviously heard it too because she popped her head around Harrison. Her little nose crinkled as she tried to peer right through the duffel's mesh sides. "What's in your bag?"

He shifted the bag to another shoulder and held it close to his side. "Nothing." They all heard the sound again.

The door to the elevator opened, and Maddie followed Harrison out, reaching for the bag. He grabbed her hand. "Wait. I'll get in trouble if you open that bag."

He hurried out the door and into the parking lot. Maddie burst out the door behind him and Mackenzie followed close behind. From the sounds coming from the bag, Mackenzie was pretty sure what was in there. And she knew it was not anything she wanted or Maddie needed.

"Maddie, if Harrison has asked you not to open his bag, you need to leave it alone."

Maddie turned her perplexed face to her mother. "Mommy . . ."

"Don't whine, Maddie."

"But why would Harry bring something in here to get him in trouble?"

She gave Harrison *the* look.

"Well," he said, "I couldn't keep it at home, or I would have gotten in trouble with my landlady."

"You got all kinds of troubles," Maddie

surmised.

Harrison laughed. He looked around the parking lot, then back at Maddie, and curled his finger at her. They followed him to his car, where he raised the trunk, setting the duffel bag on the edge. Then he pulled the zipper back, and two little furry heads popped out.

"Puppies!" Maddie clapped her hands, and her feet started to dance wildly. "Mommy, puppies!"

Mackenzie sighed. She'd been waging the puppy battle for the last year. She didn't think Maddie needed a puppy until she could take care of it herself.

"Harry, can I have one? You got two!"

Harrison looked nervously at Mackenzie, who was shaking her head emphatically. "Uh, I'm thinking I probably need to keep both of them. I actually got one for my girlfriend because she's been dying to get a dog, and the other one is for my sister."

Maddie knelt down and picked up the one that had already halfway clawed its way out of the bag. "But what if you went and got another one for your sister?" She nuzzled into its fur and started giggling when it kissed her nose. "Look, Mommy. It loves me already."

"You're easy to love, baby. But those are

130

Harrison's puppies, so we can't take them."

"Well, I would —"

"We can't take them."

The other puppy finally jumped out of the bag and walked over to sniff Maddie's nose. "It loves me too, Mommy!" Maddie scooped it up as well.

Mackenzie slowly moved toward Harrison's trunk. She couldn't help it. The little things were so dang cute. "What kind are they?"

One jumped from Maddie's arms into the trunk and walked toward Mackenzie. She reluctantly scooped it up, inhaling its sweet puppy breath. Puppy breath was the aroma that made even smart people lose their scruples.

"They're shih tzus. My girlfriend thinks they're the cutest dogs she's ever seen. Sweet, too. They love everybody."

Maddie spoke up. "But me mostest."

"Oh yes, absolutely. You mostest."

Mackenzie laughed when the one she was holding all but stuck its tongue up her nose. And within a few minutes, she and Maddie and their new shih tzu Sophie were on their way home. Gray was going to kill her, but she didn't care. And once he got a whiff of that puppy breath, he wouldn't care either.

Gray did care. He cared more than she had thought.

"You've got to be kidding me, Mack. As if either of us has time for a puppy. Maddie can't even pick up her clothes off the floor, much less take care of a dog. And you paid three hundred dollars for that thing?" he said as they walked toward their bedroom after tucking Maddie in bed.

Mackenzie nuzzled her nose against Sophie's soft fur. The puppy turned like a contortionist so it could lick her face. "Gray, you're being ridiculous." She laughed. "Here, let her kiss you." She held Sophie out toward him. "You'll fall in love with her, I promise."

He held up his hand. "I am not letting a dog lick me in the face. And we should have talked about this."

She pulled Sophie back against her. "Okay. Okay. We should have talked about this. But I couldn't resist. She's so cute. And she loves Maddie."

"I'm being serious, Mack. You should have talked to me. Puppies are a huge responsibility."

"Good grief. It's just a dog, Gray. And I

know a thing or two about responsibility."

He shook his head. "It's just one more thing right now, Mack. One more thing on top of an out-of-control budget and all these issues with my dad and us trying to have another baby. It's not right for you to just bring a dog home without talking to me."

She stalked past him and marched toward the bathroom, where she set Sophie down on the floor.

"Did you even hear me, Mack?"

She crossed over to the closet and pulled a pair of pajamas from one of her drawers. There would be no sexy nightgown tonight. "No. Honestly, I didn't hear a word you just said because I have no desire to talk to you when you're being perfectly unreasonable."

He stepped to the other side of the massive bank of drawers that separated their sides of the closet and leaned over it so his face would be close to hers. "I said, it's one more thing. I'm buried in problems right now, Mack, and I don't need a dog on top of it all."

She looked up into blue eyes that were more tired than angry. And this time she heard him. Really heard him. She laid the pajama pants on top of the cabinet and walked around it toward him. "This isn't about a puppy, Gray. What happened to-day?"

He shook his head. Her arms circled his waist. He let out a heavy sigh and his shoulders dropped. She knew the weight he had to carry outside these four walls, but she was grateful every time he could let down his guard and be just Gray inside her arms.

"They called from the nursing home again."

"Again?"

"It's just getting so much worse. He doesn't know me anymore, Mack. My own father doesn't even know my name."

There it was. She saw the hurt in his eyes and, for a moment, the humanity of this man whom even she sometimes thought superhuman. He could seemingly handle the world and then ask if anyone needed anything else. But he had his limits.

She wrapped her arms tighter around him. "Think we could get my mom to forget our address?"

He popped her on her arm, but a brief smile escaped. "Mack, I'm serious."

"I know. I'm sorry. But really, Gray, let me help you with him. I'll meet with your dad's doctors. I can take some of this off you if you'd let me."

"Thanks, babe. But I keep thinking I'll go in there and it just might be the day he recognizes me, that one moment he remembers who I am. And I don't know if I might go in one day and he'll be gone. I don't want to miss either of those moments."

"I hear you," she said. "Just promise me you'll let me know if I can help."

He wrapped his arms around her, then kissed her on the head. "I promise I — ow!"

She looked down to see Sophie chewing on Gray's foot. He gently shook her off. "How does something so little have such sharp teeth?"

She giggled, then bent and scooped Sophie up. "Want to let her sleep with us?"

His words came out quick and clear. "Absolutely not."

CHAPTER 11

"I swear, Mack, if this thing pees on my shoes one more time, she's going outside and Jeremiah can use her as a watering can!" Gray heard Mack giggling from the bathroom.

"Sophie! Sophie!" Maddie's voice came from down the hall. She burst through the bedroom door. "Daddy, where's Sophie?"

Gray looked in one of the mirrors that flanked the antique pine armoire and straightened his tie. "You mean, where is the peeing machine your mother let you get?"

Maddie stopped in the middle of the room and put her hands on her hips, the pleats of her skirt bending beneath her fingers. "Daddy, she's a baby. Babies pee."

Mack came out of the bathroom with her hands behind her neck, trying to hook her three-strand beaded necklace. "Maddie, we've got to do a better job of making sure

Sophie goes outside and does all her business. But, Gray, she is a puppy with a little bladder. And the dog trainer is going to start working with her today."

"Yeah, she's getting trained." Maddie's muffled tones came from under the round table that stood near the bay window, covered with photographs of family and friends. Gray bent down to see her curled up with Sophie, laughing as the puppy attacked her face with its tongue.

Gray had to admit he loved seeing his baby girl so happy. He crawled under the table with her. "Puppies are a lot of responsibility, Maddie."

She leaned against him, keeping a death grip on the wiggling puppy. "I know. But I'm so big, I'll take good care of her. Feed her. Pee her. Poop her. All of it, Daddy."

"Oh, you will, huh?" Gray pulled both girl and puppy into his lap. Sophie squirmed her way out of Maddie's arms, trying to get to Gray's face. He laughed when her tongue caught the edge of his chin.

"She likes you, Daddy!" Maddie squealed. "Even though you screamed at her."

"I didn't scream," he protested, handing the puppy back. "I announced."

Mack finished buttoning her gray cardigan and pulled her white tank down at the waist.

"Come on, baby girl, we're going to be late for school. Gray, have you seen my keys?"

Gray shook his head. The woman needed GPS to survive. "They're wherever your sunglasses are, I'm sure."

"Have you seen my sunglasses?"

"No, I was being a smart aleck."

"Well, I don't have time for you to be a smart aleck because I have to get Maddie to school. So, seriously, have you seen my keys?"

He climbed out from under the table. "I'll take her this morning. I'm headed to the office."

"Can Sophie come?" Maddie jumped up, Sophie all but flying out of her arms.

Gray rescued the puppy again and handed her to Mack. "No, Maddie lady, I'm not coming home after I let you off. Mommy gets to take care of Sophie today."

Mack pulled the wriggling ball of fluff up to her chest. "Mommy would be delighted. But I can take Maddie too."

He could tell that Mack was enjoying this new school drop-off routine. He wouldn't take it from her.

"You got to watch Lola too, Mommy."

"I will. I'm Superwoman. I can take care of everyone," she said with a smirk.

Gray leaned in and gave her a soft peck

on her pink-glossed lips. "The trainer is coming today, right?"

"I've already told you that three times. Yes, he's coming today."

"Just making sure." He noticed that Sophie calmed in Mack's arms as they headed downstairs. "Hope you two have a great day."

"It's going to be perfect, Daddy!" Maddie's feet bounced down the stairs and into the hall. She skirted her backpack at the garage door and headed straight to the car.

Gray picked up the backpack and held it out to Mack. "You do know who will be taking care of this dog, don't you?"

She shifted the now-sleeping puppy so she could take the backpack. Then she cocked her nose up at Gray and walked out the door.

"Just making sure," he called out as the door closed behind her.

CHAPTER 12

Mackenzie climbed the grand staircase of Conservation Hall, the "sinker wood" treads reclaimed from the bottom of the Tennessee River firm beneath her feet. Her phone vibrated, and Anna's picture popped up. "Hey."

"You ready for tonight?"

"Yeah, it's going to be a perfect evening. Eloise and I just made a final pass, and every detail is exquisite. You should see the hall."

"Make you glad the former governor's wife fought the Republicans to get it built?"

Mackenzie laughed. The new banquet facility had been a controversial addition to the former first lady's preservation-remodeling project for the mansion. It had been built entirely underground in the mansion's front yard. A huge courtyard outside the hall created a large hole in the center of the yard but afforded beautiful natural light for the otherwise-cavelike hall.

Before it was built, the mansion's maximum capacity for state dinners had been only twenty-two people. Larger events had been relegated to tents on the grounds with rented staging and portable restrooms. But the stunning new facility could hold up to 160 people, with each backside having a seat, and restrooms right around the corner. A decided improvement, as far as MacKenzie was concerned. Tennessee might be full of good old country folk, but no one really wanted to use a Porta-John at the governor's mansion.

The construction of Conservation Hall, along with many other aspects of the renovation project, had been bitterly protested by many citizens and lawmakers who felt the money was needed more in other places. Since the governor at the time was a Democrat, Republicans had been especially vocal on the issue. But whether they were right or wrong, the facility was beautiful. And tonight it would be enjoyed — along with every piece of artwork and priceless memorabilia it held — by the wonderful citizens of Tennessee.

"How did you do with your seating arrangements?" Anna asked.

"I believe I have ensured that no politicians will come to blows tonight."

Anna laughed. "You've done a marvelous job with this, Mackenzie. With everything you are responsible for these days, I can't believe you took this on."

Mackenzie reached the top of the steps and headed toward the family quarters. Passing a marble-topped altar table that rested under a portrait of Andrew Jackson, she picked up Maddie's gum wrapper and stuck it in her pocket. "It's been on my mind for years," she told her friend, "ever since the flood. I saw what the people of our city did for one another with no guidance. They just saw a need on their street or in their neighborhood and started ripping out carpet and drywall and digging through the mud. Then they did the same thing after the tornado hit and the ice storms and all. I mean, they're incredible, and they do it again and again. I just want to honor them in some way."

"You won't get any argument from me," Anna said. "Any word on protesters tonight? I know you said it was a possibility."

"Yeah, we got a heads-up this afternoon that there will be some protesting the prisoner release."

"Gray really thought that was what was best, huh?"

Mackenzie grabbed the handle of her bedroom door and stopped, the oil-rubbed bronze cool against her palm. "The other options were worse, except for completely shutting down the government. There are days I think that would suit all of us best."

Anna echoed her agreement. "Well, enjoy yourself tonight. And be sure to get me Rascal Flatts's autographs."

Mackenzie chuckled. "Oh, the benefits of being a governor's wife."

Maddie and Gray were stretched out across the bed when she entered the room, Lola and Sophie between them.

"Hey, are we solving the problems of the world?"

Maddie shook her head. "Nope, just trying to tell Daddy how nice he'll look in his tuxes."

Mackenzie walked over to the bed and sat, the brown silk quilted Ann Gish coverlet crinkling under her. She ran a hand through her daughter's fine locks. "I'm so glad you told him that. I think he looks fabulous in a tux too."

Maddie turned her face toward her mother. "He said he's cottin it."

Gray nodded as if that was exactly what he said.

"Boycotting?" Mackenzie asked.

"Yep, he's doing that to it, Mommy."

"Well, if he's boycotting his tux, then I guess that means I'll have to find some other handsome man to go as my date."

"You could take Jeremiah!" Maddie reared up suddenly, forcing Mackenzie to move her hand. "He told me 'bout one time when he took Miz Shirley to a really nice dinner, and he said he wore a tuxes. I think it might have been when he gave her a posal."

Mackenzie smiled. "When he proposed?"

She nodded.

"Jeremiah's a definite possibility." Mackenzie caught Gray's eye and winked. "He's pretty handsome, after all."

Maddie raised her right eyebrow and the right side of her lip with it. "Well, he's kind of handsome, but he's old like Gigi."

Gray laughed and pushed himself off the bed. "First, you'd better never tell Gigi she's old, or she'll make you go outside and pull your own switch from her willow tree. And second, there isn't another man in this town who's going out with my wife tonight when she's wearing that green dress of hers." He stuck his chest out. "I'm the only specimen she can handle anyway. So I will force myself to wear my tuxes and make sure no other man gets my wife's attention."

Maddie snickered. "Daddy's jealous,

Mommy."

Mackenzie touched her forehead to Maddie's. "I think we got him, didn't we?"

"Yep." Maddie grinned. "We got him."

Mackenzie stood too and headed for her closet. She heard the thump of Maddie's feet as they hit the floor and then the pounding as they barreled into the closet behind her.

"Let me watch you get fancy, Mommy. I want to see your dress."

Together Mackenzie and Maddie picked out everything for that evening — dress, lingerie, jewelry, shoes. And when every item was in place on Mackenzie's delicate frame, they did a spin around the closet and a final study in the mirror. Maddie slipped a tiny hand inside hers. "You look beautiful, Mommy. Just beautiful."

"Well, you helped me. I wouldn't look like this without you."

Gray walked into the room, and Mackenzie couldn't help but let out a slight gasp. He looked so handsome. He studied her with his eyes too — something that used to make her uncomfortable when they were newly married. Now, she loved knowing that her man was taking her in, every inch of her. It was a that's-my-girl kind of look —

one that made her feel known and appreciated.

He kissed her softly on the head. "You'll blow them away, babe." Then he knelt in front of Maddie. "You helped make Mommy this beautiful tonight, Maddie lady?"

"Yep. Sure did."

"Then you did a fantastic job," he said, hugging her close. Then he stood. "And now it's time for me to escort your beautiful mommy to this fancy shindig."

They walked out into the bedroom just as Eugenia knocked on the door. "Well, have mercy, Hannah," she exclaimed when they opened it. "Don't you two look like a stunning pair this evening."

"They look handsome, don't they, Gigi?"

Eugenia gave her gaze to Maddie. "They sure do, Madeline. Now, are you ready to go hang out with Gigi for the evening? We've got us some trouble to stir up."

"Mother," Mackenzie warned, "be good."

"What do you mean, good?" Eugenia huffed. "We are going to the playroom, and Oliver is coming over to join us in a game of bridge against me and Burt."

"Bridge?" Gray questioned.

"We can whoop her, Daddy!"

"You've taught my child how to play bridge?"

She shrugged. "It could be worse. I could have taught her how to play poker."

"Burt's coming?" Mackenzie inquired.

Eugenia puffed her chest and lifted her chin. "You want me to force Oliver and Madeline to spend the evening with Sandra or Berlyn?"

"We thank you for that." Gray walked over to the bed and lifted Sophie and Lola from it. "And y'all get to watch these characters tonight too."

Eugenia eyed the two things hanging from his hands as if they were aliens. "Doll babies I do." She snatched Lola from his hand. "Dogs I don't. I told you this when you asked me earlier."

Maddie reached up and took Sophie from her daddy's hands. "This is Sophie," she said, sticking the ball of fur in Eugenia's face. Her grandmother jerked back about the same time Sophie did. Mackenzie thought she might have heard the puppy growl.

"Does it poop?" Eugenia asked.

Maddie laughed. "All dogs go poop, Gigi. Means they're healthy, Mommy says. That's what she tells me when I poop."

"Well, I don't do dog poop."

"I'll clean it up if it goes poop."

This uplifting conversation was interrupted by the ringing of their bedroom phone. Gray left them to answer it.

"Mother, thank you for watching Maddie. And for watching Sophie." She held up a hand before Eugenia could speak. "Yes, your protest was noted, but we don't really have a choice. So, well . . . just be good."

Eugenia looked at Maddie and gave her a sly smile. Maddie giggled. "We will be *so* good. By the way, did you know Berlyn's boy finally got married?"

"Walter? Really? He's fifty years old, isn't he?"

"Yep." She laughed. "I told Sandra there was hope for her yet."

"When did this happen?"

"According to Berlyn, one very bad day. She can't stand his new wife. Says she dated the girl's third cousin once, and that should only happen in Kentucky."

Mackenzie shook her head. "Shoo, Mother." She pushed the two of them out of the bedroom and down the hall.

"Don't put that dog near me, Madeline."

Maddie giggled at her grandmother as she skipped toward her playroom.

Mackenzie walked through the bedroom. Gray was still on the phone, obviously talking to someone from the nursing home. She ached for her husband. His father had been as captivating as he was just a few years ago, but Alzheimer's had taken its toll. Hardly any pieces of the man remained. Gray had one older brother who lived in Knoxville, but they hardly ever heard from him — another situation that broke her heart.

Gray hung up the phone and joined her.

"You okay, babe?" she asked.

"Yeah. I'm okay. They had to sedate him tonight. Said he was screaming and talking about the war one minute and crying over Mom the next."

"Is he sleeping now?"

"They said he's settled." He let out a heavy sigh and held out his arm. "Now, let's go pretend we own the place."

CHAPTER 13

The door opened as the unknown heroes and the self-declared heroes of Tennessee made their way toward the governor's mansion. Average folks who had simply desired to help their neighbors lined up with senators and representatives to shake hands with the governor and his wife. Behind them, shouts and chanting marred the summer evening.

"Sounds like a pretty large crowd of protesters," Mackenzie said to Gray as they took their places by the stairs.

"Yeah, we expected this. The media has been talking about it all week. If there hadn't been so much coverage, I doubt there would be as many out there."

"Do you know how many are there?" She pressed her lips together as she waited for the first person to enter.

"About a hundred, I think."

"Security pretty tight?" Her anxiety was

evident. There had been only a few protests since they moved into the mansion.

"Sure, babe. It's just people sharing their frustration. I'd go picket with them if I could. In fact, if any are still out there after dinner, I'll probably go talk with them."

They ended their conversation abruptly when the first guests reached them.

They were still meeting and greeting thirty minutes later, when Speaker Johnson inserted himself in front of Gray. "You do hear them out there, don't you?"

Gray studied the aging legislator's sharp facial angles. The man's voice was sharp too, even though he whispered.

"Hard to ignore them, wouldn't you say, Norm?"

"We're going to encourage the VRA if you don't stop this."

"We?"

"Marcus Newman. He's our new boy."

Kurt had been right. Marcus was too pretty to be trusted. "Is that who helped you try to railroad the TEA bill today? How'd that work out for you, Norm? I honestly thought your word was your word when you gave it the other day. I had no idea I needed to be looking for the knife in my back."

"Not all teachers were happy."

"Nor were all the unions."

"Well, releasing prisoners is not going to solve our budget crisis."

Gray placed his hand on the man's shoulder. "Neither is the six million dollars in pork barrel spending projects you've racked up over the last twenty years. So I think what we're doing here is partially having to make up for your lack of self-control and long-term foresight. Will you share that with the Victims' Rights Association too?"

The representative shook off Gray's hand. "You need me on your side, Governor."

"I want you on my side, Norm. But I won't let you blackmail me to get you there."

He could feel Mack bristling and heard her mumble beneath her breath. She couldn't stand it when someone other than her challenged him. But her breathing softened at the arrival of the next guest. And for the remaining thirty minutes, no other politicians used the receiving line as their opportunity for sparring.

Gray walked into the closet and removed his bow tie. Mack sat on her ottoman, dress still on, legs stretched out in front of her. Her palms rested behind her, and a beautiful smile was on her face. Leaning beside her was a surprise gift he had presented her at the banquet, a black-and-white matted photo of a mud-encrusted Mack working in one of the worst-hit neighborhoods after the flood. The mat had been signed by all the residents of the neighborhood.

"You look relaxed." He slid his bow tie across the gold tie hanger on the wall.

"Yep," she said.

He removed his coat and hung it up. "Did I embarrass you?"

"Yep."

He raised his eyebrows and slipped off his shoes. "I did?"

"You did. But I loved your words. They were so thoughtful. You made each person feel like they were the only one in the room tonight. Including me. I was so proud of you."

He took off his socks and let his bare feet walk across the thick, cream-colored damask print carpet. He knelt in front of her and leaned over to kiss her. "Thanks."

"Meant it."

"I know." He stood and took off the rest of his clothes while she sat there. He changed into running shorts and a T-shirt and noticed she hadn't even begun to move. "I'm going to check on Maddie and any remaining protesters. In that order. Are you going to sleep in your dress?" he asked as he put on flip-flops.

"I may." She smiled.

"Be back in a minute." He walked down the hall and opened Maddie's door. Her Cinderella night-light cast a soft pink glow across her pink toile wallpaper and her angelic face. But that was all that was soft in the room, because Eugenia had crawled into the other twin bed and was snoring like a jackhammer. He studied her for a minute, trying to figure out how that sound was even coming out of her. He finally gave up and walked over to Maddie's bed. Lola was nestled underneath her arm and Sophie was curled up on the other side.

He stood there for a long time, looking, feeling a strange sadness. Did every father feel this when his little girl was growing up, this need to freeze time, to memorize her face? He knelt by her and prayed a quick prayer, brushed a black lock from the side of her face, and kissed her gently.

Eugenia let out a noise that he was certain would wake Maddie. She never stirred. Gray chuckled to himself as he picked up Sophie and headed downstairs.

A few protesters remained outside, so one of his security officers escorted him to the end of the driveway. He and Sophie spent thirty minutes listening to their concerns and offering his understanding; then he told them to head home. He assured them that they had done their job tonight and he had heard them. And he had. He honestly was as frustrated as they were over the whole situation.

When he finally made it back to their bedroom, Mack was nowhere to be found. He set Sophie down on the floor, and the puppy headed straight for the closet. Gray found Mack there sound asleep, still on her ottoman and still in her dress. Sophie licked her toes. Gray nudged her. "Come on, Mack. You need to get to bed."

Mack rubbed her eyes and stood up slowly. "Okay," she slurred and headed to her bathroom sink.

"Um, you might want to take the dress off before you brush your teeth."

She lifted her hand as if to say she heard him, then plodded back to the closet. When they finally climbed into the bed, he heard Sophie whine in her kennel.

He let out a loud exhale. He was too tired for this. He walked to the kennel to see her nose pressed hard against the black grate. "Don't look at me like that," he scolded.

She cocked her head and whimpered again.

He opened the kennel door. "If you tell anyone I did this, I will deny it." He lay down. Sophie nestled under his arm. And for the first time he caught a hint of her puppy breath.

That was when he knew.

Jeremiah

Sump'n be pressin' hard in on me this mornin'. Ain't had no clue what it was, like some ol' dark cloud done settled hard in on top a me. I tried to pray through it. Tol' the Lord if there be sump'n he need to tell me, then just go on and tell me. Then I prayed over ever'one I knowed.

I prayed hard. All day while I weedin' and prunin' and workin', I be prayin' too. When I hug Maddie Mae, I gone and hold on for a few more seconds. And when Miz Mackenzie come out and say hello, I hold her hand a li'l longer too.

Even saw Miz Eugenia this mornin' and said a prayer for her. Took me a while, though, 'cause first I had to go and ax the Lord to forgive me for all the mean thoughts I already had 'bout her 'fore that clock even got to nine in the mornin'. 'Cause by then she already been nitpickin' my garden to death.

But I did it. I pray for Eugenia too. Don't 'member what I pray, but I pray sump'n.

Governor London and his daddy was on my mind too. Was rememberin' how I used to see ol' Mr. London come outta his room and sit up there on his balcony. That was back 'fore they had to take him to that home. Sometimes, he just sit there and stare out like he ain't got no clue he livin' in the world, and other times he act a fool, like he be shootin' my boys or sump'n. But sometime he go and give me a smile. And I always used to wave at him, whether he wave back or not. Anyway, that was on my mind today too. I just felt this deep troublin' down inside a me.

If I had a way to know what this day gon' hold, I woulda buried my face in the dirt and not come up 'til God done changed his mind. I woulda torn my clothes like them ol' prophets in the Good Book, not eat one bite a food all day and just keep beggin' the Lord to change his mind.

I woulda done anything — but don't know if it woulda worked. I'm thinkin' God got his mind set. And I don't know why. Just don't know why. Alls I know is . . . it is. And it was. And it gon' be. And we still here. And we all wishin' we ain't.

CHAPTER 14

Gray's cordovan wing tips moved quietly across the diamond-patterned carpet of the Green Hills Nursing Center. After last night's call, he felt like he needed to check on his dad before the day started. He turned the corner to his father's room and was met with a new face. The young blonde looked up from tucking in the edges of his dad's sheets.

Her blue eyes flashed acknowledgment.

Gray spoke first. "Good morning. I just wanted to drop in and see how he's doing. Is Harriet off today?"

She wiped her hands against the sides of her print top and moved around from the far side of his dad's bed. "She comes in later today." She extended her hand. "I'm Tiffany Beecham. I just started — transferred from a nursing home in Franklin a couple of weeks ago. Harriet is showing me the ropes."

Gray smiled and shook her hand. Her

teeth were strikingly white. She should have been a dental hygienist. He moved toward his dad, who didn't stir. "Harriet runs a tight ship. Are you sure you're up for this?"

She laughed. "A tight ship is an understatement." Her Tennessee accent was thick and kind. "That woman is the best at what she does. I'm sure that is why she is looking after your father."

Gray turned toward her. "She has looked after Dad for five years now."

"I know. She's very fond of him." She nodded toward the bed.

"How has he been today? I heard he had a rough night."

She returned to the bed and adjusted the duvet. He noticed the French manicure on her fingernails — at least that was what Mack called it, he thought. Clean-looking and shiny, with white tips. "It takes a couple of days sometimes for new meds to get into the system. He has been sleeping heavily this morning, so I'm going to ask the doctor to look at them again. But you're right — I heard last night was pretty hard."

"Yeah, that's what I'm told." Gray pulled a chair up next to the bed. "He keeps things lively around here."

"I can assure you, we don't hurt for entertainment in this place. I'm waiting for someone to write a book about a day in the life of a nursing home. Some author is missing amazing material."

Their conversation was easy. He'd probably been a little hard on the other staff because he was so fond of Harriet. But this woman made him comfortable, and she seemed to know what she was doing. He reached out and took his dad's hand. "Mind if I have a few minutes with him?"

"You go right ahead, Governor. Take all the time you need. Let me know if I can get you anything."

"Thanks, Tiffany. Nice to meet you."

She nodded and left them alone.

His father's breathing was heavy and rhythmic. There were days he knew his father would be better off to just "go on to glory," as his mother used to say. Truth be told, he had never been the same since Gray's mother died. And when Gray's brother pretty much disappeared after her funeral — as he had most of his adult life — Gray Senior just seemed to shut down.

But even on the days when Gray thought his dad was dying, at least he still had him here. He could see him. Touch him. He pulled his father's hand up to his mouth and kissed it. He studied his dad's face. He hadn't moved since Gray came into the room. Maybe his medicine did need to be changed, but surely he didn't need to be comatose. And that was what he seemed like this morning.

"I'll check with the doctor today, Dad. This is no way to have to live. I promise I'll do whatever I can."

His father didn't respond. Gray wasn't sure he ever would again.

CHAPTER 15

If Mackenzie could stop the world on any day and time, it would be Friday afternoons. She and Gray had always loved that time of the week. Before Maddie came, Gray would take off early whenever he could, and they would sneak out to an early movie before high school kids took over the theater. Now they'd added Maddie to the equation and had to go early to avoid Gray's constituents at the concession line. But this Friday was even more important. This was a celebration of Maddie's first full week of school and Lola's first full week as the first lady's sidekick.

Mackenzie glanced at the doll as her car idled in the school line. She had been dreading this week, but it had turned into such a sweet time. Each season of motherhood had its own joys, and it was so important to savor every minute.

The sound of the door opening thrust her

back into the present.

"Mommy, it's Friday!" Maddie announced.

Mackenzie turned to see that Maddie's white polo shirt was as dirty as a football player's white pants after four quarters. "My word, baby girl, did you roll around in the dirt?"

Maddie leaned over the console between the front seats and retrieved Lola from the passenger's side. "Nope."

"No, ma'am," Mackenzie corrected.

"No, ma'am." Maddie settled back into her seat, holding Lola close. "I just fell chasing Charlie West around the playground."

Mackenzie chuckled and pulled out from the pickup line. "Charlie West, huh? And who, may I ask, is Charlie West?" Traffic was moving slowly as she drove toward Harding on her way to I-65 and the theater.

"Charlie West is my boyfriend."

Mackenzie's eyes widened, but she kept her voice nonchalant as she glanced back. "You have a boyfriend?"

Maddie never looked up; she was fixing Lola's hair. "Of course. I have lots of 'em."

"What do you mean, you have lots of them?"

"Mommy, it's school. There are lots of boys, and they're all my friends."

"Oh." Mackenzie laughed at her own relief as she pulled into the northbound lane of I-65. The drivers around her were pushing the speed limit now, aware that in thirty more minutes the interstate would be a parking lot. Mackenzie fell into rhythm with them. She glanced in the rearview mirror and saw that Maddie still hadn't buckled her seat belt. "Maddie, I have told you too many times that buckling your seat belt is the first thing you do when you get in the car. Now, I won't tell you that again." She kept her eyes on the rearview mirror.

Maddie gave a humph, tugging at her grubby top and reaching for the seat belt.

Mackenzie raised her right eyebrow. "Don't get an attitude with me, Madeline. I don't want to have to turn around and go home because you're being disrespectful when this is a day worth celebrating."

Mackenzie returned her attention to the road and gasped to see brake lights directly in front of her. She slammed on her own brakes and glanced in the rearview. An 18-wheeler was approaching her like a bullet.

She tried to swerve into the left-hand lane, but the impact was brutal. She felt the brunt of it on her side as it sent the car spinning. Everything else played in slow motion — the cars swerving to miss her, the trees spinning by on the side of the road, the impact as another car caught her front end and sent her into the concrete median. Her body braced on every side as if it could stop the car's motion.

When everything finally stopped, she was facing south in a northbound lane. The interstate looked like a parking lot for salvaged scrap. Steam poured out of what remained of her car's white hood.

She tasted blood but had no idea where it was coming from. The stench of an exploded air bag and the residue of its deployment left her feeling as if she were bathed in an inch of dust, but she felt no pain. She frantically pounded at the release button on her seat belt and noticed blood trickling down her fingers. When the restraint finally gave way, she turned toward the backseat, desperately desiring to see her baby girl's face. But the seat was empty.

She dug her knees into the hot leather beneath her, threw her body over the console, and grasped at the floorboards in the back. She could feel the screams coming from the base of her throat, but she could no longer hear them. Her world had gone silent. And Maddie wasn't there. She was nowhere.

Mackenzie looked up and saw the broken

window on Maddie's side. Panic dug its claws in even deeper. She threw her body back over her seat and pushed hard at her door. It wouldn't move. She propelled her entire weight against it, but it mocked her. She jumped over the panel into the passenger's seat and grabbed for the door handle. Her hands slipped because of the blood. But she paid no attention as she grabbed for it again and flung her weight against the door. Finally it gave way.

The sun burst into her sight as if it had just awoken. It pounded down on her, almost blinding her. Hands seemed to paw at her as she exited the car. She slapped at them wildly, her eyes frantically searching the sky, then the ground. People shouted, screamed, reached for her. But all she wanted was to find her baby. She tugged her way free, still screaming, and ran down the interstate.

The sun caught a reflection of white in the middle of the asphalt in front of her. The weight of her feet held her, her body unable to move. She lifted her right leg, but it felt heavy with lead. She pushed off on it anyway, forcing it to move, while hands once again tugged at her. She made her left leg follow. It took every ounce of her strength to get where she needed to go.

Lola lay facedown, her hand clutched inside Maddie's. Mackenzie threw herself on the ground next to her baby's tiny body. All her screams collided in the base of her throat.

Then there was nothing. The world went black.

And as she slipped away, she begged God to never let her return.

CHAPTER 16

Kurt's face registered panic. Gray noticed.

"Gray, you need to come now."

"What is it?"

"We've got to get you in the car now."

Gray stood unmoving behind his desk. "I'm not going anywhere until you tell me what it is."

Fletcher came through the door. The look on his face didn't go unnoticed by Gray either.

"Tell me now. Are we under attack?"

Kurt's face shifted. "No, Gray, it's . . . Mack and Maddie. There's been a bad accident. We have to get to Vanderbilt now."

Gray felt a sense of dread rise up inside of him. He instinctively grabbed his suit coat from the back of his leather desk chair and strode toward the door. He noticed everything from that moment on as if each of his senses had been injected with an overdose of adrenaline. Sarah was standing behind her desk in a bright-orange jacket. The smell of coffee was strong in the air, and he even thought he smelled popcorn.

The room was silent. Deathly silent. He noticed that most of all. And Sarah's eyes — the look in them was haunting. The sound of his shoes connecting with the marble floors as he walked through the door of his offices and headed down the hall thundered like explosions in his head. Sarah's words bounced toward him. "We'll be right behind you, Governor."

The Escalade was running, and he could smell the fumes when they reached the underground parking garage, the air thick and humid in the concrete cave. The car door was already open, and Gray could feel the coolness of the air conditioner before he even got inside. Voices collided against each other from the walkie-talkies of his security detail. Fletcher's and Kurt's phones rang almost in unison.

Gray slid across the black leather to the window. Kurt got in beside him.

"Tell me what happened."

Fletcher turned toward them from the front passenger seat. His words came out disjointed, his eyes darting wildly. "We're not sure . . . the details . . . just not all in." He stopped and then looked at Gray. "But it's bad."

"I need you to tell me how bad."

Kurt touched his arm. Gray saw tears in his eyes. "It's real bad, Gray." The emotion in his voice was now undeniable. "Maddie . . ." He couldn't get anything else out.

Gray felt the blood drain from his body. If he hadn't been sitting, he was certain he would have collapsed. He turned his face toward the window. "Mack?"

"She's in bad shape. They were taking her straight into surgery."

Gray kept his gaze out the window as they drove. The sounds of a police siren escorting them to the hospital seemed miles away. People on the streets went by in blurs. But he heard everything inside that car — Fletcher's sniffling, the vibration of the phone on the seat beside them, and the papers in Kurt's hands rustling so loudly, it was as if he were crumpling them next to Gray's ear.

"Do you know what happened?"

Fletcher's broken voice came from the front seat. "Eyewitnesses say there was a traffic jam, road construction. Mackenzie apparently swerved to avoid being rear-ended, but an 18-wheeler was swerving at the same time."

Gray's head turned sharply. "An 18-

wheeler hit her?"

Fletcher's gaze shifted down, then up. "It sent her car spinning. The truck hit her on the driver's side." He stopped abruptly.

"What are you not saying?"

Kurt instinctively reached a hand toward his friend and put it on his knee. It felt heavy and hot. "Maddie was thrown from the car."

Gray let the words settle. They never found a place to land. They went straight through his ears, pierced his gut, and then escaped somewhere, though he had no idea where words like that could escape to. "Her seat belt," Gray whispered.

He turned his gaze back toward the window. Pain was searing him from the inside out. Tears rushed down his face, and he was unable to stop them. By the time the car arrived at Vanderbilt Medical Center, Gray was halfway out the door. Two doctors in scrubs met him and ushered him to the surgical ward. The squeaking of their tennis shoes on the floors of the hospital corridor irritated him. The sound of their pants legs brushing together made him want to scream.

"I'm Dr. Hank Rosenberg, Governor, and this is Dr. Allen." The doctor was old and wiry and kept talking as he walked. "We took your wife straight into surgery when she got here. There was extensive bleeding, and X-rays showed that she had a pneumothorax. Do you know what that is?"

Gray shook his head.

"It's a collapsed lung due to changes in pressure within the chest. What happens is that, when she breathes in, her rib cage basically moves in reverse — it sinks instead of expands. This doesn't occur unless there is a great deal of blunt force trauma, usually when a rib either tears the lung or punctures the chest wall. Your wife had ribs broken in both the front and the back. When she arrived here, her breathing was very labored, and she was having severe chest pain. She was also expelling some blood as she coughed. It's amazing that she even got out of the car, but adrenaline can make even the severest pain seem nonexistent."

She got out of the car. Gray let the visual settle over him.

"She also has two broken bones in her right arm, with a complete break at the wrist, and, uh, several lacerations on her face. A few were pretty deep. She received a total of forty-five stitches, twenty-five to a cut on the left side, where the major impact was for her. But our biggest concern right now is her lung."

Gray could hear Fletcher and Kurt behind him. The doctor's words registered, but all he could think was that someone had made a catastrophic mix-up and they were talking about two people he had never met, not the two people who meant the most to him in the world.

Gray stopped in the center of the hall. The doctors were five steps ahead before they realized he wasn't beside them. "My baby girl. You haven't mentioned Maddie."

The younger doctor stopped and turned. His light-brown hair was brushed neatly to the side. "I'm sorry, sir. We thought you had been told."

He felt the lump heavy in the base of his throat. "I wasn't told anything I wanted to hear."

He felt Fletcher and Kurt move beside him. They were close. Really close. The doctors stepped forward. The one with the glasses and bony nose spoke first — Dr. Rosenberg, he thought. "It was instant, Governor."

Fletcher's hand came up under his left arm, and Kurt's hand held the other. Kurt turned Gray toward him. "She was thrown from the car. But she didn't suffer."

Gray turned when the other doctor, the younger one with the clear blue eyes, began to speak. "There was no pain. The blunt force trauma to the head was so severe that she died on impact."

He wanted to hit this man, to throw him against the wall and beat him. He wanted to hit anything. He wanted to scream. He wanted to run. He wanted to fall on the floor in a pile and weep.

"Would you like to see her? Your wife will be in surgery a couple more hours."

See her? See the lifeless body of his daughter? No, he didn't want to see her. He wanted to kill whoever was responsible for this. He wanted to go back to this morning and grab his baby and his wife and hold them close and not let them go anywhere. He wanted what had been. He wanted what had just been an hour earlier.

"Take me to her," he said.

Fletcher tugged at his arm. "Are you sure you want to do this?"

"It's my baby, Fletcher. What would you do if it was your baby?"

Fletcher released his grip and nodded, his tears no longer hidden. "I'm so sorry, Gray. Do you want us to go with you?"

Gray shook his head. The weight of it all was almost so great he couldn't move. "I'll do this. Alone."

Kurt released his grip on his other arm,

and Gray wasn't sure if he could stand without the support of his friend. But he did. He steadied his feet and spoke to the older doctor. "Take me to her, please."

The doctor nodded and led the way up the hall. When he pressed a square metal button on the wall, the swinging doors to the ER slowly opened in front of them. They moved into a large open room, and Gray could feel the eyes turn his way as he walked toward a glassed-in room where the shades were drawn.

"It was instant, Governor."

He stopped behind the doctors. The younger one held the door handle. "Would you like us to go in with you, sir?"

Gray shook his head. There were no words left. The doctor bowed his head and pulled the door open far enough for Gray to step through. But he couldn't move. There was something inside him that knew stepping through that door would make this nightmare real. It would take him to a reality that would change his life forever. And he didn't want any of this to be real. He wanted it all to be a lie, a mistake, someone else's story.

The older doctor came around and took his arm. "You don't have to do this."

He stepped inside the room, turned, and took the door from the doctor's hand. "Yes,

I do." And with those words, he closed it behind him.

He turned slowly, noticing the sun that streamed through the open window. How could the sun be shining if this was true? Then he forced his eyes to make their way to the gurney in the center of the room.

There in front of him was his Maddie lady. She was perfect. He moved to the side of the gurney and let his eyes take her in. Only then did he see bruising on the side of her face and caked blood nestled in the small crevice of her ear. This side of her hair was still damp from where they must have washed more blood out. He ran his fingers through her baby-soft black hair, which lay with such life against the white sheet. Her olive skin was paler but still held that hue he loved. And her face — her face was the same one he had memorized last night.

Last night. Last night he had known, hadn't he? He had known something. He had felt something. But he'd had no idea it would be this.

He leaned his head down and rested it against Maddie's cheek. It was cold. So cold. He instinctively drew the sheet up under her chin, and as he pulled, he saw Lola resting next to Maddie's arm. The side of her face was dirty. He took the lifeless doll and snuggled her under Maddie's chin, then tucked the sheet around them both.

"Keep her warm, Lola." Slightly frantic, he looked around the room. He needed a blanket. But the room was empty. No machines. No instruments. Nothing that would show they had done anything to save the life of his little girl.

He laid his head down against her again and let his tears fall across her cold forehead. He wrapped his arms around her, desperate to warm her, to bring her back to life. He nestled his nose in her hair and smelled the familiar scent of her favorite shampoo. A surge of nausea engulfed him. And the governor of Tennessee barely made it to the trash can in time for the pain on the inside to be expelled.

Gray felt a cold rag come down on his head. A strong arm fell across his back and wrapped itself against his side. Fletcher's voice fell on his ear. "Sit down, Gray."

He opened his eyes and saw the feet of both of his friends beneath him.

They never listened to him. He was the governor and they still never listened. Right now he was so glad.

He let himself cave into the arms of his

friends, and they helped him fall into a chair at the edge of the room. He looked up to see his child's body in front of him.

The baby girl who would never call him Daddy again.

That reality penetrated the room with such weight that he gave way beneath it. His friends could apparently see the torrent before it exploded all over them because they both fell to their knees beside him and encased him in their arms.

Then they wept.

The three most powerful men in the state of Tennessee wept.

Together.

Gray walked into the ICU, and his eyes took in an entirely different scene. Mack lay there with tubes running everywhere — one from her chest, apparently draining fluid, another from her mouth where they'd had to intubate her for surgery. A large bandage covered the left side of her face, and smaller bandages crossed her forehead and chin. A cast encased her right arm all the way to the top of her bicep. And monitors beeped constantly.

He moved to her side, grateful she was unaware of their new reality. He wished for a moment that she would never have to know. As glad as he was that she was there — still alive, still his — as thankful as the selfish piece of him was that they could walk through this pain together, the selfless part of him almost wanted her dead as well. Because when she woke up and had to deal with what had happened . . . well, he just wished he could spare her that.

"It's amazing that she even got out of the car, but adrenaline can make even the severest pain seem nonexistent."

Mack had gotten out of the car. *Oh, God, no. She saw everything.* He could only pray she'd seen the same Maddie lady he had. That she was able to know how beautiful and peaceful their baby girl was and that she'd experienced no pain.

He pulled a chair up to the left side of Mack's bed and laid his head down on her good arm. He realized then and there that the world wouldn't stop to let him collapse. In a few minutes he would have to console his mother-in-law and their best friends. And then he'd have to make arrangements to put his little girl in the ground.

The heaviness of it all caused him to sink a little deeper. But for now — for right now — he just closed his eyes and begged God to stop the world.

JEREMIAH

Five Days Later

There be the deepest sadness 'round here. It so deep and thick, you just know it gon' swallow you whole. I seen so many people tryin' to pull Miz Mackenzie outta it but can't pull somebody outta that kind a grief. They gots to decide themselves when they ready. And when does a body ever get the strength to do that?

The gov'nor, he be so strong through all this, even talk at his own baby's funeral. He say no one knowed her like him and Miz Mackenzie. And when he say that, I seen him break down for that one li'l moment, then gather himself up like a gentleman and talk some more 'bout his baby. I thought I was gon' go and lose it right in that there church.

There been so many tears this week. So much snifflin'. Miz Eugenia, she hurtin' so. But Miz Mackenzie, she like a stone today.

Just like one a them rocks in my garden. Not cryin'. Just sittin' there. I think she just be numb.

They had to postpone the funeral for 'bout five days so Miz Mackenzie's body could be put back together 'nough. But they still had to push her 'round in a wheelchair 'cause a her breathin' and all that bruisin'. And she gots way more bruisin' on her heart than her body. Them wounds gon' take lot longer to heal.

Grief ain't got no playbook — I hear somebody say that once. But I ain't been prepared for the way it done bust out 'round here. Been axin' the good Lord to help us get through . . . 'cause goin' through be the only way we gon' get to the other side.

CHAPTER 17

Eugenia burst through the swinging door of the kitchen with the force of class IV rapids on the Ocoee River. "Rosa, I need you to go on and get on out of this kitchen so I can get some food out there that people will eat."

"Señora Quinn, I make what I know Señor and Señora London want."

"There isn't a fried anything out there. Not a homemade biscuit. Nothing." Eugenia didn't even turn to see who had entered behind her. She'd know the sound of that crew anywhere.

"Okay, señora. But I help anyway, *por favor.*"

Eugenia didn't answer. She just walked over and started banging cabinet doors, looking for who knew what. Her three amigos fell in line behind her, each of them grabbing a cabinet door and banging too. After a good minute of endless clatter, Eugenia finally asked, "What in the world are y'all doing?"

Dimples tilted her head. The woman looked more like a cocker spaniel every day. "I have no idea. What are we doing?"

"We're sharing grief," Berlyn announced as she opened another cabinet and slammed it shut.

Sandra yanked at the ruffled collar of her black dress. If that woman was going to choke to death, Eugenia thought, now would be as good a time as any. Everyone was already here, and there was about to be food worth eating. Just what every good wake needed.

"I don't need you to share my grief," Eugenia announced. "I just need to put together some decent food. There isn't a piece of fried chicken on that table. What is a dinner after a funeral without fried chicken?"

"Or a congealed salad," Sandra added.

Berlyn nodded. "That's what I'm saying."

"Do they have lard in a governor's mansion?" Dimples asked.

"Dimples, you know very well we don't use lard to fry chicken anymore," Eugenia responded. "Now we use Crisco. And you can rest assured that if Eugenia Quinn's daughter lives here, then everything we need is on the premises." She bent down and

184

went to clanging cabinets again until she finally found a cast-iron skillet and pulled it out. She walked to the refrigerator and looked inside as if the secrets to life were held there.

Sandra scooted closer and put a hand on her arm. "It's okay to cry, Eugenia."

Eugenia jerked it away. "I don't need to cry. I need to cook."

"I always feel better after I've eaten grease," Berlyn responded.

"Eugenia, do they let foreigners in the governor's mansion?" Dimples always spoke of herself as a foreigner because she'd been born in Maryland, though her mother had moved to the real South when Dimples was two. She said she'd gotten here as fast as she could, and she'd given Dimples a Southern name to get her started. But even though Maryland was technically below the Mason-Dixon Line, Dimples still worried that she wasn't a true Southerner.

Eugenia never took her head out from the refrigerator. "The cook is Mexican, Dimples. Seriously."

"Just checking. I was thrown in jail one time for running into a fence. It was the third time for that particular fence, and the police thought I was drunk because I have to cock my head and all. And, well, while I was in there, you remember me telling you about —"

"About the big woman with spiky blonde hair who was making eyes at you? Yes, Dimples, we remember. We've heard this story a thousand times," Sandra announced. "And it's still disgusting each time you tell it."

Berlyn broke in. "And I still don't know how you thought you could tell she was making eyes at you anyway."

Dimples straightened her frail back and tugged at the hem of her black cotton sleeveless shirt, which hung loosely over her too-big black cotton skirt. "Shut up, Berlyn. I can see just fine. I see what I want to see, and you drive me crazy, so that's why I don't pay any attention to you and what you want me to look at. But that woman was looking at me with a look that ought not be shared between two women. And, well, that night traumatized me so much, I don't have any desire to spend another moment in jail."

Eugenia slammed the refrigerator door and opened the freezer. "You're not going to jail today, Dimples. So you can quit worrying." She found a package of frozen chicken breasts and pulled it out, slamming it down on the counter.

Berlyn walked to the pantry and swung open the doors. She stared for the longest time. Eugenia was about to go drag her out of there, but she finally grabbed a bottle of olive oil and set it on the counter by the chicken. "I didn't see Crisco."

"You didn't look," Eugenia confirmed.

"I did look. And all they have is this fake stuff. Your chicken's going to taste straight-up *nasty*."

"Well, you look pretty nasty in that dress. It's a funeral, for pete's sake, Berlyn, not an afternoon of speed dating."

Berlyn put her hands under her breasts, hoisting them up and then letting them go. "You can meet nice men at funerals, I'll have you know. And this was a big one. There were senators here."

Sandra walked over and pulled out a barstool. "And not a one of those senators, Berlyn, nor any man in that church who was actually looking at you — which I daresay was very few — ever saw your face because he was looking at your breasts."

Berlyn leaned against the counter. "Jealousy is ugly on an old woman, Sandra. Just ugly."

Sandra huffed.

Eugenia turned. "I want you all out of here, each one of you. I don't want you. I don't need you. I don't need to hear you talk about your breasts or senators or anything else. I just need you to get out of here so I can cook a real meal and —" Her voice broke.

Berlyn was at her side in a moment. She grabbed Eugenia's arm and led her to a seat at the breakfast table. Sandra grabbed Dimples's hand and got her to a seat at the table too. Berlyn squatted her thick legs down and knelt in front of Eugenia. "We're your friends, honey. We love you. And you need us."

"I need Madeline. I need for my daughter and Gray not to be hurting." Her tears were falling hard now.

Sandra and Dimples instinctively stood and came around behind her. Dimples laid her head on her shoulder, and Sandra gathered the sides of Eugenia's blonde bob together at the base of her neck like a mother would for her little girl.

"We're so sorry, Eugenia," Sandra whispered.

"We are." Dimples's mouth moved on Eugenia's shoulder.

"How do you survive something like this? Surviving Lorenzo's death was one thing, but a child? How do you survive losing your child?" Eugenia's words were coming out as bursts through her explosion of pain.

"There's no way to survive it, honey. A heart can't survive this kind of pain. Only thing that heals this kind of pain is heaven itself," Berlyn said, her meaty arms on top of Eugenia's legs. "So we're gonna pray for you. Right now, girls."

Berlyn's eyes looked past Eugenia to the two women behind her, and then she started praying. Her prayer was as loud as her Pentecostal roots. It was as fiery as a preacher during a tent revival, and it was as needed as water for an empty well. Eugenia rested her head on Berlyn's thick bosom and let the words wash over her.

When she was finished, Berlyn raised Eugenia's chin so she could look her in the eye. "Remember when our husbands died and we wondered how we were going to make it through the day? And somehow we did? We'd wake up, and it would be a new day, and we had survived? And then, day by day, the pain got a little easier and easier? Well, that is how we'll get through. It's like there is something pulling us to the next day."

Eugenia looked at Berlyn and wiped her eyes. "I can't get through this one, Berlyn."

Berlyn stood and pulled Eugenia into a tight hug that stuffed her face back into that hefty bosom. "You can and you will."

And Eugenia rested in the safety of her friend, knowing there was a huge probability of suffocation if she stayed there very long. But there was an aching piece that wouldn't really care.

JEREMIAH

Ten Days Later

Ain't nothin' green 'bout this here valley today. Valley gone dark.

Miz Eugenia pretty near moved in by now. Miz Mackenzie's best friend Anna been here for a week too, helpin' out. And you should see all the flowers and notes and such. But most people, they stayin' away.

I seen that before. Folks don't know what to do with this kind a grief. I think they 'fraid, like it sump'n you can catch. Like admittin' it mean it can happen to you. So a lotta folks clutchin' they own and grievin' at a distance.

Gov'nor been tryin' to get back to work. Guess he don't know what else to do. All the rest a us just movin' slow 'neath this dark cloud that gone and settled over us. We just tryin' to get by. Rosa cookin' and cryin'. The gov'nor's friends ain't even raised they voices at one 'nother since that sad day. And Miss Jessica ain't had her a twitch, neither.

We all just deep in the griefs. We down so deep, don't know if we ever comin' out. Like God done took the one bulb outta the lamp been keepin' all a us lit up. Like he forgot that be the one thing we needin' the most.

I ain't never understood that 'bout God. He always doin' things that in the natural don't make a lick a sense. And in middle a all that craziness, he go and ax us to trust him.

Trust him? Today I ain't even sure I like him. I been arguin' with him, givin' him all my meanness and madness. And he takin' it — ain't striked me or nothin'. Just sittin' up there, listenin' to an ol' man question his 'bility to manage this here world. 'Cause it feel like he done took his eye offa us. Way offa us.

I ain't gon' stay mad long. Never do. Me and God got a deal. He make me mad, I tell him. I make him mad, he tell me. He winnin' on the scorecard I been keepin'.

I been thinkin' a lot these days 'bout my ol' daddy. He the one taught me 'bout talkin' to God. Taught me a lot 'bout flowers too. He always say, "God can handle my yellin', and flowers can win a heart."

This white woman he work for, ol' Miz Moss, she be mean and gruff and ugly. And I don't mean just heart ugly. She just plain beat-by-the-ugly-stick ugly. And Daddy, he her yardman. Anyway, he tol' me, after he had all a her he could stand, God started layin' flowers on his heart to give her. Flowers that got meanin'.

He learned 'bout the meanin's of flowers when he worked for a flower shop, way back 'fore I come along. So he'd write the meanin' down on a note and stick the flower and the note by her door.

She ain't ever spoke one nice word to him 'bout them flowers, but he knowed she liked 'em. Said he saw it in her eyes. And sure 'nough, when my daddy died, ol' Miz Moss gone and paid for ever' part a his funeral. Took care a my mama, too, 'til the day Miz Moss died. Then Miz Moss's son took care a Mama the rest a her life.

God been speakin' to me 'bout flowers too. Couple a months ago, I ain't knowed why but felt like growin' me some white hyacinths from bulbs. Today, it like God be whisperin', "Today the day." So I take her one a them hyacinths. That mean I be prayin' for her. Ain't gon' tell her arguin' been more like it.

But she wadn't out there to take that hyacinth from me, 'cause she don't come outside to pray that prayer no more. Guess she don't see the point, since there ain't no little hand gon' be holdin' hers.

God, we gots to help her back to her point.

Gov'nor took that flower and put it in water and took it up to her, I s'pose. And I did see her sad face starin' out that there window one day. But she ain't seen me. She seen *through* me, but she ain't seen me. Don't know when she gon' see nothin' again.

I prayin' that one day, one day, Lord, our Miz Mackenzie be able to see sump'n other than her grief.

Though alls I seein' right now be mine.

CHAPTER 18

Mackenzie hugged the pillow against her body, and it seemed to press against every ache in her being. Her mother had come in that morning and opened the draperies, even though she wanted them closed. If she had the strength to get up, she would close them herself. But she didn't. All she had the strength for was tears, and fresh ones were falling down familiar paths they had all but carved on her face. They fell into her hair and then onto the pillow.

She hadn't been out of their room since the funeral. She had gone through that service with some strength she couldn't define, but as soon as she got home, she crawled into bed and had only come out to go to the bathroom. She still wore the pajamas she had put on after the funeral.

Everyone had tried to get her to take a shower — Anna, Gray, her mother. But she refused. She hadn't washed her hair, either.

And she wouldn't have eaten had her mother not force-fed her.

She was supposed to go to the doctor to get the stitches out of her face and her head, but she'd told Gray that the only way they were coming out was if the doctor came to her.

The doctor had come — almost a week ago. According to Gray, he was coming again today.

Anna did her best to love and support her, but Mackenzie could barely raise her head when she entered the room and didn't have much to say when she was there. So her friend simply sat in the chair at the bay window and read. Mackenzie knew Anna was praying too; she could hear her whispering under her breath. In those moments she wanted to scream at her friend to just get out of the room, but she didn't even have the energy to scream.

Most of the time, though, Mackenzie was grateful Anna was there. Not to talk to. Just to be. There. And yet she was also relieved when Anna left because that removed her from having to think of anything else but her own pain. Though Anna's absence only made her mother's presence increase. So Mackenzie wasn't sure what was worse.

And Gray? He had been sweet, supportive.

But she knew — she knew way down deep — that he blamed her. She could see it in his eyes. It was all her fault. She was why their baby was dead. She was the one who wasn't paying attention. She was the one who modeled the bad habit about seat belts. She was the one whose last words to her baby girl had been scolding, threatening to take away her Friday treat.

The tears fell faster now, stinging the half-healed cuts on her face. She never raised a hand to wipe them away. Gray might say he loved her, try to coax her from bed, kiss her at night, and wrap her in his arms. But there was no way he could truly love the woman who had taken the life of his little girl. And more than that — the woman who was incapable of giving him another child. How could he love that?

She heard the door open. "You're getting a bath today, Mackenzie," her mother announced as she made her way to the bathroom. Mackenzie heard her mother's shoes on the tile floor and then the sound of water as it began to fill the tub. Then her mother's presence was at the side of her bed and standing between her and the window, her substantial shadow blocking the sun. Mackenzie closed her eyes.

"You're not asleep, and you're not letting

a doctor see you like this. I love you. I know you're hurting, but you stink. And your sheets stink. So you're taking a bath, and we're getting these sheets washed."

Eugenia pulled at Mackenzie's good arm. It dropped limply to the bed. She simply pulled harder. "Come on. I'm telling you, you're not going to meet the doctor looking or smelling this way. You're getting a bath if I have to get in there with you and wash you like I did when you were a kid. And I'm pretty confident you don't want that happening."

She pulled at the arm again and finally got Mackenzie out of bed. But it hurt. Even rolling over hurt. Getting up could be excruciating. Mackenzie held her ribs and winced as Eugenia put one arm underneath her and struggled to get her to the bathroom. "You could help me by picking up your feet."

Mackenzie offered her very little. Eugenia deposited her on the ottoman in the center of the bathroom and checked the water temperature. It must have felt adequate because she walked over to Mackenzie and picked her up, stripped the white cotton shorts from her, and gingerly pulled the red tank top from her body. Her ribs were still wrapped tightly, and Eugenia removed the bandages with the utmost care. She pulled a white trash bag over Mackenzie's cast and put a rubber band at the top of it so the cast wouldn't get wet. Then she put her forty-year-old daughter in the bathtub. Eugenia sat on the ottoman across from the tub, while Mackenzie leaned her head back against the bath pillow and let the hot water settle over her.

The sensation was instantly familiar, and it felt surprisingly good. But the warmth of the water also seemed to push the pain from the inside up to the surface. Overwhelming grief roared to life and brought with it piercing wails that were deep and loud and painful.

Mackenzie heard something hit the water and then felt her mother's strong arms wrap around her, the fabric of her white linen jacket resting against Mackenzie's heaving body.

She heard Gray's voice in the bedroom.

"I've got her, Gray. Her mama's got her. Let me get her cleaned up, and I'll tell you when we're done. She'll be ready for the doctor."

Fully clothed and fully soaked, her mother held her until the wave subsided. "Breathe, baby. Breathe."

"I can't, Mama. It hurts. It all hurts."

"I know, baby. I know."

"I can't live through this."

"Now you listen to me." She felt her mother's grip tighten around her. "You did live. And you will live. We're going to make it through this together somehow. All you need is today's grace. And when you get to tomorrow, God will have all the grace you need to get through that day too."

She shook her head. "There's not enough grace for that."

"We'll get you through. Your mama will get you through. I promise you."

Mackenzie reached her hand up and grabbed hold of her mother as hard as she could. She felt in that moment that if she didn't hold on, she might slip beneath the water and let it swallow her, washing away the ache in her soul.

"I'm going to wash your hair now. Lean your head back here."

Mackenzie moved her head the best she could, grateful for a moment that this was a mighty big tub.

Eugenia carefully sprayed water from the nozzle across Mackenzie's head. "Remember how I used to do this when you were little?"

Mackenzie nodded slowly.

"Even back then, if there was a day when

your dad or I were in the pits, you'd find the pearl in it. You'd dig it out if you had to, but you always found something we should be happy about." Eugenia's thick fingers dug into her scalp. "I remember one time your father was out there mowing my lawn, not paying a lick of attention, and he ran right over the new heads of my tulips. I walked into the house ranting and raving. But you walked outside, surveyed the damage, and came right back in. You didn't miss a beat. You just said, 'Well, Mama, at least Daddy's still healthy enough to cut something.'"

Mackenzie felt her mother's stomach move slightly as a soft laugh washed through her. "I remember standing right there in the kitchen and laughing. And forgetting all about how angry I was at your daddy."

Mackenzie closed her eyes. Maddie had possessed that same magic, but she couldn't see it anymore. All she could see was the empty backseat, the flash of white. She couldn't get rid of those images in her mind. "Make it go away, Mama. Please make it go away." She clinched her eyes tighter.

Her mother wrapped her broken body in another embrace. "It's okay, Mackenzie. It's okay. Let's just get through this moment.

And then we'll get through the next moment."

When her body relaxed, her mother rinsed the shampoo, and she felt warmth as the water ran over her scalp.

Eugenia climbed out of the tub, grabbed a towel, and wrapped it around Mackenzie's clean hair. Then reached for the shaving gel and began to shave her grown daughter's legs.

Mackenzie opened her eyes and took in her own mother's pain. There were no tears. If there were, Eugenia would never let her see them. But her pain was real and thick and present in the paleness of her face, the lines around her mouth, the way she breathed. Mackenzie leaned her head back on the pillow, grateful for her mother's presence — in this moment, at least.

"Time to get out." Eugenia helped Mackenzie stand, wrapped a warm towel around her body, and sat her down on the ottoman to dry her off. She bundled her in a fresh, dry towel while she tended to herself for a moment — stripping down to her wet bra and granny panties, wrapping towels around her own head and body. Then she turned her attention back to Mackenzie.

She combed her daughter's hair and blew it dry, then dressed her in a pair of black cotton lounge pants and a white T-shirt. She'd leave rewrapping the ribs to the doctor, in order to allow Mackenzie a moment of freedom from yet one more reminder of the tragedy. After washing her face carefully, she applied vitamin E to the scars, then added a touch of mascara and lip gloss before leading her to a chair by the window.

Mackenzie turned her face and looked through the window to the gardens below. "Thank you, Mama," she whispered so quietly that she knew her mother would never hear her.

"You're welcome, baby girl."

She felt her mother's lips come down on top of her head and her mother's hand rest on her shoulder. She reached up and grabbed the hand. She didn't want to ever let go. Not ever.

CHAPTER 19

Gray sat in the hallway outside the bedroom, his head against the doorframe, his eyes closed, his insides screaming. The last two weeks had been a nightmare — first the funeral, then shutting that box on his baby girl, then each day having to watch the vastness of Mack's grief and the way she seemed to move farther away from him.

He was grateful for Eugenia. Without her, he wasn't sure he would have ever gotten Mack to eat anything. Eugenia had forced her, threatened an IV drip if she didn't open her mouth. Now she was in the bathroom with Mack, forcing her to clean up. He had heard the blow-dryer going, though now everything was quiet.

But he knew how much Eugenia was hurting too. She would put on some kind of supernatural strength to take care of her daughter, never shedding a tear, but he could hear her pain as soon as she came out of that room. He had found her in Maddie's bed the other night, clinging to her granddaughter's pillow, sobbing. But that woman was a fighter, and she was clearly determined not to let her daughter slip away without a battle.

Sophie stretched in his lap, and he looked down at the sleeping ball of fur. He had hated the thought of the dog when Maddie and Mack brought her home. But he couldn't describe what she had done for him. She had forced him up in the mornings because she had to be taken outside and then fed. She demanded his attention. And she was the only one desiring it or requiring it right now, so she was getting it. He'd gotten in the habit of taking her everywhere he went.

Which hadn't been far this week. The little bit of work he had accomplished had been done from here at the house. Mack's condition was too frail for him to leave her and go to the office. His team was handling as much of the state's business as they could without him, and what they needed him for, he took the time to oversee. But the preliminary hearing on the VRA lawsuit next week would require him back in the office.

The entire state had stopped and grieved with him and Mack until the funeral was over. But they had already begun to move on, and they would expect him to move on soon as well. For now, he and Sophie were taking lots of walks around the grounds while he prayed that somehow God would either stop the world or stop the pain.

Eugenia came out the bedroom door and almost tripped over him. She wore one of his bathrobes and had a towel wrapped around her head. The sheets from his bed were wadded up in her arms. "My word, boy, could you give me a little room to get through the door next time? Mama's a big girl."

Gray pushed his body up the wall until he was standing in front of her. Sophie shifted in his arms. He took his other arm and wrapped it around Eugenia. He pulled her close and held her tight. "I love you, Mom."

She patted his back. "I love you too, Gray."

He leaned back. "How is she?"

"Clean."

"That's huge progress."

"I don't know how you slept with her like that."

"I didn't realize it was that bad."

"Well, I knew love was blind, but I never knew it was incapable of smelling too."

He and Sophie followed her down the hall toward the laundry room. Ever since she moved in, Eugenia had refused to let the house caretakers touch the laundry. She said she had never had a person in her life touch her underwear except her, and while she was here, it was going to stay that way.

"You going to appoint that dog your chief of staff? You're with her more than your two sidekicks these days."

Gray put his nose in Sophie's fur. "She's a sweet little dog, Eugenia."

"Key word: *dog*." She opened the washer's lid and dumped the sheets inside.

"She likes me. I think I needed her."

Eugenia poured in detergent and turned to Gray, studying him. Then she reached out and patted Sophie's head as if it were a hot burner. Sophie's eyes popped open. "I think she needed you too," Eugenia said softly. "The doctor on his way?"

Gray checked his watch. "Should be here in about fifteen minutes."

"Well, I've sat her in the chair by the window. Why don't you go spend some time with her?"

"Okay." He held Sophie out to her. "Watch her for me?"

She shook her head and moved past him, heading back up the hall. "No. Y'all are the two *needing* each other. I don't need her at all."

He looked at Sophie. "Looks like we're going to see Mama." As he turned to follow Eugenia, he spotted the white hyacinth in a vase on the hallway table. Jeremiah had brought a flower each day this week, but Gray had forgotten to take her this one. Mack used to get a flower only on Mondays. Obviously Jeremiah had felt the need to change things. Gray tucked Sophie under one arm, picked up the vase, and headed to see his wife.

She didn't even move when he opened the door. Sophie squirmed beneath his arm. When he set her down on the floor, she instinctively ran to Mack's chair, her little hind legs still wobbly in getting her where she wanted to go. He walked over and placed his vase on the round table, right beside another vase that held two wilted hyacinths.

Maddie's face stared back at him from five of the ten pictures scattered on the table. His favorite was a black-and-white one where they had colored in her blue eyes and the creamy dollop of vanilla ice cream on her nose. His shattered heart seemed to fracture even more just looking at that picture.

He turned his gaze toward Mack. She still wouldn't look at him. She had hardly looked at him since the funeral. He sat on the edge of an ottoman and pulled her legs into his lap. He put his hands beneath the soft fabric of her pants and ran his hands up and down her smooth skin, physically aching to be able to pull her into his arms and have her respond in some way.

"Hey, babe." He reached up and moved a strand of dark hair behind her ear. The cuts on her face still looked painful, but he knew they were healing. If only that were true of the rest of her.

"You look beautiful," he told her.

She still didn't move. Her brown eyes remained fixed on the view outside.

"Kurt and Debbie came by today. They wanted you to know how much they love you, and they'll do anything you need, okay?"

He waited. When there was nothing, he continued. "Thad's going to be here in a minute. Can I get you anything? Would you eat something if I had your mom make it?"

Sophie was chewing on the laces of his tennis shoes.

She shook her head. "I'm not hungry."

He understood that. Food was nothing more than a nuisance to him these days too. If it wasn't needed, he wouldn't eat either. Poor Rosa made all their favorites, and Eugenia cooked some as well, but there was no flavor, no satisfaction in any of it. Eating was simply an element of survival. That's all anything in life was.

Even right now, this moment with Mack, was about survival. The next sentence. The next movement. The next moment. Life had boiled down to nothing more than surviving each moment.

"Will you talk to me? Tell me what is going on inside of you? No one in this world understands what you're experiencing like I do, babe. Please, just talk to me. I need —"

A soft knock on the door interrupted his plea. He stood instinctively. Sophie jumped underneath the table. "Come in."

Their friend and family doctor Thad Tyler walked into the room. He didn't say anything, simply wrapped Gray in a tight hug. When he stepped back, he kept his right hand on Gray's arm.

Thad turned his head toward Mack. His green eyes filled with an unavoidable compassion. "How is she?"

"Tough week. But it has nothing to do with her physical injuries."

"Well, let me check them out for her."

Thad worked and talked with Mack for the next hour, checking her wounds, listening to her lungs, and rewrapping her ribs.

Gray sat quietly on the edge of the bed with Sophie in his arms and watched as Mack lifelessly answered Thad's questions and summoned the strength she required to survive her own moment.

When Thad left, Mack turned toward the window again. She stayed there all day, cared for periodically by Eugenia, until he put her to bed. When he curled up beside her, he wrapped his arms around her waist as softly and gingerly as he could.

"I love you, babe," he whispered, burying his face in her hair. "Feel like talking?"

She never said a word.

CHAPTER 20

Even the sound of her mother fluffing a cushion for the wicker rocker on the veranda made Mackenzie want to cry. "This will do you good," Eugenia puffed as her arms beat wildly against the cushion.

"I just want to be left alone," Mackenzie protested, yet no fight resided in her tone.

"You've been alone enough. You look pasty and need some vitamin D." Eugenia placed her hand under the upper part of Mackenzie's arm and helped lower her to the chair. Mackenzie's ribs still ached with each movement. And each time they ached, so did her heart. Because the ache was a reminder of what now was.

That was one reason she wanted to be left alone, because solitude brought fewer reminders of how utterly empty her life would forever be.

It had been two weeks since she had been outside, and her mother was waiting no longer. She'd come into her room that morning at eight o'clock, forced her into the bathroom for a shower, carefully rubbed sunscreen on her facial scars. Then she'd brought her out here to the spot where she held her little girl's hand every morning and prayed.

It was a spot she'd sworn never to visit again, a prayer she could no longer manage. And yet here she was, sitting in a wicker rocker, a glass of sweet tea beside her.

She raised her face to the sun, its early September heat an undeniably welcome sensation. It fell across her arms and moved down her bare legs to her uncovered toes. The white tank top and soft blue Nike shorts had been Eugenia's choice. Everything she wore these days was Eugenia's choice.

For nearly three years, Mackenzie had picked out her wardrobe a week at a time. She'd taken her calendar to her closet on Saturday mornings before Maddie was up and chosen a complete outfit — clothing, shoes, jewelry, handbag, even underwear — for every coming event. Once she'd hung the outfits in a special section of the closet, her week had been set. Organizing her wardrobe had been something she enjoyed.

It was a girl thing. But now it was a Mama

thing. Because if it were up to Mackenzie, she'd just give it all away and go dig her baby up and climb inside the coffin with her. That's what she'd wanted to do the day of the funeral — just crawl in there with Maddie and tell them to close the lid. She would never care again what she wore.

"Your pastor's wife called," Eugenia said. "You want me to get the phone so you can call her back?"

"No thank you."

"She said there's a lady at church who lost a child and it might be good for you to talk to her."

"I'm not interested."

"Mackenzie, darling, you seriously need to —" Her mother's words stopped when the door opened. "Jessica's here."

Her assistant came into view and walked over to a chair next to the table. Mackenzie was exceptionally grateful for her presence, only because it cut her mother off.

"Good morning, Mrs. London."

"Good morning." She motioned to the other chair. "You can sit." Mackenzie could only imagine what her absence had done to Jessica's nerves. But she didn't have the energy to worry about it. Jessica was a grown woman. She'd have to figure it out for herself.

Jessica sat slowly. "We've missed you," she whispered. "And we're all so sorry."

Mackenzie looked at the young woman. A woman who had never had children. A woman who didn't know what this kind of pain was like. A woman whose biggest issue when she woke up this morning was whether to wear her taupe suit or her gray one, whether to put her hair in a bun or a ponytail.

"Thank you." Mackenzie could barely get the words out. And she said nothing more.

"Well . . ." Jessica shifted uncomfortably and finally stood. "Just know we've got everything under control in your office and, um . . . well, just let us know if we can do anything."

Mackenzie nodded but didn't answer. Jessica's eyes filled up, and she quickly turned and went back into the house.

"She's hurting for you," Eugenia said. "So many people are hurting for you." She pulled Mackenzie's hair from her neck and put it in a loose ponytail. Then she leaned over her shoulder and whispered in her ear. "I'm going to make you something to eat. I'll be right back."

They both looked up at the same time to see Jeremiah climbing the stairs to the veranda.

"Since he's headed up here, why don't you tell him that I checked on his *Lilium Loretos*. They need more shade. He's going to assassinate them."

Mackenzie stared ahead. "What is a *Lilium Loreto?*"

Eugenia patted her daughter's head. "I've taught you nothing. My horticultural talents are going to die with me because my child refuses to tap into her heritage." Her footsteps walked away, and the door opened. "It's a lily, Mackenzie. A lily."

The door closed, and Mackenzie focused her eyes on Jeremiah. His lanky, lumbering movements were strangely relaxing as he ascended the expansive staircase toward her.

He didn't look the same. No one looked the same. Mackenzie didn't see people now as she once had. No, now she saw them through her memories of them with Maddie. She couldn't help it. Every shattered piece of her heart was attached to that child. And so anyone who desired to enter her world had to pass through Maddie's memory.

Jeremiah was passing through it now. She could see Maddie so clearly, twirling around in her little skirt and telling Jeremiah all about her big day. The tears didn't even ask permission.

He reached the top of the stairs, close enough that she could see beads of sweat perched atop his upper lip. "Mornin', Miz Mackenzie."

She scanned his familiar, freckled face. "Morning, Jeremiah."

"Sure good to see you out here in the sunshine."

Mackenzie tried to smile, but her face just didn't work that way anymore. She had nothing to offer him. She was grateful he didn't force her to.

"Picked you sump'n this mornin', ma'am."

She looked at the multiple stems of multicolored blooms in his hand, then back at him. "Jeremiah, in three years you've never given me anything but roses — and those only on Mondays. Why have you changed all of a sudden?"

He shook his head and tugged at the left side of his overalls with his free hand. "Well, flowers have meanin's, you know. Each one mean sump'n. And today, these mixed Zahara zinnias be what I wanted to say to you."

She reached her hand out and let Jeremiah slip them to her. He held her hand with both of his and made sure she had a strong grasp before he let go.

"So what do these mean?"

He pulled out a faded blue hankie and swiped at his lip and forehead. "They mean I be thinkin' of a friend that ain't here no more."

The words thudded onto her heart. *He might as well give me these for the rest of my life.*

"Miz Mackenzie, ain't no words big 'nough to tell you how my heart be achin' for you and the gov'nor. Ache so deep down inside." He held a hand against his chest, and tears puddled in his lower eyelids. "I loved that chil' so much."

Mackenzie felt the knot clench more tightly inside her. She was tired of talking. "Thank you, Jeremiah."

"You 'member how you gone and loved me and took care a me and prayed for me when my Shirley died?"

That was different. "I remember when Shirley died."

"Well, I be gon' take care a you however you need. If you need me, I be right out here tendin' to our garden. I'd go and take up all your burdens sure 'nough if you could just go and hand 'em on over to me."

She didn't know what to say to that. So she just said thank you again.

He nodded the way he always did when they finished their conversations. But this time he reached down and took her free hand and placed it between his own. The warmth and gentleness and roughness and strength of it, all combined, swept through her. Then he let go. She watched his aged gait as he made his way down the stairs.

"Did you tell him about the lilies?" Eugenia's voice interrupted the silence. She set a piece of peanut butter toast with homemade preserves in front of Mackenzie.

Mackenzie kept her eyes on Jeremiah. "No, I didn't tell him."

Eugenia reached over and took the flowers from her hand. A smirky smile came over her face. "I thought he only gave you roses."

"That is all he's ever given me for three years."

"For three years? Every day?"

"Every Monday, actually. Red rosebuds with all the thorns taken off. Don't know where he found them in the winter," she mused.

Eugenia looked at Mackenzie. "He took off the thorns?"

"Yes, why?"

"Red rosebuds mean 'pure and lovely.' And when all the thorns are taken off, it means that it was love at first sight."

Mackenzie looked toward Jeremiah's

disappearing figure. "Oh," she said. "What do white hyacinths mean? He's been sending those up to me ever since the funeral." She glanced at the zinnias. "Until today, that is."

She watched as Eugenia looked out toward Jeremiah. A softness that Mackenzie rarely saw swept across her face. "They mean 'I'm praying for you.' "

Mackenzie leaned her head back. It was a good thing someone was because she wasn't sure when or if she ever would be able to again.

CHAPTER 21

Gray took off his readers and rubbed his eyes. They burned beneath his touch. The camel-colored leather of the antique desktop blurred, and he rubbed harder.

He hadn't been in the office for almost three weeks, but it was time. He was the governor, and that was the end of it. Eugenia had gotten Mack out of the room today, so life was now entering a different phase. He hoped.

"We don't have to do this now." Kurt leaned back on the sofa, laying a sheaf of printouts on the caramel velvet cushion beside him. Sam Foster, the commissioner of finance and administration, sat beside him. "It's still early days to put the budget together."

"This isn't going to be an ordinary budget." Gray's words were sharp and uncharacteristic. "We can't spend our way out of this economic slump. The housing market still hasn't recovered. The flood cost us billions of dollars, and the tornado up north and then all the weather last winter haven't helped things. We lost millions in state revenue when Opry Mills wasn't rebuilt. And the Assembly keeps trying to sneak pork through here when I've let men who are behind bars go free just to make sure we don't have to shut the lights off or cut our teacher workforce in half. Remember the 2002 government shutdown?"

Kurt nodded. He obviously remembered. Sam's face made it clear he remembered as well.

"Well, I will do it again. I will stop classes at state universities. I will close state parks. I will stop road construction." His voice was escalating as his hand made a sweeping motion in front of him. "If that's what it takes for this government to get control of itself, I will do all of it. Even in an election year." He made the last statement before Kurt posed the question.

Sarah put her pen down and straightened her back in a French antique side chair. Fletcher tugged at his bow tie. Gray felt their anxiety.

Kurt slumped back. His boyish good looks seemed to have faded some in recent weeks. "We won't even have the agency requests until October, and we won't be able to make any real decisions until we've got those numbers. But we're already looking at a shortfall this year, and it's only September. Next year's going to be even tougher."

"I know." Gray's sigh came out heavy and long. "And each decision we make affects everyone. But the senators and representatives in this state are going to have to give up something too, whether they want to or not. Or they will find themselves twiddling their thumbs back in their hometowns."

"We'll go through everything with a fine-tooth comb, Governor," Sam said, making a note in the leather portfolio on his lap. "We'll weed out everything that isn't essential."

Gray got up suddenly and pulled his dark-green suit coat from the back of his leather chair. He felt like he wanted to climb out of his skin. "We have to. Or come July, the lights in the capitol and the mansion are going to be cut off if I have to turn the switch myself."

"You going somewhere, Gray?" Kurt sat forward on the sofa, his face showing concern.

Gray was stuffing papers into his briefcase. "I'm sorry, guys. I thought I was ready. But I have to be close to Mack. Right now I just . . . need to know where she is."

The compassion in the room was both felt and seen. He knew these people had his back, his front, and his sides. Over the last few weeks he had fought to maintain any semblance of himself. He was grateful that these four people knew the Gray beneath this grief that he wore.

"Go home, Gray." Sarah spoke like a mother.

He nodded and headed for the door. "I'll read through those numbers you've given me, and maybe we can get together again in a day or two."

"We'll get it done. I promise." Kurt got to his feet and walked with him out the door. As they exited the office, he heard a rush of activity that reminded him his people wouldn't let him down. Their work to save this state from complete collapse and their work to help their governor and friend survive were mutually inclusive.

Sophie ran in front of Gray — or maybe *hopped* was more like it. She took each step as if she were a lion pouncing on its prey and claiming its domain. Though when she came down on the grass, you could barely see her. So small and so full of life. Gray

looked up and let his eyes take in the backyard.

They were gone.

The grass still held the dented remains of
where the trampoline and swing set had
been. Apparently Jeremiah had put them in
storage. Only the playhouse still stood, but
without its bench and the array of outdoor
toys that usually surrounded it.

Gray wished Jeremiah could take the
playhouse down too. But he was sadly grateful for the gesture. If God dared to bless
them with another child, Jeremiah would
get the play equipment out again. But right
now he didn't want either him or Mack living with those looming reminders of what
they had lost.

Gray had spent so much time out here
with Maddie, pushing her on the swings,
listening to her squeals of delight on the
trampoline. He missed the sound of her
voice, hated the painful silence that had
settled over the mansion. Maddie and Mack
used to fill the house with more words than
a full set of encyclopedias held. Now Mack
said almost nothing. The staff didn't seem
to know what to say either. If it weren't for
Eugenia, Gray thought he might go mad.

Sophie stopped when a butterfly swooped
down to check her out. She instinctively

backed toward him.

"It's a butterfly, Sophie, not a pterodactyl."

"Governor!"

The child's voice pierced Gray's insides. He and Sophie turned toward the thick garden of rosebushes and saw their little neighbor coming toward them, his head bouncing up and down as he ran. Gray felt his heart sink slightly. He was very fond of Oliver, who had shown such concern for the family and had even attended the funeral, his little face right there in the front-page photo. But he was also a reminder of what wasn't and what would never be. Gray had wondered if someday his Maddie lady might marry Oliver. Now his presence just announced the reality that Maddie would never grow up to marry anybody.

But none of that was Oliver's fault. Gray put on a smile. "How are you, buddy?"

The boy stopped in front of him, his curls strewn wildly about his head and his plaid shorts and blue shirt looking like he'd slept in them for the last two days. His breath came out in rapid bursts. "Sophie!" Oliver yelled when he caught sight of the puppy at Gray's feet. Sophie bounced wildly in response.

Oliver dropped to his knees and scooped

the dog up, her tongue dancing across his face. Gray's heart melted at the child's laughter. He squatted down and patted Oliver's curls. He wanted desperately to wrap Oliver in his arms. To feel the warmth of a child. Any child.

Oliver raised his face up to Gray's, his gray eyes big and bright. "I miss Maddie."

The words stung. Badly. But Gray knew the little one had to be grieving too, and to tell the truth, he was grateful for a chance to talk about her. He sat on the thick grass. "I do too, buddy."

"My mom says she's not coming back."

"I'm afraid that's right." He said it carefully, not sure what else Oliver's parents had told him or what he was truly capable of understanding about death.

"Never?"

"Well, we get to see her again in heaven one day."

Oliver scratched a red rash on his leg. The child got poison ivy more than anyone Gray knew. "My mom said that too. But heaven is real far away. I mean, I know Superman can get there and all, but I don't want to wait until I get like Superman to be able to see Maddie again. We were going to have a lemonade stand, you know."

Gray hadn't heard about that. "You were, huh?"

"Yeah, right outside the gate. We were going to make us a load. I need a new baseball glove, and she wanted to buy a dog." Oliver stopped as if he had realized something. "You think that's why she went on to heaven? 'Cause she already got her a dog and now she didn't need any money? You think she forgot I still needed my glove?"

Gray could only wish for such a simple truth. "I can assure you she didn't forget about your glove. And I'm sure that's not why she went." Gray ran his hand through the grass. "I just know it's going to be lonely without her."

"Well, I'll keep coming to see ya. I'm pretty good comp'ny."

Gray smiled. "You sure are. I've loved your visits."

Oliver stood, making it clear the conversation was over as far as he was concerned. He patted Sophie on the head and started singing one of his recently composed ditties as he danced back to his house. The child didn't need an audience. The world was clearly his stage.

He turned back as if remembering something.

"Governor!" That's what Oliver had called

him since they'd moved in. And it came out determined, with each syllable getting its own emphasis. "I learned a new French word."

"You did, huh?"

"Yep. Wanna hear?"

"Love to."

"I learned how to say puppy."

Gray sat up straighter in the grass. "Really? Well, you've got to let me hear that."

Oliver turned his nose up as well as any Frenchman Gray had ever encountered. *"Poopy."* He said it as if he were versed enough to teach the language himself.

Gray smiled. "That is awesome, Oliver. You're amazing, you know."

"I know," Oliver said as he took off through the sea of roses.

Gray heard a chuckle. He turned to see Jeremiah behind him.

"Quite a chil', ain't he?"

Gray looked toward Oliver's disappearing form. "Yeah, sweet kid." He sensed Jeremiah's weight shift as he came closer and felt Sophie's excitement escalate at the new presence. "I haven't thanked you, Jeremiah." Gray turned his face back toward the gardener. A couple of inmates' orange jumpsuits caught his eye across the lawn.

"Don't need to thank me for nothin',

229

Gov'nor. I be doin' what I love, and I just grateful I can do it at all."

Gray felt a lump rise hard and fast in the base of his throat. "Not for this. For Maddie's grave. I know what you did. Thank you for taking care of our baby."

Jeremiah bent over and dug his index finger and thumb into the base of Sophie's neck. Her little head leaned in hard for the attention. "I did what my heart be achin' to do."

"My heart aches too, Jeremiah." His words came out vulnerable in Jeremiah's paternal presence. "At times I feel like I'm not going to be able to catch my breath. I need to work, but I just want to be here. Wish I could get past this grief."

Jeremiah shook his head. "Grief ain't sump'n you wanna rush. It be God's way a helpin' us get out the pain. He know if we ain't got some way to get it all out, we gon' explode. So he give us grief, give us tears. All them things we need to get it out."

Gray brushed at tears that had slipped down his cheeks. "It's never going to be the same again. That is what's so hard for me to wrap my mind around. I'm never going to see her again — not here anyway. And life is never going to be the same."

Jeremiah lowered himself all the way to

the grass. Sophie jumped on top of his green overalls. "You right. Ain't ever gon' be the same again. Gon' be different the rest a your life. But you gon' be different too. Better, maybe." He shifted Sophie in his lap. "You strong, Gov'nor. Gentle, but strong."

Gray shook his head. "I don't feel strong."

"Strong don't mean lack a pain. Strong mean livin' spite of it."

Gray blew out hard, trying to relieve some of the tension that had built up in his chest. "What do I do with Mack? It's like she doesn't even want to live."

Jeremiah thought a minute. "Out here, when some a my flowers go and get diseased, I hafta start doctorin' 'em all up. And some, it like they be beggin' me to take the sick from 'em so they can get on with life. But others just want me doin' what need be done, then leave 'em alone. Grief don't always look the same, y'know. Miz Mackenzie ain't gon' do it the way you do."

Gray let out a soft laugh and wiped his face again. "You got that right." He reached over and pried Sophie loose from Jeremiah's pocket button, which she had been chewing intently.

"Just let her grieve however she need to right now. And give it time, 'cause ever'thing still fresh."

"Well, I suspect you're right." Gray tucked Sophie under his arm and got to his feet. He reached a hand down to help the older man up. Jeremiah took his hand and rose with ease.

"We ain't gon' let her go, Gov'nor. Gon' fight long and hard for her. And we gon' get her back. She gon' bloom again." He patted Gray's arm. "And you gon' too."

"Thank you, Jeremiah. I needed to hear that. All of it."

Jeremiah dipped his head again, and Gray turned toward the house. He looked up to see Mack's face in the window. She never saw him.

He could only hope that someday she'd see him again.

JEREMIAH

I seen me lots a grief in my day. I seen growed men stripped from they families and weepin' like chil'rens. I seen evil and pain so deep and dark and thick, it take years for some to dig they way out. Knowed my own share a troubles too. Bad troubles.

But this here be different. Maybe 'cause my heart gone and got so 'vested in Miz Mackenzie and the gov'nor and all. And maybe 'cause my heart done spread so wide and took in all that love sweet Maddie brought down here for us to know. Or maybe 'cause she so li'l and innocent. But chil'rens — chil'rens s'posed to be safe. Live long and old.

This kind a trouble make you feel sure God done lost all his good sense. Like he ain't watchin'. And we all feelin' that 'round here.

Miz Mackenzie, she not gettin' any better. Fact, she gone and made herself sick. Pale's a ghost and can't eat nothin', Rosa say. Then she caught a bad cold, and now she throwin' up all the time. Maybe got the flu or sump'n. They callin' the doctor in today to check on her.

But 'nother bad part, it just keep Miz Eugenia 'round. Can't get rid a that lady for nothin'. And you'd think, with all this cryin' and grievin' and sadness, she be more quiet. Not her. She incapable. Just chewin' the fat all the time.

That woman got more words in her than one a them word-processin' machines. And them words, they so know-it-all. Even now, with all she needs to be focusin' on, Eugenia always gots to find a way to focus on me and what I doin'. I seen her the other day out here messin' with my hydrangeas. Had me a good mind to go and sock her — and I ain't never socked no woman in my 'tire life. Beat me a good man a time or twos, but ain't never socked no woman. Shirley woulda had my hide.

But this one. Lord, you gon' have to help me, 'cause I think I'm gon' lose what left a my good mind. She just always on that last nerve.

I know I been prayin' me some selfish prayers lately. Ain't selfish to pray for Miz Mackenzie's healin' and all. But her healin' gon' get that crazy lady outta this house faster. And God help me, I be prayin' for that too.

CHAPTER 22

"Mackenzie Quinn London, I know you're sick, but you've got to eat something anyway. You're practically skin and bones as it is, and you'll never get over this whatever-it-is without some nourishment."

Mackenzie stood in the closet staring at her clothes. "Mama, I'm serious. I can't. The mere thought of food makes me sick." She wiped her nose with a Kleenex.

Eugenia threw herself down on the ottoman. "I give up. I didn't know I could be worn down, but you have officially worn me down."

"Thank the Lord," Mackenzie whispered. It was as close to a prayer as she had spoken in weeks.

"I heard that. You may have worn me down, but I can still hear."

Mackenzie faced her mother, her voice flat. "Mother, I'm in the closet looking at my own clothes. This moment holds the potential of me actually getting myself dressed. I would think we have made huge progress. So I would appreciate it if you would surrender the drama. I'm not in the mood."

"I'm incapable of surrendering drama. I'm from the South. We created drama. To surrender it would be to amputate a limb. And I'm fond of myself."

"You're full of yourself too," Mackenzie said. As soon as the words came out, she felt a churning in her gut again. It was intense and rising quickly.

She ran past her mother and flung herself across the commode. The orange juice Eugenia had pushed on her at breakfast burned as it came up. She would never drink orange juice again.

She heard her mother at the sink, water running. As Mackenzie leaned over her new porcelain friend, she realized that the sickness had at least gotten her mobile again. For the last week she had been scurrying from the bed to the toilet, from her chair to the toilet. If her limbs had been about to atrophy before, she was well on her way to becoming a track runner now.

The thought fluttered across her mind again — the same crazy thought she'd been playing with for days. She had flung it away at first. It was crazy. It would be too hopeful. And yet it kept coming back, teasing her.

A wet rag came softly against her forehead. She reached up and patted her mother's hand. "Thanks, Mama."

Eugenia kissed the top of her head. "You're welcome, baby. I'm sorry you're suffering like this. We'll trust the doctor will let us know what's wrong. He was pretty confident it was your nerves or some bug, but I'm not letting him out of here today until he tells me what's wrong with you. You've probably contracted some horrible intestinal virus because of that gardener and some mutant species of flower he's brought you, or because of some crazy Mexican thing Rosa has made you eat."

Mackenzie felt the nausea subside and sat on the stone floor. Her breast brushed against the toilet, and that familiar pain was there again. "There is nothing wrong with Jeremiah's flowers, Mother. He is a fabulous gardener. And Rosa's a wonderful cook. Now hush and help me get dressed."

Eugenia jerked the wet washcloth from Mackenzie's forehead and took her good arm to help her up. The cast on her right arm still had another four good weeks. "It's not nice to tell your mother to hush."

Mackenzie headed back into the closet while Eugenia stood in the doorway. "It's not nice to torment your daughter when she's throwing up." She used her good arm to sort through her clothing, her eyes settling on the comfortable clothing of the last several weeks. But she resisted the urge and chose a brown cotton wrap dress. She tugged at the sleeve of the dress, trying to pull it over her cast.

Eugenia laid the washcloth down on the dirty clothes hamper and came to her rescue, successfully getting her arm through. "I put a cold rag on your head; don't forget that."

Mackenzie's head was pounding. She closed her eyes and rubbed her temples.

"If you have typhoid fever, I promise the good Lord above that I am firing Rosa and you will only eat what I cook."

Mackenzie simply shook her head as she went to stand in front of the mirror. Everything about her looked foreign. Her eyes. Her skin. Her drawn face. She had probably lost twenty pounds in the last six weeks, and this wasn't helping.

"You should put a little makeup on," Eugenia offered.

Mackenzie pulled her hair back in a ponytail and sat at her bathroom counter.

"I look horrible, Mama. Have you seen these dark circles under my eyes?"

Eugenia walked over and took the concealer from her hands, then began to dab it underneath her eyes. "You've been through a time, baby girl. I'm proud that you are dressed and have clean hair. Today we will celebrate that."

Mackenzie let her mother dab some blush on her cheeks, color on her lips, and mascara on her eyelashes; then she walked to her familiar spot by the window. And as she looked outside, she realized that for one brief moment she had forgotten. For one brief moment in that closet, trying to find a dress, she had let go of that day six weeks ago that had brought her life to a screeching halt.

It was only a moment, though, because it was all back now — every piece of it. The blood, the broken window, the smell of gas, the reaching hands. The white figure on the pavement . . .

The green grass blurred into an ocean before her.

"I'll come back when the doctor gets here."

Mackenzie nodded but never turned. The doctor. He was coming because she was sick. But perhaps she wasn't. This felt . . .

240

different. And familiar. And if what she was thinking was true, she didn't know how she was going to feel about that. She kept teetering between joy and terror, unable to land on either.

"She's in here, Doctor." She heard her mother's voice through the door. She looked up to see Thad Tyler following her mother into the room. "And take it in. She's dressed in real clothes. We're believing this is going to be a daily occurrence now."

Thad gave her mother a kind smile, then saved them both. "Thank you so much, Mrs. Quinn. Do you mind if I check Mackenzie out alone?"

Eugenia gave him a look. A Eugenia look. "That's my baby girl over there, Doctor. I hear her scream one time, and I'll be in here quicker than you can say *stethoscope*."

Mackenzie wasn't sure if that was fear or humor she saw in Thad's eyes. Eugenia pointed two fingers from one hand at her eyes, then back at the doctor. That this was a grown woman often amazed Mackenzie.

"Mother. Go."

Eugenia walked backward to the door and finally out, leaving them alone.

"I came from that," Mackenzie said.

Thad chuckled. "You've been through a lot. She's just worried about you."

Mackenzie shifted in the chair. "I'm think-ing you're about to do a checkup on the wrong person."

He shook his head and grinned. "I've known your family a long time, Mackenzie. And I don't think I'm the right kind of doc-tor for her." He pulled the ottoman from the edge of her chair and sat down, leaning his elbows on his knees. "Now, tell me how you're feeling."

"I'm feeling pregnant," she said matter-of-factly.

His eyes registered surprise, and he straightened. "Pregnant?"

"Yeah. It feels just like . . . last time."

"Are you still on the Pregnyl?"

She shook her head. "I haven't taken it since Maddie died. I've barely wanted to brush my teeth, let alone have a shot re-minding me of . . . everything."

He pulled his stethoscope from his bag. He placed the cold instrument against her chest. "Breathe in."

She obeyed. Life was easier these days when she was being told what to do. Even being told to breathe helped.

"When was the last time you and Gray were intimate?"

She didn't have to think about that. She remembered. "The week Maddie died."

Everything in life would now be defined by that experience. Before Maddie died and after Maddie died.

"Were you on the Pregnyl then?"

She nodded.

He moved the stethoscope to her back. "Deep breath now."

She breathed in deeply, and when she released it, she felt light-headed. And nauseated. The wave came hard. She barely made it to the bathroom. At least now she was well-dressed as she hung over the toilet. When the wave subsided, she stood and went to the sink to wet a washcloth and wipe off her mouth. She pulled out her toothbrush and brushed.

Thad came to the door and walked over to the counter. "We'll do some blood work to see if you're right. But in the meantime you could have Gray go buy a pregnancy test for you. They're rarely wrong."

Mackenzie spit and rinsed, then straightened to look at him in the mirror. She slowly reached down and opened her bottom drawer. Five pregnancy tests sat neatly in a row inside. "They had a special on them," she quipped.

"Been a lot of trying, hasn't there?"

She could buy a car with the money she had spent on those boxes over the years, and the mere sight of them made her knees weak. "Lots."

He reached into the drawer and pulled one out. "I'd like you to take this for me."

She shook her head. "I don't want to."

"I know you don't, Mackenzie, but let's just see what it says."

She caught her reflection in the mirror. The look on her face was panicked. "What if it's negative?"

"Like I said, we'll do blood work as well. That will tell us definitely. But this could save some time. We need to find out what is causing this nausea anyway."

She took the box from him as if it contained a nuclear weapon. He gave her a reassuring smile as he slipped from the bathroom.

She hated these things. For her, they held such unfulfilled possibilities, such crushing disappointments. Five times, she'd seen tiny pink lines, and only one time had the little pink line actually resulted in life. The other four times, the pink promise had ended in miscarried pain. Still, each time she'd seen a pink line, even knowing that heartbreak could follow, something inside her had come to life in a completely new way.

She pulled the wrapper from the box. The noise felt like it echoed from every corner of the room. She did what you do to get the results on things like these and then stood up to wait. As she waited, she realized this was different from any time before. Every other time, she'd had Gray waiting right outside the door. This time she hadn't even told him her suspicions. She had just watched him grieve with her and over her for the last six weeks. And now he was consumed with worry since she had gotten so violently sick.

She wasn't sure why she hadn't told him. But she hadn't wanted to tell *anyone.* It was another piece of this new life that she had decided to keep to herself. Just like her anger, her fear, and her pain. Sharing with anyone, even Gray, felt too dangerous, like opening a wound that would never stop bleeding.

The edge of a pink line forming on the stick in her hand arrested her thoughts. She felt her breathing stop. And she didn't exhale until a completed pink line was staring back at her.

CHAPTER 23

The stainless steel handle was cold beneath Gray's fingers, the light of the refrigerator bright in the dark kitchen. "Thad was here today," he said into the phone, "but I don't know what he said. I was at the office until about an hour ago, going over some budget stuff with a few of the clerks. Did you get my message about Raymond Field's $150,000 project to study the life cycle of cicadas here in Nashville?"

Kurt's voice came through the other end. "Are you kidding me? Wouldn't his district love to know when the state parks close or we have to lay off police officers that at least we're figuring out when the next round of cicadas are coming?"

"I can tell them that for free." Cold air from the refrigerator filtered out onto Gray's face. "Some come out every thirteen years and some come out every seventeen, depending on what kind of cicadas they are.

There, I just saved us $150,000."

"Get some rest, friend."

"I will. Talk to you tomorrow."

Gray ended the call and laid his phone on the counter. He turned back to the contents of the refrigerator and realized that two months ago everything there would have looked good to him. Tonight he just knew he needed to eat because he had worked through dinner and his body required food. He closed the door, deciding to settle for a banana. That at least would quell the growling.

He turned and jumped at the shadowed figure in front of him, illuminated by the outside lights shining through the large bay window. It was Mack.

"You're working late tonight."

He walked around the island that separated them, his hand sliding across the wooden top as he went. "What are you still doing up? I thought you would have gone to bed hours ago. You think you could eat something? I'll fix you something." He took the edges of her white cotton robe beneath his fingers.

She patted his hands. "No, I'm good. I actually got some soup down tonight. Thad gave me some medicine that seems to have stopped the vomiting, but it knocked me out. Just woke up a couple of hours ago."

"Do you want to tell me what he said?"

Mack pulled out a barstool and sat, so he pulled one out for himself. She was quiet, and in the darkness it was hard to make out the expression on her face. She finally spoke. "Babe, I've never hurt like this before."

His hand instinctively went to her knee. His hunger had completely dissipated. "I know," he said. "Me neither."

She placed her hand on top of his. "I'm so sorry. I've seen your hurt. I've felt it in bed at night. But it's been all I can do to breathe, let alone feel for someone else."

"But I needed you." He heard the break in his own voice. "No one around here but you understands how hard this is. Not really. I don't want to eat. I do everything in my power to work because I know I have to. Then I come home, and I can't even talk to you. I can't ache with you. I can't cry with you. Instead, I've felt like you just want to grieve alone."

She laid her head against his arm. It felt so good to have her near him simply because she wanted to be. And yet he couldn't help feeling a little angry too. A little hurt. The way she had pulled away, shut him out, had torn at his heart.

"I'm sorry. I'm so sorry." She let the tears fall. "I love you so much, Gray."

"I love you too, babe. It's okay." He bent to kiss the top of her head, his own tears falling into her hair. She clung tightly to his arm. And he let his body absorb every ounce of her presence.

"Nothing feels the same," she whispered.

He savored her words. There had been so few since Maddie's death that he wished she would sit here and talk to him all night. "It will never be the same. But we still have each other, and we can't forget that."

They settled in this place for a long time before she spoke. He felt the movement of her lips against his arm. "I've got something to tell you."

"You can tell me anything."

She pushed herself up. "I'm pregnant, Gray."

He blinked. His mind fired off thoughts like an AK-47. *When? Where? How? Why now?*

Finally he found his voice. "How — when did you find this out?"

"Thad called and confirmed it tonight, but I had been thinking this past week that was where the nausea was coming from."

He sat up straight in his chair. "Why didn't you say anything?"

"I had to know for sure. I didn't want to speculate about something like that."

Gray stood, his flip-flops slapping against his feet as he paced across the tiled kitchen floor. He ran both hands through his hair over and over. "This is crazy, Mack. I can't believe this. I don't even know how to feel."

She didn't move. "I know. I don't either."

He walked over to her. "All these years. We've been trying for the last three years, and this is when it happens? This is when God decides to give us another baby?"

She shook her head. "I know. I've gone through all those same thoughts all week. I haven't known whether to be ecstatic or angry. But I think this might be our miracle, Gray. I think it might be God's gift since we've suffered so much. Our restoration. I can't help but think that."

He sat down again and pulled her toward him. She rested her weight on the front of his barstool and leaned her head on his shoulder. He wrapped his arms around her neck. It had been his initial thought too, but he'd been afraid to verbalize it. Mack's body had rejected so many children. If this pregnancy failed, he couldn't imagine how devastated she would be.

"I don't know," he said. "I can't even begin to understand God's mind. I just know that this is where we are. This is what is happening. And I'm going to choose to be happy about it."

She leaned back and looked at him. Her face was so different from the face he had seen the last several weeks. This one had a spark, almost a smile. And he was so grateful. If this life inside her could bring her back to him, then he would do everything in his power to make sure it arrived safely into this world.

Her body softened in his arms. "I love you so much."

"I love you too."

He studied her wounded but hopeful face, then leaned over and kissed her. At first it felt awkward, but gradually she responded as she had so many times before. He picked up her tiny frame in his arms and headed to their room. And that night he made love to his wife in that way of knowing that only a shared grief — and a shared hope — can bring.

CHAPTER 24

Six Weeks Later

Mackenzie nuzzled her face in the crease of Gray's neck. "Do you know what today is?"

"No," he said. "What's today?"

"It's the end of the first trimester." She popped up to sit cross-legged on the bed. "We actually made it. I knew we would."

Gray rolled onto his side and propped his head on the palm of his hand. "You kept saying it, didn't you, babe? And you were right."

She leaned down and kissed him softly on his lips. "I've just felt from the beginning that this was our gift. Our restoration. We've been through so much, you know." Her hands pulled at the hem of her red silk pajama top. "It's time, Gray."

"Time?"

She punched him. "You know what I'm talking about. It's time to make our announcement. You don't keep stuff like this quiet, Gray. You share it."

They'd had this conversation before. From the moment they learned about the pregnancy, she'd wanted to shout the news from the rooftops. She said that the people of Tennessee had grieved with them and should now be able to celebrate with them. Because of their track record, he had asked her to wait at least until the first trimester was over, and she'd gone along with his request. But she just knew. She knew in her gut that this was the boy they had longed for. And now she was ready to tell the world.

"You sure you don't want to wait a little longer?" he asked with a gentle smile. "Are you ready for the public attention? I mean, after —"

"I'm ready." She hopped out of bed, and he followed her to the bathroom. Sophie let out a yip from her kennel in the closet when she heard them.

"Just a minute, girl," Gray called to the puppy. "Hang on." He walked to his side of the counter and pulled out his toothbrush.

"It's going to be a busy week," she told him. "Things have been hopping since we agreed to host that luncheon for the Duchess of Wilshire in a couple of months. Jessica might as well be preparing for the queen. She'll have a heart attack when I ask her to put together a press release about the baby, but too bad. She'll just have to work it in."

Gray turned to look at her, his eyes serious. "I want to read it before it goes out."

"Sure," she said through a mouthful of toothpaste. She finished, wiped her mouth, and walked to the shower, opening the door and turning on the shower to warm the water. "What's your day look like?"

"Full. The budget requests have all come in, and we're in the beginning stages of going over everything." He rinsed his toothbrush. "What about you? Besides the announcement, I mean."

Mack slipped from her pj's and into the warmth of the streaming water. "Well, I've got a trip to the baby store with Anna. I'm buying something today to celebrate." Steam began to filter out of the shower. "We're going to meet Tina and Heather for lunch. And then I'm working on writing the foreword for the Junior League's new cookbook. I'm pretty sure my mother got me that gig."

Gray put down his towel and walked over to the shower. "I bet you'll smile all day," he said through the door.

She giggled. "I've smiled the last two months. I've even done everything Jessica has told me to do. Can you believe that? I haven't changed her schedule one time." She poked her wet head out. "Until today."

"I wondered why she was humming the other day." He gave her a quick smile and disappeared into the closet, where Sophie gave another yip.

She slipped from the shower, grabbed her towel, and picked up a bottle of baby oil. And for just a moment she remembered. It all came back. She opened the pink top, thinking of how soft the oil had made Maddie's skin. That was why she'd started using it on her own.

But she couldn't go there. Not now. She pushed the thought away and replaced it with a new, positive one. She imagined how wonderful it would be to slather oil on the new baby.

She wrapped a towel around her body and walked to the closet just as Gray stepped out with Sophie in his arms. The puppy had grown so much over the last two months. Her shaggy hair fell in front of her eyes and was about ready for a ponytail holder. She wiggled wildly.

Mackenzie reached out her hands. "Let me take her."

Gray's shock was evident.

She laughed. "Don't act like that. I have

been very sweet to her lately."

"Sweet, yes. Dog walker, no."

She wiggled her fingers. "Come on. Let me take her."

"No," he said flatly.

Her brow furrowed, and she dropped her arms. "Gray, I just want to take our dog for a walk."

He answered again. "No."

She was getting frustrated. "You're being ridiculous. Seriously."

"Mack, you're wearing a towel."

She looked down and burst out laughing. She had completely forgotten. "Well, I guess I am." She crinkled her nose. "Maybe I'll take her tomorrow."

He chuckled. "Yeah. I'll help you remember that."

She walked into the closet smiling. Her outfit for the day was hanging up and ready to go. And so was she. She had been on a full schedule for six weeks now. From the time she knew life was inside of her, life seemed to have come back to her. Her brown slacks swished softly as she made her way to the small balcony off their bedroom. The location had changed, and so had the prayer. But she couldn't help but return to praying after the gift she'd been given.

She raised her face to the sunshine, the

soft leather of her jacket rubbing at her neck. And then, when she was finished, she headed downstairs to the garage. In minutes, her new car was headed for Anna's house and then that quaint baby store in Belle Meade.

She had a nursery to decorate. And for the second time in her life, she was going to enjoy every minute of it.

JEREMIAH

The last few months 'round here be sweet. Miz Mackenzie seem to come back to life, and I knowed why even 'fore they gone and finally told. Any man seen his wife with his seed planted inside her know what a woman with chil' look like. I ain't said nothin' 'bout nothin' 'til they ready to 'nounce. But I still knowed. And I knowed it be a miracle.

They havin' a gatherin' here at the mansion today. That feel like a miracle too. After Maddie Mae died, I be wonderin' if this house ever do any celebratin' again. But then they gone and had 'em a coupla Christmas parties. And now what they havin' be some kinda ladies' tea honorin' a dignitary from England. Some relation to the queen, I hear.

You'd think that kind a highfalutin stuff would keep the crazies out. But Miz Eugenia and her three cronies been up in here all day fussin' 'bout. Eugenia even insist that her and her friends gon' do the flowers, and Miz Mackenzie say okay. Don't know what she was thinkin'.

That Dimples 'bout near destroyed my magnolias. Probably maimed 'em for life with all the leaves she gone and cut. But Eugenia bringin' all the rest herself. All she had to do is ax me — I gots me plenty a flowers winterin' in the greenhouse.

But she ain't done it. She too proud.

'Course, them crazy women the least a our worries 'round here. The gov'nor, he be 'bout near through with his budget, I hear. He tell me he find 'nough manure in that thing to keep my gardens fertilized 'til Jesus come back. I tol' him at least that be one less thing the gov'ment gon' have to go and pay for. He just laugh the way he do. An' that fine with me. I just glad to hear him laugh at all.

But I be a li'l worried 'bout him and Miz Mackenzie too. Not my place to say nothin' 'bout it. But it seem to me the healin' that need to be happenin' ain't really happenin'. Seem like it was at first. But now, there just lots a 'stractions. They 'stracted from they pain with this new baby comin' and all. They 'stracted with gov'ment stuff too. But there be a piece a me know, way down there deep in my knower, that this here grief ain't

259

finished yet. 'Stractions can only 'stract for so long.

Always hard to understand why life happen like this to good people like Miz Mackenzie and the gov'nor. But I heard a preacher man say one time that when God call you to sump'n big, ever'thing in your life gon' be big. Your mountains and your valleys — they all gon' be big. And this here valley, it be as big as any I ever see. But maybe that just 'cause they both made for greatness.

Still, I can't help but wonder what God gon' use to get that grief out. I kinda scared to know. Because that last grief so deep, they almost gots lost in it.

Had to dig hard that time just to find 'em.

Can't 'magine where we might have to dig next time.

CHAPTER 25

Spring had been birthed in the middle of January. Outside, the winter winds were bitter. But inside the governor's mansion, it was a breathtaking April day.

Eugenia put her hands on her hips and surveyed the dining room with satisfaction. Two gorgeous chandeliers hung over the two twelve-seater round tables that were covered in crisp ivory linens. Mackenzie had been bound and determined she was going to add two more seats to the stated capacity of the dining room. So she had moved the long dining table out and had two rounds brought in. It had worked perfectly. Each chair was wrapped in beautiful moss-green silk fabric gathered in the back with a large ivory bow. In front of each chair was a place setting of new custom-made Pickard china decorated with the state flower, the purple iris. And on every conceivable surface in the mansion there were blossoms.

That was Eugenia's doing. She had proclaimed herself chief florist for this event the minute she found out that royalty was coming to Nashville. She was excited to use her talents to make sure Mackenzie shined. Of course she had no doubt her talents would shine as well.

"I got these from out there." Dimples's head was slanted toward the back door. Her hands were full of glossy magnolia leaves. "But that Jeremiah told me I couldn't have any more."

"No matter. We're finished with the centerpieces." Eugenia straightened the stone-colored cashmere hat she was wearing. Its large cream flower nestled on the side. "So Jeremiah can just can it."

Berlyn shook her head. "I swear you're going to go to your grave battling with that man. It's the dead of winter, not a bloom in sight, and you just can't give it up."

Eugenia gave Berlyn the evil eye. "Did you check the china?"

Berlyn let out an exasperated groan. "Eugenia, you're a control freak. I checked the china; I checked the silver. I checked the stem-ware for water spots, even though Eloise gets *paid* to do all that. I also sampled the fried-chicken tea sandwiches you made, just to make sure they were worth eating.

My word. Next you're going to have me tell the chef to bend over and cough."

The water Sandra was sipping spewed from her mouth, and her ivory wool hat nearly flew off her head.

"Well, Sandra," Berlyn announced, "you are human after all. That is the most ungraceful thing I've ever seen you do. There is now hope for the free world. Do that in front of the queen, won't you?"

"Hush up." Sandra dabbed at her mouth with a hankie that had been safely tucked inside the ruffled sleeve of her maroon dress.

Eugenia walked over to the dessert table while the three ladies followed. "Sandra, I do believe that is as close to cussing as you're ever going to get. One day I wish you'd just cut loose and let 'er rip. And it's not the queen, Berlyn; it's one of her relatives. Get it right."

"Oh, queenie-weenie — who cares?" Berlyn grabbed Dimples's arm to keep her from running into a chair. "And why didn't you ask me to taste the desserts too? I would've been glad to do that."

Sandra stepped in front of her as if she felt a need to guard the cake. "You sample any more cake, and you're going to need to get that stomach surgery that makes it where you can't eat anymore."

"Do I look like a woman who feels bad about the way she looks?" Berlyn stuck out her chest, the red flowers on her bodice looking as if they were holding on for dear life. She reached for a silver fork and twirled it in her fingers.

"Don't you even think of taking that home with you." Eugenia straightened the serving utensils. "You two act like children. Can we please pretend we're the adults today?" She snatched the leaves from Dimples's hands, and Dimples nearly tipped over. Sandra reached out quickly to steady her. "Go get the two vases off the welcome table," Eugenia ordered. "I want to make some arrangements."

The three of them flitted around as if Eugenia had hired them herself while the chef and mansion staff continued to tend to final details of what would be a glorious event. The centerpieces were beautiful moss-covered boxes with moss-colored silk ribbon, magnolia leaves, and bunches of fragrant paperwhite narcissus.

Eugenia cut the stems of forced forsythia as she arranged them in a vase with purple Dutch iris from the florist, her thoughts straying to a *Good Housekeeping* article she had read during yesterday's visit to the beauty shop. The magazine talked about postpartum depression and how it often resulted from unresolved emotions accentuated by hormonal changes during and after pregnancy.

What if that happened to Mackenzie? Lord knew the poor girl had unresolved emotions. In fact, once she knew she was pregnant, it was like she'd put all her grieving on hold. Went from sitting in that chair all day to being a busy governor's wife again.

She'd never even cleaned out Maddie's room. She'd just closed the door. And that worried Eugenia. Because if there was anything she'd learned in her years of living, it was that you couldn't just close a door on grief. It would end up seeping through the cracks.

"You gonna let us take home the leftovers?" Berlyn's voice interrupted her thoughts as she put the last stalk in the vase.

Sandra lifted a vase of forsythia and irises and walked toward the dessert table. "You don't need leftovers, Berlyn. You need a personal trainer."

Berlyn's eyes lit up as if that might actually be something she was interested in. Sandra must have noticed the look on her face. "They work you out, Berlyn. They're not for your personal enjoyment."

Dimples wasn't paying attention to any of

them. She dug an envelope from the cream leather purse that hung at her side. "I got lottery tickets for the queen."

Eugenia turned and looked at her. Poor soul needed to be taken shopping. Her green wool suit hung on her as if she'd bought it for a woman two sizes larger, and the tiny green beret sitting atop her head made her look like some Army sergeant's great-grandmother. "Are you afraid someone's going to steal your purse, Dimples?"

Dimples clutched her bag tighter to her side as if afraid Eugenia would make her put it down. "You never know. It's tough times around here. Paper said that Gray's new budget that comes out tomorrow is going to make everyone have to shut off their electricity."

Sandra ran her fingers through the high cream ruffles around her neck. "Your electricity isn't going anywhere, Dimples. And why in the world would you buy a lottery ticket for someone who doesn't even live in this nation?"

"It's practical," Dimples insisted. "She actually might win, and all the money for lotteries goes toward education. I am officially helping Mackenzie and the new baby."

Eugenia shook her head. "Seriously,

Dimples. You weren't supposed to bring a present for the guest. Mackenzie already has something that is representative of all Tennesseans. It will be as if it is from you."

Berlyn snatched a square of blackberry crumb cake. "Well, if she's got my name on it, I want to see what it is."

Sandra slapped her hand. "You should just be grateful it isn't a gift you had to buy."

"I can't help it if I'm on Social Security." Berlyn's words came out muffled as she chewed, crumbs dropping in her ample cleavage. She saw Eugenia notice. "I'll get that later," she said.

"Why are you here?" Eugenia muttered as she moved around the dessert table to the other side of the room. "Honestly, why are any of you here?"

Dimples started teetering slightly on her feet. "Think I can take a nap before this shindig starts?"

Eugenia turned to survey her work. "Why not? And take the others with you. If there is a God in heaven, he will be merciful enough to us all that you sleep right through it."

CHAPTER 26

Some of the faces staring back at Gray London had one desire — his blood. Others wanted simply to report the news. A newbie raised his hand. "Governor?"

Gray acknowledged the reporter from a local NBC affiliate. "Yes, Davis."

The young man jumped up quickly and adjusted his wire-framed glasses. His pad shook slightly in his hands. "So why did you decide to deliver this budget via e-mail?"

Gray didn't miss a beat. "Because I know some legislators around here who are afraid to check e-mail. I'm hoping they'll simply pass it without ever reading it."

The tension in the newbie's face released with the governor's relaxed response. "Honestly, Davis," Gray went on, "getting rid of the paper version was just another way we could cut costs. And that is what my team and I have spent the last couple of months doing. We have gone through this budget like a hillbilly plucking a chicken. We haven't left anything we thought we could get rid of. And I'll be honest with you, some of the cuts are going to hurt. I wish we didn't have to make them. But I made it clear when I ran for governor, and I'm making it clear again today: I am here to protect this state. That is my job. And if that means some people aren't happy with me, then I'm sorry. But this is the job the voters elected me to do, and it is what I have done."

When the reporters knew he was finished, hands shot up wildly in front of the sea of video cameras that were airing this broadcast live across the state and taping it for the noon and nightly broadcasts.

"Bonnie. Yes."

The well-known journalist from the *Tennessean* stood, her presence immediately taking over the space around her.

"I seem to be graying quicker than you these days," Gray added before Bonnie had time to ask her question.

The reporter nodded. "I think your job is tougher than mine, sir. I just report what you do. You have to do it. Speaking of that, what are your plans regarding the VRA lawsuit now that they've been given the go-ahead to actually take their case to court?"

"My plans haven't changed from what

they were at the beginning, Bonnie. We are focused on one thing: getting our state out of the red. If we can't get a handle on this, there will be far worse things to deal with than some nonviolent prisoners going free. So we will go to court and face what we have to face."

He leaned a little closer to the cameras, his eyes still focused on the reporter who had asked the question. "As governor, you try to weigh the possibilities of what can happen before you make the decisions that can cause them to happen. We knew going to court was a likelihood. But releasing prisoners wasn't something we wanted to do. It was something we were forced to do. With this new budget, we are trying to prevent it from ever happening again. But that means our legislative body has to learn how to make tough decisions too — tough decisions that possibly won't get them reelected. And I'm hoping the people of this state are more important to our senators and representatives than their own political futures."

Gray reached for his water and took a long sip. The last forty-five minutes of presenting his new budget and fielding questions had left him parched. One of the reporters raised her hand.

"Vivian. Yes."

"Governor —" the white-haired reporter's twang revealed her east Tennessee roots — "Marcus Newman has just announced his official bid for governor. Elaine Wiggins and Matt Kubitza have been unofficially campaigning since spring. So are you running for reelection or aren't you?"

"Well, first, Vivian, you look beautiful today," Gray said with a smile.

"I didn't vote for you the first time, Governor, so sweet-talking me won't change a thing."

The room erupted at the freedom her age afforded her. Gray laughed too. "One can always hope. But today is about the budget. I will make a decision in the next couple of weeks, and when I do, I will let you know. And whether Marcus Newman or anyone else has chosen to run will have no bearing on my decision. Okay, one last question."

Hands darted up like they belonged to a pack of first graders.

"Yes, Jeremy?"

"Governor, how are you and Mrs. London coping these days — with the new baby, I mean, and the loss of your daughter?" The young reporter's blue eyes were filled with sincerity.

Gray felt the sting of what he meant. He

271

still felt it every morning. No matter how much their joy over the life in Mackenzie's womb tried to edge it out, the pain was still there, gnawing and real. "It's a painfully beautiful season, Jeremy." The words were more transparent than he intended. He gathered himself. "Now, that's all. The rest is up to your representatives. We'll see what they do."

Fletcher held the door open as Gray walked through it. Kurt followed on his heels. "Good job, Gray."

Gray draped an arm around the shoulders of Fletcher's brown suit coat. "I need a big lunch." He looked at his watch. "It's only noon, but I want steak. How about you fellas? Let me treat you to a big, juicy piece of red meat. And I won't even charge the taxpayers. We'll let Kurt pay for it."

"There are already reports out about some legislators' responses to the budget," Kurt said, his pace almost pressing behind Gray. "We'll want to respond quickly."

Gray stopped in the middle of the carpet and turned to his friend. "Kurt, we have worked tirelessly for months on this budget. I just spent almost an hour going over it and fielding questions about issues I haven't even made decisions about. So could we please, for an hour or two, do something we haven't done in a long time?"

Silence rose quickly between the three of them. They each knew how long.

"I just want to go eat together and be normal guys having lunch."

"You're the governor," Kurt responded quickly. "Nothing's normal about that."

Fletcher slapped Gray's shoulder and glared at Kurt. "Yes, Gray, for two hours we can go be normal. I'll call Fleming's and see if their chef will let us have an early dinner."

"It's noon, Fletch," Kurt reminded, even though the chef had done it for them numerous times before.

"He likes Gray. And he tolerates you. He'll be glad to see us back."

"I'll call for the car," Kurt said in a surrendered tone.

Gray threw his hands up. "Alas, he caves. He is a mere mortal. And we have had the privilege of finally discovering this truth."

Kurt gave his shoulder a mock punch. "Shut up."

"Hey, you're talking to the governor."

"No, I'm talking to Gray, the guy from college who for some unfathomable reason got himself elected as the governor of an entire state. Have you even learned all the counties yet?" Kurt's sly smile darted across his face as he turned and headed to the garage. He pulled out his phone to call the driver.

"Anderson, Bedford, Benton, Bledsoe . . ." Though Fletcher repeatedly begged him to stop, Gray didn't give up until he had gotten through the whole alphabetical list.

CHAPTER 27

Mackenzie closed the folder in front of her and let the routine that had once again engulfed her have its way. "I think that looks good, ladies. We have successfully charted out the next four months. Thank you for all your hard work."

She stood and nodded gratefully to the staff. They were the ones responsible for making sure the causes Mackenzie believed in and wanted to promote were benefiting fully by her presence in the mansion.

"Thank you, Mrs. London," Chandra said as she and Susan walked toward the door. "We'll see you shortly at the tea."

Jessica closed the door behind them.

"Will the tours be over by two thirty?" Mackenzie asked her.

"The last group comes in at two. We will have them out before the duchess's car arrives. I'm going to run to the bathroom, then grab a cup of coffee. Do you need anything before we go over the tea events?"

"No. No, I'm good. If I drink anything else, I'll just have to pee again."

Jessica smiled. "I'll be right back."

Mackenzie turned from her glass-topped worktable to the hand-painted French desk that overlooked the north lawn. The tea was at three, but she had some business to tidy up before she met her guest, the Duchess of Wilshire, at the north entrance. She slid another one of her monogrammed thank-you notes inside its envelope. The notes were going to all the volunteers who had given of their time to decorate the mansion for Christmas.

She was grateful the holidays had come and gone. Maddie's absence had been so glaring then. She'd rammed into it every time a child laughed or a commercial for a toy appeared on television. She and Gray had actually fled to Florida for Christmas, relying on the change of scenery to keep their focus away from what they had lost and on the new life inside her. Their gift from the ruins.

Now that January was here, though, things were easier. She and Gray were even talking seriously about his upcoming reelection campaign. Gray was created to be governor. Mackenzie had no doubt of that. And she was created to love people, serve them, believe with them. Championing their causes. Listening to their stories.

She ran her hands across the small pooch in her stomach. Her yellow wool dress clung to it. She loved being pregnant. And she loved the freedom she'd had the last two months to let it show.

Over the weekend, the last bit of furniture had come in for the baby. Several times a day, Mackenzie or Gray would walk past Maddie's closed door — she still couldn't go in that room — and visit the now completely decorated nursery.

It was their little shrine of hope.

Eugenia walked through the door and right to a sofa, throwing herself on it with an exasperated sigh. "If I ever say I'm bringing those women anywhere again, just shoot me."

Mackenzie didn't even turn as she placed a stamp on the last of the thank-you letters. "You take them everywhere, Mother."

"I know. I'm pathetic. I need to get out more. Burt took me to a show the other night."

"The movies?" The shock in Mackenzie's voice was evident as she turned her head.

"No, child, a show. The theater. I don't go to the movies. I'm not going to pay to watch people shoot people, drink their blood, or flaunt their fake boobs. I get enough of that with Berlyn. I live with characters far more entertaining than I'll ever see at the movies." She paused and looked up toward the ceiling. "Unless of course Gena Rowlands is in it. You know I —"

Mackenzie cut her off. "Favor her. Yes, I know."

"Or a movie about Southern women. I love those movies."

Mackenzie turned her chair around to face her mother. "If you hate all movies other than ones with women who look like you or act like you, then why exactly are you in charge of the Franklin Theatre restoration project?"

Eugenia shook her head as if Mackenzie could ask the dumbest questions. "Because who else would do it like I would? Seriously, child, who raised you?"

Mackenzie let out a soft laugh. "Do I have options?"

Eugenia rolled her eyes. Then Mackenzie saw them cut over to the round antique side table and come to rest on Maddie's picture. Eugenia reached over and picked it up.

Mackenzie knew what was coming. She turned her chair back around. "I don't want to hear it."

"Hear it you will." Mackenzie heard her mother rise from the sofa. "You haven't finished grieving her, Mackenzie."

"I didn't do anything *but* grieve, Mother. Until —"

"No, you didn't grieve. Not really. You just stopped breathing for a while. Then you found out about the baby, and it's like you just . . . forgot. Just picked up your life again and left Maddie behind."

Mackenzie ignored the catch in her mother's voice. She couldn't go there. Couldn't afford to go there. Not now.

"I did not forget. I will never forget." She kept her voice cool and hard. "You're the one who hid your tears, remember? Do not lecture me on grief."

"I'm your mother. I will lecture you until the day I die. And I may have hidden my tears from you, but I didn't hide them from *me.* I felt them. Every one of them. I still feel them. That's why when y'all try to push Burt down my throat, it's such a tough pill to swallow because I've still got all that love for your father down deep —"

"How do you know I don't hide my tears from you?" Mackenzie's words came out with more sarcasm than she intended.

Eugenia hesitated an instant. "Like I said, I'm your mother. I have eyes in the back of my head. And giddy and grief don't usually cohabit." She stood and put the picture back on the table. "Anyway, your flowers are beautiful. Your attitude isn't so hot. But your flowers look like a million bucks." And with that she marched out, closing the door hard enough behind her to reiterate her frustration with her daughter.

Mackenzie turned. The door cracked open again. "Mother, I mean it. Not another —"

Jessica's head peeked through. "Do I need a white flag?"

Mackenzie's shoulders dropped. "No, sorry. Just my mother. How did she get here again?"

"You invited her, remember?"

"Right. I can only blame myself. Shoot, I wanted to blame you." Jessica didn't smile. "I'm joking, Jessica."

Jessica sat down on the edge of her chair, notepad on her lap, a single strand of pearls around her neck, the hem of her baby-blue sheath dress tucked under her, and those impossibly long legs crossed neatly. Eugenia would so approve.

Mackenzie did her best to wrestle her mind around again and focus on the new baby. On the strand of hope that was keeping her sane. On the work she had to do.

"Did the humane society find a new chair

for their event next month?"

"They did, but they still have requested you be listed as honorary chair."

Mackenzie sat back. "That's so sweet of them. Tell them I'd be honored. And I would love to attend."

"I will."

Mackenzie leaned back in her leather desk chair, plopped her hands up on her stomach, and laced her fingers. "There are days I still can't believe it, Jessica. Any of it. I just wish my mother didn't try to spoil the entire thing."

Jessica looked up, obviously noticing that Mackenzie was no longer talking about work. "We all needed a miracle around here, Mrs. London. And this child gave us one." She smiled. "Your mother will come around. As soon as she holds that little one in her arms, she'll come around."

Mackenzie shook her head, trying to shake off the frustration that lingered. "I know. You're right." She stuffed the frustration down. She'd worry about her mother later. Eugenia wasn't going anywhere.

"Can you believe that in just four months I'll be holding a new baby in my arms? It doesn't seem possible. I should be feeling it move pretty soon." Mackenzie ran her hands across her stomach. Then she pushed her chair back from the desk and stood. "Let's eat. I'm starving."

Jessica looked at her watch, a nervous twitch starting at the base of her neck. "The tea is in two hours. We'll be eating then. Plus, I've already gained weight since you got pregnant."

Mackenzie walked toward Jessica's chair and grabbed her arm. "You can't gain weight on lettuce."

"No, but you can on banana splits."

Mackenzie pulled her from her chair. "Well, you needed to gain some weight."

"That's what your mother says."

"Of course she does. Now, let's go give this little miracle a bite to eat."

The two women headed toward the kitchen. As Mackenzie made her way across the hardwood floor, she felt something warm roll down her legs. She looked and saw a streak of blood start from beneath the bottom of her skirt and run down to the top of her Michael Kors honey-colored snakeskin shoes.

She gripped Jessica's shoulder. "Call Gray. Now." She could barely get the words out.

She watched as Jessica turned and caught sight of the blood that was now running down the side of Mackenzie's shoe.

"Oh no," Jessica whispered. She frantically pulled her phone from her pocket and dialed while Mackenzie watched the hope drain out of her body and onto the floor.

CHAPTER 28

Gray closed the bedroom door behind him once he and Thad and Sophie were on the other side. He felt as if he were closing the door on any hope of life inside the walls of this mansion again.

"It should help her sleep. But monitor this medicine, Gray." Thad's warning tone encased his words as he extended the bottle. "Do you hear me?"

Gray nodded solemnly. His eyes burned. He patted his friend on the shoulder and walked him toward the top of the stairs. He could feel Sophie at his heels. "I don't know what's going to happen to her now. I honestly don't know."

Thad stopped and looked at Gray, his eyes full of deep hurt for his friend. "This isn't just about her loss, you know. You've lost something here too. You need to remember that. And you need to talk to someone. I mean it. Even governors can't carry everything. Y'all have been through too much."

He pulled a card from the side of his bag. "Ken Jantzen is a good friend of mine. He's a wonderful grief counselor. Call him." He placed the card in Gray's palm and wrapped an arm around his shoulders. His words came out softly. "I'm so sorry, my friend."

Gray embraced him back. He needed someone else's strength, if only for a moment. Thad released him and stepped back. "I'll see myself out. You go take care of Mackenzie, and I'll call tomorrow and check on you both."

Gray watched his friend walk down the circular staircase. He looked toward the opposite end of the hall from his bedroom at yet another closed door. He hadn't been inside that room since they'd set up the new crib in there. He didn't know if he ever would because it was just another reminder of what was never coming home.

He had tried to get Mack to realize they could lose this baby. But she had determined the pregnancy was a gift. A reward or consolation or something. And she had been so adamant about announcing it, celebrating it, preparing for it. How could he deny her that? It wasn't fair for her to have to keep secret one of the greatest joys a woman could have.

She had looked so beautiful. The changes in her body only made her more beautiful. And she had loved every minute of it. He knew she was still stuffing down the loss of Maddie. But he didn't care. To have her happy, to have her available to him was worth it. Truth be told, he had helped her.

He couldn't take his eyes off the door. Something drew him. Something internal tugged at him. He walked toward the door and turned the knob. He pushed the door open and entered the nursery.

It looked like something from a magazine. Mackenzie's friend Lucinda Walters, who had decorated the governor's mansion back in the Lamar Alexander days, had helped her add the finishing touches in ivory and a funny green color — "celadon," Mack called it. Gray could barely pronounce it, but he figured it was in the celery family.

Gray walked over to the pine armoire and opened it. It was already lined with little white hangers. He shut the door and moved to the pine dresser. He pulled open the top drawer and saw a row of diapers lined up perfectly. Stored next to them was everything needed to give a baby that smell that makes every parent melt.

Mack had paid attention to every detail. The room had everything. Everything except a baby.

The pain of this insurmountable loss raced through him. Then he caught sight of the antique rocker in the corner. It was Maddie's rocker. The chair that he and Mack had rocked their baby girl in almost every night for two years . . .

He slammed the door shut and closed himself inside the room. A guttural scream came from depths he didn't know existed in the human soul. It was angry and bitter and desperate. He pounded his fists against the dresser until it seemed the wood was bending beneath the force of his blows. Pain shot through his arms, but he didn't care. He would beat that dresser all the way to hell if he could.

It was the pain inside that forced him to his knees, forced the words to spew out of him.

"Why? Why?" he demanded. "What are you doing to us? Do you hate us? Do you want to destroy us? Did we do something so horrible that we need to be punished? Punish me if you need to — but don't punish Mack!"

His words were venomous, and spittle flew as he wept and yelled, his fists now beating the fluffy rug Mack had placed over the hard wood. But heaven was silent.

"You can't speak?"

He wouldn't wait for a response. He already knew the answer.

"Of course you can't. There's no defense for this. There's no answer for this!" His face was raised toward the ceiling, and his words were coming out with a force that made his head hurt.

"How will we get through this? Do you think we're superhuman? That we can just take anything you dish out? Mack barely made it through last time — and now you expect her to survive this! And I —" pain surged through him, pushing his tears harder and forcing his chest to heave in a frantic attempt to make room for the hurt — "I'm not that strong. I can't do it this time."

His body lowered with his defeat. "I don't have anything left to give. I can't make it okay. It's *not* okay. This is too big for me."

He brought his head down and buried his face in the rug, the newness of it filling his nostrils. His body gradually lowered until he was fully prostrate.

As he turned his head to the side so he could breathe, Sophie's hot breath came quickly toward him. And his body surrendered. Sleep came over him, strong and deep. When he awoke, the room was dark.

Sophie's head popped up when his did. Apparently she had decided to take a nap too. He raised his head and felt a salty residue still on his face. His hands dug into the carpet until he was able to push himself from the ground. His body ached.

He walked back down the hall and opened the bedroom door. Mack was sitting by the window, staring into the blackness of the night. He walked over to her and sat on her chair's ottoman. He pulled her body into his arms and held her tightly there.

She never moved. The life that had rekindled for a brief instant might never be found again. And if he were being honest, he wasn't sure his would either.

CHAPTER 29

One Month Later

The fur of the winter coat was soft against Mackenzie's face, but she couldn't feel it. The air was as frosty as a snow cone in July, but she felt hot inside. The smell of the pine trees was as rich as a Christmas morning, but she had no sense of Christmas. And chickadee songs were as whimsical as an aria from *Don Quixote,* yet they barely registered in her ears.

This was the first time she had left the house since . . . since her hope had died. She didn't even know why she was out here. She'd just wrapped a coat around her pajamas, slipped on some boots, and walked. Maybe deep down she thought she could walk away from the pain, the noise, the silence. The . . . world.

Maybe she would never stop walking.

A flash of setting sun caught her eyes, and she squinted. Then she cursed the brightness. It should be raining. It should pour from now until God decided to get off his duff and get back to doing his job. At this point, though, she doubted if there even was a God.

And if there was, she was pretty sure she hated him.

She turned toward the azalea garden and heard a mumbling sound. She jumped instinctively when a figure suddenly straightened up in front of her. She pulled at the edges of her coat. A scream escaped her lips.

"Just me, Miz Mackenzie. Just me." Jeremiah's voice was easily discernible before his face registered.

"You almost scared me to death."

"Sorry, ma'am. Ain't mean to scare you." He gestured toward the ground. "Just makin' sure these gon' be ready for spring. What you doin' out here this afternoon, Miz Mackenzie? Though it sure 'nough good to see you up."

"I . . . needed some fresh air." She wrapped her arms around her chest. "What were you mumbling when I came up?"

"Oh, just prayin'. I do that a lot when I'm workin' out here."

She stared at him. "What do you pray about, Jeremiah?"

He let out a soft chuckle. "Just 'bout

ever'thing, I guess. I pray 'bout the boys that work with me. I pray 'bout life. I pray my bones don't give out. I pray 'bout you . . ." The last part came out soft.

"What do you pray about me? I mean, what do you pray for?"

"I pray for your heart. That it won't ache forever."

She felt a sudden fury rise up inside her. She didn't want to feel it, didn't want to feel anything, but there it was. "Don't waste any more of those prayers on me, Jeremiah."

She watched him shift his weight slowly, back and forth. "Ain't prayed nothin' I figure to be a waste. Only wasted prayers to my way a thinkin' be the ones you ain't gone and prayed."

Her words fell as more of a whisper. "Then you've never heard mine."

Jeremiah reached down and pulled a leaf from the camellia shrub at his feet. He twirled the green leaf between his fingers. Mackenzie watched as it moved slowly in the fading sunlight. "This here be a camellia leaf. Now, the flowers on this here bush ain't gon' bloom 'til spring. But y'know what them flowers mean? They mean 'you be a flame in my heart.' And I done lived long 'nough to learn a thing or two 'bout the heart."

He paused as if waiting for her to respond. She didn't.

"Knowed me a lot of people through the years. They hearts be all shut down. Y'know what that look like?"

She shook her head.

"A shut-down heart's 'bout the saddest thing I ever see. 'Cause we all come out the womb with our hearts wide open. All sweet and trustin' and close to God. It like we got this line runnin' straight up to heaven.

"But life can start cuttin' into that there line. Li'l cut when we li'l and sump'n sad happens or we find out somebody can do things better'n we can. More li'l cuts when we go and get married and our husband or wife does sump'n to hurt us — or maybe we don't never marry and we lonely. And it just keep comin'. When we lose sump'n or hurt somewheres or get lied on and betrayed — all that just keep sawin' at that line from heaven to that li'l alive heart. And finally it don't want to stay open no more, so it just clench up."

He held his tightened fist out in front of her, soil still clinging to it. "That be to me what a shut-down heart look like — all sad and scared and bitter, all them things. But the real sad thing is, it don't have to shut down. 'Cause even with all them cuts, that line to heaven still there. If it go and close up, that be our doin'."

Mackenzie shifted her boots. But still had nothing to offer.

"God okay if you mad, Miz Mackenzie. Way I figure, he hear ever'thing, so ain't much we gots to say gon' shock him. But when you take that heart he gone and placed inside you and shut it all down, well . . . don't know if there be anythin' make him ache more."

Mackenzie's eyebrows rose, then lowered.

Jeremiah twirled the tiny leaf again through his fingers. "Can't pretend I know where your heart be. Just know from my own 'periences that when life come at you hard, like it done come down on you now, be easy to quit livin'. And I don't want you to do that. Not when there more livin' left to do."

She had heard enough. "Have a good day, Jeremiah." She turned before he could respond.

"I sure will. Seein' you already make it perfect." He paused for a moment. Then his words shot through the gathering darkness. "Miz Mackenzie, you know what a pink camellia mean?"

"You already said. Something about a flame in my heart."

"Guess I did, but that what a *red* camellia mean. A pink one, it mean 'longin' for you.' " He paused. "That's what I figure God be doin' when we tryin' to shut down the flame in our heart. He longin' for us."

She stared at the outline of his figure for a moment longer, then turned again and headed toward the house. Heavy clouds had rolled in as she talked to Jeremiah. A snow-flake skirted in front of her.

She paid it no attention. Nor the hundreds that would fall before morning.

JEREMIAH

I ain't never forgot that smell 'round here after the Tennessee flood. The soil was soppin'. I wore muck boots just to get it all cleaned up. The boys and me worked so hard, pullin' up dead things, transplantin' wet things. Just stank like death.

Kinda how it smell 'round here now. Like death.

I'm always plumb near amazed at how tragedy can swallow people whole. I 'member that dark day for me almost thirty years ago. I thought I would die. I wanted to die. But I didn't die. I lived. And when I knowed I was gon' live, I decided to do just that.

Live.

Couldn't change what happen. Couldn't change the lies told 'bout me. Alls I could do was live the life I been given to live. I ain't wanted to live it this way. This life ain't looked like the picture Shirley and me had for our lives. But it what we get. And Shirley and me, we just dig in. We dig in for the pain, and we dig in for the healin'.

But ain't no healin' 'round here right now. Them two ain't doin' nothin' but diggin' in to dyin'.

Lord know good and well I ain't got a lot to give. And he know good and well that there be days when I see Miz Eugenia stroll out here and wanna ax her what Sanford ax Esther. You know: "How you doin'? How you feelin'? When you leavin'?" Or tell her what Ralph always tol' Alice: "I gon' give you one right in the kisser."

So reckon I do got sump'n to give. It just ain't what I needin' to give. But I don't know how to pull 'em up outta 'emselves. And Eugenia, she do try. She try harder'n most folks I know. She love that girl and boy so deep and so wide.

Trouble is, Eugenia just a lot a woman to be lovin' on anybody.

She keep tryin' that hard, might well smother 'em to death.

CHAPTER 30

Berlyn pulled Eugenia out the front door of her house. Eugenia slapped wildly at her hand. But Berlyn was a brute. She hauled Eugenia onto the sidewalk where Sandra and Dimples waited, then pointed her toward Main Street. Snow fell softly while they walked.

Eugenia had come home to check on things and grab some clean underwear. She hadn't planned on having to fight a seventy-one-year-old woman intent on kidnapping her.

"We're getting you out, and that's that. You've been living at the mansion full-time for the last month, and it's time for you to have a day for you. Plus, you're getting skinny and I am not going to be in the healthy club all by myself."

"Since when did obesity become healthy?" Sandra quipped.

Berlyn snapped, "Since when did full-figured become obese? I wish you would tell Marilyn Monroe that or Betty Grable. Or Oprah."

Sandra puffed, "You are no Marilyn Monroe or Betty Grable. And Lord knows you're no Oprah."

Berlyn ignored her and tugged at the sleeve of Eugenia's royal-blue coat. While Eugenia huffed down the street, Dimples was pulling up the rear, trying desperately not to take a tumble over her too-big black galoshes.

"Get her!" Eugenia barked at Sandra, pointing to Dimples. "Last thing we need is her in the street."

"She needs egg salad," Berlyn announced.

Dimples instinctively licked her lips.

Sandra walked back toward Dimples, taupe leather pumps squishing in the snow, matching handbag dangling from her wrist, and the mink collar of her taupe coat encasing her like she had a beaver wrapped around her neck. Franklin's Main Street was bustling, its sidewalks crowded with people wanting to enjoy winter's first snowfall in one of Tennessee's most picturesque towns.

Eugenia had always loved living in Franklin. Long before it was featured in *Southern Living,* she'd known the town was a treasure.

Something about it always felt soothing to her. And now, walking down Main Street with her friends, she realized how much she'd missed being home. She'd almost forgotten there was a world outside the walls of the mansion. Her soul needed this so badly.

They walked past Chico's, where most of Eugenia's wardrobe came from. She had tried to get Berlyn in there. But the low-cut floral pantsuit Berlyn wore under her bright-pink coat was proof that if it didn't come from the Tacky Palace, Berlyn wouldn't wear it. The pantsuit was orange and fuchsia, for goodness' sake! Frederick's of Hollywood was conservative to Berlyn.

They crossed Main Street, and Eugenia could see bubbles floating outside the homemade soap store. Maddie had loved that bubble machine. The thought made her heart ache. Just as it had ached since the moment she first got the news about Maddie.

Had that really been six months ago?

The pain had been so great at times she wasn't even sure that she was going to survive it. She'd never tell them, but if it hadn't been for these three crazy women, she wouldn't have. Their calls, notes, meals, even their bickering, renewed her. They could drive her to drink, but she'd have died without them. And without their intervention today, she wouldn't have been able to tear herself away from the mansion. She was afraid of what she might find when she returned. The thought made her shudder.

When they walked through the door of Merridee's Breadbasket, the smells of butter and yeast accosted her senses. The warmth of the place seemed to press against the perpetual chill she had been living with. She closed her eyes and let momentary delight overtake her. Standing here now, basking in it, she realized she'd forgotten what delight even felt like. Her soul was grateful for the distraction and eternally grateful she had a place like Merridee's to visit.

The shop's founder, Merridee, had been destined for the baking business. Her grandmother had once been a baker for Pillsbury. And everyone in Franklin rejoiced when she decided to bring her baking gifts to this Southern town in 1984. The place was a carb lover's dream. And Eugenia and her friends had always loved carbs.

"I'm only eating pie today," Berlyn announced as she finally let go of Eugenia's arm.

Dimples braced herself against the counter

and stared into the glass-paned display case. "Me too. Just sweets today. We're on the doorstep of death, and I haven't had my own teeth in years, so why not enjoy myself?"

"You're drooling, Dimples." Sandra pulled at the fingers of her leather gloves. "I'm having a salad."

Berlyn stared at her in disgust. "You're going to die without ever enjoying life."

"At least when I get to heaven, I won't get scolded for having abused my body."

Berlyn's eyes widened, and she leaned her head back. "Excuse me, but just about every time I read about Jesus in the New Testament, he's somewhere eating. So I'm thinking he's going to tell you that you wasted a lot of wonderful opportunities to enjoy yourself."

Eugenia ignored them and focused on the cashier. "I want a double egg salad, a bag of chips, a fruit cup, and a piece of rhubarb pie. And I want these women to pay for it. They've driven me crazy in less than three blocks, so they should have to foot the bill."

Eugenia turned to look at Sandra, whose expression went as tight as Berlyn's thong — or at least the thong Berlyn tried to convince Sandra she wore. Sandra scurried to the counter. "Oh my . . . well, now . . . I think we're going to have Berlyn here pay for it —" she motioned toward her — "because she was the one who decided we all needed this outing. I will have the chicken salad on lettuce with your strawberries and house dressing."

Berlyn moved up to the counter and scooted Sandra over with a push of her ample right hip. "Oh, phooey . . . just put it all on mine. I'm on Social Security, and there won't be any left in there soon, so let's live it up now. If it weren't for me, they'd all be six feet under by now, anyway. Or sitting in a nursing home, gurgling and hoping someone rolled them over."

The poor cashier must have been new because her face registered horror.

"I'll have a piece of your chess pie and a piece of your chocolate pie," Berlyn announced. "And Dimples here wants your mint fudge brownie and a piece of pecan pie. We have both decided that life is better if you lead with dessert."

The young cashier rang the order up quickly and turned gratefully to the people behind them. Eugenia and her friends waited until their names were called, grabbed their food from the counter, and found a six-seater over by the window. Neither Eugenia nor Sandra liked to sit too close to other people. Eugenia's excuse was hot flashes. She'd been using it for twenty years. Sandra's excuse was germs.

Sandra sat down and immediately informed them it was time to pray. They complied as usual, though Berlyn always kept her eyes open to torment Sandra. Sandra was convinced Berlyn was the biggest heathen she knew. Yet Berlyn was the first person Sandra called whenever she wanted company.

As soon as the amen was given, Berlyn grabbed five packets of Splenda from the tabletop dispenser and stuck them in her purse.

"That's stealing," Sandra snapped.

"Mind your own business, old woman."

Sandra sniffed and turned to Eugenia. "How is Mackenzie?"

Eugenia's fork played in her fruit cup. She watched as a strawberry tumbled over cantaloupe. "Pitiful. I don't know what to do. I feel like a failure as a mother." Her voice cracked.

Dimples reached across the table to take her friend's arm. She missed by a mile in her first attempt but patted her hand around until she safely landed on Eugenia's arm. "You're a wonderful mother, Eugenia. We don't even want to hear that nonsense. If it weren't for you and her jewel of a husband, the poor child would have wasted away by now. You are doing all that you can."

Berlyn pulled a bottled Coke from her handbag and popped off the cap with her bottle opener. "Have you considered a shrink?" she asked right before a big bite of chocolate pie and meringue entered her mouth.

Eugenia snorted. "My child doesn't need a shrink."

Berlyn chewed just enough to make sure none of the pie spewed from her mouth when she talked. "It's not time to be self-righteous, Eugenia. It's time to be realistic. Mackenzie and Gray have both been through hell. And when you go through hell, sometimes it helps if you have someone other than a family member to talk to. That's all I'm saying. We may not have grown up with all that counseling stuff, but —" she looked at the three women sur-rounding her — "that might be the reason why y'all are all screwed up."

Eugenia's back softened against the wood lattice behind it. She was still mulling over Berlyn's previous statement. "Mackenzie barely leaves the house. Her doctor, Thad, has her on these antidepressants."

Sandra sniffed again, and Berlyn eyed her

suspiciously. "What are you turning your nose up at now?"

Sandra wound a strand of pearls around her neck tighter. "I happen to think that depression stuff is nothing but nonsense."

"Well, some people think uptight old women are nonsense too," Berlyn retorted, "but it doesn't make them any less real."

Eugenia spread her napkin over her lap. She ran her hands across it as she spoke. "You aren't saying a thing I haven't thought, Sandra. That's just not how we were raised — to take pills when we had problems. I even begged Thad and Gray not to give that stuff to my baby."

Dimples picked up her fork and stabbed at the pecan pie in front of her. She caught a smidgen of the edge.

"But he told me that depression is kind of like potholes in the brain."

Dimples never looked up. "A pothole in the what?" She stabbed at her pie again and managed to get a forkful.

"In the brain, Dimples. The brain. Now will you eat your pie and let me finish?"

Dimples already had a mouthful, but she smiled and nodded. Eugenia went on. "Thad said that when a person suffers trauma, what it does to the brain is sort of like a pothole. And —"

"Oh my stars! Sandra, now we finally know!"

Sandra furrowed her brow. "What in the world are you talking about, Berlyn?"

"We finally know what your problem is. When your mama dropped you on your head, it made a pothole in your brain. That's what is wrong with you."

Sandra's eyes squinched up. "If I weren't a lady, Berlyn . . ."

Eugenia threw her hands up. "That's it! I can't even have a normal conversation with the three of you because y'all are incapable of having one. I don't know why I thought I could do anything normal with crazy people."

Berlyn shifted her large bottom in her seat. "Go ahead, Eugenia. We're listening. But I just couldn't help it. It was such a revelation."

"I'm not saying another word."

Dimples gnawed at her pie. "No, seriously. We want to hear, Eugenia."

"The only way I will speak again is if none of y'all open your mouths until I'm through."

Dimples ran her fingers across her lips as if she were zipping them. Berlyn followed suit. Sandra just sniffed one more time and stuck a bite of chicken salad in her mouth.

Eugenia pointed two fingers at her eyes, then back at them. "Like I said, trauma creates potholes in your brain. And when you keep going through difficult things one after the other, it's like your body can't fill up those holes fast enough, so you get depressed."

Dimples looked up from her plate. "Fill 'em up with what?"

Berlyn rolled her eyes. "With asphalt, Dimples. What do you think?" But she looked expectantly at Eugenia. Obviously she didn't know either.

"It's this brain stuff — Thad called it serotonin. He said the antidepressant kind of fills in the pothole until your body can produce enough serotonin to take over. And I don't know —" she lowered her head — "it just made sense to me. My baby needs some help filling her potholes. If those pills help do that, then I'm for them." She lifted her eyes and fixed them on Berlyn, who was opening her mouth. "And I don't want to hear one wisecrack about anything I just said."

Berlyn's mouth closed slowly.

"How is Gray?" Sandra asked.

Eugenia's eyes moistened again. "Hurting. And brooding, it seems. He's not himself. And he still hasn't officially announced he's running for reelection."

"He's got time," Sandra responded. "And this state loves him. They know what he and Mack have been through. Plus, people respect what he's done with the budget. It had to be done. I know the politicians are behaving like juveniles, but no one needs money spent on how to teach college students to watch television. Did you know some senator from Knoxville actually had that in his budget request for UT? I was in education for forty-five years, and I assure you the kids had no problem watching television. I'm glad Gray has been willing to do the difficult things. Truth is, we need him."

Eugenia shook her head. "Well, not everyone thinks he is a hero. And I know he's a smart man and he's been a wonderful governor. But honestly, I don't know if Gray and Mackenzie can handle a reelection campaign. I'm not sure they should try. My children need to grieve and they need to heal."

Dimples hacked into her napkin before she spoke. "Mackenzie has been a wonderful first lady. What she's done for that rescue mission has been just beautiful." She smiled, chocolate from her brownie covering her top teeth.

"Well, I'm voting for Gray, even if he pulls out," Berlyn announced. "I'll write his name in if I have to."

"You can spell?" Sandra quipped, a gnawed lemon between her fingers. She kept her eyes on Berlyn.

Berlyn stabbed her fork into her pie. "Have you ever been hit, Sandra? I mean right-smack-dab-between-the-eyes, stars-flying-over-your-head, bells-ringing-in-your-ears hit? Because that is what the experience is going to be like when my fist comes up against the side of that French twist of yours. Just because you were a school librarian doesn't mean other people don't read."

Sandra patted her hair. "You're a Neanderthal."

"No, I'm a little redneck and a little Southern, which means I could deck you and then offer my hand to help you back up. The delight will be the same."

CHAPTER 31

The alarm went off by Gray's head. He reached over and pressed a button on top of the clock. A green fluorescent light backlit the numbers.

Six thirty. He thought he had set it for seven. He was tired these days. He hadn't seen five thirty in over a month.

He looked at Mack. She was sleeping. It used to be, when he woke up first, he'd slide over, slip one arm under her head and the other around her waist, and just hold her for a few minutes. He'd loved that sense of closeness in the first moments of his morning. But he hadn't touched her in weeks. And if he was being honest, he didn't want to. When she shut him out this time, it had felt too much like a betrayal. She knew he needed her too, and yet she acted as if she was the only one who had lost anything.

He wanted to shake her out of it. Make her respond. Make her feel . . . something.

Even if it was anger, maybe that would bring her back to the land of the living. Back to him.

But he couldn't do that. He couldn't shake her. So there didn't seem to be much that he could do.

He climbed out of bed and went into the bathroom to get ready. He set Mack's pill on the counter. Per Thad's orders, he was overseeing the disbursement of her meds. Then he stepped into the shower.

Ten minutes later, while he was shaving, Mack scooted in to use the restroom. She went to get her pill but dropped it. He watched her bend down and pat her hand across the stone floor, but she couldn't find it. He told her he'd leave her another one. But those were the only words they spoke to each other.

He didn't even kiss her when he walked out of the room. He knew he should. But he didn't.

Why? Because he simply didn't want to.

"Come on, Sophie, let's go to work." Gray opened the car door, and Sophie hopped in. They had their routine down pat by now, and with the help of the dog trainer, the puppy had more or less mastered the basics of being a good canine citizen. Sometimes

Gray wished his fellow politicians had manners as good.

A black Toyota Avalon was what Gray was driving now. He only used a driver on long car trips when he had meetings to prepare for, and he had traded in the black Escalade for something more practical and fuel efficient. The state paid his gas bills, and he wanted to use that privilege wisely.

Sophie stretched out in the passenger's seat for the fifteen-minute jaunt to the capitol as snow fell from a gray sky. The thought crossed his mind that schools were probably out because of the snow. A fact that no longer mattered to him except as one more reminder of the gaping wound that still sliced through his heart.

He reached over to scratch Sophie, and she instantly rolled over to give him unobstructed access to her belly. Her fur was soft as cotton, her presence healing. Truth be told, she got him out of bed more days than his job did. She depended on him, and he depended on her too. Several members of the household staff had offered to help with her, but he craved her unhindered desire to be with him.

Every now and then, he did feel a little self-conscious about having a shih tzu by his side instead of a golden retriever or

Great Dane. But most people knew Sophie's story, so there were few remarks.

The most disparaging remarks about Sophie, in fact, had come from Mack. To her, the puppy was simply a reminder of Maddie's last days. She had wanted Gray to get rid of Sophie right after the accident. Later, when she was pregnant, she had finally warmed up to Sophie a little. But since the miscarriage — well, Mack desired nothing these days. Not Sophie and certainly not him.

The counselor Thad recommended, Ken Jantzen, had started coming to the house to see Mack twice a week. According to Eugenia, Mack wasn't responding to him either. The counselor was worried that Mack was dangerously depressed, so Thad had started her on an antidepressant, but Gray saw no sign that it was working. Thad had encouraged Gray to meet with the counselor too, and he'd promised to think about it. He had — thought about it, that was. And decided he wasn't going. He didn't need therapy. He simply needed his wife back.

He had never been a man to use his work as an escape from his home life. Until now. More and more, he found himself escaping to the one place where he knew he was wanted.

A state trooper assigned to the underground parking garage opened the door when Gray pulled in. Gray climbed from the car, and Sophie jumped out behind him. He scooped her up and headed for the elevator.

Fletcher fell in beside them in the corridor outside Gray's staff offices and handed over a file.

"What's this?" Gray asked.

"Something we don't need right before we announce a reelection campaign."

The door to the suite opened, and Kurt appeared. "I know you don't need anything else on you now, and we would handle this ourselves if we could. But the news will break at lunch hour. Thankfully, it happened too late to hit the morning news cycle. And it would be another random killing to most people in the state if Marcus Newman and his people weren't looking for a way to keep you from running for reelection."

Gray kept walking, gave a brief hello to Sarah, grabbed a cup of coffee, and walked into his office. Kurt and Fletcher followed, and Kurt shut the door. Sophie went straight to her water bowl, tucked in a corner next to an antique dresser that dated back to the Lamar Alexander administration.

Gray opened the file and thumbed through the police reports. A convenience store clerk had been murdered at three thirty that morning, the suspect quickly apprehended. A mug shot stared back at Gray, the suspect's pale face hard.

"Should I know this man?"

Kurt leaned over Gray's desk. "You should know that he was one of the men released because of budget cuts."

Gray sat down. "What?"

"He was a nonviolent offender who apparently became violent. He did this right after he pummeled his wife."

"Does he have a family?"

Fletcher squinted his eyes. "He beat his wife, Gray. Obviously he has a family."

Gray's eyes darted up in irritation. "The victim, Fletcher. I'm talking about the man who got shot. Did you forget there was a man who got shot? Or are you just worried about what this is going to do to a campaign?"

Fletcher's eyes widened. "No, um . . . sorry. I honestly hadn't really thought about his family. Want me to find out?"

Gray felt his anger rise. It seemed to be sitting right on the surface lately. He tamped it down and flipped through the file again. "Yes, find out. And find out about the prisoner's wife too."

"We *were* more focused on the campaign," Kurt said, obviously trying to smooth things over. "That's our job — to make sure that you are represented accurately."

Gray tossed the file down on his desk. "How do you represent this accurately, Kurt? How do you accurately represent the fact that a prisoner we allowed to go free has beaten one person and killed another? And that somewhere right now a mother or father or wife or child is heartbroken over a family member who went to work last night fine and is never coming home again? How do you represent that any more accurately than what it is? It's horrifying. And it's our problem."

Kurt and Fletcher shared a look. Then Fletcher opened his notebook. "So how do you want to handle our statement to the press?" he asked carefully.

"We'll handle it like we've handled everything else that has come out of this office — honestly. We'll tell them this is part of the tragedy of what is happening to our state. Assure them that we continue to monitor the prisoners we released, but that there's always the risk of these men and women doing something we hope they won't do. When they get out and see how difficult the economy really is, they probably have little hope for things getting better."

Kurt sat in a chair beside Gray's desk. "I think we need to connect this with something in the Newman camp — make it clear who spent us into this mess."

Gray shook his head. "A man just died, Kurt. A woman was 'pummeled,' to use Fletcher's word. And Newman wasn't even in Nashville when all of this happened. So, no, we're not pinning this on him. Plus, I'm thinking of not running."

Fletcher's pen about fell out of his hand.

Kurt stood. Sophie jumped slightly at his sudden movement, then walked over to her pillow and lay down. "You're what? We've been working on this for months. Constituents have been patient because of all the loss you've suffered. But people have already invested in a campaign."

"Well, they may have to uninvest." His words were sharp.

Kurt was visibly trying to calm himself down. "Look, I know that this has been a —"

"Don't you dare say it, Kurt." Gray stood. He was close to Kurt now. "Don't you dare say you know what this season has been like.

You have no idea. You go home every day to Debbie, you tuck Carly and Tyler into bed, and you kiss them good night. You wake up in the morning and watch them eat breakfast and take them to school. And when you get home, Debbie has dinner on the table and she kisses you and she's glad you're there. And at night she crawls in bed with you and wants to hear what your day has been like. So don't you ever say again you know how I feel. You have no idea."

Kurt's hurt was evident on his face. Gray didn't care.

"Gray, I'm sorry. I was just —"

"Get out." Gray motioned his hand toward the door and sat down in his chair. "Just get out. Fletcher, make the statement I told you to make. And I'll let you both know when and if I decide I'm actually going to run in this election."

Fletcher stood quickly and slapped his notebook shut. Gray was aware his behavior was different from anything his friends had ever experienced from him. But *he* was different. He would never be the same. They should know that. They should all know that.

Kurt opened the door and turned back toward Gray. "We have nine months until this election — less than that, really. The people deserve to know your decision. *We* deserve to know your decision."

"Yeah, people deserve a lot of things," Gray muttered. "But people don't always get what they deserve, do they?"

Kurt let Fletcher walk through the open door, then followed him out, closing the door behind them.

Gray picked up the phone and dialed Sarah. "Can you get the phone number of the family of the victim from last night's convenience store shooting? I want to call them."

"Sure."

"Thanks." He knew exactly what he'd say. He'd say what he wished people would say to him.

Gray leaned against the edge of his desk and stared at the television screen in his office. He could see dust on the left side of the screen because of how the light hit it. He thought of Philippe, who usually cleaned his office. His wife had been in the hospital with cancer. He and Mack had gone to see her in December before . . . well, before all of this. But he hadn't thought about Philippe's family since the miscarriage — not until this moment. He needed to check on them.

The ringing phone interrupted his thoughts. Sarah was on the other end with the information he had requested. He hung up with Sarah and dialed.

A voice on the other end answered weakly. "Hello?"

"Is this Mr. Gooden?"

"Yes, it is."

"Mr. Gooden, this is Governor Gray London."

There was a long silence. "Um . . . yes."

"Sir, I just found out about the tragic loss of your son. And I want you to know how sorry I am."

Another silence, then finally, "Thank you. Um, that's nice of you to call."

"I hope you know that if you need anything, you can reach us. We will do everything in our power to make sure justice is served to the man who did this."

Gray heard the man's voice crack. "Thank you."

He worked hard to control his own. "You're welcome, sir. . . . Well, that's really all I called to say."

"Okay, then."

"Okay . . . good-bye."

"Bye, now."

He knew that in the grand scheme of things his call mattered very little. Why would that family care for his condolences when injustice had already fallen with all of its cruelty on them? But somewhere in the back of his mind, a thought pricked that the whole situation was just a little . . . convenient. A murder. An election. A released prisoner — one whom Gray had released. A bit extreme for Tennessee politics, but he'd heard of such things before.

Sophie scratched at his leg, pulling him back from his ridiculous thought. He reached over and rubbed the top of her head, then picked her up to let her sit on his desk. A delicate knock sounded on the door.

"Come in." His hand still rubbed Sophie's head.

Sarah walked through the door. "I just wanted to check on you. You okay?"

He nodded. "Yeah, I'm good."

She walked toward him. He knew she wanted to talk, but he didn't feel like talking. The only problem with his staff was that they all went so far back together, they sometimes crossed the employee-employer line and got right into his personal space. He had never really minded that much. He did now.

"How's Mackenzie?" Sarah asked carefully.

"Alive."

Sarah tilted her head. She was beautiful for sixty — petite, classy, always put together and soft-spoken. But all that could fool you because there was a tiger mama in there too. And with Mack and her daughter Anna being such good friends from childhood, Sarah seemed to feel that both he and Mack were part of her den.

"And how's Gray?" she added.

He moved his hand from Sophie's head. She shot up and headed for the edge of the desk. He caught her before she could jump. "I'm fine."

"That doesn't sound like fine, Gray. And you don't look fine. You've been through a lot, you know."

Her hand came up on the side of his arm. She rubbed it with the affection of a concerned mother. "It's okay to feel all that pain. And it's okay to not be okay." She paused for a minute. "And it's okay if you don't want to go through with this election. There isn't a soul who would blame you."

Gray laid his head in his hands. "Yeah, I know." A sudden thought sent his pulse racing again. He raised his head. His words came out measured. "Is someone in our camp not wanting me to run? Are people other than Newman's camp talking about this?"

Sarah removed her hand but kept her voice soft. "No, Gray. This is me talking to you. Your mother's gone, your father isn't available the way you need him to be, and you and I have been through a lot together. I'm just saying there is nothing wrong with backing down if an election feels like too much."

Gray fought the feeling of panic that rose in his throat. Sarah was hiding something. He could feel it. Someone out there was talking. They thought he was weak, thought he couldn't handle his family losses and an election too. "I am more than capable of following this through. The people need me in this house. They need what I have to offer." His voice was peppered with anger. "I may not be able to keep my children from dying, but I can certainly maintain a political campaign."

Sarah's expression turned to pity. He didn't want her pity. "Okay. I want you to do what you think is best. And whatever you decide, I'm behind you 100 percent."

She gave him a tender smile, one he didn't want — and didn't return. She walked out the door without saying anything else.

He sat there for several minutes, breathing hard, then picked up his phone. "Kurt, what happened today is going to burn out in a couple of weeks at the most. Let's not give it any legs — not talk about it anymore after Fletcher does the news conference this afternoon. If our opponents bring it up, we'll address it. Otherwise it is a dead issue to us."

He slammed down the phone before Kurt could respond. He shook at the torment that was raging through his body. Scattered thoughts ricocheted through his head. He felt like he might be going mad. It was crazy — the thoughts, the frustration, all of it. He wanted to crawl out of his skin. That was the feeling. If he could just get away from everything that was inside, maybe he could survive this.

He put Sophie down on the floor, left her in the office, and headed to his car. He didn't want to run for governor. He wanted to crawl into a hole and not come out. But there were things inside him that were more powerful than that desire. They felt new and real. They were his pride. His anger. His intense need to be needed. Somewhere. Anywhere.

He didn't know what to do with any of those. More than that, he wasn't sure what they would do with him.

But maybe they weren't new at all. Maybe, just maybe, they'd been in him for a long time. It had just taken the perfect storm to wash them to shore.

Chapter 32

Mackenzie walked to her window and looked out, mildly surprised to see a snowy landscape. If not for the snow, she wouldn't know if it was spring or winter. Nor did she really care. The clock on the bedside table said four o'clock. She had slept the day away.

She had hoped she would never wake up.

She had dropped her antidepressant pill on purpose this morning, then lied and told Gray she couldn't find it. He'd given her another one, and she'd taken both.

The whole idea of medication was something new for her. She had been raised in a home where you rarely took aspirin when you had a headache. But things were different now that she knew the reality of depression. She'd thought that taking two pills at once might give her a jolt of life, or maybe they would just sweep her away. They had done nothing but make her sleep a little longer than usual. And her mother hadn't come in to bother her.

When she climbed back into bed that morning, she had wanted Gray to kiss her. To touch her. To do something. He hadn't even tried.

That was new. Gray had always touched her. Used to be, he couldn't pass her without some kind of touch. A kiss on the head. A pat on the rear. A tug on her arm to pull her close to him. But this morning, he'd just walked out.

Mackenzie knew why. She was a walking tomb. She so disgusted him now, he couldn't even touch her or hold her. He barely spoke to her. And she didn't blame him. She disgusted herself.

She sat down in a chair, and her body dissolved in it. She wished it could swallow her whole. Her hand fell to the suede book holder that sat beside her chair, her fingers brushing one of the books. She fingered its corners and knew immediately what it was. Her Bible. She wanted to throw it out the window because everything inside was a lie. Everything that professed to be a promise was nothing but hollow clanging.

After Maddie died, Gray had begged her to go to church with him, and she'd refused. She had gone back willingly after she found out she was pregnant. Now, Gray never bothered to ask. She didn't even know if he went. But she did know she would never go again. Because no one knew her pain. No one knew the depth of her loss. She wondered in this moment if stories like Job were even true. Because no human could survive losing ten children.

She had lost six. *Six.* And she wouldn't call what she was doing now surviving.

A gentle knock came at the door, jarring her from her thoughts. "Come in." She didn't even look up.

Soft steps came up beside her. "Hello, Mrs. London. Jeremiah gave me this to bring to you."

Mackenzie turned to see Jessica holding a mirrored container with an orchid inside. Five dainty blooms hung from its bending stem as if they too desired to simply fall away.

"Who did you say gave you this?"

"Jeremiah Williams. Want me to set it right here?" Jessica motioned toward the table.

Mackenzie nodded and turned back to the window.

"Can I get you anything else? Are you hungry? Rosa made some chili."

Mackenzie shook her head.

"Okay, then. Well, I guess I'll leave you alone."

Jessica's footfall was quiet across the damask carpet. Mackenzie heard her bracelet hit the doorknob. "Why an orchid?" Mackenzie asked.

"Excuse me, ma'am?"

"An orchid? Why an orchid?" Mackenzie now stared at the flower. "He's always given me a single-stem flower. There has never been a potted plant." She turned quickly toward Jessica, who stood at the door, her gaze gently landing on Mackenzie. "Tell me what an orchid means."

"What an orchid means?" Jessica's eyes registered her puzzlement.

"Yes, you know, that every-flower-has-a-meaning stuff. I want to know what an orchid means."

Jessica shook her head. "I don't know, Mrs. London. I didn't even know flowers had meanings."

"Would you get my phone from the bathroom and look it up for me?"

"You want me to look it up?"

"Yes, please. Just look it up." Mackenzie laid her head back. She felt as if that short conversation had drained the very little bit of life she did have out of her.

Jessica walked into the bathroom and

330

returned with Mackenzie's iPhone in her hand. "Okay, let's see here." She squinted at the screen. "Orchids mean 'love, beauty, refinement, beautiful lady, Chinese symbol for . . .'" She stopped in midsentence.

The silence was long and obvious. Mackenzie raised her head. "Chinese symbol for what?"

"Um . . . okay, here are a few more: 'thoughtfulness, maturity, charm.'" Jessica clicked the phone off and returned it to the bathroom. "That's all."

Mackenzie knew that Jeremiah could say all of those things to her, but she also knew that since he had quit giving her roses, his flowers had conveyed very specific messages. And each one had, in a strange way, given her a little peace — dare she say, the only peace anything had given her.

"Chinese symbol for what?"

Jessica emerged from the bathroom and shook her head, her lips pursed so tight her eyes bulged.

"Jessica —" Mackenzie slowed her words — "what did you not read to me?"

Jessica's shoulders slumped. "I'm sure he didn't know this one."

"Jeremiah knows everything about flowers. What are you sure he didn't know?"

Jessica paused, her eyes darting toward

the window as if Mackenzie might forget her question. Finally she let out a slow sigh. "Orchids are the Chinese symbol for many children."

Mackenzie's eyes narrowed. Surely she hadn't heard right. "Did you say 'for many children'?"

Jessica nodded slowly. "Yes, they are a symbol for having a lot of children."

Mackenzie felt the anger start from her toes and work its way up as if it were going to come out of every orifice in her head. She pushed her body hard into her chair, scooted the ottoman out from under her legs, and stood up quickly. She snatched the container from the table and walked past Jessica, bumping her as she did. She headed down the stairs, slipped her feet into boots at the back door, and walked straight outside, the cold instantly beating against the exposed portions of her arms. The wind seemed to slice straight through her. But her anger had her virtually on fire.

"Jeremiah!" Her loud call echoed through the meandering garden lanes.

"Have you seen Jeremiah?" she asked two young men in orange jumpsuits who were shoveling snow from the terrace. They looked at each other as if scared to answer, then pointed in the direction of the back of the property.

Jeremiah was bent over, large pruning shears in his hand. She came up behind him and stopped just inches away. "What were you trying to say with this orchid?"

Jeremiah rose slowly, his left hand pressing the small of his back. "Hope it ain't gone and made you angry."

"What were you trying to say?" she repeated. "After Maddie died, you sent me hyacinths and some kind of daisy and —"

"Zinnias. Zahara zinnias."

"Okay, zinnias. But each one had a different meaning, right? Then when I got pregnant, you went back to the roses like you had always done. And since . . . since . . ." Her words softened slightly. "Since the baby died, you've gone back to giving me different flowers. And trust me, my mother tells me every day what they mean. But today . . ." Her back stiffened. "So what were you saying today with that orchid?"

Jeremiah pulled his work gloves from his hands, revealing a slight tremor before he placed them in his pockets. "Now, Miz Mackenzie, I need you to know I ain't had no desire to give you that there orchid. But I just keep gettin' this thought stirred up inside a me that this be the flower you be needin'. And, yes'm, I know very well what

it means. Well, I know what meanin' you re-
ferrin' to and all."

"The one about many children?"

"Yes'm. That one. That be the one just
couldn't quit diggin' in my gut. I can't
explain it none. Alls I know is that I felt like
I s'pose to give it to you today."

"Do you think this is a joke, Jeremiah?"

He shook his head, his face solemn. "No,
ma'am. Ain't never thought none of this be
a joke."

Her face was burning. "Do you think this
is some game you and I are playing?"

"No, ma'am. Don't think that at all. Just
be doin' what I feel I'm s'posed to."

She threw the container against a tree. The
mirror cracked instantly, and the orchid
flopped against it, its stem broken in two by
the time it landed on the snow-covered
ground. "I don't want another flower. Do
you hear me?"

He looked at her steadily. "Yes'm."

"Don't try to tell me anything. Don't try
to give me some message. I don't want to
hear any of it. All I want is for you to leave
me alone. Do you hear me?"

"Yes'm. I sure am sorry, ma'am. Ain't
mean no disrespect or nothin' — just
thought it might give you a li'l hope."

She let out a mocking laugh. "Hope! For

children! Don't you know my track record?"

He didn't speak.

"This body can't do children! And this woman can't either! When I finally had one, I couldn't even protect her." The break was hard in her voice, and tears began to stream down her face. "I couldn't even protect Maddie! No child deserves me, Jeremiah! No child deserves me!"

The emotion was deep and raw. It left her scared as she ran down the path toward the mansion and cut through one of the rose beds. A large thorn caught her arm, but she paid it no attention. Her tears flowed as fast as her feet ran.

She passed Jessica, who was standing at the back door, and never said a word. She went straight to her room and into the bathroom, where she jerked the bottom drawer with such force the items resting in it bounced in unison. Dropping to her knees, she reached inside and began to grab wildly at the pregnancy tests that sat in a line as if ridiculing her. She threw them across the bathroom with all her might and let out a scream as they flew through the air, hitting the far bathroom wall and then scattering across the stone floor. Then she stared at the bottles of Pregnyl and the needles.

She jerked her chair out from under her makeup counter and flung it behind her. It toppled over with a crash. She yanked out the trash can, gathered up the medicine, and threw it in with all the force her arms would allow. Heaving tears shook her body as she flung the trash can back underneath the counter, only to watch it topple over, its contents spilling on the floor.

Weariness washed over her as she slowly got to her feet. She walked into the bedroom and threw her body across the bed. A trickle of blood from the cut on her arm created a small red splotch on the duvet beneath her.

JEREMIAH

I knowed it. I knowed Miz Mackenzie gon'
go and have that freak-out.

Well, maybe I ain't knowed it for sure. A
piece a me thought maybe she wouldn't
even notice. But she notice. She *really*
notice. That's why I ain't wanted to do it.

'Course, maybe that anger be a good
thing. Maybe it prove that sump'n still alive
up in there, that she still gots a li'l fight in
her. Anger be part of healin' too.

Did hurt a li'l though. Miz Mackenzie
ain't never talk to me like that. Come to
think of it, I ain't never hear her talk to
nobody like that. Ain't seen her brow all
scrunched up like that neither.

Alls I ever seen her doin' is smilin' — 'til
this past year, anyway. Ain't been much
smilin' this year.

I still don't know 'xactly why God made
me go and give her that orchid. But him
and me sure done stir up a nest a angry

hornets, look like. Maybe that what he want. Maybe he want Miz Mackenzie to go and feel sump'n. Just ain't quite figured out why I be the one had to do it. One thing sure — I gon' be hearin' from Miz Eugenia 'bout this. She gon' say sump'n nasty and mean and probably gon' get me fired too. That woman'd just love to get me outta what she think is her own garden.

Well, alls I gots to say is, the good Lord gon' have fun fixin' this one. 'Cause I ain't gots nothin' can calm down a woman like Eugenia Quinn when she up on her high horse. Can't get rid a her neither. I gots stuff to take care a beetles, mites, borers, caterpillars — you name it — but I ain't find nothin' yet to get rid of Eugenia Quinn.

Sometimes I think the Lord be keepin' her 'round 'cause I needs some thorn in my flesh. But last I check, I gots plenty a them thorns already.

So next time she show up here in my garden, I just gon' step back and let God handle her. Ain't even gon' say nothin'. 'Cause all this be his bright idea anyway.

CHAPTER 33

Gray felt heaviness crashing down on his shoulders as he pulled into the mansion's garage and walked with Sophie down the long basement corridor. He had told security that he was going by the nursing home and might be gone for a while. Then he'd spent the day sitting at a local sports bar in Green Hills, had found a seat in the corner and turned his back to the rest of the patrons. The college student who waited on him apparently had no idea who he was, so he'd guzzled one too many beers while eating chicken wings and watching a basketball game.

He hadn't had a beer in years. But today he'd needed one. Okay, a few. He'd needed something. When he returned to the capitol to get Sophie, he'd used the back entrance and made a special effort not to breathe on the state trooper stationed there. Now he just needed to sweat some of the alcohol out.

On his way to the basement workout room, he heard a noise down the hall. A light was on in Jeremiah's workroom.

Gray looked at his watch. Five o'clock. He hadn't thought about Jeremiah still being here and he didn't feel like talking, so he moved quietly through the workout room and into his private bathroom, where he kept his workout clothes. He put them on, walked to the treadmill, then punched buttons and got started while Sophie wrestled one of her ropes in the corner. But halfway through mile one, Jeremiah's head popped through the door.

"Home kinda early tonight, ain't you, Gov'nor?"

Gray's words came out in puffs. "Needed to get some stress out."

"Well, I sure 'nough glad you gots you some time. Keep that heart good and healthy."

"Yeah." Gray nodded dismissively, but Jeremiah didn't leave. He just stood there watching him, a pair of pruners in his hand, the silence awkward between them. Gray kept running, staring straight ahead at the television in front of him.

After a moment, Jeremiah walked in and

placed a hand on the treadmill's railing. "Saw Miz Mackenzie today. She not doin' so good."

Gray didn't say anything. He just gazed straight ahead, his feet moving at a quick clip. Sweat already rolled down his face.

"I'd say you both be hurtin'." Jeremiah fiddled with the pruners.

"Grief usually hurts, Jeremiah."

The old man shook his head slow and steady. "Yep, it sure 'nough do. Get you real good. Sometimes it even get worse 'fore it get better."

"Thank you. That's reassuring." Gray didn't even try to soften the sarcasm, but Jeremiah didn't seem to notice. He just pulled a handkerchief from his pocket and ran it down the blades of his pruners. "I been out prunin' roses today, y'know. Lots a folks don't know it, but roses, they sturdy creatures. Treat 'em right, they hard to kill. But my azaleas out there, they ain't like that. Gots to baby 'em along. You ever knowed the Chinese meanin' of azalea?"

Gray's arms moved in rhythmic motion with his feet. "Can't say I do."

"It mean 'womanhood.' Some say another meanin' is 'fragile.' " He paused. "Miz Mackenzie seem real fragile to me right now."

"Well, she's been through a lot."

341

"Yeah, I know it been real tough. We're all feelin' the hurt 'round here. That's what gots me thinkin' 'bout them azaleas, how they so different from roses. Gots to have lots a shade, gots to be watered all the time, soil gots to be just acid 'nough. Sometimes they ain't even feel worth all the trouble."

Gray wiped sweat from his forehead. His feet were feeling heavy, and alcohol seemed to ooze out his pores. He watched Jeremiah through the mirror in front of him, wishing for five thirty to come.

Jeremiah stuffed the handkerchief into his back pocket. "Y'know, after the flood come through here, I done lost a bunch a them blasted azaleas. They roots so shallow, they just come right up outta the ground — left big ol' holes in the plantin's out by the front gates. I just wanted to throw my hands up and give up on 'em. I mean, after I gone and worked so hard with 'em and all.

"But I ain't done that, Gov'nor. I didn't give up on them azaleas. And y'know why?"

Gray shook his head. "No. Why?"

" 'Cause ever' spring, they just bust out with this gaudy display a color — kinda like Miz Berlyn's dresses."

Gray smiled slightly at that.

"And people come drivin' by just to look at 'em. And y'know what else?"

Gray wasn't sure if Jeremiah was looking for a response or not, so he just shook his head and kept running.

"Not one person notice the holes from what's gone 'cause what still there so dang beautiful."

Jeremiah dropped the pruners down to his side. "All life's gots holes, Gov'nor. Some holes be bigger than others. But that don't mean you don't keep takin' care a what you gots. And you know what's crazy? Spring always come. Never found me a year yet that ain't had a spring. It always come. And when it do, when it show up, I be so grateful I ain't give up on them temperamental, ornery shrubs."

Gray blinked sweat from his eyes. He heard the old man. He just didn't feel like admitting it.

"Yep, y'know, Gov'nor, them azaleas be so beautiful, they worth the trouble. They worth tendin' to. Fightin' for. And a really wise gardener, a gardener that know he don't know it all — he get real good at listenin' to what heaven tell him 'bout *how* to tend 'em."

Gray still didn't answer. Finally Jeremiah nodded and turned toward the door. "Well, I headed out now. See you tomorrow."

Gray nodded as the old man walked away.

"Good night."

Jeremiah stopped at the door and turned. "Oh, them azaleas have one more meanin' I 'bout near forgot."

"What is that?"

"They also mean 'take care of yourself' —" he paused — " 'for me.' "

With that, he left the room. When he was gone, Gray hit a button on the treadmill and brought his feet to a stop. He walked to a bench and sat down. Sophie came up beside him and swung her rope wildly at his feet. He bent down, wrestled it from her mouth, and threw it across the room. Her little feet floundered underneath her until she got enough traction to propel herself across the room, grab the rope between her jaws, and carry it back to him, nearly tripping over the end that dangled beneath her. Gray pulled the loose end of the rope while she growled and jerked madly at the other end.

He and Mack *had* been through a flood. And for some unknown reason, they had survived, despite their desires to the contrary. He had never felt so ravaged, so broken. And there were more holes in Mack than in anyone he knew. She was like an open pasture full of holes left by detonated land mines.

He let go of the rope and stretched his body across the top of the padded bench. Sophie dropped her end too and began licking his arm. He lay there a long time.

He knew Mack needed him. But in that moment, it all felt too hard. He didn't have it in him to fight for her. Not anymore.

So he made the conscious decision simply to take on a fight he thought he could win.

Becoming governor again.

CHAPTER 34

Mackenzie watched Gray come into the room. He said nothing when he entered, nor did he even look in her direction. She watched him walk into the bathroom and then heard water as it fell in the shower.

Darkness had settled an hour ago, but moonlight on the snow outside made it easy to see in the unlit bedroom. Mackenzie lifted herself from the chair and walked into the bathroom. When light hit her, she saw caked blood on the side of her arm. She got a washcloth from the linen closet and walked to the sink, letting water soak the brown fabric. She placed her hand on the travertine countertop and wiped at the blood.

In the mirror she saw Gray's outline through the steam on the glass shower door. He looked foreign to her. She had once known him so well and been curious to know more. There had always seemed to be something new to uncover, something about the way his mind worked that she had never realized, something about his heart that she had yet to explore. Now she was curious about nothing. Except what it would take to make all of this pain go away.

She secured a Band-Aid across the scratch on her arm. Gray opened the shower door. Steam poured into the bathroom and immediately attacked the mirror in front of her. He reached for a towel and dried himself off. When he looked up, he saw her.

"Mack! I didn't even know you were there."

She had obviously startled him. "Sorry. I didn't mean to scare you."

"Where were you?"

"I was in my chair when you came in. But I have a cut on my arm, so I was just getting a Band-Aid for it. A rosebush caught me," she said before he asked.

He rubbed his head wildly with the towel, then wrapped it around his waist and walked into the closet. She could hear drawers opening. The distance between them felt more like a canyon than the length of the bathroom. He came out dressed in his warm-ups and started past her.

"Where are you going?" she asked.

He stopped. "It's seven o'clock at night,

Mack. I'm going to eat some dinner and watch some television and do some work. I'm going to do what living, breathing humans do."

She stared at him. His eyes looked bloodshot and tired. She didn't remark about that, just reached down to throw away the Band-Aid wrapper.

"Mack," he said, and she looked up. He leaned against the doorway. "You need to know a few things. I've decided to run for reelection. I think we've accomplished a great deal with the budget, and I really think that the people believe in what we're doing."

His words fell against her, and as they did, she realized she hadn't thought about his campaign once in the past month. The mere thought of it now made her want to throw up. "As long as you don't plan on me campaigning with you."

She noticed his countenance change immediately. He stepped toward her. "You know what I expect, Mack? I expect you to get dressed in the morning — in real clothes. Then I expect you to meet with Jessica and set up appointments on your calendar. I also expect you to know that as of this coming Monday, this mansion is going to be open once again to public tours. And I expect you —" he stepped even closer — "to realize that life is moving on, and you and I are going to move on with it. Whether either of us wants to or not."

She stood there frozen as his words collided against her. In sixteen years of marriage, he had never used that tone. He didn't say another word, simply stepped around her and strode out of the bedroom.

The faint smell of alcohol lingered long after he passed.

CHAPTER 35

Soft, warm hair brushed against his face. He opened his eyes, feeling a spark of something inside, only to have it quickly extinguished when he realized it was Sophie. He nudged the puppy. "Get down, girl."

She obeyed, jumping off the end of the sofa. Gray pushed his blanket to one side and put his feet on the thick carpet. He raised his hands above his head and stretched . . . long . . . hard, then rubbed the back of his neck. He hadn't slept on a sofa in years and had never slept in his office at the capitol. But after his conversation with Mack he just hadn't wanted to be at home. He was tired of it all — tired of the tears, the heaviness, and the lack of intimacy.

He had never spoken to Mack the way he had last night. They'd had fights, of course, because they were two passionate people, but he had never given her orders, never spoken harshly.

But maybe he should have. Because it really was time for her to snap out of it.

He folded the blanket and draped it over the end of the sofa. He fluffed the pillow and switched off the fan he'd brought from home to help him sleep. He and Sophie both had business to take care of. He put on his tennis shoes and took care of his before they headed out to take care of hers. He pulled on his warm-up jacket and walked into the main offices.

Sarah was already at her desk. She looked up, her face showing her shock. "You're here early." Her eyes scanned his outfit.

He looked down at his black Under Armour workout pants. In all the years Sarah had worked with him, he had never been to the office without a tie, much less looking like this. His hand reached up to rub his face and felt day-old stubble.

He obviously hadn't thought his entire plan through. He always kept an extra suit and toiletries in his bathroom at the office, but he'd never realized just how early Sarah got to work.

"Um, yeah. Up pretty early." He pointed awkwardly to the door. "I'm just going to take Sophie out to the bathroom."

Sarah eyed him, then walked over and

scooped Sophie into her arms. "How about you let me do that for you? Me and Sophie are good buddies, aren't we, girl?" Sophie's tail wagged profusely, and her tongue licked Sarah's fingertips. "Top right-hand drawer," Sarah added. "Blueberry muffins. I made extra. Fresh coffee is in the coffeepot over there."

She took such good care of him. Better care than he was taking of himself these days. He patted Sophie on the head, grateful that Sarah was the only one in the front office. "Thank you."

She winked at him and left with Sophie. He walked to her desk and pulled out a plastic container, still warm underneath. He carried it into his office and closed the door. As soon as he sat down on his sofa, he pulled the top off the container. The aroma of freshly baked sweets warmed him and took him immediately to Maddie's blueberry pancakes. The choke hold on his throat came without warning.

And that was the story of grief. It could give you a moment of reprieve, and then from nowhere, it would blindside you and take your breath away. He picked up a muffin, refusing to let the past take hold of the day.

A knock sounded on the door as he took

his first bite. "Come in," he garbled, expecting Sophie to pounce at the smell of food.

"Hey, you're here early." It wasn't Sarah with Sophie. It was Kurt, carrying a newspaper under his arm and folders in his other hand.

"Yep. Want a muffin?" Gray extended the container.

Kurt never reached for a muffin. Instead, he just stood there staring, obviously caught off guard by Gray's appearance.

"Yes, I slept on the sofa last night." Gray stood and crammed the rest of the muffin in his mouth.

"You and Mackenzie have a fight?"

Still chewing, Gray set the container and lid down on his desk and walked to the window. He could see Sophie picking through the snow, trying to find the perfect spot to do her business, while Sarah sat on a bench, giving her time to do what she needed to do. "You can't fight with a corpse."

He felt Kurt come closer. "Is the counselor helping?"

The rising anger was beginning to feel familiar. "The counselor would help if she'd actually talk to him."

Kurt placed a hand on his shoulder. "What about you, Gray? Why don't you talk to him? Debbie and I saw a guy for years when we were having problems in our marriage — you remember that, right? Anyway, it really helped us. You've been through a lot more than I could even imagine. You need someone to help you come to terms with everything that's happened."

Gray pulled away from Kurt's hand. "Won't that look great for a reelection campaign? Headline reads, 'Governor Seeking Professional Help While Governing State Affairs.' "

Kurt's eyes widened. "First, there isn't a person in this state who wouldn't understand your getting counseling after what you've been through. Second, are you saying you've decided to run?"

"Yes, and I'm going to win."

"Listen, buddy, I've thought all night about what you said yesterday. Maybe you were right then. Maybe you should think about whether this race is the best thing or not."

Gray's head turned sharply in his direction. "Okay, let me get this straight. Just yesterday all you could think about was the election. The last words you left me with when you walked out of my office were about the election. And now today you don't think I should run. What are you *not* saying?"

Kurt held his hands up instinctively. "Calm down. I'm just being your friend, and your friend sees that you're in pain. And I need to apologize. I'm sorry I've been pushy. Right now, all I care about is seeing you and Mackenzie heal."

Gray pushed Kurt's raised hands aside and moved past him. "You're full of it, Kurt! There's no way you would be desperate for me to run one day and not care the next. Did you find a more formidable candidate to work for?" Gray turned back, jerked the newspaper from beneath Kurt's arm, and opened it. The killing of the convenience store worker and the fact that the suspect had been a released prisoner was splashed across the front page.

Gray slammed the paper down on the desk. "The backlash from this murder too much for you? Well, you know what? I do death. It follows me like the plague. So get used to it or get out!"

Kurt stepped back. "Listen to yourself. This is ridiculous. We've been friends for twenty-five years. I have always and will always have your back."

"Easier to turn the knife from there, isn't it?" Gray saw the look on Kurt's face as soon as the words came out, but he didn't care.

"I'm going to forget you said —" Kurt began.

"Don't." Gray stepped closer. "I meant it."

Kurt stood face-to-face with him. His head looked freshly shaved. "You need help, Gray. And I'm not going to support your running for reelection when you're like this. The people will understand if you don't run."

"I don't want anyone's understanding! And don't make this about something it's not. You're just ready to walk — and how convenient for you. Now you can go support whoever promises the easier path for your promotion. It's always been about you anyway, hasn't it? Riding my coattails because you don't have any vision of your own."

Another knock sounded on the door. "Come in." Gray's words echoed through the office. The door opened, and Sophie bounded through. Sarah stood in the doorway, a cup of coffee in her hand.

"Get out, Kurt." Gray pointed toward the door. "The door's already open for you."

Sarah shot them a bewildered look as she

walked toward Gray's desk to set down the coffee.

"You too, Sarah. Get out."

Kurt started toward the door. "We'll talk later when you're more in control of yourself."

"I'm in perfect control, and we won't talk later. Clean out your desk now. You're fired."

"Gray, what are you doing?" Sarah asked.

"Stay out of this, Sarah."

"It's okay," Kurt said. "He isn't thinking clearly."

Gray got up in Kurt's face. "I'm thinking perfectly. And I want you out. You are fired. Do you understand?"

He saw emotion behind Kurt's eyes but he didn't care. "Do you understand?" he asked again.

Kurt's response was almost tender. "Yes, Gray. I understand." But his calmness only caused a fresh wave of fury to boil up from deep inside Gray.

"It's 'Governor'!" he shouted as his fist connected with Kurt's right cheek.

Kurt's head flew back sharply. Sarah screamed and ran toward him. "What in the world is wrong with you?"

Kurt's hand instinctively reached for his mouth. Blood trickled from the corner.

The quickness of it shocked even Gray,

but he refused to give in to empathy. There had once been an endless supply of that in his soul, but now he felt as barren as Mack's womb.

Kurt swiped at the blood on his mouth and locked eyes with Gray. "I'll have my desk cleaned out in thirty minutes, Governor." The sadness in his eyes was all Gray could see as he walked out of the room.

Sarah never said a word. Her tears were falling too hard for her to speak.

Gray strode into the familiar corridor of the Green Hills Nursing Center, Sophie tucked under his arm. His nerves were still frayed. And his pulse felt as if he had just finished running sprints.

"Good afternoon, Governor," the elderly gentleman who sat at the front desk said as Gray passed by. But before Gray could answer, he heard a commotion from up the hall.

". . . can't keep us down. We'll fight to the death!" His father's voice echoed through the halls straight at him. Gray followed the sound and found his father fighting hard against two nurses who were trying to hold him. Gray hurried into the room, deposited Sophie on the floor, and threw his weight across his father, being careful not to injure his frail body. Harriet Purvis quickly raised a sleeve of Gray Senior's baby-blue pajama shirt and inserted a needle into the wrinkled and sallow, thin skin of his arm.

Gray lifted his weight as his dad's body succumbed to the sedative. He pulled Gray Senior's sleeve down and raised the sheet up to his dad's chin. He pulled the green coverlet up too, then folded the sheet over the edge and patted it down. As if straightening his father's covers could straighten out the mess that had become his life.

Harriet brought her round, sixty-year-old frame next to him. Her smooth dark hand patted Gray's. "He's getting a lot worse. We're going to have to make some more changes."

He sat in a chair by the bed and shook his head. "I know. I'll have a talk with his doctor this week and see what we need to do. We can't have him hurting himself or either one of you." Gray nodded to the nurse who had been helping Harriet. Tiffany — that was her name.

She walked to Harriet. "He's still pretty strong, you know, and we just can't hold him down. He's even difficult for the male nurses at times."

Gray's eyes took her in. She was beautiful — he hadn't realized quite how beautiful until now. Couldn't have been more than thirty. Her body tight and her eyes soft. "Yeah," he told her, "I'm really sorry."

Harriet's voice wrestled his brain back from where it had landed. "The only way to control him now is to keep him sedated all the time. It's gotten to that point. Anytime he's lucid, it's not pretty."

He shook his head again. "Maybe you're right, Harriet. Why don't you and Tiffany take a break and let me spend some time with him. Let the doctor know I'm here if he has time to talk."

Harriet moved to the sofa by the bay window and picked up an orange tray that held Gray Senior's uneaten dinner. "We may have to go to tube feeding too. I know you don't want to hear it, but he hasn't eaten anything much the last week."

She patted Gray's arm. "But we'll get the doctor in here. Maybe he can take a quick look at you too — you don't look so great."

Gray smiled weakly. "I'm sure the doc doesn't have time for that."

Harriet gave him a sharp glance and shrugged. "Well, call me if you need me." She picked Sophie up and plopped her in Gray's lap. "You know I'm not going to let anything happen to the ornery cuss. When he remembers me, he likes me, whether he admits it or not."

Tiffany caught Gray's eye as she cleaned up the nightstand. Her blue uniform couldn't conceal the soft curve of her hips. She walked toward the bed and her eyes settled on him. He could feel it. Something churned inside him.

She leaned over his father and straightened the coverlet, then approached Gray and touched his shoulder softly. "Yes, please let us know if you need anything else, Governor." She let her hand fall away.

His insides shook as she left the room. He hadn't been touched like that by a woman, a beautiful woman, since — well, since the day Mack lost their baby. And he hadn't looked at a woman that way since he met Mack.

The frightening thing about it all was . . . Tiffany had noticed too.

CHAPTER 36

If hell had steps, Eugenia Quinn would march right down them just like she was marching down these veranda steps into the garden. Because if anyone bugged her more than Satan himself, it had to be that man with the pruning shears and dingy old blue handkerchiefs. She didn't know what it was about him that drove her so crazy. But something about him rubbed her the wrong way. She just didn't trust him, especially with that history of his. She knew people, and she was convinced that under that aw-shucks exterior was somebody calculating and mean. Besides, his blasted garden wasn't all that, in spite of the fact that it had won the most beautiful garden contest among governor's mansions.

Her black pumps stopped when she reached a line of holly trees. "Ahem."

Jeremiah's head turned toward her. "Well, good afternoon, Miz Eugenia." He nodded as he slowly got to his feet. "You sure lookin' lovely in that blue coat a yours."

"Don't try to butter me up, Jeremiah," she shot back. "How dare you?"

"Now, Miz Eugenia —"

"Don't Miz Eugenia me. I don't know what you're trying to do. As if Mackenzie wasn't hurting enough, you have to go make it worse by sending her that orchid."

"Well, I didn't —" he began. But she wasn't having any of it.

"I'm telling you right now, mister — you'd better not send her anything else. Not a pansy, not a marigold, not a weed! Do you understand me?"

She saw the change in his face. She hadn't bargained for pain, and that bothered her a little. She shook it off. This man wasn't going to manipulate her.

"Yes'm," he said quietly. "Didn't mean no harm."

"Give me a break," she huffed and turned to go.

"Miz Eugenia, what is it 'bout me you can't like?"

His question startled her. Her friends were as forthright as they came, but she'd had a relationship with them for all her days. Most other people knew better than to try and go a round with her.

Her anger rose. "You ought not be here," she spat. "I don't know who thought letting you keep the lawn of the governor was a good idea. You don't know what you're doing anyway."

The look of hurt was gone now, replaced by an expression she couldn't read. "Well, you might be right about that, ma'am. Probably ain't gots no business bein' here. And I sure 'nough ain't gots no business interferin' with your family. Guess all these years workin' here in this beautiful place made me lose track a my place."

She froze, unsure how to take his words. Did he mean them, or was he mocking her? She just couldn't tell.

"Well, I got my eyes on you," she finally said. "And I mean it. Not another flower to my daughter." She pivoted on her heels to march back to the house.

"She all but dead, y'know."

His words came around and arrested her. She turned toward him, and her eyes narrowed, causing everything in her line of sight to converge on Jeremiah. "What did you say?"

"I said, she all but dead."

" 'She all but dead.' " She danced her head as she repeated his phrase back to him. Her hands flew up in the air. "Don't you think I know that? Don't you think every day I'm fighting for her to come back? I've done everything I know to do for her, Jeremiah." Eugenia felt her voice quivering. She worked desperately to control it. "She's all I have. I have nothing else in this world but her."

"I ain't tryin' to hurt her," he said softly. "I ain't never want to see Miz Mackenzie hurt. I be tryin' to encourage her. Show her she got sump'n worth livin' for."

She stepped closer. "And you don't think I'm trying to do the same thing? I've lost my husband. I just put one grandbaby in the ground and lost another one in less than a year. And now I can hardly find my daughter inside this shell of a human being she's become. But I sure in God's name am not going to let her think that children are going to bring her back to life — not when she may never have another one. What were you thinking, Jeremiah?"

"It weren't me that thought it."

"Well, that much is true. You didn't think at all —"

"I done it 'cause he gone and tol' me to." He shifted his eyes to the sky.

She moved her eyes upward too. "Who? God? I don't care if God himself came down and wrote it on the branches of one of your pitiful holly trees." She grabbed a limb and shook it wildly. "If you want to know my opinion, the Almighty's got a lot of explaining to do for all he has allowed my family to go through."

Her voice broke for good this time, and she shook her fist upward. "A lot of . . . explaining . . ."

Her hands flew to her face. She didn't want to break down. Not now. And certainly not here. But she couldn't help it. It was all too much. Just . . . too much. Her shoulders shook with heaves.

She felt Jeremiah's thin but strong arms curl around her. His hand patted her back in unrhythmic poundings. It felt strange, foreign. She never let Burt hold her. In fact, it had been a long time since she had let a man other than Gray touch her. And if she was going to get back in the letting-men-touch-her business, this was not the man she wanted to be doing it.

Yet she needed him. In this moment, she needed him badly. The tears shook her hard, but his arms never gave way.

When a final wave washed over her, she collected herself. Pushed herself from his arms and patted her face as if a few Southern flitters could wipe away the residue of grief.

"We on the same side, Miz Eugenia." Jeremiah's voice was quiet. "I know what you think a me, and maybe you right. Maybe I don't deserve to be here, but I here anyway. Been here these last twenty-five years and grateful for ever' day. Ain't done nothin' but love the families come through here. And Lord amercy, I sure 'nough love this one."

She wasn't used to not knowing what to say. She just stood there looking at the ground, willing her tears to dry. Finally she shook her head. "Well, no more flowers, and I mean it."

She turned and this time wouldn't stop even if he did call out to her. She could never let anyone know she had just cried on the shoulder of a man who had no business being gardener at the governor's mansion.

JEREMIAH

In all these years, ain't nobody called my hollies pitiful. I swear, Lord, if that woman ain't collapsed in my arms, I mighta just gone and punched her.

I knowed she was gon' come out here too. I done tol' you that already. Soon as she heard 'bout that orchid, I knowed she be comin' out here all riled up with bees in her bonnet and hornets in her britches.

I know she hurtin' though. Guess I ain't realized just how much. She tryin' so hard to pull Miz Mackenzie outta her pit, she just 'bout fell right down in it with her.

But that don't give her the right to say all them mean things to me, do it?

Do it?

Guess I need to pray for her, huh? Don't want to. Want to shake her. Slap her. Sure don't feel like prayin' for a woman who'd go and say all that to me.

But she need you too, Lord. Y'hear me? I

say she need you. And she ain't none too happy with you, neither. You really gone and stirred up some waters 'round here. And maybe Miz Eugenia be right 'bout me not belongin' here. I know the likes a me ain't deserve no place like this. But for some reason this where you planted me a long time ago, and I'm thinkin' you got me right where you want me. Ain't sure why — but I purty sure this whole thing bigger'n me.

Maybe this what the last thirty years been for. Maybe this why I gone through ever'thing I gone through, see ever'thing I see, hear ever'thing I hear. 'Cause this family need me. 'Cause there be some way I can make a difference, even if it's only prayin' for an ornery ol' woman.

So okay. But, Lord, please don't ax me to go give Miz Mackenzie no more flowers. 'Cause I have me a feelin' if I do, that Dimples ain't gon' be the only one walkin' 'round with one good eye. Purty sure Miz Eugenia gon' try to slap me cross-eyed too.

CHAPTER 37

Mackenzie stood at her bedroom window, her anger as thick and choking as the black necklace around her throat. Gray had never spoken to her the way he had yesterday, the way she still heard him in her head. His words bounced around inside, feeding the fury. And yesterday she hadn't needed anything else to make her angry because Jeremiah had already successfully unearthed the simmering rage she hadn't even known was there.

But Gray's stupid words had done one thing for her. They had given her something to rage against. Something to do. If Gray wanted a dutiful wife, that was what he would get. She exited the family quarters and headed to the top of the stairwell. And caught sight of her mother coming like a force.

Eugenia jerked off her coat and flung it across the curve at the bottom of the banister. Her size nines thudded against the stair runner.

"I handled it, Mackenzie." She held on to the brass railing, pulling her body weight as she plodded upward. "There will be no more flowers from Jeremiah."

Eugenia was breathing hard by the time she reached the top of the stairs. She stopped in front of Mackenzie, still puffing, and her eyes widened. "You're up . . . and dressed. Is Jesus coming back today?"

Mackenzie let out a slight puff of her own. "I'm going to work. Apparently we have a campaign to win." She moved past her mother and started down the stairs, black high-heeled boots silent on the carpet.

"Who picked out your clothes?" Eugenia's voice came behind her.

Mackenzie fiddled with the belt of her fitted plaid jacket. "I did. I'm not an invalid."

"May as well have been for the last month or so."

Mackenzie whipped around. "Well, I'm not, okay? And you know what? I can take care of myself. I'm a grown woman, and I can very well feed myself and dress myself." She tugged at the sleeves of her jacket.

Eugenia gripped her arm, and Mackenzie winced. Her mother might be aging, but she still had some power in her. "Now, let's get one thing straight, missy. I have taken care of your behind, even washed it when necessary, over these past six months. And I don't know what little switch has flipped in your head, but the 'sass your mama' switch better get turned off quickly. Now, you can either tell me what happened, or I can beat it out of you. I'm still not afraid to turn you over my knee."

"Mother." Mackenzie pulled free and continued down the stairs.

Eugenia was hot on her heels. "I'm serious. Tell me what happened."

Mackenzie's heels connected with the marble foyer, and she spun around. "Gray made it very clear that he has one objective right now, and that is to win reelection. So that's what we're going to do."

"Mackenzie, darling —" Eugenia's voice softened — "you're in no state to be campaigning. And honestly, Gray isn't either."

"You obviously haven't talked to Gray lately."

"Gray's not himself. He's grieving just like you are."

"Well, he can grieve by himself. I've got work to do. Then I'm going out for lunch with Anna. And then — who knows? — we might go to the mall." She placed her hands on her mother's shoulders. "Now, you go back to your life. Thank you for taking care of me. Thank you for all you've done. But there will be no more counselors. There will be no more medication. There will be no more mothers feeding me soup. I'm a big girl, and I can take care of myself."

"Big girl, my backside. Big girls know what they need and are brave enough to admit it. You've just apparently found another way to run and hide. And if you want to know my opinion, the way you've been hiding, all holed up in your room and despondent, might actually be better than this. Because broken has all kinds of faces, darling. And some are far more dangerous than others."

Mackenzie's face hardened into a smile. "Go home, Mother. I'm fine."

Eugenia studied her with narrowed eyes. "I *am* going home. Truth be told, I miss my bed and my bathtub. But you'd better know, this is not healing. Not as long as you're still running away."

"Okay. Sounds good. I'll call you later."

Eugenia stood with hands on hips, her exasperation obvious. She reached for Mackenzie and pulled her into an embrace. Tight. Then tighter. Her mouth rubbed past Mackenzie's ear. "Pain has to be faced eventually. It has to be talked about. It has to be gone through. It can't be avoided or masked or denied."

Mackenzie patted her mother's back until she released her. As Eugenia walked out the door, Mackenzie dug her phone out from the pocket of her crisp black jeans.

"Jessica, it's time to get to work."

CHAPTER 38

"You cried on his shoulder?" The straw in Dimples's sweet tea slid across the side of her face. She grabbed it and stuck it in her mouth.

Eugenia stiffened. She hadn't planned on telling them, but they had hounded it out of her. When they retired from meddling, they should all become spies for the CIA. "Only after I gave him a piece of my mind."

Berlyn brought her elbows to the edge of their table in the Franklin Mercantile Deli. She pushed her trio of pimento cheese, tuna salad, and chicken salad away from her. Then she clasped her hands, causing the red rose clipped to the cleavage of her white fluffy sweater to all but take flight.

"So you went out to the gardener and yelled at him, told him never to give Mackenzie another flower, and then you cried on his shoulder. You're a train wreck, Eugenia. I told you that you need to start taking yoga with me. It will relax you." She pressed a Coke bottle to her lips and raised it as if she were going to chug a beer.

Sandra raised a fork in front of her face, studying the prongs as if to make sure they were clean enough for her liking. "Yoga is New Age. You shouldn't be doing it."

Berlyn dropped her bottle and snatched the fork from Sandra's hand. "New Age— phew age. Yoga is what you make of it. And I don't sit there channeling spirits. I sit there wondering how in the tar hill I'm going to get my legs above my heart without suffocating myself." She glanced down into her cleavage and shrugged.

Eugenia let out a huff. "That sounds like just the relaxation I need."

A bell chimed on the restaurant door. A young mother in a pink peacoat came in with a bundled-up toddler in tow.

"You need to quit talking so ugly to people, Eugenia. It's not proper," Sandra scolded.

Eugenia turned toward the noise. "The man gave my daughter an orchid, Sandra! An orchid! Poor girl can't have children, and he gives her a flower that could mean 'many children.' And you want to lecture me on what's proper?"

Dimples looked up. A piece of bacon hung

from her mouth, the remainder of a BLT in her hand. "I don't think it was such a bad idea."

Their heads turned quickly. She shifted her eyes, aware that all the attention was now on her. She usually wasn't crazy about that, but Eugenia watched her back straighten. She chewed hard on the bacon, then set her sandwich down with a determined slap. She picked up her napkin and wiped her mouth. "Don't look at me like that, Berlyn."

"We weren't. We were looking at that piece of food stuck in the corner of your mouth."

She swiped at it with her napkin. "Don't try to change the subject. I know a thing or two about life in spite of what y'all think. And I know that sometimes people need hope. If you don't have hope, you ain't got nothing left."

"Don't say *ain't*," Sandra retorted.

"Shut up, Sandra." Dimples turned back to Eugenia, who gaped at her. Dimples had never told anyone to shut up. "Mackenzie needs her some hope. And if the good Lord himself told that man to go give her some hope, then who are we to question it?"

Eugenia started to answer, but Dimples wasn't through. "You more than anyone else, Eugenia Quinn, ought to be glad someone loves your daughter enough to try. Besides, all you've been doing hasn't accomplished much. As of yesterday morning she was still in her pajamas at noon. Sounds like that gardener went and stirred up a fire in her that got her out of bed and dressed —"

"It's because she's angry, Dimples, not because she has hope."

Dimples picked up her sandwich and swung it slightly as she talked. "Maybe that's not so bad. Maybe she *needs* that anger. And if Jeremiah wants to give her flowers, if he wants to help heal your girl's heart, you'd be stupid not to let him." A piece of lettuce flew out of her sandwich and onto the table.

Sandra snatched the lettuce and put it back on Dimples's plate. "Quit flinging your food, Dimples. They're going to think we just broke out of the home up the street."

Eugenia moved a fork around her salad. "That flower broke her heart."

Dimples set her sandwich down again. "Her heart's already broken, Eugenia. But what if? What if there are more children out there for her? Would it be so bad for her to believe it's possible? Everyone needs something to believe in. If you convince her there is nothing worth believing in, then may as well put her in the grave. And if you don't believe there is something beautiful out there for her too, you're as pitiful as she is. Angry or sad, without something to believe in, there ain't nothing worth living for."

Sandra's lips parted, and Dimples raised a crooked, bony finger at her. "Sandra, I swear, if one word comes out of your mouth, I'm gonna deck ya."

Sandra turned her glare to Berlyn as if Berlyn had been giving Dimples lessons on sass. Berlyn just shrugged. Eugenia studied Dimples's good eye, which was still locked on hers. In all these years, she'd never seen Dimples confront anyone. Truth be told, this outburst was a miracle in and of itself.

Berlyn's interjection halted her thoughts. "I'm believing for something."

Sandra rolled her eyes. "Oh, do tell."

Berlyn turned toward Sandra. Eugenia could see the rise and fall of Sandra's thin chest beneath the ruffles of her navy-blue blouse.

"I'm believing one day I'm going to wake up, and Krispy Kreme is going to announce that the Hot Now sign will be on twenty-four hours a day."

Eugenia chuckled. She felt it coming up. She hadn't chuckled in a long time.

Maybe she'd been half-dead too.

And maybe Dimples saw more with one good eye than Eugenia had seen with two.

Chapter 39

Soft music sifted through Anna's car like waves lapping in a pool. Slow and rhythmic. Anna's question came out laced with apprehension: "You sure you feel like doing this?"

"Yes, I'm sure. It's the mall, Anna. It's lunch. It's what they call living."

"Well, it's a good place to start, I guess, but we could just go to lunch now and maybe go to the mall next week. It's okay to take things slow, Mackenzie. You don't have to do everything at once. It's not like there are huge expectations here."

"You apparently haven't spoken to Gray either. Trust me. Gray has expectations."

Anna pulled her Tahoe into a parking space in front of Macy's and let it idle beneath them. "I don't think Gray meant you had to do everything in one day. Maybe he just meant start somewhere."

Mackenzie released her seat belt and

opened the car door. "I'm tired of talking about Gray."

Anna followed her lead, and they made their way inside the store. Colors of spring exploded around them like an Easter basket as they walked through the door. Every sweater, shirt, necklace, and pair of pants screamed that winter was a has-been and it was time for spring to stake out its territory. They wandered by habit toward a familiar corner of the store.

"Have you ever wondered what ninety-five-year-old woman purchases clothes for the petites department?" Mackenzie said as she scanned the offerings.

Anna shrugged. "Can't say that I have."

"Seriously. If it's not a button-up sweater, floral top, or khaki capris, you won't find it here."

"I'm taking that to mean you have no desire to buy anything here."

Mackenzie looked into her friend's face. The tension melted. "Sorry. I'm being catty. I usually don't do catty."

Anna nudged her. "We're only allowed to do catty when we're PMSing and need chocolate or a gallon of sweet tea. Then catty is completely permitted."

Mackenzie smiled.

"Nice to see that." Anna wrapped an arm

around her friend's shoulders as they walked out of the department store and into the mall. The activity was nowhere near what it would be on a weekend, but it was still filled with people and movement.

"Smell that?" Anna asked.

"What?"

"Those pretzels." She pointed toward an Auntie Anne's store in the middle of a large open area surrounded by tables and peppered with partakers. "I love those things."

Mackenzie shrugged. She no longer loved any kind of food. "I didn't even smell it."

"Want some?"

"We're eating lunch in an hour."

"It can be our appetizer."

Mackenzie shook her head. "You get one if you like."

"I don't want it if you don't."

Mackenzie nudged her. "Go. I'm fine. I'm just going to walk over there and look in the window." She pointed toward the Sephora store directly across from Auntie Anne's.

She left Anna and wandered to the window. An acrylic stand inside displayed three tubes of lipstick in vibrant pink, orange, and red. She rubbed her lips together. Today was the first time she had put on lip gloss in . . . well, forever.

Pain jolted her Achilles tendon. She

reached down instinctively.

"Oh, I'm so sorry. I just wasn't paying attention."

Mackenzie turned to see the small wheel of a stroller wedged against her foot. A red-faced young woman gripped the stroller's handle.

"It's okay." Mackenzie absently rubbed her heel, jolted again by the sight of a sleeping baby nestled inside the carrier. "I'll take a wound for a little one."

"I really am sorry."

Mackenzie laid her hand on the stroller. "How old?"

"Six months. It's such a great age."

"They're all great." The comment came out without Mackenzie even realizing it.

"You have children?" the woman asked.

A fog settled over Mackenzie quick and thick. She shook her head slightly. "Um . . . no, I don't . . . Well, I . . ." She straightened. "It's a long story."

"Well, I'm sure you would be a wonderful mother."

Mackenzie wasn't aware that dams could burst without warning, without at least a brief sign. In all her years of being self-controlled, a planner, a think-before-you-speak kind of soul, she had never experienced anything close to what happened next. In that moment, every crack in her soul collided with the onrushing reality of the world that now was hers, and it was more than she could endure. The floodwaters simply let loose, and she had no ark to ride out the deluge.

She whirled and took off in a full run toward the department store. She heard Anna's voice calling out to her as if it came from a lifetime she no longer resided in. Her wails came from a deep place where excuses were never given and where people's opinions were of no consequence. She tried to maneuver a corner and ran into a metal rod displaying silk dresses. It dug hard into her shoulder before crashing to the ground.

She never let it stop her. By the time she broke free into the parking lot, she was already hoarse from her screams.

Chapter 40

Bloodshot eyes stared back at Gray from the mirror of his father's bathroom. He rubbed his stubbled jaw. The careworn face in the mirror accused him. He was losing it. Hanging on the edge of a cliff. Dangling over a desperate place he didn't want to go and Mack didn't deserve.

Jeremiah was right. Mackenzie needed to be loved back to life. But he did too. He deserved to be loved too. And for a brief moment he had realized just how easy it would be to grab for the wrong kind of love.

He turned on the faucet and watched water circle down the drain. His life felt like it was going down just as quickly. He dipped his hands into the stream, lowered his head, and splashed cold water against his face. His nerve endings came alive with the impact and so did his senses.

I'm the governor of the state, and I just assaulted my chief of staff. One of my best friends, no less. And that nurse . . .

He placed his hands on the edge of the Formica countertop. Water dripped from his face. He pulled a white towel from the plastic ring that held it and dried his face. Then he heard his father moan.

He walked into his dad's room. Gray Senior had been asleep for at least three hours. The doctor was coming over later this afternoon, and Gray had decided to wait for him.

Gray sat down and put his hand on his dad's bed. His father's eyes were open but remained locked on the ceiling.

"Hey, Dad, how're you doing?"

His father's eyes slowly focused on Gray's face and seemed to study it. Then a soft smile made its way to his lips. "Hey, Son. I'm doing good. Where ya been?"

Gray's heart melted. It felt like it could ooze right from his fingertips. A lump came to his throat with such force that his tears couldn't be stopped. "Been right here."

"Yeah? Well, I'll be. I've missed ya."

Gray let out a soft laugh, then wiped his nose. "It's okay. You've been resting."

"Then why do I feel so tired?" He rubbed his eyes.

Gray couldn't help it. He was a boy and this was his dad. He laid his head on his father's chest and wept. After a minute he felt his father's hand rubbing his scalp.

"Hey, what's wrong? Why are you crying?"

"I'm sorry, Dad."

"I told you to never apologize for that. Not a thing wrong with a grown man crying. Tears have to come out. It's the way God made us."

"I've just missed you too; that's all."

"Well, then, we don't need to go so long without seeing each other."

Gray lifted his head and nodded. His tears had left a wet spot on his father's pajama shirt. Gray forced himself to sit up. He didn't want to miss this moment of lucidness with his face buried. He wanted to look into his father's eyes so he could remember what it was like to have him present. Just in case this was the last time it happened.

"Dad, can I ask you a question?"

"You can ask me anything."

Gray took his father's hands and held them in his own, the green coverlet wrinkled beneath them. "When you hurt really bad, how can you take care of someone else? How can you be there for someone else when you can't even figure out how to heal your own heart?"

He felt his father's fingers squirm loose from his hold. He held on a little tighter, worried his father was getting agitated and about to have another fit. "Son, can you let my hands go for a minute?"

Gray laughed and released him.

"You having a hard time these days?" his father asked.

"Really bad."

"Mackenzie too?"

Gray nodded.

"Want to tell me why?"

He couldn't tell his father what had happened. The brunt of it might send him away again. Gray just shrugged.

His father shook his head. "Healing takes a lot of energy, you know. Sometimes it feels like your whole body is focused on that one gaping wound like it can't even think about anything else. And that's okay. There are seasons for that. But pain can also make us selfish. We can let it swallow us up until there isn't anything left to offer. And the only way to avoid that is to keep on giving even in the middle of your own pain."

He reached to grip Gray's hand. "You hear me, Son? If Mack needs you, you need to be there. I have a feeling that seeing her heal will help heal you too."

Gray leaned down and kissed his dad's hands. He let his lips linger there a few moments. When he looked up, his father was fast asleep. He kissed the top of his head before picking up Sophie and leaving the room.

Out in the hallway, he shifted Sophie to one arm and pulled out his cell phone as he proceeded to the parking lot. He climbed into the car, placed Sophie on the passenger seat, and closed the door. Then he dug through the console between the seats and found the card for the counselor Thad had suggested.

He needed help. And he needed to heal. He didn't know how you even started to heal wounds as big as his. He dialed the number on the card.

A man's voice came alive on the other end. "This is Ken Jantzen."

"Ken, um . . . this is Gray — Gray London. You know — Mackenzie's husband — the, um, governor . . ." Gray lowered his head to the steering wheel. His voice cracked as he said, "I think I need to come see you."

His call-waiting signal beeped, and he checked the display. Why in the world would Anna be calling him?

CHAPTER 41

"Hey, Mack. Babe, it's okay. It's okay."
Gray's words were soothing as he knelt in
front of her in the tiny lounge of the ladies'
room.

Mackenzie sat in a green fabric chair with
her legs curled underneath her. She rocked
back and forth, staring at Gray and Anna,
but her mind was a world away. They might
as well have been strangers.

"She ran out into the parking lot." Anna
shook as she spoke. "It was all I could do to
get her in here. I've never seen her like this.
We've got to get her some help."

"It's okay." Gray's voice kept the same
soothing tone. "I've got her. Will you make
sure no one comes in for a few minutes?"

Mackenzie's eyes darted around the room.
Even this bathroom mocked her. The changing table attached to the wall. The seating
area for nursing mothers. Everywhere she
went, the world seemed to scoff at her.

Gray placed his hands on her knees. "Let me take you home, Mack."

She slapped at his hands. "Don't touch me."

He moved his hands. "We just need to get you home."

She jumped up from the chair. "I don't want to go home. I don't ever want to go home." Her tears started in a fresh surge. She walked over to the changing table and jerked at the latch. The long plastic table bounced as it fell open. She tugged at its straps in a desperate attempt to wrench the table from the wall.

She felt Gray's hands encase her. "Stop. Please. Stop."

"Let me go!" Her words came out with a venom she didn't know was in her. "Let me go!"

He held on tighter. "I won't. Come here." His words were almost a whisper. "Babe, come here."

Her grip on the nylon straps was almost like an animal's, but he was finally able to pry her away. He pulled her back toward the chair, and she flailed wildly in his arms. "Let me go."

"Mack, you're going to break something or end up hurting yourself."

"I don't care! I just want to die! I should

have died! Not Maddie! Not our —" Her voice choked with another burst of tears.

"I know. It hurts so bad."

She kept jerking within his grasp, and he finally let her go. She stood there shaking in front of him. "It wasn't supposed to be this way!"

His own tears were falling now. "I know, babe. I know."

"I should have been a mom so many times by now. I should have children everywhere. But I don't! Do you know what I have?" She walked back to the changing table and slammed her fist on it. "I have a diaper bag with nowhere to take it! I have an empty baby book with nothing to record in it! No first tooth. No first haircut. I have baby hangers that will never hold baby clothes."

She grabbed the table and began slamming it up against the wall over and over. "This is all wrong! My life wasn't supposed to be this way! I want to die! I want all of this over, and I just want to die!" Her body collapsed in desperate sobs.

She felt Gray bend down and encircle her again. "I'm glad you didn't die. I need you."

Mackenzie all but spat her words at him. "You need someone to help you win a campaign! You don't need me."

He shook his head adamantly. "No. That's

not true. I was wrong with what I said last night. I was just hurting. I do need you. I do. But none of this is going to change anything. It won't bring Maddie back or get us another baby."

"You blame me! Go ahead and say it — it's all my fault. You've been wanting to say that since Maddie died. Tell me what you really feel, for once!" Her fists pounded his chest. "Tell me what you've wanted to say to the woman who killed your child!"

Gray grabbed her hands. "That's not true. I don't blame you. It was an accident."

"You're lying! Say it, Gray! Say it!"

"I love you, Mack." His words came out through his own tears. "That's all I'm going to say. I . . . I love you."

He held on until her body could no longer fight. Finally she gave way beneath his strength and felt her body fold. She had nothing left. For a little while there, she'd thought the anger could help her survive. But life was too big. The pain was too great. The blackness of it seemed to swallow her whole.

She woke in the middle of the night and found herself in bed, in a soft pair of pajamas. Gray's arms were tight around her. She fell back asleep, desperate to never wake up.

JEREMIAH

Ain't got no words to tell God how grateful I be today. I waked up, and there ain't been one flower pressed in my mind to give Miz Mackenzie. Thought sure I be off the hook. Then I seen Miz Eugenia marchin' down the basement stairs this mornin' with a box in her hand. And my mind gone straight to thinkin' I 'bout to be dropped right there in the middle a my trays a seedlin's.

But Eugenia, she gone and surprised the stew outta me.

"Here," she say when she marched into my workroom. She stuck that box plumb into my chest. Almost made me jump.

I opened it. It be white handkerchiefs. White handkerchiefs! What a man gon' do with white handkerchiefs when he work in the dirt all day long and sweat like a pack mule? Ain't no bleach gon' take care a such a thing.

I got my manners though. I tol' her,

"Thanks."

She flick her hand like she wavin'. "Yours are filthy. You needed new ones." But even though she try to act like it were nothin', I knowed Eugenia Quinn givin' me handkerchiefs was sump'n.

So I ax her, "What you go and give me white ones for?"

She got that all-puffed-up look. Looked like the buttons on that pink sweater a hers done stretched or sump'n. She snatched the box from my hand. "Well, aren't you an ungrateful old cuss."

"I ain't ungrateful. I just thinkin', if you gon' give somebody a gift, might wanna figure out 'xactly what they need. And anybody can see a man that work in the dirt all day ain't need him no white handkerchiefs. He need dark ones."

She wrinkle her forehead and pull that box tighter to her chest. "Well, a proper man would know to just say thank you when he's given a gift, not tell the person who gave it to him what the gift should be."

"Guess that make me proper, then, 'cause I did say thank you first."

I watch her beady blue eyes get all slantedlike and think for a minute her lips gon' squinch up so tight, gon' need my shovel to pry 'em loose. But I shoulda knowed they'd find a way to open up. Ain't that much green ever coursed through my valley.

"You're incorrigible," she say with one a them ol' huff things she do. "I wanted to tell you that you can give Mackenzie flowers if you want."

My eyes 'bout bulged outta my head when she say that. "What?"

"You heard me, Jeremiah. Give her flowers if you want."

"Like any kind a flowers? And you ain't gon' shoot me?"

"I'm not saying I won't eventually shoot you." And from the look on her face, I be believin' she mean it. "But it won't be because you gave her flowers." Then she mumble sump'n, sound like she sayin' I be right. But I know there ain't no way this side a heaven or hell that Eugenia Quinn gon' admit I be right 'bout sump'n.

"If getting angry keeps her alive, we'll settle for anger for a while. And hope . . ."

Her words gone and trailed off then. Her eyes couldn't look at me. And there be one li'l moment there where all that live inside a me want to break out whoopin' and hollerin' and laughin' and just rub that woman's face all up in the fact that she had to go and she be wrong.

But I ain't done it. Lord amercy, I wanted

to, but I ain't. I just shake my head, let her move on with what dignity she think she got left. "I like me some hope" be all I say.

She shifted all antsylike then and got all weird actin'. "Well, all right, then. . . . That's all I needed to say." She flitted her hand the way she do up 'round my flowers. "Now go back to tending whatever it is you tend. 'Cause the good Lord knows that garden out there needs to be tended to. Ought to have a gardener to come behind the gardener."

And off she prance. Prance away like she done her deed. Like she been keepin' a tally for all the good deeds she need to do this year and she fulled it up in one big swoop when she hand me them dumb handkerchiefs.

She ain't knowed there always been a Gardener who come up behind me. And as soon as she leave, I heard him. God done tell me to give Miz Mackenzie that other bulb I been growin' in the workroom.

I been worried he might gon' do that. 'Course, it won't be bloomin' good for another coupla of weeks. But Lord help us when it do — 'cause I know what that flower mean. And if that orchid made her angry 'fore, I ain't even wanna know what gon' happen next.

CHAPTER 42

The world had lost all its landmarks.

Mackenzie sat in her chair, unable to identify anything that passed in front of the window. All she could focus on was what was going on in her mind, and that was nothing but torment.

She knew by now that grief was a cruel companion. It didn't care how tired or weak or desperate you were. It hovered and mocked and rarely yielded. It might pull back for a brief moment, only to swoop in again through an unsuspecting word or glance or memory.

The moments of respite felt almost crueler than the constant pain because they could end in a split second, and you never saw the attack coming.

But now there were no more respites. Somewhere in the numberless days that passed her by, the darkness had thickened. Every waking minute, it whispered in her ear how utterly hopeless life was.

She had thought her surge of anger would last, that she could use it to her advantage and somehow outsmart her grief.

She had been fooling herself.

Before she threw that orchid at Jeremiah, she had never thrown anything in her life. Afterward she had wanted to throw everything she touched. The deep rage had felt like it was coming from her toes. But once she expended it, it had left her expended. And since then she had nothing. Absolutely nothing.

There were still moments when the present would press in. She'd hear a word, catch a glimpse of something that actually registered. But for the most part she lived in this empty well. A pit of black and heaviness and tormenting voices in the key of "if only."

If only she'd stopped the car and made Maddie put on her seat belt.

If only she'd set a better example.

If only she'd taken better care of herself when she was pregnant, not tried to do so much.

If only . . .

The voices beat at her mercilessly until she took the medicine Thad had given her. Then they simply echoed more quietly, joining the voices of all the people who kept trying to intrude on her silence.

More than anything, she wished that the voices would all stop. Just leave her alone.

Gray seemed different, though. That much she noticed. He was there almost all the time now, trying harder to reach her. But he was just one more distant voice calling her to stay in a world she wanted with all her heart to escape.

And in those rare moments when the voices silenced long enough for her to hear the sound of what she thought might be her own heart, she realized this world of nothingness was far scarier than the world of fury. She was certain that when she reached the bottom of wherever she was headed, there would be no retrieving her.

She didn't know what that meant, and in this torturous occurrence of yet another day, she wasn't sure that she cared. But she did for a moment wonder if there could be a darkness darker than what she was now living. And something inside her stirred the thought that there actually was.

CHAPTER 43

When Gray woke up the morning after Mack's breakdown, she had reverted back into her shell. He had tried to engage her, talk to her, but she'd given him nothing.

He had hung around anyway. For the last two weeks he had done everything for her and had made it clear to everyone that was how he wanted it. He brought her breakfast. He brought her lunch. He bathed and dressed her.

Jeremiah's words about the azaleas rang over and over in his mind: *"They worth tendin' to. Fightin' for. And a really wise gardener, a gardener that know he don't know it all — he get real good at listenin' to what heaven tell him 'bout* how *to tend 'em."*

It had taken him a while, but now he felt he was finally listening.

Because after Mack's meltdown at the mall, when he finally got her to the car, he had heard heaven whisper. And it had clearly said, "Love her." That's what he was trying to do in every moment. He was loving her the best he knew how.

Whether it would be enough, he just didn't know.

Another couple of weeks remained before the house and senate were due to deliver their final budget bills. His lawyers were working diligently on the VRA court case. And he had told Fletcher they would not hire a new chief of staff — not yet, anyway. For the next few weeks, Fletcher was simply to remain on message. And the message right now was that the governor was taking a respite with his wife to make a final decision about running for a second term.

He had assured the public he would let them know before the April filing deadline. And it was already the first week of March. Newman was rising in the polls, but Gray's numbers were descending faster than Bradford pear trees could bloom — and around here that was practically an overnight occurrence. But with Mackenzie this way, he knew there was only one thing he could do — be the husband he had committed to be. In sickness and in health.

The bedroom door opened. "Get out," Eugenia's voice instructed him.

He looked at her over the top of his readers and put down the book he had been reading to Mack. "I'm not leaving, Eugenia. I told Fletcher I'd be back in the office Monday, and I will. But it's Wednesday, not Monday."

Eugenia picked Sophie up as if she were a sewer rat and handed her to Gray. "Go. You need fresh air, and I need to spend some time with my daughter. You've had her long enough."

He took his readers off, set them on the table beside him, and looked at Mack. She sat unmoving in her chair by the window, looking out at God only knew what.

He did need to get away. To breathe. To live, even if for just a minute.

"Sure you don't mind?"

She nudged him out of the chair. "I wouldn't have offered if I minded."

He leaned over Mack and kissed her on the head. "I won't be gone long, babe. Just going to take Sophie out to walk."

She never moved.

Eugenia touched his arm. "Go, son. I'll take care of her."

"Thanks, Mom." He kissed her before he left.

He and Sophie were headed to the front of the house when the yellow school bus stopped next door. He watched Oliver's coffee-colored curls bounce as he darted down his driveway.

Every time Gray saw Oliver, Maddie's memory offered no grace. It roared to life with maximum impact. And it was so vivid. He could see her and Oliver jumping on the trampoline, playing on her swing set, entertaining Gray and Mack with dramatic performances on Sunday nights after pizza.

He refused to push away the memory. He let the grief pass through him and felt the ache it produced in his gut. That's the promise he had made to himself in his father's room, a promise his sessions with the counselor had reinforced. He wasn't going to run from his grief any longer. Instead, when grief showed up, he was going to run into it. He would hold it, feel it, absorb its impact. Then he'd move back into the life that, for whatever reason, he'd been left to live.

Live — he had forgotten what that really meant. When Maddie was still with them, every moment vibrated with life. In his grief, his anger, his self-pity, he had forgotten what life actually felt like, and he was just now realizing it. He hadn't watched a single football or basketball game except the one that day at the sports bar — and he hadn't really seen that one. He hadn't had a belly laugh since he couldn't remember when.

He lifted his face to the sun as it pressed gently against his skin. He hadn't been aware of that sensation since Maddie's death had removed his ability to feel anything except pain.

Then he opened his eyes and called Oliver's name. He had just thought of something that would make him feel unimaginably alive.

The boy turned at the sound of his voice. His hand shot up. "Governor!"

Gray stepped closer to the black wrought-iron fence that separated the mansion grounds from Oliver's house. "Hey, buddy! Can you come here a minute?"

Oliver flung his book bag to the aggregate stone of his driveway and broke into a lanky trot, his skinny knees flashing white under khaki shorts. Gray smiled. March had brought them nice weather, but not shorts weather. Obviously second graders were impervious to chilly temps.

Oliver reached the fence. "What ya got, Governor?"

Gray squatted down so he could be closer to Oliver's eye level. Sophie stuck her head between the rails of the iron fence, straining to get as close to the boy as she could. She caught Oliver's attention first. "Sophie!" he hollered. He knelt and rubbed Sophie wildly on the head.

Gray sank into the soft grass on his side of the fence. "Oliver, I was thinking. Since you and Maddie never got to have that lemonade stand, what do you say you and I make ourselves a lemonade stand this afternoon?"

Oliver cocked his head. Sophie did too. They both seemed to be wondering if they could take Gray seriously.

"Like you and me on the sidewalk?" Oliver looked toward the street. "Okay, we don't have sidewalks. So . . . like on your driveway? But wait! You're the governor, right? I bet you could get someone to put us some sidewalks in real quick."

Gray laughed. "Well, I don't know if we could have them in by this afternoon, so how about we just do it right over here on the driveway? I'll go ask Rosa to make some lemonade, and I'll get a table —"

"And I'll make the sign!" Oliver jumped up so his feet could do a little dance. Then he stopped abruptly. His brow furrowed. "But I've gotta tell ya, Governor. I think we should ask for a buck and no less. This economy is killin' us."

Gray had to bite his lip. "You don't think

a buck is a lot for a cup of lemonade?"

Oliver's bushy eyebrows pulled together, almost making one full brow across his head. He twisted his lips back and forth and scratched his head as if this was the biggest decision he had made since starting second grade. "Nah," he finally said. "With you being the governor and all, I'm sure we can get a buck."

Gray decided there was no budging Oliver on the price. So he'd just find some big cups.

Oliver leaned toward the fence and whispered as if they were plotting the next great military attack. "Meet in an hour. Right here. We're gonna kill it, Governor. By the time we go to bed, Warren Buffett's gonna be jealous."

Laughter had to be released with that statement. And Gray felt it. All the way to his soul, he felt it. The boy must have been listening to his economist father. Maybe Gray should hire Oliver and his dad to help fix the budget. Right now, though, he had a lemonade stand to run. "I'll see you in an hour," he said.

Oliver pointed a finger at him. "Make sure Miss Rosa doesn't use any of that fake stuff. We're going real lemons, real sugar all the way."

Gray nodded. "Got it. Real lemons, real sugar. No fake stuff."

"Get on 'em, Governor!" And with that, Oliver was off.

Gray eased himself up from the grass, groaning slightly from the effort, then looked at Sophie, who was already whining for Oliver to come back. "We'll be millionaires by bedtime, girl. Budget crisis solved."

He started toward the house. She gave up and followed. And as they walked, a little piece of his heart felt like it was headed home.

The lemonade sale had been a success in so many ways. Oliver made forty bucks in the span of two hours. Of course one of his customers had given him a twenty just to get him to quit talking. And a little girl who stopped with her mother in their minivan had given him five dollars mostly because she thought Oliver was cute. And two troopers from Gray's security detail had drunk two glasses apiece just because they had to stand out there with them.

Oliver was clueless about those dynamics, of course. As far as he was concerned, he and Gray were bona fide lemonade tycoons. Gray let him think it. The whole experience had done his heart good.

They had just begun to tear down the stand when a black van pulled up. "It's a buck," Oliver said as he extended a plastic cup.

Gray recognized a familiar clicking sound and looked up to see the zoom lens of a camera extending from the back window. The driver stuck his arm out, something black clutched in his fingers. The troopers moved in quickly. "Hey, hey," the kid behind the wheel protested. "It's just an iPhone."

One of the officers jerked it from his hand. Gray stepped forward quickly as he moved Oliver out of the way, lemonade splashing on the pavement as he did. "It's okay, Clint. Give him back the phone. He's a kid who didn't have anything else to do but come check on the governor today."

The officer handed back the device, and the young man extended it toward Gray. "Governor, any comment on the budget that the house and senate are about to pass?"

Gray knew the phone's recording function was on. He had a phone just like it. He shook his head.

"So is this what you do with your respite — play at a lemonade stand with neighborhood boys?"

Oliver bowed out his chest. "Hey, I'm not a boy. I am a young man."

Gray bit his lip, trying his best to hide his growing anger. "I'm doing what people do when they take a break. I'm relaxing."

"Do you really think this is a time for the governor to take off? People are losing their homes. You're asking everyone to cut back, and you're getting a paid vacation from the taxpayers."

Gray felt his pulse quicken. "For over three years I've held this office, and I've taken a total of only twenty-one days off to be with my family. Frankly my wife needs me right now. And I don't have to — no, I won't apologize to you or anyone for it."

"So making lemonade is taking care of your wife?" The question came out snide and smart-alecky.

"It's time for you to go," Gray said calmly.

"Yeah, if you ain't giving us a buck, you need to get to the getting," Oliver announced. Then he added with a wave of his hand — accurately, for a change — "Au revoir."

The two young men drove off, and Gray made sure Oliver was okay before he sent him home. He could only imagine what stories the boy would come up with from this or what the reporters would do with what they'd discovered.

But Gray knew what he'd gotten from the afternoon. For the first time in more than six months, he'd actually had fun.

CHAPTER 44

Eugenia brushed the thick black hair that fell across her daughter's back as she'd brushed it a thousand times. "Baby girl, you've got to eat. Rosa has told me that your plates are coming back untouched, and you can't do that. Your body needs food."

Mackenzie's head tilted back slightly as Eugenia pulled her hair into a ponytail. Eugenia glanced at a vase filled with white violets. It was all Jeremiah had brought Mackenzie since Eugenia had told him that he could start giving her flowers again. They meant "let's take a chance."

Eugenia knew what he was trying to say with the violets. He was trying to call her daughter back out, encourage her to take a chance on living. And in the depth of her soul, she appreciated him for it. Mackenzie had never once bothered to ask what they meant. But Eugenia made a point of telling her anyway.

As Eugenia pulled the ottoman out, Mackenzie shifted her feet to make room.

"You can't survive this way, and I need you to survive."

Mackenzie turned her face toward her mother's. Her eyes were sunken dark circles. "I don't want to survive."

Eugenia felt her breath leave her. Hearing Mackenzie say it out loud caused fear to race through her like blood through her veins.

"You can't say that!" She grabbed Mackenzie by the shoulders. "If you were supposed to die, you would have died. But you didn't. And I'm not going to let you. Do you hear me?" Eugenia's tears broke loose with such force that she threw her head across Mackenzie's lap, wrapping her arms around her daughter's bony legs.

Mackenzie didn't move. Eugenia's dam of strength burst and seeped out across her daughter's bedroom. But she didn't care. She no longer cared. If it took her daughter seeing her heartbreak, she'd let her see it.

She finally raised her head and saw that Mackenzie wasn't even looking at her, just staring out the window. She stood and quietly walked to the bathroom.

She heard the bedroom door open.

"Mom?" She could hear concern in Gray's voice.

"In here."

He came around the corner, relief apparent when he caught sight of her. Then his face fell. "What's wrong? Did Mackenzie say something?"

"No!" Eugenia didn't care who heard her. She pointed toward the bedroom. "She doesn't say anything! She is dying, Gray. My daughter is dying."

Gray pulled her into a hug, and she let her head fall to his chest. "You've got to get her some help. We can't just let her shrivel up and die."

He held her tighter. "I know. Thad and I have already talked about it. He's arranged for a wonderful psychiatrist to come evaluate her on Monday. He said that what he's had her on doesn't seem to be working, and he wants to bring in a specialist."

He pushed back and held her shoulders, looking into her eyes. "I don't know what will happen. The doctor may try another medication — and give her a little time to see how that works. Or he might think she needs to be in the inpatient program at Vanderbilt. But I'm committed to doing whatever it takes to get her back. You know that, don't you?"

Eugenia studied his clear blue eyes. They looked so different now than they had just a couple of weeks ago. Calmer. More focused. More *there.*

"Of course I know that," she said quietly. "I've never doubted how much you love my girl, Gray." She rubbed her eyes. "All that psychiatrist stuff — I don't know much about it. But I know my baby is sick, and I'm for anything that will get her well."

He nodded and released her. "I know you are. Now, you go home. I'll take care of her tonight. But come back tomorrow because I have someone I need to go see."

Eugenia wiped her nose. "Okay, but please get her to drink or eat something."

"I'll do my best."

Eugenia walked into the bedroom to her daughter. She leaned down and pressed her head to Mackenzie's. "I will not let you die. Do you hear me?" When Eugenia raised her head, she saw a tear roll down one of Mackenzie's sallow cheeks.

A glimmer of hope seeped through her. If Mackenzie could cry, she was feeling something. Tonight Eugenia would take that.

CHAPTER 45

Mackenzie didn't try to stop the tears. Her mother's words were true. Mothers did everything in their power to help their babies live and not die. She knew that. And she also knew that she was the ultimate failure.

She had heard Gray and her mother talking and knew what was being planned. But she didn't care. If they put her in a hospital room and pumped drugs inside her for the rest of her life, she would be grateful. Anything to help her forget.

Gray lifted her from the chair. He carried her into the closet and began undressing her so he could put some pajamas on her. He had done this every night since her breakdown. She had done nothing, felt almost nothing. In fact, this was the first tear she had shed since that day.

Gray lifted her T-shirt over her head. "You remember when we first met? You would always fall asleep in the car on the way home from our dates, and I would carry you inside your apartment?" He didn't wait for her to respond. He knew by now she wasn't going to. "You could fall asleep anywhere. And the car was like a drug to you. Kind of like it was to Mad—"

He stopped himself, and his eyes darted to hers as if he expected her to break down. She didn't. But she knew. Maddie could fall asleep anywhere. Anywhere . . .

He apparently decided he was willing to continue on that track. "Maddie was like that, too, wasn't she?" He slipped off her bra and helped her put her arms in a cream silk pajama top. He talked as he buttoned her up. "I miss her so much, Mack. I miss her laugh. I miss her in my arms. I know you miss all that too. And it's okay to miss it, you know. It's okay to cry over it, yell over it, all of that. But we need to go through it. Experience it. Not just shut the pain out."

He pulled her jeans off and helped her into the matching pajama pants, then raised his face up to hers. She looked at him, but she couldn't see him. Not the way she used to. Not in that knowing way.

"We can't go on like this, Mack," he told her gently. "*You* can't go on like this. So this is what needs to happen. If you don't do something to pull yourself out of this, then we're going to have to call another doctor, maybe even put you in the hospital. Do you hear me?" He wrapped his hands around her arms. She felt his fingers press into her flesh.

"I know what is inside of you. And if you could just talk to me or go with me to see Ken or something, I think we could walk through this healthy. But you are drifting to a place that I am petrified you're not going to be able to return from, so I've got to get you some help."

He cupped her face in his hands. "I'd love you back to life if I could, but at some point you've got to want to live. I can't do that for you, Mack. I wish I could, but I can't."

She simply stared at him. She could see the pain in his expression and hear the desperation in his voice. But she couldn't reach out to it, respond to it even if she wanted to. The parts of her that did such things seemed to have been ripped out of her.

He stood and stretched out his hand. She took it and let him lead her to the bathroom.

"Need me to brush your teeth?"

She shook her head, found her toothbrush, and brushed her teeth. When she climbed into her side of the bed, Gray's body came up behind her, warm and encasing. But she had no energy to move to him. She just lay there.

At some point in the middle of the night, when he had retreated to his side, she moved her fingers until they barely touched his arm. It was a move that took everything that remained alive inside her. And way down deep, in places where the unspoken and often-untouched things of the soul resided, it was her heart's last attempt to survive.

Because it felt as if one more drop into despair would prevent her from ever coming up again.

And Mackenzie London would be gone . . . forever.

CHAPTER 46

Gray had no idea what he would get behind this door. He lifted the knocker of the renovated farmhouse off Hillsboro Road. Debbie Green answered, a red-and-black dish towel hanging from her hand and a warm smile spread across her face. Without a word, she wrapped him in a big hug. He let her. When she released him, she said, "He's out on the deck."

He stayed on the front stoop, his feet on the large *G* in the center of a sea-grass doormat.

"Is he going to hit me?"

She laughed. "If he does, I'm going to let him."

"I'm sorry, Debbie."

"He understands. We both do."

"It's no excuse."

She pointed to the back door. "You're right. Now, go tell him."

Gray kissed her full cheek as he stepped

inside. "I love you."

She patted his arm. "I love you too. And, Gray?" Her hazel eyes showed concern. "How's Mack?"

He shook his head. "Not good."

She closed the front door, then nudged him toward the back of the house. "Go."

The pool area could be seen from the foyer through three French doors that lined the rear of the house. Kurt sat in a chair underneath an umbrella, his glasses propped on the end of his nose, a newspaper in his hands. His son, Tyler, sat on the edge of the deck, throwing a tennis ball for the family's Labrador puppy.

Gray walked to the French doors and let himself outside. Kurt looked up, his gaze instantly conveying a welcome. He set the paper on the table in front of him and moved his chair back to stand and greet Gray.

Gray caught sight of the front page. A picture of him and Oliver stared back at him. "That was quick."

Kurt looked at the paper. "Newman is going to use anything he can. He is capitalizing on your 'time off.' "

Gray shook his head. "Let him." He raised his eyes to Kurt's. "I've got to ask you a question."

"Shoot."

"Why did you choose this time to listen to me?"

Kurt's eyes narrowed beneath his tortoiseshell glasses. "What do you mean?"

"You never pay attention to anything I say. So why did you make this the one time you decided to listen to me and let yourself be fired?"

Kurt scratched his head. "Well, you've never actually punched me before."

Gray walked over to his friend and wrapped his arms around him. "I'm sorry, Kurt. Please forgive me."

Kurt's arms tightened around him. "You're forgiven." They stood there for a few moments until Tyler made a joke about their embrace. Of course he did. He was thirteen now. They all laughed.

"Sit down." Kurt motioned to a chair on the other side of the table. Gray sat, and the awkwardness immediately evaporated.

"I need you to come back," Gray said.

"I know you do."

"But not to run the campaign."

"So you're really not going to run?"

Gray placed his elbows on the table and rubbed his hands together. "I can't, Kurt. It's Mack. She's bad. If something doesn't happen, I don't know what I'm going to do.

The depression is deep. I just can't reach her."

Kurt leaned forward. "I'm so sorry." He shook his head. "Not about the election. About Mack. And you. And all of this nightmare you've endured. You're doing the right thing."

"I have to." Gray could hardly speak. "Mack's all I have. I can't lose her. The day I . . . well, the day I . . ."

Kurt helped him out. "Hit me?"

"Yeah, that. Again, I'm sor—"

"I heard you the first time. No more apologies."

Gray rubbed his head. "Okay, well, the night before that, I was already starting to lose it, I guess. And I said these ugly, awful things to her." His voice broke.

"Gray, Mack knows how much you love her."

"But I told her basically that the only thing I cared about was this campaign. That she was going to have to pull it together. Sort of shape up or ship out. And after that — that was when it all fell apart. I just threw her away."

"Gray, you didn't. You just . . . lost yourself there for a minute. It could happen to any-one."

Gray nodded. "I know. And I'm getting

help. I am. But I still need you and Fletch. I can't walk the rest of this without you." He paused and looked at his friend. "And I don't want to."

"You know I'll walk with you anywhere."

"Do you think y'all could draft a statement for me so we could announce that I'm not going to seek reelection?"

"Absolutely. What specifics do you want in there?"

"I want it to say that my family is the most important thing to me. And right now that has to come first, so this isn't the right time for me to be focused on anything else."

Kurt nodded. "We'll have it ready by the middle of next week — make the announcement together on Friday."

"No," Gray said. "It has to be sooner. Any way you could have it to me by tomorrow so I can announce on Saturday?"

Kurt considered. "It's not usual to make a big announcement on Saturday, but these are special circumstances." He nodded. "We'll do it."

"Thanks." Gray rubbed his eyes and shook his head. "It's like Mack's gone even farther into that dark place she had retreated to. And I don't have a clue what will pull her out of it."

"All we can do is love her, Gray. We don't

have anything else. And we'll trust the doctors will have wisdom to know the rest."

"I don't want her to be in a psych ward somewhere." He didn't even try to stop the tears that surged at the thought.

Kurt reached over and grabbed his wrist. "We won't let that happen."

Gray's eyes never left his friend's. "It might be too late."

Gray pulled in to the garage and walked down the basement hallway. He saw light coming from Jeremiah's workroom. "What you got there, Jeremiah?"

Jeremiah looked up slowly, his long fingers pressing down black dirt inside a green ceramic container in his familiar, unhurried manner. Everything Jeremiah did seemed slow. "Gettin' me a flower ready for Miz Mackenzie."

Gray studied the flower. "That's not one of those white flowers you've been giving her."

"Nope."

"So you're going to get adventurous again with your flower giving?"

Jeremiah chuckled. "Guess so. Sound crazy, don't it? But Miz Eugenia gone and give me permission. And I figure she scarier than Miz Mackenzie."

Gray had to laugh too. "No truer statement has ever been spoken." He gazed around the workroom, taking in the long table, the flats of seedlings under their grow lights, the mini fridge and hot plate in the corner.

"Rosa still bring you bologna in here to fry?"

Jeremiah smiled. "Yep, love havin' me fried bologna for lunch. One a my favorite things."

Gray laughed, then nodded at the flower Jeremiah was working with. "What is that anyway? I've seen one before . . . at Christmas, right?"

"Yeah, mostly for Christmas. It be an amaryllis. But I had me a bulb ever since then, put it in some water back in January, right after y'all lost the baby. Took a while, but now it bloomin' good, and the good Lord done tol' me to give it to Miz Mackenzie."

Gray watched as Jeremiah took some green moss from a box and placed it on the dirt. His hands worked with the delicacy of an artist. Every time he did something different — packed the dirt, covered it with moss, pulled out a ribbon and tied a bow. Each movement seemed to be a stroke that created a perfect picture. And there was

427

something about the ease and grace with which he did it. Such simplicity made an impact.

"Jeremiah, can I ask you something?"

Jeremiah pushed the finished amaryllis aside. The thick stalk and three bright-red blooms held themselves proud and stately as if they knew the power of their presence. "Ax away, Gov'nor. I ain't in all that much hurry to get home."

Gray nodded. He understood. He had felt that way a lot lately. "I've decided I'm not going to run for reelection."

Jeremiah dug his hands in his pockets and shifted back on his heels. "Hm."

"Yeah, at first I thought it would be the best thing for me. You know, keep my mind off everything we've been through." He gazed at the old pine worktable that spanned almost the entire length of the room and fingered some of the loose dirt left from where the container had been.

"Be a 'straction, you mean?"

Gray pressed his lips together. "Yeah, probably. Anyway, Mack's in bad shape, and I just think it's best I don't run. She needs me right now." He paused, still feeling the pull of the decision. He loved his wife desperately. She mattered more to him than anything in this world. And yet the finality of closing this door was real and heavy. "I'm doing the right thing . . . right?"

Jeremiah turned. His tools from the day's work were laid out on the other end of the table. He walked to the sink and took a towel from the shelf above his head. He ran some water over it, picked up his pruning shears from the table, and began to wipe the blades. His wrinkled hand was steady and strong as it ran hard across the blades.

"I 'member years ago when my daddy had his garden. One night he be out real late tryin' to catch this rabbit that be wreakin' havoc on his daisies. I ax him why he spend so much time tryin' to catch that rabbit when there always be another rabbit after that. Know what he tol' me? 'It's 'cause this be the rabbit that's here now.'

"I know sometimes, when you gots one thing after 'nother, don't feel like even botherin' with what you goin' through now 'cause you figure you gon' be goin' through sump'n else soon's this one be over with. And you probably right. But this be the one here now. And the only way it gon' quit eatin' your daisies be if you take time to catch it."

Gray heard him. And what he spoke was so true. If Gray was meant to be governor, the opportunity would come back. But what he needed to do now was be Mackenzie London's husband. For better or for worse.

Jeremiah interrupted his thoughts. "Anythin' else, Gov'nor?"

Gray looked into Jeremiah's rich, dark eyes. They weren't rushing him. They were searching him. "No. Just really appreciate you and your honesty. You know that, don't you?"

Jeremiah's eyes flickered with mischief. "You 'preciate me 'nough to take this here amaryllis up to Miz Mackenzie?"

Gray smiled. "You chicken?"

"Yep" was all he offered.

"Sure."

Jeremiah placed the container in his hands.

"Want to tell me what this flower means?" Gray asked.

Jeremiah pushed his lips out as if he was thinking. He finally shook his head. "Nah. Figure you be findin' out soon 'nough."

CHAPTER 47

She heard the door open but didn't turn to look. She heard Gray's soft footfall on the carpet, the jingle of Sophie's dog tags. Then he was next to her, setting a flower on the table beside her.

"Jeremiah sent this."

She didn't care.

"It's different from what he has been sending you the last couple of weeks." He smiled at her.

Her lips couldn't even form one anymore.

"Do you think this flower has a meaning?"

She was certain it did. But she never asked what it was.

CHAPTER 48

Eugenia saw it before she saw Mackenzie on Friday morning. It wasn't Christmas. What in the world was Jeremiah thinking, sending Mackenzie an amaryllis?

She looked at the flower sitting there so strong and proud and sucked in a breath. He was not saying . . . was he?

He was.

She took a few minutes to make a phone call. Then she marched down the veranda stairs and straight to the garden. She caught sight of the backside of his overalls with that ridiculous blue hankie sticking from his left pocket. He was bent over, his head in a patch of tulips.

She leaned over, spreading her legs for balance. Then she reached down, grabbed a pocket with each of her hands, and pulled as hard as she could. She jerked with such force that she landed on the ground with Jeremiah right on top of her.

"Get off me, Jeremiah!" she hollered as she struggled and squirmed.

Jeremiah shifted around, trying to stand up but having a hard time himself. He finally said, "Well, Lord amercy, woman, if you be still, I might be able to get me some traction."

She finally quit flailing, and he managed to get to his feet. He reached a hand down to help her up only after he gave her a look that let her know he thought she had lost her mind. She slapped his hand aside and pushed herself up, wiping grass off her kelly-green cardigan and picking at blades that had adhered to her white tank.

"Now, I don't know what in the tar hill this be 'bout, but you gone and tol' me I could give Miz Mackenzie a flower. Any flower."

She pulled at the hem of her sweater. "Yes, I did. So if you're going to declare my daughter is prideful, you're going to be part of the remedy." She snatched his hand and yanked him through the gardens as they headed toward the house.

"Where you takin' me?"

"We're going on a field trip."

"But I can't be leavin' —"

"The governor is my son-in-law. We can do whatever I want."

"You gon' get me put away the rest a my life with no time off for good behavior."

"You wouldn't get time off for good behavior anyway because you make it your mission to drive me crazy."

"Don't hafta drive you. You done already arrived."

She stopped at the back door and faced him. "I'm going to forget you said that."

"Forgettin' ain't ever made sump'n less true."

She grabbed his hand again and tugged him right through the main part of the mansion and out the front door. She had parked in front of the north entrance in the large circular drive.

Jeremiah dug in his heels. "I ain't gettin' in that."

A black Cadillac sedan sat in front of them. She opened the passenger door. "Get in, Jeremiah."

He didn't budge. "I ain't doin' it."

"You are."

"I ain't. I tol' you — I can't leave. 'Sides, that look like a funeral car, and for alls I know, you plan on killin' me."

She jerked his arm and pushed him into the front seat using all her force, and when the final piece of him wouldn't budge, she used her backside. He couldn't have fought

434

that if he'd tried. She finally got him inside and slammed the door, beeping it locked. She ran around to the driver's side and climbed in.

"We're picking up some friends," she said as she turned the key in the ignition and put her foot on the accelerator.

Sheer force pressed his head against the headrest. "Lord amercy, help us," he muttered.

"He already has," Eugenia said. "I think he already has."

"Don't touch me!" Sandra hollered from the backseat.

Eugenia twisted the rearview mirror and watched as Berlyn wiggled even closer to Sandra. Sandra slapped her.

"Could you two stop it? Seriously!" Eugenia scolded like a preschool teacher.

Dimples sat on the other side of Sandra with her teeth in her hand. She had one eye on them, and Eugenia swore the other one was watching the trees fly by on the interstate. "Dimples, you too. Put your teeth back in your mouth."

Jeremiah shook his head and put it in his hands. "I gon' call the police and tell 'em I done been kidnapped."

"We ain't kidnapped you." Dimples

gummed the words out. "We're just borrowing you."

"Don't say *ain't*." Sandra grabbed Dimples's hand, the one that held her teeth. "And put those back in now, or I swear I'm throwing them out the window. That is disgusting."

Dimples crammed them back in her mouth. "I had a piece of chicken in them," she said, offering Sandra a mocking expression. "And ladies don't swear, Sandra," she added, sticking out her tongue for emphasis.

"The maturity level here is killing me!" Eugenia announced. "Sandra, don't touch her. And next time, Dimples, get a toothpick." She adjusted the mirror back to its original position.

Berlyn leaned forward as far as her seat belt would allow. "So where are we going?"

"We're going to remind my daughter that she is not the only one in the world who has problems."

Jeremiah turned sharply. "What you gon' do, Miz Eugenia? Miz Mackenzie don't need no foolishness right now."

"Well, you're the one who gave my child an amaryllis in March," she reminded. "Far as I know, that flower means 'pride.' So if that wasn't what you were insinuating, then do tell me now." Her hands tightened around the steering wheel. Berlyn's head whipped to Jeremiah as if the tennis ball had just been hit into his court.

"Well, I give it to 'er 'cause that what I be tol' to give 'er."

"Who told you?" Berlyn asked.

"Don't ask," Eugenia said.

"The Lord tol' me."

"The Lord?" Berlyn said. "As in . . . God?"

Sandra punched her. "Don't use the Lord's name in vain."

Berlyn shook her fist in Sandra's face. "Hit me again. I dare you . . ."

"Y'all crazy," Jeremiah hollered to the backseat. "Yep, God done tol' me lotta things out there in my garden. He like to hang out there."

"And God told you to give her an amaryllis because he was saying something about pride, right?" Eugenia responded.

His dark eyes looked at her as if they were studying whether answering yes could actually cut his life short. But he still responded truthfully. He knew no other way. It was one of the things about him that drove her crazy.

"You right. Don't know 'xactly what, though. I mean, I be a smart man and all, and I know what grief look like — done had my share. I know Miz Mackenzie be havin' her some real grief. But grievin' can go and get itself mixed all in with pride and self-pity, and them things can swallow you whole after a while. Maybe that be what God tryin' to say. But Lord amercy, Miz Eugenia, I ain't him. Don't always un'erstand why he tellin' me to do sump'n. Just know I gots to do it."

Eugenia jerked her head toward the street in front of her again. "Well, my baby is not going to be swallowed whole by anything as long as I'm alive to see about it. Those doctors may be going to take care of her head, but I'm going to go in after her heart."

Dimples slid up to the edge of the seat too and pulled on Jeremiah's headrest. "So are we like Charlie's angels or something?"

"Or something," Eugenia said.

"If we are, I'm Farrah Fawcett," Berlyn declared quickly.

"She's dead, you know," Sandra informed her.

Berlyn turned her head to Sandra. "It can happen to the best of us. Anytime — when we least expect it, when we're not looking, even by someone we know." She cast a significant look at Sandra, who hugged her black patent-leather purse a little tighter to her chest.

"We're going to the Nashville Rescue Mission," Eugenia announced.

"Do they have men there?" Berlyn asked.

Eugenia saw Jeremiah's brow furrow. He looked at her. She just shook her head. "Don't ask."

"Don't wanna know."

"It's not about men, Berlyn," Eugenia said. "Mackenzie used to bring home single mothers with little ones and let them spend the night in the guest rooms when the mission was short on beds. Rosa would fix them big dinners, and Mackenzie would teach Maddie what it meant to take care of other people. That life isn't all about you and that you should share what you have and bear one another's burdens. It was one of the things that brought her the greatest joy."

Eugenia's voice softened. "But she hasn't even been back to the mission since she had that miscarriage." She steeled her shoulders once again. "Jessica told me yesterday that the head of the Family Life Center at the mission called, and they don't have enough beds for a family coming in today. They wanted to know if we could have them at the mansion. Jessica didn't know what to tell them. But I have decided we're bringing the mission to Mackenzie tonight. She's going to remember how to live by realizing everyone goes through difficult situations in life, not just her."

"Why the gov'nor's car be followin' us?" She heard fear in Jeremiah's voice.

"That isn't the governor's car. It's my friend Burt. He's going to bring the family to the mansion because we don't have room in here with all of us."

She saw Jeremiah's shoulders relax. Then his lips slowly curved into a smile.

"What're you smiling at?" she asked.

He just let out a soft chuckle.

She didn't look at him again until they parked in front of the Family Life Center. When she did, she saw he was still smiling. A very irritating smile, if she had to say so herself.

And she did.

She always had to say so herself.

JEREMIAH

Crazy got a face. I seen it. It look like four ol' women runnin' through a homeless shelter grabbin' up some poor woman and her three chil'rens and tellin' 'em they goin' to the gov'nor's mansion. Eugenia been barkin' orders like she the gov'nor herself. Dimples been samplin' the spaghetti dinner. And Sandra, she just tryin' to keep Berlyn from goin' in the men's restroom.

And me, I just hangin' on. Ain't much else you can do when you with crazy people. You just hang on and see where in the good Lord's name they gon' take you.

They crammed that family into that car — kids' hair be all dirty and the mama look so tired — then they put they clothes and stuff in the trunk a Eugenia's car. Guess it'd been a while since they had a chance to wash them clothes 'cause they made that prissy Sandra's nose wrinkle up good. She even whisper sump'n 'bout head lice, though thank God she ain't said that too loud.

I been prayin' the whole way I ain't gon' get in no trouble for leavin' my post. I know Eugenia's the gov'nor's mother-in-law and all, but I still gots me a job to do — a job I proud to hold and one she ain't ax my boss if I could leave. I know he a good man and he trust me, but rules is rules. And Miz Eugenia, she don't ever think rules apply to her.

I ain't figured out why she want me there anyways. If she wanna go and drag somebody 'long, should go after the Lord himself 'cause that amaryllis be his idea.

But I gone and had me a thought while all that mayhem was goin' on. Maybe this flower ain't 'bout Miz Mackenzie after all. God knowed good 'nough that Miz Eugenia gon' be stickin' her nose in my flower business, so maybe that flower be for her. Maybe it s'posed to shake her up, make her good and mad. 'Cause sometime you gots to get mad 'nough at the devil to make him stop stealin'. And Miz Eugenia sure 'nough tired of that ol' devil stealin' from her.

So maybe God knowed just what would get up in her craw and get her to thinkin' a sump'n that might work. Sump'n that ain't just about coddlin' hurt. 'Cause there do come a moment where hurt ain't need to be coddled no more. Hurt need to be put in perspective.

So I just prayin' this whole day be worth sump'n. Please, Lord, let the fact that I had to spend two a the precious hours a my life with these here women be worth sump'n. And, Lord, if you be wantin' to tell me sump'n, you just gots to help me have eyes to see and ears to hear.

'Cause at this point, I just ain't seein' it yet.

CHAPTER 49

This was what it came down to. More than three years of serving the people of Tennessee, and this one speech would mark the beginning of the end.

Kurt had called Fletcher as soon as Gray left his house, and they'd begun drafting a statement. They had scheduled this evening's meeting so he could look over it. He would read it tomorrow at a hastily scheduled press conference. That way he would have all this pressure off his shoulders and be able to be with Mack all day Monday.

He had no idea what Monday would entail. But he wasn't going to let her go through any of it alone.

Fletcher stood at the edge of his desk in perpetual fidget.

"Seriously, Fletch. Could you be still for one minute?" Gray laughed as he made a note on the current draft of his statement.

Fletcher pushed at his wire-rimmed glasses. "Yeah, sure." His leg still twitched.

Gray slipped off his readers and set them on the leather top of his desk. He handed the papers to Fletcher, who had traded in his usual bow tie for a long-sleeved UT T-shirt. "The statement looks great. You did a wonderful job. Now, how are we doing at keeping this from leaking out before *we* leak it?"

"Well, when I set up the press conference for tomorrow, that of course triggered a million questions. Everyone seems pretty confident that you'll be launching your campaign. They knew you'd announce your decision when you finished your respite. But far as I can tell, no one knows for sure where you are going to land."

Kurt spoke. "We're going to do a private announcement for leaders in the house and senate, who need to know prior to the news conference. I've set that up for ten in the morning. That way they will feel like they heard it from us first and they can get a step ahead of the media frenzy that will ensue after the press conference at noon."

Kurt studied Gray. "How are you?"

Gray ran his hands through his hair. "A little tired. A little sad. All of those things."

"Any doubts?" Fletcher asked, his hand

fiddling with change in his pocket.

Gray shook his head. "No. No doubts. Mack was in bed when I left. Eugenia came over so I could meet with you guys."

Fletcher nodded. "Well, Marcus Newman's new ad hit the airwaves today. He doesn't mention you, but the insinuation is evident."

Gray leaned against his desk and crossed his arms. "What is this one about?"

"This one reminds the public that a released prisoner killed a store clerk. The family of the victim is actually in the commercial."

Gray felt a tightening in his chest, a flash of anger. He had called them. He had talked to them. The tightening loosened. They had lost someone they loved. They were angry. "It's okay," he said. "I understand. I just hate that they are being taken advantage of in their grief."

"Well, it doesn't matter now. At least it can't be used against you," Fletcher responded.

"It's out there now, though. People will either think I did the right thing or think I didn't. But I will always know that I did the best I could with what I had. Budget still on schedule?"

"Yep," Kurt said. "Hope you have your

red pen handy."

"I do. And I intend to use it."

"Well, the good news is that we should have enough votes to keep your vetoes from being overturned."

"We have our work cut out for us, then, as we leave our final mark around here, huh? Good job on the statement, fellas. You said it exactly like I would. How do you know me so well?" He smiled.

Kurt and Fletcher both shook their heads and walked out the door.

Gray moved to the floor-to-ceiling windows behind his desk. He peered out over the capitol lawn, thinking about Mack curled up in bed, covers pulled up to her chin, looking like a child herself.

He wanted to rescue her. He wanted so desperately to pull her from her pain. Pain in his own gut struck with the thought.

Then came a revelation. In all of this, in dealing with his own pain, in reclaiming his own heart, there was one thing he hadn't really done for Mack.

The realization hit him so hard he had to sit down. "I can't believe I haven't prayed for her."

He had thrown prayers up, sure. "God, help us. Lord, give me wisdom." He had done those. But he hadn't pressed in. Not the way he should have. Not the way that desperate times in people's lives demanded.

Jeremiah had told him a story one time about when his little boy was sick with spinal meningitis. Jeremiah said that he went into his bedroom, closed the door, and didn't come out until the doctors said the boy was fine. Said that he'd prayed and fasted for three full days. That he'd felt like King David did when he did the same thing over his son.

Gray walked to his personal study. Sophie studied him from her pillow as he passed her, closed the door, and locked it. He pulled his Bible from a side table, then knelt in front of the sofa. And there, in Tennessee's state capitol, the governor of that state battled for the very life of his wife.

CHAPTER 50

Eugenia burst through the doors of the mansion, scaring the heebie-jeebies out of Joseph. She could tell by the way he grabbed his chest when the door swung open. "It's okay, Joseph," she told the steward. "It's just me."

She hollered out the door to Berlyn. "Bring them in."

Berlyn turned her broad behind around, displaying the equally broad hot-pink rose that was splattered across it.

"I'm buying her nothing but stripes for Christmas," Eugenia muttered to herself.

Dimples and Sandra climbed out of the car. Sandra was huffing and puffing and acting like she was dying.

"Get the laundry," Eugenia barked. "You're doing it, Sandra."

Sandra's top lip pressed hard against her bottom lip, but Eugenia knew her friend well enough to know that her Southern manners or Southern pride, however you wanted to define it, would never let her say, "There's no way on God's green earth I'm doing that stinky laundry" in front of the very people it belonged to. So Eugenia had handled that perfectly.

Jeremiah got out of the car slowly. The man needed a piece of dynamite stuck to his rear end. Dimples came around the corner of the car and ran into the bumper. Eugenia popped the lid to her trunk with a little button in her hand, and it shot upward, about scaring poor Dimples's left eye straight.

Berlyn held the hand of one of three little girls as she led them in the front door. "It's okay. Come right in. You get to stay here until beds open up at the shelter."

The mother of the three girls stood a head above Eugenia. She had to be at least six feet tall. But she was kind of scrawny and ostrichlike. And her poor hair must have been running from shampoo. If she even had any shampoo.

Jeremiah brought up the rear and grabbed Eugenia's arm right before she headed upstairs to get Mackenzie.

"Where you goin'?"

"I'm going to get Mackenzie. Now, let me go."

"What if she ain't gon' come?"

"Then I'll drag her out of the bed."

"What good that gon' do? Same bed be there tomorrow."

She jerked her arm free from his grip. "Do you think I brought this woman and her children here for me?"

"Nope. Be pretty clear on why you brought 'em here. Just maybe you ain't thought through what you need to do now that they here."

She shook her head in frustration and stomped her foot. "Speak English, Jeremiah. English. What are you trying to say?"

"That flower do mean pride, Miz Eugenia. It do. I knowed that when I give it to Miz Mackenzie. And I knowed self-pity's one a pride's ugliest and meanest faces. But alls you can do for somebody when they all tangled up in hurt is give 'em a chance to heal. And if you think you can do more'n that for 'em, well then, maybe that flower wasn't for Miz Mackenzie."

She could feel her brow furrow. "Are you saying me? *I've* got a problem with pride?"

" 'Bout as English as I can say it. Control be pride, Miz Eugenia. Lettin' go . . . now, lettin' go is healin'."

Eugenia was too flustered to think. She had just brought a homeless family to the

451

governor's mansion. Sandra had all but thrown up when she heard she had laundry duty. Dimples needed as much taking care of as the woman and her children. And Berlyn couldn't be trusted in the governor's mansion; she always left with a souvenir. And now Jeremiah had the nerve to suggest Eugenia had gone to all this trouble because she was too full of pride?

Jeremiah must have read her mind. "Alls you can do is lead her to the water, Miz Eugenia. She the only one can decide to take a drink. You gots to leave all that in the Lord's hands. He a big ol' God."

Eugenia ran her hand across her face and then tugged both hands through her stiff-sprayed bob. "Go, Jeremiah," she said. "Just go!" She marched up the stairs, right past a flustered-looking Jessica, still feeling his eyes on her. But she was Eugenia Quinn, and every day was Burger King for her. So she would have it her way.

Mackenzie's door was closed. Eugenia opened it slowly to find her daughter still in bed, the covers tucked around her. It was as if she were still seven, sleeping there all safe and sound, back when Eugenia and Lorenzo could keep her safe. Tell her what to do. Make her do it. Mackenzie had always been an obedient child — a little stubborn sometimes, but she would eventually do what she was told. Even if she did it her own way.

Eugenia walked to the window, keeping her eyes on her daughter. Mackenzie had needed her these past six months, and she had been there. There had been moments when she needed to be pushed, and Eugenia had pushed her. And there had been moments when she simply needed to be loved and held, so Eugenia had loved her and held her.

But Jeremiah was right. Eugenia knew it.

That was why she hated it so much — because it had come from him. She flipped her hand in disgust and walked to Mackenzie's bed. "Mackenzie, I want you to get up."

She saw Mackenzie's eyes move slightly.

"Come on. I know you can hear me. I need you to get yourself out of that bed and get up. You've got company to tend to." She reached for her daughter's arm.

Mackenzie's embrace around her pillow tightened.

"Now you listen to me, Mackenzie. Your mother has told you to do something, and it's time to do it." Her voice shook, and she could feel her fear rising rapidly. "Now, come on. You need to get up and get dressed and come help me take care of these visitors we've got."

Even as the words came from her mouth, she knew they were useless. Banging gongs. Clanging cymbals. Biscuits made without Crisco. Useless. But she was a mama, and mamas didn't let their babies drown. They dove in after them and would pummel sharks with their bare fists if that was what stood in their way.

She was leaning down to tug again at Mackenzie's arm when the tug of something else arrested her. Her body moved back instinctively. She felt it again. It was pulling her away from Mackenzie. A thought fluttered through her soul — *I've got her.*

She pushed against it. But she knew where it had come from.

"I can't trust you with her," she whispered. "Not now. Not after all of this."

She moved closer to the bed. Mackenzie stirred. Another thought dug deeper still. *Broken worlds hold broken things. But only one can put it all back together.*

Eugenia stepped back. She knew it was true. She knew this world was broken and cruel and nothing like what had originally been intended. And she also knew from losing Lorenzo that heaven was the only place big enough to put the kind of agony that travels through your insides and doesn't stop until it has removed half your heart.

It was time to let go. Strangely, it felt like she'd known that for a long time, long before Jeremiah had said anything. But knowing it and doing it were not the same thing.

She retreated to the bay window and stood there a long time, watching a sky that still held the fleeting blue of day. Finally she spoke. "Father, I'm good at a lot of things. I'm good at gardening — better than Jeremiah. I'm good at deciding and dictating. Without me, those three down there would be lost. And I'm a good mama. You know that. You made me one. But I have never been good at letting go. I can beat a dead horse, pick it up, and then beat it again."

She chuckled to herself. "At least that's what Mackenzie always says, but I guess you made me that way too."

She felt the knot grow large in her throat, and she had to wait for it to subside. "Father, my baby girl is broken, and I can't fix her. I see that now. I really do. I've done everything I know to do. I'm all out of fixing."

She shook her head and then stood silent for what seemed like days. Finally she cupped her hands and raised them toward the blue of the sky. "All right, Lord. You gave that baby girl to me. Now I give her to you. She's in your hands."

Tears fell freely down her face. "But please, if you can bring her back to us — the real Mackenzie, our Mackenzie —" she had to fight to get those words out — "Gray and I would sure appreciate it." The next pause was long, and what transpired in the middle of it would redefine Eugenia Quinn forever. "But whatever you think is best for my baby girl . . . I'll trust you."

When she finally knew her surrender was complete — or as complete as she was capable of — Eugenia walked to Mackenzie and kissed her softly on the cheek. And with that, she left her alone.

As soon as she closed the door, she heard a scream.

Obviously Sandra had gotten the laundry out of the car.

JEREMIAH

I knowed soon as I let go her arm, that woman ain't gon' listen to a thing I say. So I gone and did what I knowed to do. Marched right down them stairs to my workroom and tol' them boys to leave me be for a few minutes. They all knowed why. When I clear 'em out like that, it be 'cause I gots business to do.

I knowed the gov'nor and Miz Eugenia wanna save Miz Mackenzie. I wanna save her too. But she gots to want to be saved. So this be Miz Mackenzie's fightin' place too. This 'tween her and God.

And so I do the only thing make a lick a sense. I get down on my knees, grateful they still good 'nough to be gotten down on, and I start prayin' for all a them. Prayin' for the gov'nor, prayin' for the crazy lady, and prayin' for Miz Mackenzie. That each one a them find strength to let go they pride if they got any.

And pride hard, 'cause it like to pretend it sump'n it ain't — like a rescuer or a protector or a griever or a pitier. I'm thinkin' sometimes pride can pretend to be an ol' man tellin' gov'nors and such what they oughta do.

But no matter what it pretend to be, pride be such a liar. It make us *think* we sump'n we ain't. Make us think we can get by without God.

Way I see it, God thought it'd be okay to get all a life started in a garden. Then, after ever'body thought he gone for good, he show back up in another garden. Women that saw him after he raised up from the dead, they thought he be a gardener. Always did love that story. Way I see it, he be a Master Gardener. So now, good Lord, please help us all to keep our prideful hands outta your garden and get outta the way a all the growin' things you be tryin' to do.

CHAPTER 51

A shrill scream pierced through the haze in Mackenzie's mind. She blinked hard. The sun was still up. She had no idea what time it was, when Gray had left, or whose scream had just awoken her.

She tried to pick up her feet to move them to the edge of the bed. They felt like they had soaked in concrete all night. She finally got them over the side and managed to sit up. Everything hurt. She shouldn't be surprised. Her body had spent more time against that mattress than it had anywhere else. It was a miracle her muscles hadn't atrophied completely.

Loud voices sounded down the hall. A knock landed on her door, loud and forceful. "Mrs. London?"

She didn't respond. She just sat still on the edge of the bed.

Another knock, harder this time, and the

voice at her door was louder. "Mrs. London?"

"Would you stop it! She's resting!" Her mother's voice was loud enough to wake the dead, let alone someone sleeping in the other room.

Mackenzie pushed to her feet and picked up a white fluffy sweatshirt that was draped over the foot of the bed. She realized that Gray had known what she'd want when she got up. She'd want her sweatshirt. That sweatshirt. And he had left it there for her.

She put on the sweatshirt and looked around. Something felt . . . different. Her senses seemed more alert than usual. She walked to the door and opened it.

Jessica and her mother stared at her, wide-eyed. She immediately knew why. Her mother had seen her this morning, practically dead to the world. Jessica had seen her yesterday, sitting in her chair like a zombie. Right now she didn't feel so great, but she was neither of those people.

"Oh, Mrs. London," Jessica said. "I'm sorry. I didn't know you were sleeping. I just . . ." Her words trailed off.

Mackenzie leaned against the doorframe. "It's okay." She wrapped her arms around herself. "What's going on?"

Jessica's look was uptight. Her words followed the same pattern. "Did you decide you wanted to bring a family in today from the mission?"

"I decided for her," Eugenia said.

Mackenzie rubbed her eyes. "What do you mean? What family?"

"There is a family here. A mother with two girls —"

Eugenia interrupted. "Three."

Jessica turned toward Eugenia and shook her head. "Okay, there are four people downstairs, all seemingly here to be fed and housed for the evening. And I know you've done this in the past, but usually you run things like this through me."

Her head kind of tilted toward Eugenia as the last sentence came out, a subtle declaration of what belonged in a home.

Mackenzie moved past them and down the hall. She looked over the railing to the foyer below. A tall, dirty woman with three scraggly redheaded children waited there. One girl sat on the floor, another at the bottom of the steps, and the other ran wildly through the foyer, arms stretched out and airplane noises coming from her little but boisterous mouth.

Dimples chased her as best she could, barely missing the wall. Berlyn was sitting on the steps with a child's head resting on

461

her large bosom. And Sandra was in the corner holding on to her purse. Bags of dirty laundry sat across the foyer from her, and every now and then she'd pat the running child on the head as if the girl were a porcupine.

"Yes," Eugenia responded in a rather mild tone. She walked to Mackenzie's side. "But it's not for you to worry about. We've got it under control. So just go back to your room. And, well, me and the girls and Jessica —" she grabbed Jessica's arm and pulled her toward the stairs — "will handle it. Just trying to help some people out here."

Jessica looked at Mackenzie, her eyes pleading, as Eugenia dragged her down the stairs. Mackenzie watched as her mother hit the foyer and went into her familiar drill sergeant routine. Much more her style.

"So," she said, "Rosa informs me we've got some time before dinner. That'll give us time to get y'all settled."

The mother took a step toward Eugenia. "If we're going to be staying here for a little while, ma'am . . ." She seemed to hesitate. "Would you mind if me and my girls could wash up somewhere?"

Eugenia patted the woman's arm. "Sure, honey. We'll get you all taken care of." She turned to her friends. "Dimples, why don't you and Berlyn take the kids upstairs to the guest bathroom and get them all bathed."

The littlest guest stopped in the middle of the foyer, studying the woman handing out bathing instructions. The look on her face made it evident that she had no interest in a bath. She raised her face to her mother. "Ma, do we have to?"

The mother patted the little one and leaned down to whisper in her ear. The little redhead's shoulders slumped, but she started toward the stairs.

"Mother, I'm going to take you to the other guest bedroom, let you have some time all to yourself," Eugenia said. Then hollered, "Rosa!"

Rosa came out of the kitchen.

"We need it big and bold and —" she stopped and gave Rosa that look — "preferably fried. And plenty of it."

Rosa gave her a smile and disappeared behind the swinging wooden door.

"Joseph, make sure the table is set for dinner. And show Sandra where the upstairs laundry is." She looked at Sandra. Sandra just glared at her but bent to gingerly pick up a bag. One of the housekeepers hurried over to help her.

Eugenia wasn't through. "Berlyn, you and Dimples need to slather, smother, and cover these children. Make sure they scrub in places they didn't even know they had. And be sure and use bubbles — kids like bubbles. Do you understand?"

"Yes, ma'am!" Berlyn stood and saluted, then leaned over to the oldest girl. "She always tells us what to do. She came out of the womb bossy."

"You got it!" Dimples tried to clap her bony legs together, which only made the extra fabric of her baggy, celery-green pants seem to billow in the wind. The tops of her white socks showed as her black orthopedic shoes clomped together. She tried a salute but missed her head by an inch.

"Jessica!"

Jessica's head turned hard toward Eugenia.

"You go do whatever it was you were doing. I've got this under control."

Mackenzie could see Jessica's twitch from upstairs. Eugenia took the mother's arm, and in less than a minute, the busy foyer was silent again.

And that was how quickly it could happen. Mackenzie had seen it. One minute, life filled every crevice, and the next it was snatched away. Gone in an instant. Mackenzie stared at the empty space.

But this particular life had not gone away.

It was heading up the stairs toward her. Mackenzie leaned back instinctively as they all trooped by. The children eyed her curiously as Berlyn scurried them to the bathroom.

"Grace, this is my daughter, Mackenzie." Eugenia introduced the children's mother. "Excuse us, darling. We'll try not to disturb you."

"Nice to meet you, Grace." Mackenzie dredged up a smile, as much as she had given anyone in the past six weeks. She saw Sandra at the bottom of the stairs with an arm wrapped over her mouth, tugging a bag of laundry in one hand while the housekeeper waited behind her.

The commotion down the hall couldn't be ignored. Mackenzie followed the noise to the guest bathroom. Berlyn was leaning over the tub, testing the water, her behind high enough in the air to prop a small child on. Dimples was entertaining the children — or horrifying them — by popping her teeth out and sucking them back in.

"What's wrong with your eye?" one of them asked.

"Not a thing," she answered. "God gave me two eyes that could move in opposite directions so I could keep better eyes on kids like you."

One of the older children shrugged. One took a step back toward her sister.

Dimples started tugging a sleeve of the youngest, the child's head caught somewhere in her dingy yellow long-sleeved T-shirt. Dimples yanked while the little one hollered, "Ow! You're going to kill me in here."

Mackenzie reached over and took the sleeve from Dimples's hand, pulling the shirt up gently. Red curls popped out with a bounce, and big blue eyes were wild with animation.

"Thank goodness you showed up, lady."

Mackenzie looked at the three sisters standing in a line. Three stair steps, each with wild, curly red hair and a grimy, freckled face. And in that moment something inside her shifted, turned, dislodged. Something small but key.

She knelt by the smallest one. "Hey, what's your name?"

Wide blue eyes turned toward her, then looked at the floor and spoke softly. "Suzy."

"That's a beautiful name."

The eyes popped back up. "I got it 'cause it's my aunt's name."

"Really? Well, is she as beautiful as you?"

"Yeah." Her head bobbed up and down. "And know what?"

"What?"

"She's got red hair too."

Mackenzie touched a bright-red curl. "Your hair is certainly beautiful."

The child nodded as if she knew that too. "Yeah."

The middle sister tugged at Suzy. "Hush," she scolded.

Mackenzie studied her face. It was way too serious for one her age. She couldn't be more than seven or eight. "It's okay, honey. I was just asking her questions."

The oldest turned around then. And something else turned over in Mackenzie's soul. For one brief moment it wasn't about death or loss or dying, not about the past or the bleak, endless future. It was about right now, in this moment. It was about three little girls and one woman who, more than anything in the world, loved taking care of little girls.

"How about you three come with me," she said. "I've got another bathroom down the hall with a big ol' tub that I bet you all could fit in at once."

Suzy's smile grew. The other two looked hesitant. Mackenzie stood and leaned toward the oldest. "It's okay. This is my house." She smiled at them and placed her hand on the oldest's back. "Berlyn, I'm going to take them with me for a minute. I think they might like my bathroom more than this one."

Berlyn raised a bubble-covered hand. "That'll work. Me and Dimples here can go help Rosa with dinner."

Dimples's tongue ran across her lips at the mere mention of food. Mackenzie had no doubt they would enjoy those activities far more than the ones they had been ordered to handle. Whether Rosa enjoyed their help was a different matter. She steered the three girls out of the bathroom and down the hall.

"I ain't never seen a house this huge before," Suzy said.

"Don't say *ain't*," the oldest sister scolded.

"What's your name?" Mackenzie asked her.

"I'm Lily, and this here is Toby." The mama of the bunch pointed to the middle sister.

"Our daddy wanted a boy," Suzy announced.

Toby punched her. "I told you not to tell everyone that."

Suzy rubbed her arm and furrowed her brow. "Still true."

Mackenzie felt a bubble of laughter somewhere inside. It never escaped, but it existed.

And it struck her as both foreign and beautiful. She took them into her bedroom, which they beheld with the wonder of children on Main Street at Walt Disney World.

Suzy ran straight for the window and looked out over the backyard. "Is that a pool?"

Mackenzie walked behind her. "It is."

"You swim in it, lady?"

"You should ask her name," Lily said.

Suzy shrugged. "What's your name, lady?"

Mackenzie laid a hand on Suzy's soft curls. "My name is Mackenzie."

"You swim in it, Mackenzie?"

Lily joined them. "*Miz* Mackenzie."

Suzy huffed. "Gee whiz." She rolled her eyes before she was willing to obey. "You swim in it, *Miz* Mackenzie?" She emphasized it clearly for her sister's sake.

Mackenzie felt the revelation rise hard in her throat. Suzy was like her Maddie. She was a little full of herself. She said whatever passed through her mind. And she was captivating. The girl couldn't be any more than five herself. Looking at her was like staring at a strawberry version of Maddie's chocolate. And Maddie had always wanted to swim in the reflecting pool too — they'd had to watch her like hawks when they first moved in.

Tears came to Mackenzie's eyes before she could stop them. They clustered on her eyelashes and blurred her vision. The pool turned into a backyard of blue. "No, honey, we don't really swim in that pool."

Suzy looked at her and crinkled her nose. "You mean you got a pool out there like that and you ain't swim in —" she looked at her sisters — "I mean, you don't swim in it? That's crazy."

Mackenzie looked out the window. She blinked at the tears, and the beauty of what rested below suddenly seemed to pop out at her. The colors were greener, brighter, the water in the pool bluer. The clouds gleamed an impossible gold in the setting sun. "Yeah, kind of crazy, isn't it, Suzy?" She continued to stare out for a moment until she felt Suzy fidget beside her. She looked down.

The child's hand was between her legs. "I gotta go pee."

"Oh yeah, sure. Let's go." Mackenzie led them into the bathroom and let Suzy take care of her business while she filled the bath to the brim with warm water full of bubbles. Just like Maddie always liked it.

While the three girls climbed in, Mackenzie went to the linen closet and opened it. A bottle of baby shampoo was still inside.

She pulled it out and steadied herself as she walked toward the tub again. Reminders were everywhere.

She soaked the girls' heads and began to scrub them with shampoo. As she scrubbed, it seemed that the adult weight that had been on the older two's shoulders washed away with all the dirt that had been on their little bodies.

She got out some of Maddie's bath toys from the cabinet too and sat on the floor as the girls talked and played and laughed and blew bubbles. At one point she turned on the whirlpool jets. Each of them was startled for a moment, until the whirling water began to make more bubbles fly to the surface. Then their amazement turned to delight.

"Miz Mackenzie, you got any babies?" Suzy asked through the bubble mustache she had made for herself.

Mackenzie's stomach clenched, but she knew the question came from an innocent place. "No, sweetie, I don't."

"Don't want any?"

She froze. She couldn't talk about this. She had holed it up inside her, in the place where dead things dwelled. But blue eyes were looking at her. "Well, I had one," she finally said. "A little girl, actually."

The older two stopped playing. Suzy grabbed a handful of bubbles and blew them. The bubbles flew right to Mackenzie's feet. "Where did you put her?"

"Well, God took her, I guess." She hadn't mentioned God's name in many weeks.

"Suzy, don't ask no more questions." Lily's maturity was quickly returning.

But Toby obviously thought the reprimand was for Suzy alone. She put her hands on the side of the tub. "Did she die?"

Suzy stopped all movement when Toby spoke. She came to the edge of the tub and put her hands over the side as well.

How did you ignore children? How did you explain to them that some questions in life were too personal, some pain too private? Granted, Mackenzie had invited them into her bathroom, but she hadn't invited them into the private places of her heart.

She answered anyway. "Yes."

Suzy's eyes were big and wide. Mackenzie felt her heart snap. She let the words come out as they willed. "My little girl, Maddie, was about your age," she said, nodding at Suzy. "And she was beautiful, just like you." She rubbed the girl's arm. And the next words that left her mouth were ones she had never before spoken, at least this way. "She was killed in a car accident."

All three girls stared at her, their faces solemn, their blue eyes large and now old. "You miss her?" Suzy finally asked.

Mackenzie bit the inside of her lip to stop the tears. "Every day."

Lily seemed to study her for a moment, then lowered her head and spoke softly. "I miss our dad."

The other two heads snapped toward her, and pain registered immediately on their faces.

"Oh, honey, did your father die?" Mackenzie asked.

"No, ma'am. He's in jail."

"Shot a man and killed him." Suzy said it so matter-of-factly, it was clear she really didn't understand what it all meant.

"He had just gotten released from jail too," Lily added. "Said he was going to help Mama take care of us the right way. But he couldn't find a job. Looked and looked for a real long time. Then one night he got in a fight with Mama, beat her up real bad, and then went and robbed a gas station. He killed the man that was working there. So they put him back in jail."

Instantly Mackenzie remembered. The prisoner release. It had been all over the papers for quite a while, and there was even a lawsuit, but she didn't know what, if anything, had happened with it. And the children affected by this nightmare were soaking in her tub.

Mackenzie saw tears well up in Lily's eyes. She watched her desperately try to fight them, but she couldn't. Mackenzie reached through the bubbles and wrapped her arms around Lily. Toby hugged her sister too, and Suzy waded through the tub to get near them.

Lily spoke through her tears. "Daddy did all that and never got any money. And once Mama got out of the hospital, she lost her job too. Then we couldn't pay our rent anymore or anything, so she had to bring us to the shelter so we could get food and someplace to sleep."

"It'll be all right." Suzy kissed her sister's wet curls. "Mama's gonna get a job, and we're gonna get us a house and have all the macaroni and cheese we can stand."

Mackenzie looked at Suzy and gave her a soft wink. "You're exactly right. She sure will. But you three are going to become prunes if we don't get you out of here."

Suzy protested. "Aw, man."

"Come on," Lily coaxed.

All three climbed out, and Mackenzie wrapped them in towels. Then she led them toward the laundry room, where the first load of fresh, dry clothes was coming out of the dryer. Sandra held them out to the girls as if they carried the plague, but they didn't seem to notice. Once they were dressed, they went downstairs with Eugenia to enjoy what they were told was a Mexican fiesta, with a special request accompaniment of macaroni and cheese.

Mackenzie returned to her room and stood in her closet, surprised to find she actually wanted to put on real clothes. She stepped into dark-wash straight-leg jeans and pulled on a white V-necked T-shirt. Her red flats with the brushed-gold buckles sat at the ready, and she slipped her feet inside.

She went to the mirror and studied her face. Her eyes seemed virtually hollowed out from the weight she had lost. She must have looked as scary to those girls as Dimples's teeth.

She took a few minutes to put on some makeup and brush her teeth and for a moment act as if she were alive. For the first time in so long, she actually felt she might be.

She walked from her bathroom and saw the bright-red amaryllis standing tall in its container on the table. She remembered Gray bringing in something from Jeremiah, asking her if she knew what it meant. She hadn't known. And until this moment she hadn't really cared. She wondered about the meaning of that flower all the way downstairs.

Her mother's face registered a brief shock at her arrival in the kitchen. But as usual, Eugenia acted as if everything was normal. "You want to help that little one with her plate before it ends up on the floor?"

"Sure. I'd be glad to."

And the rest of the evening she helped her mother, her mother's crazy friends, and a far-less-frantic Jessica — who had stayed late without even being asked — to take care of those three girls.

While Lily, Toby, and Suzy ate ice cream at a long table by the bay window in the kitchen, Mackenzie sat down by their mother. "Your children are beautiful."

She nodded modestly. "Thank you. I believe they are as well."

"I'm sorry." Mackenzie shook her head. "I can't recall your name."

"It's Grace."

"Yes, right. Grace. Well, I'm sorry for what you've been through."

The woman turned her remarkable gray-green eyes toward Mackenzie. "We'll get through. That's what we do. We go through."

"Yep, not around or under. Right,

Mommy?" Suzy's face was still stuck in her bowl.

Her mother laughed as she ran her hand down the top of Suzy's clean head. "That's right, baby. Just through."

Mackenzie's hand dropped to the table as the impact of the words settled on her. They echoed in her mind as she sat there listening to childish pleas for more ice cream. Finally Grace announced that dessert was over and it was time for bed.

When Eugenia rose to clear the table and walked by, Mackenzie grabbed her mother's arm. "What's the amaryllis mean, Mama?"

Her mother looked at her, her face revealing nothing. "It means 'pride,' Mackenzie."

Mackenzie felt the force of the word. "Pride?"

"Yes, darling. And seems like we've all been dealing with our own form of it."

"How am I prideful, Mama?"

Eugenia shook her head gently, the way a mother would at her baby girl when she doesn't want to hurt her. "Self-pity can be pride. I'm not saying that's where you are now, but in any kind of loss, it can come hunting for us."

These words struck harder, the weight of them pressing Mackenzie deeper into the cushioned seat.

"It does have another meaning, though, that I think you should consider."

"Yeah?"

Eugenia shifted the sticky ice cream bowl to her other hand. "It means 'determination.' Something I always instilled in you." She picked up another bowl and walked toward the sink.

Mackenzie rose slowly. Suzy jumped from her chair. "Can we sleep with you, Miz Mackenzie?"

Mackenzie hesitated a second, then smiled. "I've got something even better than that for you." And before she had thought it through, she was standing at Maddie's door with Lily, Toby, and Suzy right behind her.

Her hand shook as she stood there. She felt one of the girls jostle another and whisper something. Then she opened the door slowly, revealing the room that had been virtually sealed as a tomb. Her baby girl's smell no longer lingered, but every ounce of her still seemed alive in that world of pink.

Mackenzie closed the door quickly. Her pulse raced.

"You okay, Miz Mackenzie?" Lily's hand was on her shoulder.

She looked down at the expectant face and exhaled slowly. She wanted to retreat.

Just run to her room, climb in bed, and pull the covers over her head. But she couldn't. Not now. If she did, she was pretty certain Suzy would come looking for her with twenty questions.

For some reason, that thought calmed her. She turned the knob and opened the door again. "Let's get you girls put to bed."

She tucked the two older girls into the twin beds and fixed Suzy a pallet on the floor — or a "palace," as she called it. Then she found a book and read them a story. Before she was through, each of them had fallen asleep.

Mackenzie pulled the covers up tight under Suzy's chin and marinated in the magic of a five-year-old. She didn't want to let it go. She wanted to grab it and bottle it up to pull out and enjoy whenever she wanted.

The light in Maddie's closet shone through the door she had left cracked at Suzy's suggestion. She walked to it and held the knob in her hand. These were waters she hadn't even dreamed of traveling. She let go of the knob and just stood there.

Not around or under. Just through.

She pulled it open, wide. Everything in there was just like it was the day Maddie died. She hadn't touched it, not one piece of it, though she suspected that Eugenia or the housekeepers had dusted and vacuumed.

She entered the closet and closed the door behind her. She ran her hands along the edges of Maddie's tulle "princess skirt" on its hanger. Maddie's shoes were all still neatly placed side by side, and the papers from her first couple days of school still sat on her bottom shelf.

Mackenzie took a construction paper booklet from the shelf. The first page read, *My World, by Maddie London.* Each following page held a drawing of how Maddie saw her world. There were stick figures of Mackenzie and Gray. A pretty good depiction of a fluffy dog, a wild-haired child she had to assume was Oliver, and a picture of Rosa's pancakes. And a tall, dark figure holding a flower.

It was Maddie's world, all right. It had been Mackenzie's world too. But grief had swallowed it whole. She had allowed that to happen.

She'd had a picture of her world too, a picture in her mind. She and Gray and at least two kids living out their lives together, doing what they were created to do, loving people, loving God. And then, when they were old, sitting on the front porch with their grandchildren.

It was such a beautiful picture. A perfect picture. And her life hadn't turned out anything like it. For that, she had rebuked heaven. Ever since Maddie died, in one way or another, that's what she'd been doing.

In that moment, the truth of how she'd lived the past six months washed over her and she knew: only she could have allowed it. Yes, the grief was real and thick. But she had chosen to let it all consume her. And only she could dig her way out.

She pulled more papers from the shelf and carefully studied them one by one, letting the pain and loss of what lay before her be felt. Telling herself, minute by minute, *Go through. Go through.*

Tears ran in steady streams down her face the whole time. Then she reached the last page, a half-drawn picture. The irony wasn't lost on her. Maddie's picture had never been finished. Nor had hers.

Mackenzie crumpled to her knees, pulling one of Maddie's shirts from a hanger as she did and stuffing it against her face to stifle her cries, cries that came from deep inside her. It felt like they'd been pushed so far down they had clogged up her soul. But as they were dislodged, so was something else.

Something even deeper. Something . . . healing.

Bursts of grief rushed through her for at least thirty minutes. When the tears finally subsided, she felt spent but somehow alive. The pain hadn't killed her. In fact, feeling it, experiencing it, going through it had actually allowed her to know she was alive.

She lowered her body to the floor and curled up on her side, the fine fiber of the carpet pressed against her cheek. "Forgive me," she whispered.

She spoke it for so many different reasons. But she spoke it first to herself. She had to in order to live. If she didn't let go of what she was holding against her own heart, she could never move forward. Then she spoke it to Maddie, as she had done many times before. But she determined this would be the last time. It had to end somewhere, and she was choosing for it to end here. *I'm so sorry, baby. Please forgive me.*

Finally she spoke it to heaven. She was coming to realize that heaven hadn't been holding her prisoner. Yes, God had allowed her to be crushed beneath a weight of grief she didn't feel anyone should have to carry, but it was she who had imprisoned her own soul. With self-pity? Yes, she knew it. It was self-pity that had held her in a prison of grief.

Not that the pain wasn't real. But somehow it had welded itself to resentment over the fact that real life didn't match her picture of it. She had assumed she deserved to have the life she wanted, and when that didn't happen, she had wanted to give up. For that, she told heaven she was sorry.

She lifted her head slightly and pulled the half-finished picture toward her. As she studied it, a soft seed of hope stirred, a thought that maybe, just maybe, an incomplete picture meant that there was something left for heaven to work with.

She couldn't imagine what her new picture might be. In fact, just believing that there might *be* one would be the biggest step of faith she had ever taken. And in that deep place in her soul, where the black pit that had all but swallowed her whole still existed as a reminder of what she could choose, she made a decision.

She didn't just take a step, though. Mackenzie London leaped.

CHAPTER 52

Eugenia kept her ear by the door of Maddie's bedroom while Mackenzie tucked in the three sisters. Dimples had told her earlier that Mackenzie had taken the girls to her bathroom. At least Dimples thought it was Mackenzie. "If it wasn't," she'd said, "there was another real attractive brunette rummaging around here, and you might want to call the police."

Berlyn assured Eugenia it was Mackenzie and told Dimples it was time for a new hearing aid to go with her one good eye. So the three of them had gone to check on Sandra in the laundry room. They found her stripped to her bra and granny panties and waiting on her own clothes to dry because she was certain they had all been contaminated. She swore she'd seen lice.

Eugenia confirmed her suspicion. She was pretty sure there were no lice, but at this point Sandra had driven her crazy, so saying there were lice brought satisfaction and some entertainment. The three friends watched Sandra strip off her remaining clothes quicker than they would have come off on her wedding night if God actually had a man on earth who could tolerate her. Eugenia had to fetch some of Mackenzie's sweats just so they wouldn't have to look at her.

Everybody had finally gotten settled for the night. Jessica had even come up with a big basket of bath oils and lotions and some nice pajamas to help Grace feel pampered and comfortable in the guest room. Eugenia had to admit that Jessica had more to her than anyone suspected. Not just starchy organization, but practical caring — and there was a lot to be said for practical caring.

When Mackenzie went into Maddie's room, Eugenia had felt a thud of panic collide with her airway. She wasn't sure how the events of the day would actually reveal themselves in Mackenzie's emotions. And she certainly hadn't planned on telling her about the flower. But Mackenzie had asked. Eugenia might have her faults, but she'd never believed in protecting people from the truth.

Life was what it was, and this was Mackenzie's life. So she had told her. Besides, she was still trying out this whole surrender thing too.

She stood there in the hallway for a long time, praying for Mackenzie. And when she finally heard stifled cries coming from inside, she'd felt some of her panic subside. Other than the day at the mall, Mackenzie had shown virtually no emotion since the miscarriage. As far as Eugenia was concerned, real crying was almost always a good thing. And though it took everything she had not to rush in there and wrap her arms around her baby girl and let her know everything would be okay, she knew Mackenzie needed this grief more than she needed her mama. She needed to feel the pain of everything she had lost.

Besides, truth be told, this day had worked out much better when Eugenia had surrendered it. Not that she'd ever in a million years tell Jeremiah he'd been right.

It was a while before she heard Mackenzie's sobs subside. And then there was nothing. Eugenia cracked open the bedroom door and saw light peeking out from beneath the tightly shut closet door.

She knew what the loss of Maddie had done to her own heart. But as a mother she had no idea what it was like to bury your child — let alone lose five more. As much as she tried, she couldn't fully understand Mackenzie's pain. All she did know was her deep pain at seeing her daughter hurt.

That was when a whisper came to the deepest place of her heart. *Mine too.* And then she realized. She knew that all this time there was a Father in heaven who had only one desire as well — to heal his children's hurt.

Eugenia looked up to the ceiling, where Maddie's fluorescent stars danced through the pink hue of a night-light. "Take care of her."

Never stopped.

JEREMIAH

My ride come and got me at five thirty like it always do. But I still keep prayin' after that. Ever'body know by now just to leave me alone when I prayin'. So when I got to my room, I just kneel down and keep on goin'.

Fought that battle good and hard. Let the Spirit pray through me like he ain't gone and prayed in a long time. He groan in ways only God know what he be sayin'. But I sure 'nough glad God know.

Don't know what happened to make that burden lift. But there come a moment in the middle a my prayin' when I knowed what need to be done, be done.

So when I climb on my bed, them springs squeak like they do, and I laid there and just had some knowin' come up all in me.

I knowed what tomorrow gon' bring. For the first time since our world's been rocked with that news 'bout our baby Maddie, we gon' have us some peace. That deep kind a peace. That peace our minds ain't able to understand. And I knowed what flower say all that best.

I laid there starin' up at that white ceilin', wonderin' how God done it all. Wondered what 'xactly he done. Best guess, Eugenia gots her hands all up in it like she do, but I ain't knowed for sure. Maybe God go pass him a real big miracle and get Eugenia to stay outta it.

One thing I know — I sure glad God let me be in on all this ruckus. Workin' at the mansion ain't 'xactly been my life's dream. But there ain't one day go by that I ain't grateful he let me work there. Ain't one day. And today I 'specially grateful.

CHAPTER 53

Darkness had settled before Gray felt a peace that the war he had been fighting could be surrendered — at least for now. In his entire life he had never prayed the way he prayed today, and he had never fasted. But the stakes had felt higher too. He truly felt that for the first time in his life he had fought something otherworldly.

He opened the door to find Sophie staring at him with that "Please take me out to the bathroom and then feed me" kind of look.

"Need to go potty?"

She jumped halfway up his leg.

"I'll take that as a yes."

On the way to his car he stopped and let her relieve herself, then assured her he would feed her once they got home.

The house was quiet except for a commotion coming from the kitchen. He pushed the swinging wood door and encountered

Eugenia and her cohorts, along with Rosa and Jessica, lounging around the breakfast table and chatting like schoolchildren. The rich aroma of coffee filled the room, setting his stomach to churning. He felt like he could eat now.

Rosa jumped from her seat. "Señor London, good evening, sir."

He motioned for her to sit. "Rosa, enjoy yourself. Whatever it is the six of you are talking about, it sounds way too good to interrupt."

"Please, señor, let me make you something to eat."

He placed his hands on her shoulders and gently pressed her back into her seat. "Sit, Rosa. I'm a big boy. Your workday is over. I'll get myself something."

She finally, reluctantly, sat.

He rested his hand on the table and looked at the women. Each had a sly expression on her face. "You all would be pitiful at poker."

Berlyn cleared her throat. "I'm actually the best one at my church."

"Your heathen church," Sandra added.

"Shut up," Eugenia shot out without looking at either of them. She stood, her eyes focused on Gray.

"Mack okay?" he asked.

"You should go see her."

His shoulders slumped. "Bad day?"

She took his hand between both of hers and patted it softly. "Perfect day. Go see her. She's in Maddie's closet."

He didn't understand. "Maddie's closet?"

"Just go see her, Gray. And pay no attention to the children in the room," she offered as he headed toward the kitchen door.

He heard Jessica snicker as he stopped and turned. He had never heard Jessica snicker. He had a feeling nothing would ever be the same after whatever had gone on here today. And he wasn't too sure all of it was a good thing. Not with Eugenia's friends involved.

"What have y'all done?" he asked.

Eugenia's smile was warm. "We just opened the door, Gray. But Mackenzie walked through it."

"Yep, opened it wide and she walked clear through it," Dimples confirmed. "At least I think it was her. Lord knows it could have been some other woman, but from best I could tell it was her."

Gray noticed that Sandra wore a pair of yoga pants and a red V-necked T-shirt. He stared at the miraculous — and strangely familiar — sight. "Sandra, your outfit — what are you wearing? Is that . . . Mackenzie's?"

Sandra looked down nervously at her clothes, then ran a hand across her bare throat before a rather satisfied look came across her face. "Well, I do believe it is. I'll be — I have a neck."

Eugenia was the first to laugh. And from there, laughter rippled across the table until even Sandra was laughing. Gray just shook his head. He wasn't sure he had ever seen Sandra laugh. He would check the liquor cabinet on the way upstairs.

Maddie's door was open a crack, and a stream of pink filtered out from her nightlight. He opened the door wider and saw three curly redheads — one in each of the twin beds and one on a pallet on the floor. It was Goldilocks on steroids. He had a moment of concern that whatever had happened here today would end up in the *Tennessean* by morning.

He tiptoed around the little body lying on the floor and walked to the closet. He pulled the door open as quietly as he could and found Mack asleep on the floor with one of Maddie's shirts tucked under her chin and a paper in her hand. How this could be good was beyond him.

He closed the door behind him and sat beside his wife. He ran his hands through her dark hair, the motion stirring her. She blinked, obviously trying to figure out where she was.

"Hey, babe. Gone to sleeping in closets now?"

She pushed herself up to a sitting position, and he noticed the change immediately. It was gone. That hopeless, lost look was gone.

She threw her arms around him and clung as if for dear life. "I'm sorry. I'm so sorry," she whispered over and over in his ear.

"It's okay." He pulled her close, kissing her hair. "It's okay."

"I'll do anything, Gray. I'll talk. I'll eat. I'll do anything. Please don't give up on me." Her words came out desperate against his ear.

He squeezed her tighter. "I would never give up on you. Don't even say that."

She held on for the longest time, and he savored her presence, her fear, her emotion — all of it. When she finally released him and leaned back, he cradled her face in his hands. "What happened, Mack?"

She shook her head. "I don't know. These kids were just here. And they kept asking me questions. And forcing me to respond."

"But who are they?" The confusion on his face must have been obvious because a hint of laughter filtered out of her.

Then it hit him: she had laughed.

He'd just heard Mack laugh.

He grabbed her head again and pulled it toward him, hugging her hard. She laid her head against his chest. And there in his embrace, she told him the entire story of the day.

". . . and then you woke me up."

He released her so he could study her face. It looked so different — like there was a piece of something alive there. But then fear rose up inside him.

"Where do we go from here, Mack? What is tomorrow going to look like? I don't want to lose you like that again. I thought —" his voice broke — "I thought I'd never get you back." His tears wouldn't obey his command not to fall. They didn't care if he was still the governor or not.

She wiped them away. "I don't know where we go from here. I'll start meeting with Ken again. I'll even meet with the psychiatrist. I know I need help with all of this. I can be willing to do it, but I can't do it by myself." She patted her hand gently on her chest. "I don't know what to do with all of it. All the pain that's still in here."

He nodded. "I know. Me neither."

"Can we do it together?"

"I'll do anything with you, Mack. You

495

know that."

She leaned her head on his chest again and let it rest there. "I need to ask you something though."

He ran his hand up and down her back. "Sure. Ask me anything."

"Do you blame me?"

"Blame you?"

"Yes, do you blame me for Maddie's death? It's okay if you do." She sat up as the words came out quickly. "I understand if you do. I just . . . need to know."

He stretched his legs out and brought them around her. He encased her waist with his arms. "I've told you this before, and it's true. I never blamed you. Never. What happened to Maddie was an accident . . . a horrible accident."

"But I —"

He placed a finger against her lips. "Babe, nothing in life is as it was meant to be. It was meant to be perfect, like the Garden of Eden. But that's gone now. What we've got now is a world full of broken people. And hurts and pains and sickness and accidents and death . . ."

His last words trailed off softly, and he leaned his head against hers. "But God has been right here in the middle of it all, with us. He's been grieving with us, fighting with us, cheering for us to hold on."

"But I've been so angry at God," she said. "I hated him, Gray."

He laughed. "I'm sure he knows that."

A soft smile swept over her face. "I thought he owed me the baby."

"I did too."

She hung her head. "He doesn't owe us anything, does he?"

He raised her chin. "Not a thing."

"Anything we have is just a gift, isn't it?"

He nodded. "Just a gift. But he sure gave us a beautiful gift in Maddie, even if we only had her for a little while. Think of it. Of all the people in the world to trust with her, he entrusted her to us."

Tears rushed to her eyes. "I didn't want to give her back. I still don't."

Gray's grief rose to life with her words. "Me neither."

And in that moment, for the first time, they shared grief. Truly shared grief. There on the floor of their baby's closet, they wept . . . together, as husbands and wives were meant to.

After a while Mack wiped her face with the sleeve of her T-shirt. She picked up Maddie's shirt, which had fallen to the floor beside her. "I've got to let go. If I'm going to make it, I've got to let go. That little girl out there, the one asleep on the floor — her name is Suzy."

"Suzy?"

She smiled. "Yeah, Suzy. But she — she's just so Maddie. I mean her spunk, her wit, her questions. Oh my word, that child asks more questions. Anyway, she and Maddie are about the same size. So I was thinking, would you mind if I packed up Maddie's clothes and sent them with her? And I could pack up some of Maddie's toys for her and her sisters and send the rest on over to the mission."

Gray tilted his head. "You sure? We can take this one step at a time."

She nodded. "I'm sure. It's time, Gray. I've got to live again. And I can't do that by holding on to the past or pretending the whole thing never happened."

Gray pulled her a little closer to him. "What if there never is another child for us, Mack? What if we've had all we'll ever have?"

He could see the thought settle on her, and he wondered if he had pushed too hard. Maybe he shouldn't have even gone there. Could one word propel her back to that horrible place where she had been just that morning?

"There are always children to be loved,

Gray," she finally said, "whether they come from this broken body or someone else's. If I love them for a day or a lifetime, there will always be children to love. And I think I'm supposed to do that."

His heart settled back into place as she smiled at him. "And I'm good at it. I'm good at loving babies, Gray."

He kissed her softly. "Yes, you are. You are so good at it. Now, are you ready to go sleep in a real bed?"

"I'm actually tired of sleeping in that bed. And I just had a nap."

"Well, then, are you hungry? 'Cause I'm starving. And two of the best cooks in Nashville are still down there in our kitchen."

She licked her lips. "I want chocolate gravy and biscuits."

His eyes widened. "And bacon."

They were on a roll now. "And fried eggs." Her chuckle was thick and rich.

He stood and pulled her from the floor. He knew they still had a long way to go. And yet he allowed himself to think the words he'd wanted to say for so long now: *My Mack is back.*

CHAPTER 54

She held the tiny pink ballerina skirt in her hands and didn't even attempt to stop the tears. Cleaning out Maddie's closet was one of the hardest things Mackenzie had ever done. Both Gray and her mother had offered to help, but she knew this was something she needed to do herself. She needed to feel every feeling, relive every memory before she let them go. So while her mother and her allies had Grace and her children downstairs, feeding them a big old Southern breakfast laden with cholesterol and starches, she was packing up her baby's clothes. She'd send the toys later. This was all she could do today.

After she had told Gray the story about who the girls' father was, they knew they needed to do something. She had asked Grace to meet with them before leaving the mansion. Even though Gray had told her last night that he was no longer going to run.

"Did you want to talk to me?"

The tall woman hesitated at the entrance to the family room. Her gaze strayed to three large boxes beside the couch where Mackenzie sat.

"Come in," Mackenzie said as warmly as she could to the stranger in her doorway.

"Thank you." The woman's words were also warm, though her eyes were wary. She stepped into the family room, the toes of her flats completely rubbed free of their brown faux leather.

"Please sit." Mackenzie motioned to the other sofa. Grace sat down, and Mackenzie moved to sit beside her. Gray remained across from them. "Grace, thank you for spending the evening with us."

A gentle smile swept over the woman's thin face. She pushed away a strand of hair that had fallen by her left eye. "Your home is beautiful. We appreciate it so much."

Mackenzie smiled. "I loved every minute of it." She paused and gestured toward the boxes. "I had a little girl. She was so much like Suzy. And, well . . . she passed away last year. And Gray and I had never gotten rid of her clothes. Would you be offended if

I gave them to Suzy?"

Compassion and a shared sorrow were immediately evident in Grace's green eyes. "Oh my, that's a lot of boxes."

"Yeah, one is nothing but dress-up clothes. Maddie loved to be a princess."

"My Suzy is certain she is Cinderella." Grace's countenance shifted. "It's really sweet of you to offer, Mrs. . . . um, First Lady."

"Call me Mackenzie."

Grace reached down and pushed at the velvet cushion beneath her as if resituating herself. "Well, the thing is, we just don't have nowhere to keep all that stuff."

Gray finally spoke. "We've thought about that."

"Yes. My mother's friend Berlyn has a guest apartment that isn't being used right now. It's not huge or anything, but it would be a good place for you and the girls to get back on your feet. Her husband died a few years back, and if you have your license, she never got rid of his car, so you could use that. And we could help you find a job."

The woman stood up quickly. Gray and Mackenzie stood too.

"No, no, this is too much. I mean, it's really nice, but if you knew what my husband had done, you'd never —"

Gray and Mackenzie exchanged glances. "Grace, we do know," Gray said quietly. "In fact, we know all too well what your husband did. But we also know that you and your babies had nothing to do with it."

Mackenzie placed a hand on Grace's shoulder. "We want to help you and your girls, Grace. They're so smart. And so polite. And so sweet. You did that. Your influence, your parenting created these inquisitive, charming children. They came from you. And we just want to help you catch a break. Will you let us do that?"

Grace shifted from foot to foot. "I can't do it for free. I'll have to pay you something."

Mackenzie nodded. "Berlyn already has some ideas for places you can get a job. Some of them are even within walking distance of her house. And the schools are good. We can get the children enrolled immediately."

Tears surfaced in Grace's eyes as the impact of the offer settled over her. "What can I say?"

Mackenzie wrapped her arms around her. "Nothing. Your babies did something for me last night that no one has been able to do. Please just accept this as a gift in return for the gift you gave me."

■ ■ ■ ■

Over the next hour, they piled Grace and the girls into Berlyn's car and finally got all of them out of the house. Eugenia was the last to go, but that was because poor Dimples had gashed her head when she misjudged how far the front door was open. When the cut was bandaged and the circus finally left town, Mackenzie and Gray stood at the door and let out simultaneous sighs.

Mackenzie turned and started up the stairs. "We need to talk" was all she said.

Gray followed her to their family room. "What is it?" She heard the concern in his voice.

She sat on the sofa and tucked her legs underneath her. "I don't want you to drop out of the race."

The tension on his face eased. He sat beside her on the sofa. "Mack, I know you feel better, but there is still so much healing for us to do. We talked through all that last night. You are in no condition to rush anything here. We have to deal with everything that has happened to us. It's been so much."

She nodded slowly. "I agree. We need all of that. But if there is anything inside you that wants to run, I want to do this with you."

He shook his head. "We're too broken to be running a state."

"Look, if what's real doesn't have the opportunity to reside in this house, then how can it reside in any other house in our state? We're not perfect, and we shouldn't act like we are."

He dropped his jaw in mock astonishment. "What? You're not perfect? I thought you were."

She slapped at him. "I'm serious. We've been through a lot. We're not superhuman, and people need to see that. They need to know it's okay to hurt and to get help."

"Well, we can't work though this and be out on a campaign trail."

She shook her head. "You can't win an election without campaigning."

"No, Mack. I'm not doing it. When we found out you were pregnant, we pushed all of that Maddie pain down and didn't deal with it, and look where it got us. This is fresh and new, and we're not doing that again."

"But —"

He held up a finger. He bit his bottom lip and turned his head slightly. She could tell he was thinking.

"What?"

He shook his head as if it were a crazy thought. "How about this? I'll only run under one condition — no campaign trail. At least not the way we've ever done it before."

"Then how do you propose to campaign?"

"You want us to be transparent and honest?"

She hesitated. "Yes."

"Do you really? Do you really want to offer this state something it's never seen?"

She really did. This time her voice was strong and sure. "Yes. I do. With you."

"Then we'll do one interview that can be aired on all the stations in the state. And we'll do one commercial that can do the same. And we will simply be honest about everything. About this last year. About our pain. About our continued battle for our family. About my decisions for balancing the budget and why I made them and about the tragedy that was a part of it. That's it. No bus. No road trips. No twenty-four-hour days and endless pummeling to our bodies or our minds. And if we win, we win. If we lose, we lose."

She laid a hand on his knee. "Are you going to tell them what we've done for Grace and her kids?"

He didn't hesitate. "No, there's no need. People will think we've done it for publicity. And they've been through enough."

"What if someone finds out?"

"I don't care," he said. "For the first time in my life, I truly don't care what anyone thinks. I have lost my daughter. I almost lost my wife. They can have this house, they can have this title, or they can have a man who isn't perfect but is committed to fighting for them. We're going to share our stuff. All of it."

She could tell by the look on his face that he was serious. "It's not pretty stuff, is it?"

He threw an arm around her and pulled her close. "No," he said, "but it's ours."

"Aren't we lucky," she said as she buried her head in the middle of his chest. He softly kissed the top of her head. And there was no place on earth she felt safer.

They canceled Gray's scheduled press conference and set up the interview for the following Friday. Gray wanted to start meeting with a counselor before they moved forward. The state could wait or move on. Either was fine with him.

And on Monday morning, Joseph brought a beautiful bouquet of white tulips up to Mackenzie, along with a scrawled note. It was clear it was from Jeremiah.

Miz Mackenzie — ain't gon' make you go and search for what these here flowers mean. They be tulips, you good and well know. Be the flower of spring. And they mean "perfect love." That be the only thing could do what been done 'round here. They mean "forgiveness" too, 'cause without it, can't no healin' ever really happen.

She ran her fingers across a silky white petal, grateful for both the flower and the man who sent it.

CHAPTER 55

Eugenia straightened her clunky gold necklace as she got out of the car. She'd told Mackenzie she would pick her up and take her to the rescue mission tonight, but first she had something to do. She walked straight out to the back gardens and found Jeremiah sitting under a tree, drinking bottled water.

She tossed a bag at him. "There. I had to go everywhere but Timbuktu to find those."

His long fingers reached inside the bag and pulled out a box of navy-blue handkerchiefs. A big white smile stretched across his freckled brown face. "Well, I'll be. You gone and found me some handkerchiefs I can sweat on."

She huffed. "It's ridiculous. I've never seen a man so adamant about what kind of handkerchiefs he needs. You're worse than a woman."

He pushed himself to his feet, then wiped

dirt from his backside, holding on to the bag with his other hand. "Know why these be so special to me?"

She poked at a stiff blonde strand the breeze had rearranged. "I have no idea."

"My Shirley bought me some right after we got married. Ain't cared nothin' 'bout 'nother color since."

Eugenia had forgotten he had lost his spouse too. The loss was pretty fresh, like hers. She crinkled her brow. "You told me you used them because of the dirt."

"That sure 'nough true. But ain't why I first gone and got 'em." He put a new handkerchief under his nose and inhaled long and deep. "Ah. Love me the smell a new stuff."

She had no idea how often Jeremiah actually got new things. And seeing him with his nose against a fresh blue handkerchief, she suddenly felt a twinge of pain for how she had treated him. She looked at her gold watch and saw that she had to go.

"Well, enjoy," she said, turning on her heel. "But you'd better get back to work because your Lenten roses look like . . . Well, I'm Southern and a lady, so I won't say it, but it starts with a *c* and ends with a *p*."

The snide comment seeped out of her as

effortlessly as her hands could make a seven-layer chocolate cake. Sure, she felt a twinge of guilt over it — but only a twinge. And as she walked away, she heard him chuckle.

She didn't let him see that she chuckled too.

CHAPTER 56

Mackenzie's friends were waiting in the foyer of the mission after she came through the metal detector. It was the first time she had been back since she lost the baby. She had asked Eugenia to bring her.

"Mama, I've got to do the hard things or I'll never do them again," she'd said. Eugenia had agreed. So they were here — with some reinforcements. Eugenia had decided her friends needed to come too. She'd told them that they were getting old and narcissistic and needed to think of somebody else for a while. But she suspected they'd agreed to come because they were getting bored with Skip-Bo.

"Welcome back!" Anna pulled Mackenzie into a hug. "We held the fort down."

Mackenzie leaned her head on her friend's shoulder. "I had no doubt."

Eugenia pushed Mackenzie and Anna toward the elevator and up to the kitchen, where Harrison had already put Berlyn, Sandra, and Dimples to work. Berlyn was slicing tomatoes. Sandra was putting silverware out. And since Dimples wasn't allowed to play with sharp objects, she was wiping off dinner trays.

But Dimples was sneaky. When Sandra wasn't looking, she grabbed a fork and snagged a carrot from one of the steam trays.

"If you take another one, I'll fork you." Sandra held up her own utensil and turned it in her hand, making sure Dimples saw it no matter which eye she was looking with.

Harrison looked at Mackenzie. "How'd you come out so normal?"

She pulled a plastic cap over her hair. "Who knows?"

Eugenia brought a large tray of lettuce to the serving line. "Girls, if you can't act right, I won't take you out anymore."

Berlyn put her knife down. "Well, I vote that the next time we go out, we at least go to a place where there are men — preferably men with jobs."

"Yeah," Dimples said. "Social Security is *tight*."

"Y'all don't need men. You need to be put in a home," Sandra quipped as she patted the bobble necklace that hung in the deep *V* of her blouse.

Berlyn giggled. "As long as it's a home with men."

Harrison stuck his fingers in his ears and started singing.

Mackenzie laughed. "You're scaring him."

"Scaring him?" Eugenia flailed her hand in Harrison's direction. "They're scaring *me.*"

"Hey, you brought them," Mackenzie reminded.

Berlyn turned to Sandra. "Why are you acting so self-righteous, anyway? We finally got you set free from high-collared shirts. Now it's time to find you a man."

Eugenia nearly gasped when she saw Dimples's good eye wander toward Harrison. "Dimples, don't even think about it," she whispered sharply.

Dimples lowered her head quickly and scrubbed hard at the tray in her hands.

"I just started going through the change," Sandra said. "That's why I had to wear cooler tops."

"Change-schmange, Sandra. You're practically the same age as me," Berlyn shot back. "You haven't had the use of your girl parts for as long as I've gone without sex."

Eugenia could see Dimples trying to do the calculations in her head. If she didn't stop her, she might hurt herself. Berlyn must have seen it too. "It's been fifteen years, Dimples. Herbert died fifteen years ago."

Berlyn raised her eyebrows at Eugenia. Eugenia shook her head. She could only hope it had been fifteen years.

"I have all of my parts, for your information," Sandra said.

Harrison glanced at the clock. "Oh, looky there — we've got to go to work."

The doors opened, and women and children began filing in. A little girl with black curls was at the front of the line, balanced on her mother's hip. Eugenia looked up just in time to see Mackenzie disappear around the corner.

And her heart stopped.

Mackenzie knew what she had to do. It was one of the reasons she'd wanted to come to the mission tonight — to get it over with. One more first time among all the first times that remained ahead of her.

The first visit to an elementary school for a curriculum meeting.

The first movie with Gray and without Maddie.

The first warm spring day without a child to go to the park with.

One at a time, she was determined to tackle them all. It was all about going through. In fact, she was beginning to realize that it was in the going through — not the avoiding — that God had promised to be with her.

Letting the kitchen door close behind her, she approached a young woman in the front of the line, the one with the beautiful black-haired baby. "Can I hold your little girl while you fix your tray?"

The woman studied Mackenzie and finally nodded. Mackenzie took the little one in her arms and pulled her close to her chest. Her friends serving in the line all seemed to be holding their breath, waiting for her to collapse, scream, do something that they thought looked like the face of grief.

But this was grief too. She was doing grief, doing it the way she had to do it in this particular season. She was holding the very thing she didn't have and realizing that babies were still going to be born in this world. Every day, someone was going to have one. She was going to encounter them in grocery stores and gas stations and here at the mission. And those babies would never be hers. She had no choice about that. She could only choose to run from them or run to them.

"Hey, pumpkin," she said, bouncing the baby on her hip.

The girl reached up and pulled at Mackenzie's long hair. "Yeah, that's my hair. I wish I had your curls, though," she said, fingering black ringlets.

The baby jumped in her arms as she spotted her mother coming with a tray, her little face lit up with excitement. Mackenzie followed the mother to a table and settled the little one in a high chair. For the rest of the evening, she did this with baby after baby after baby.

There were a couple of moments when all the what-ifs wanted to rage to the surface. But she mentally set them aside, knowing the what-if game would rob her of the ability to live in the what-could-bes.

This was her life.

And she had chosen to live it.

"Thank you, Lord," Eugenia whispered under her breath when she saw Mackenzie walk into the cafeteria. She had feared for a brief moment that they might be carrying her daughter out on a stretcher, and without thinking, she had started after her. But then she stopped, feeling strongly that she wasn't to follow her. That this was now about Mackenzie's journey to her own healing.

Besides, once they started serving, she was too busy to worry about Mackenzie. It was her job to fix the salads. Berlyn dipped the whipped potatoes and gravy. Sandra served the veggies. Harrison served the meat, and Dimples passed out rolls, most of which actually made it to the plates, while Anna and the other volunteers kept them all well-stocked with food.

From her vantage point, Eugenia could see bittersweet delight on her baby girl's face and tears that she swiped throughout dinner. She felt a lump rise in her throat at the thought of all that the last year had brought her and her family. Then she looked at the faithful friends beside her and felt how truly blessed she was. She also thought about Jeremiah, the steady and faithful man who was as kind as she was ornery. How he had been so steady in loving her family. She might even find it in her heart to cut him some slack about that garden.

A loud clang came from the end of the line and stirred her thoughts back to the present. She looked down the aisle to see Dimples pop up from underneath the counter. She rose with two rolls in her hand. "It's all good!" she announced.

And it was. Their hearts would never be the same. Broken like that never heals completely, and Eugenia wouldn't want it to. She didn't want to be the same.

She wanted to be better.

She was standing here with her good friends, serving food to people who needed it. And looking out into the dining room, watching joy and sorrow and determination do their dance on her daughter's face as she ran headlong into her healing. And she had just given Jeremiah Williams a box of handkerchiefs. Blue handkerchiefs.

If that wasn't a sign of *better,* she didn't know what was.

CHAPTER 57

Lights had taken over the living room, along with three cameras that had been set up to deliver Mack and Gray's story to Tennesseans. Dan Miner, an anchor for the NBC affiliate, adjusted his lapel mic and checked his notes, preparing for the interview.

It had been a long week. Kurt, Fletcher, and the rest of the staff had been working on the launch of Gray's unusual campaign — making plans, talking to donors and supporters, as well as trying to keep the business of state rolling along. More importantly, Gray and Mackenzie had been to see Ken Jantzen three times this week. The sessions were exhaustingly painful, yet hopeful too. Getting out pain that severe could wear you out, but it also freed you.

Every night that week, he and Mack had crawled into bed at nine. The first couple of nights, he'd been afraid to close his eyes. Afraid that in the morning she would decide it wasn't worth getting up anymore. But every morning, there she was.

There were tears, of course, and anger, but she was getting up and facing each day. And he was too. They were doing it together.

Mack walked into the living room, her spring-green dress moving softly against her hips. She was still too thin, but her beauty was undeniable, and he loved seeing a hint of color in her cheeks. She extended her hand to the news anchor, and a wide gold bracelet dangled from her delicate wrist.

The reporter turned to him. "Well, Governor, we're ready if you are."

Gray looked at Mackenzie. "You ready, babe?"

She nodded, apprehension evident on her face. He leaned toward her, his voice low. "We don't have to do this. It is not too late for us to change our minds."

She shook her head firmly. "No. We can do it. Like Ken said, this can be part of our healing." She straightened his baby-blue tie. "Did you wear this for me?" She smiled. "Because it makes your eyes look electric."

He nodded. He had. He loved to wear blue for her, and he loved it even more that she was finally noticing him again.

"Okay, then." He took her hand and led her to two chairs that sat in front of a large window overlooking the gardens. Gray unbuttoned his khaki sports coat and pulled at the bottom of his tie as he sat. Cameras started rolling, and Dan began.

"Governor, the people of Tennessee know that this has been a difficult year for you and your wife. And we are here today because you requested this. What is it that you and Mrs. London want to share with the state of Tennessee?"

Gray and Mackenzie simultaneously let out deep exhales. Then he began to tell their story. He covered everything from Maddie's death to the miscarriage to the counseling to their decision to run for reelection without a traditional campaign.

"And are you concerned about the lawsuit from the Victims' Rights Association that goes to trial in a few weeks?" Dan asked.

"We are confident the court will see that we were making decisions based on what we believed was best for all Tennesseans. And we had been left with few options."

"What about the new budget that the General Assembly has passed? Do you plan on vetoing any of it?"

"I am committed to my original statement. If the Assembly has kept in earmarks that I believe are detrimental to this state and its budget, I won't let them remain, and

I believe we have enough votes for my vetoes to stand. And then these grown men and women will be left to face the voters as well for the decisions that they have made."

"And your opponents?"

"My opponents are formidable and, I believe, capable. I can tell you, moreover, that this will not be a campaign of mudslinging from my camp. I will engage in open and honest debate, and my team will not respond to anything other than that."

The anchor turned his attention to Mackenzie. "Mrs. London, as we wrap this up, are you sure you're ready for this campaign?"

She looked at Gray, then back toward Dan. She shook her head. "No. Honestly, Dan, I'm not sure what I'm going to feel like ten minutes after you leave, much less what I'm going to feel like tomorrow. I'm just at the point where I'm making myself get out of bed every morning and not wishing my life away. I have no guarantees for anyone."

She reached down and clasped her husband's hand. "All I know is I'm alive. For some reason, I wasn't killed in that car accident that day, which in and of itself is a miracle. My grief didn't kill me, though sometimes I wished it would. But it appears

I'm going to live. And right now, in this moment, that is what I'm doing. I'm living."

As the interview ended, the cameras shut down, and the room emptied. And thus began a new kind of campaign.

One that Gray and Mackenzie London would deal with one day at a time.

CHAPTER 58

Election Day

Gray looked at his friends, who were crammed into the family quarters living room. All eyes were glued to three televisions — one tuned to Fox, one to CNN, and the third to the local NBC affiliate. The news that Gray had won reelection had been announced on the NBC affiliate first, but within seconds Fox started carrying it, and right after that, CNN announced it as well. An explosion of cheers burst forth with each announcement.

The shirttail of Gray's blue oxford shirt had come out of his pressed khakis three hours ago. It was nearing midnight now. He had downed multiple glasses of Eugenia's fruit tea and OD'd on Rosa's chili con queso.

Kurt grabbed him first, his bald head looking even shinier than it had four years ago. He wrapped his friend in a tight hug and patted his back hard. "I'm so proud of you," he said.

Gray hugged him back. "Thank you, buddy. I couldn't have done it without you."

"You are the one who did it. You took the risk on the budget, and it paid off. And your transparency about the prisoner release was key in making the VRA case go our way."

"Hear, hear!" Fletcher joined them, the ends of his bow tie hanging loosely around his neck, his top two shirt buttons undone.

"Look," Gray announced, "we even got Fletcher loosened up."

Everyone laughed, and Gray gave his friend a hug. "You kept the information flowing out there, Fletch. Thank you."

"You and Mack made it easy, Gray."

After everyone had kissed and hugged and high-fived, Gray and Mack waved them off and returned to the wreckage of their victory party. Plates and cups were strewn about. Most of the staff had celebrated with them, but Gray and Mack refused to let them clean up afterward. Gray had told them that after everything was prepared and served, they were off duty and allowed to do nothing but have a good time. They really had seemed to enjoy themselves and were thrilled with the outcome. Their response had spoken to Gray more than any other constituents'.

Mack surveyed the damage. "Well, did you think your first act as a second-term governor would be cleaning up your living room?"

He laughed. "At least I get to do it with the first lady. Don't tell her husband, okay?"

She eyed him. Her lips curled. "Mum's the word." As she began to stack plates, he went downstairs to get a trash bag from the kitchen.

"I didn't know if it would work," she said when he reappeared.

"Honesty?" he asked.

"Yeah, honesty. It is politics, you know."

He chuckled. "I think that's why it did work. It's so rare. It took everyone by surprise."

She dropped a stack of plastic plates and empty cups into the large black bag. "Fine dining at the governor's mansion." She laughed. "I'm a great hostess, aren't I?"

He kissed her on the nose. "Perfect."

When the last plate was thrown away, they headed toward the bedroom. He stopped at the door. "I'm going to go make a phone call real quick, and Sophie needs to go out."

"Go ahead. I'm going to bed."

Gray walked to his office with Sophie at his heels and picked up the phone. He dialed and sat on the edge of his desk to wait for someone to answer. A man's voice came on the line.

"This is Governor London. I know it's late, but is there any way I could speak to Jeremiah Williams, please?"

"Yes . . . um, sure, Governor. Hold one moment."

It was quite a few moments before he heard Jeremiah pick up the phone. "Gov'nor." Jeremiah's voice was just as fresh as it had been when he had left. "Hear you gots sump'n worth celebratin' tonight."

"Yeah. Sure wish you had stayed with us tonight. I could've gotten you home, you know."

Jeremiah chuckled. "You the gov'nor — I know you could. Just needed to come on with my ride, though. But I seen it all on the TV. Real proud a you and Miz Mackenzie, Gov'nor. Real proud."

"Thanks. Just wanted to tell you you're stuck with us for four more years."

"Hee-hee. Well, I guess I can live with that."

"That means you'll have Eugenia too."

"Ooh, Lord amercy. Well, some things in life worth the sacrifice they come with."

Gray hesitated a minute, knowing how much meaning was packed into those words. "Yes, they are, my friend," he finally said.

"Sleep well. I hope I didn't mess your night up too much."

"I'll get up for a call from the gov'nor anytimes," he said. "Anytimes."

Mack was in the bathroom doing her thing when Gray and Sophie came back to the room. He leaned into the doorway. "You sure are cute."

She was slathering some kind of cream onto her face. Her bare legs showed underneath her short black nightgown. "Why, thank you," she said.

"Want to make love to the governor?"

She looked at his face in the mirror and shook her head. "Nah."

His eyes widened. She hadn't turned him down since she'd come back to life.

She turned around with mischief on her face. "But I would love to make love to my husband." She walked over to stand very close. "Now he, well, he is quite a man. Have you met him?"

"I think I have," he said. "Tall, good-looking fellow. I'd call a man like that a specimen."

She giggled. "Yes, he is. Definitely a specimen. And he has gorgeous blue eyes." She brushed past him and headed to her side of the bed.

"Yeah, I hear they really pop when he wears blue." He started unbuttoning his blue oxford.

"They do. He really does it for me."

"So you're sure you'd rather have him than the governor?"

She climbed into bed and pulled the covers up to her chin. He reached down and straightened his side, pulling the top sheet over the duvet as best he could.

"Absolutely," she said. "Who wants the governor when you can have a specimen like I have." She bit her lip, obviously trying not to let laughter break loose.

"Well, you had your shot."

"I appreciate it."

He laid his shirt on the end of the bed and took off his belt. "Mind if I go find your husband?"

"Not at all." She curled up on her side, watching him.

He picked up his shirt and walked into the bathroom. He came out in a T-shirt and a pair of nylon running shorts. "I hear you've been talking about me."

"Good thing you're here. The governor tried to seduce me."

"Oh, he did?" He punched on the fan and slid beneath the covers, trying to keep his side of the sheet as straight as he could. He had long ago given up trying to straighten her side. Besides, with what he had in mind, the sheets were bound to get a little out of place.

He lifted his arm and she slid underneath it, settling her head next to his. She nuzzled his ear. "Didn't work," she whispered.

"He doesn't know the specimen I am, does he, babe?"

"Nope." And with that, she lost it. The laughter came from her toes and sent her rolling to her side of the bed. And everything they had gone through and fought for and fought through was worth that laughter.

Gray grabbed her and pulled her back toward him, but it was no use. She was useless. It would be ten minutes before she got control of herself, and he enjoyed every minute.

When the laughter had subsided and the lovemaking was over, she nestled under his arm again. "I love you, Gray London."

"I love you too, Mack. So what are we going to do these next four years?"

She pressed her mouth next to his ear. "Live," she whispered.

He couldn't think of anything he'd rather do.

Or anyone he'd rather do it with.

CHAPTER 59

The shipment came to the front door. Joseph brought it up to Mackenzie. And it was perfect. She had searched everywhere for just the right one. It would grow beautifully in the garden, but now wasn't the right time of year. She had chosen the container a while back and knew it would be perfect in Jeremiah's workroom if that was where he needed to keep it. In the winter months he spent just as much time in there repairing tools and taking care of bulbs as he did outside.

She looked for him downstairs first. The workroom was dark and quiet. So she headed out into the coolness of the November morning and found him tending to some broken slate in one of the walking areas around the pool.

She extended the container, the flower hanging from it in an elegant yet humble way. Which didn't surprise her, since "humility" was one of its meanings.

"This is for you," she said.

He unfolded his long legs and stood — a little more slowly than last year. "Oh, Miz Mackenzie, that be just 'bout the purtiest lily a the valley I ever see. But ain't that time a year. How you get it?"

She smiled. "I searched high and low, but I finally found one. It was the only flower that said what I wanted it to say."

He took it from her hands.

"Jeremiah, do you know what you mean to me?"

The look on his face showed he did. She saw the whites of his eyes expand and tears flood them quickly.

"We wouldn't have made it through all this without you. Not any of us. Not me. Not Gray. Not even my mother, though she'd never admit it."

He shook his head. Hard.

She laughed. "I know — right? No words for that."

"Ain't gon' lie, Miz Mackenzie. If I was a drinkin' man . . ."

"I know. My father used to say the same thing. 'If I was a drinking man, I'd have drunk myself to death by now.' "

They both laughed. "I know I don't have to tell you what a lily of the valley means," she said.

He cocked his head. "Can't say I do know what that one mean."

She played along. "It means 'return to happiness.' That's what I feel has happened with us. And you are a huge part of that."

He shook his head. "Ain't done much 'cept raise flowers and pray."

"Act humble if you will, but it's true. You pressed us. You pushed our buttons. You opened our hearts. Then you dug in like the gardener you are and tilled our very soil until a seed came to life."

"Ain't never found hearts more worth diggin' in."

She stood on her tiptoes and wrapped her arms around his neck. "And I haven't found a man worth loving like I love you since I met Gray London." The tears came quickly as she hugged him.

She leaned back, and he handed her a blue handkerchief. "They new. Well, sorta new. Your mama gone and bought 'em back in March. 'Bout near killed her, but she done it."

Mackenzie laughed and blew her nose. "It has another meaning, you know. The lily of the valley."

"Really? What that be?"

"It also means 'you've made my life

complete.' "

He bowed his head low in that humble
way of his. She lifted his chin. "I mean it,
Jeremiah. Our life here would not be complete without you in it. I'm sorry you've
gone through what you've gone through to
get here. But I am selfishly grateful that you
are here."

"Ain't nothin' happened to me ain't gone
through him first." He pointed toward the
brilliant-blue Tennessee sky. "Figure if he
think I can handle it, I can handle it. But I
do thank you. Ain't never heard words any
kinder."

They stood there for a moment, smiling,
the flower between them in Jeremiah's
hands.

"Okay, then." Mackenzie clapped her
hands together. "Jessica has a plan for my
day."

" 'Course she do." He grinned. "And I
bet for tomorrow too."

JEREMIAH

Inauguration Day

"Big day, huh, Jeremiah?"

I laid my suit coat on the metal table. "Yep, Harvey. Big day."

"Back to the real world now, huh?"

The concrete wall stare back at me like it always do. "Sure 'nough."

"Hate to do this to you."

"Don't 'pologize for what you do. Man gots to work." He always do it fast, though, and I always grateful 'bout that. But it don't never get less humiliatin'.

I pick my clothes up off the table and walk through them metal doors. They lock behind me as loud and sure as they have ever' day these last thirty years. And there ain't been one day since then that my body ain't jolt when they do.

I take me a cold shower — ain't no such thing as a hot one 'round here — and walk to my cell. They fed us so good today, I ain't even a li'l bit hungry. I full up and bone weary.

I gone and sat down on my bunk, mattress as thin as the skin on the back a my legs. I lay my ol' tired body down and look up at that ceilin', and it like the whole day play out in front a me. Gov'nor on that platform bein' sworn in. Miz Mackenzie standin' by him in that gold dress a hers. Ain't never seen her purtier. And that happy smile on her face — I ain't never thought I gon' see that smile again.

Miz Eugenia, she be all decked out too. Even smiled at me once. I 'bout near thinkin' she got her a crush on me. Make me shiver just thinkin' 'bout it.

They even invite me to that big ol' luncheon in the capitol rotunda. Most a them men ain't even knowed who I be. Ain't knowed I wake up this mornin' in a cell. Just 'cause I be at that lunch, they prob'ly think I somebody 'portant.

And know what? It be true. I 'portant to the gov'nor and Miz Mackenzie — so 'portant they sat me and Rosa right at the same table with Eugenia herself. And she ain't been able to say one word to me 'bout that pitiful centerpiece 'cause florist from downtown do it.

I ain't never had people been so good to

me as the gov'nor and his family — 'cept maybe that warden show up here 'bout the same time I did. He like me — ain't never knowed why. He always say, "J. W., I know you ain't done what they say."

And I ain't. I ain't killed the owner a that flower shop where I be workin'. But thirty years ago, black mens all look the same to old white women. We ain't had real faces or real names. We just be black. All it take was her sayin' she seen me come outta there late one night, and the next mornin' they found him dead. Twelve white people done believe I did it. Judge give me seventy-five years, no chance a parole. Sentence like that, I be dead 'fore I ever saw light a day.

But that warden knowed I didn't do it. Shirley knowed. And my babies knowed. And I knowed. That be what really matter. And when that warden get me the job at the mansion, I ain't never felt freer. Not 'cause I really free. But 'cause somebody seen who I really be.

That be the day I set myself free too — 'cause that the day I knowed God knowed I innocent too. And once that happen, I seen myself different. Ain't walked 'round shameful. I walked 'round with some respect.

My Shirley, she always say that when God make you innocent, can't nobody make you guilty. I knowed that even if I did pull that trigger they swore I pulled, God could still make me innocent. And he really did, I guess. 'Cause in all the years I been workin' at the mansion, ain't nobody ever gone and talked 'bout my past.

Ever' gov'nor and his wife I work for been aware a my story. And ain't a one treated me like a guilty man. I just figure they thinkin', if the warden here trust me with the first family, then maybe I worth trustin'. I also be wonderin' if maybe God help 'em a little — help 'em know what be true.

Gov'nor and Miz Mackenzie the only ones that trust me with they baby, though. Guess that be why I love 'em so much. But I liked that gov'nor before Gov'nor London too. He the one bought me them there green overalls. Said I ain't looked good in orange. But I knowed what he really sayin'. He want me to see myself like he saw me.

That done my heart more good than I ever be able to tell him. Give me a piece a my dignity back. Give me hope maybe someday they find out who really gone and killed that florist fella.

I was prayin' they'd find out sooner so I could close out life with Shirley in our own bed, kissin' my own babies and grandbabies, livin' without these here metal bars.

But it ain't work out that way. And a coupla gov'nors even tried to go and pardon me. But can't pardon a criminal in Tennessee 'less he done all his time. And I be dead 'fore that happen — 'less they can do fancy with that DNA stuff I hear 'bout. And at this point, I thinkin' that ain't likely.

I always knowed that these bars gots me wrapped up ain't s'posed to be mine. But they all the bars I gots left 'cause I done let go a the ones on my heart a long time ago.

I knowed that old woman ain't picked me outta that lineup 'cause she had some kinda grudge. She just think it be me. And I gots to admit, I spend me some time bein' real angry with her and the judge and the lawyer and all them jurors.

But I finally let go a bein' mad at 'em. Finally 'cided one prison in one lifetime be 'nough.

Now I sure glad I do that.

'Cause the way I see it, I rather be a free man in prison than a 'prisoned man who think he free.

AFTERWORD

Now that we've completed our journey together through this book, you might be looking for some profound reason as to why I wrote it. I'm still not sure that I know. I do know the idea came to me from out of the blue, and it was Jeremiah's voice I heard first. (Yes, that's proof to all my friends that I do hear voices.) I knew Maddie would die. And I knew that if I was ever going to write a story like this, I needed to write it before I ever had children. I had no idea that during my first few weeks of writing this, I would meet a wonderful man and eventually become a "bonus" mom to five beautiful children.

I discovered as I began to write about Gray and Mackenzie's pain over losing Maddie that I was able to use much of my own personal pain about not having children. That had been a deep ache in my heart for so long. Although I don't know what it is to have birthed children and lost them, I do know what it is to grieve the children I thought I would give birth to.

Another thing I know is something life has taught me: God owes me nothing. Oh, I thought for a long time that he did. I thought if I was good enough, kind enough, or did enough, he would surely make sure I got the long end of the stick at least 90 percent of the time. Now I am very aware that this isn't true. God owes me nothing. And the fact that I have anything good at all is simply because he is so exceptionally kind. In his love, he shows up with unexpected blessings, amazing friendships, beautiful opportunities. And yes, sometimes he allows inexplicable pain.

Another thing I've learned is that God will give us beautiful companions on the journeys through our pain if we are willing to open our eyes and look for them. Sometimes they will come with the wisdom of a Jeremiah. Or they'll have the persistence of a Eugenia or the steady hand of a Gray. However they come, they too are God's gift to walk with us, love us, and "go through" with us.

My prayer for you is that in the seasons where you need a Jeremiah (or a Eugenia or a Gray or an Anna), you will find him. And in the seasons where someone needs you to be a Jeremiah, that you will be him.

ACKNOWLEDGMENTS

Many thanks to my amazing Tyndale family for believing in this story with me and helping me sharpen it into what it has become: Karen, Stephanie, Babette, and Vicky.

To Anne Christian Buchanan, my fearless and detailed editor: You took my muddled mess and helped hone it into a beautiful story. Thank you for your diligent work and thoughtful insight.

To my agent, Greg Daniel: You are a gift to any story.

To Jenny Sanford: Thank you for giving me insights into what it's like to be a governor's wife and to live in a governor's mansion while raising children.

To Brenda Farris and the staff at the Nashville Rescue Mission, especially Michael Davenport, my fabulous tour guide: Thank you all for your kind hospitality to me and for the amazing work you do for our city.

To my sweet husband: Thank you for putting up with my breakdowns during deadlines, my countless words (yes, you'd think I'd be out of them by now), and my still-healing heart. You love me patiently and kindly. You are my Gray. And I thank God every day for the gift of you.

To my beautiful children: I'm glad this book is finished. And I'm glad I now know what it is to sit in a carpool line, read bedtime stories, and curl up on the sofa to watch *American Idol* with a group of kids I can call mine. You have made my life rich and full.

And to my heavenly Father: You may owe me nothing, but you have given me everything.

DISCUSSION QUESTIONS

1. Gray and Mackenzie struggle with balancing Gray's role as the governor — his job — and spending time together as a family. Have you ever experienced a similar struggle to balance work and family life? How did you handle it?
2. At first, Gray resents the fact that Mack gets a dog without talking to him. But later, Sophie saves him from his grief in some ways. Why do you think that is? In times of grief, have you had anything or anyone that was a lifeline for you?
3. On p. 140, in a moment of frustration, Jeremiah says, "I ain't never understood that 'bout God. He always doin' things that in the natural don't make a lick a sense. And in middle a all that craziness, he go and ax us to trust him." How would you respond to someone who asked you how to trust God even when he allows tragedy to come into our lives?

4. Mackenzie tells Gray that she thinks her pregnancy is their miracle, a gift from God since they've suffered so much. Do you agree with that reasoning, that God punishes and rewards us? Why or why not?

5. Even though Jeremiah doesn't want to give Mackenzie the orchid, he feels God nudging him to do so and listens. Have you ever experienced a similar "nudging," a feeling that you're supposed to do something? Did you listen? What were the results?

6. How did you feel about the description of depression as "potholes in the brain"? What are your thoughts about medication versus other methods for treating depression? How much of a role do you think Eugenia's friends play in her recovery from grief and possible depression?

7. Eugenia wonders if Mackenzie has put her grief on hold and if that will lead to postpartum depression. She reads an article that "talked about postpartum depression and how it often resulted from unresolved emotions accentuated by hormonal changes during and after pregnancy." Have you ever experienced postpartum depression, or do you know someone who has? Do you think it can result from unresolved emotions?

8. Eugenia thinks that "if there was anything she'd learned in her years of living, it was that you couldn't just close a door on grief. It would end up seeping through the cracks." How can grief work differently for different people? Can grief be controlled or delayed? What might be some effects of "closing the door" on grief?

9. Near the end of the story, Jeremiah finally convinces Eugenia that what Mackenzie needs most is tough love. Did you agree with him? Have you ever had to show tough love to someone you cared about? How did you know that's what they needed? What helped you reach out to them in that way?

10. "Strong don't mean lack a pain, Gov'nor. Strong mean livin' spite of it." Do you agree with what Jeremiah says? How have you seen this reflected in your life or the lives of those you love?

11. After Jeremiah gives Mackenzie the amaryllis, he tells Eugenia that self-pity is one of pride's "ugliest and meanest faces." What does he mean by that? Do you agree? How did you see that play out in the story?

12. Much of Mackenzie's grief is a result of resentment that she let build up — anger that her life didn't turn out as she ex-

pected, as she deserved. Reflect on your own life. Have you ever faced similar disappointments? Have you ever felt resentment against God when you expected things and didn't get them?

ABOUT THE AUTHOR

Denise Hildreth Jones has spent the last six years writing fiction that has been hailed as both "smart and witty." Her ability to express the heart of the Southern voice has led to her being featured twice in *Southern Living* and receiving the accolades of readers and reviewers alike, but it is the simple joy of writing stories that keeps them coming. Her previous books include the Savannah series, *Flies on the Butter, The Will of Wisteria, Hurricanes in Paradise,* and *Flying Solo.*

Denise makes her home in Franklin, Tennessee, with her husband, five bonus children, and two dogs. And on her days off, she will settle for a long walk or a good book and a Coca-Cola.

Visit Denise's website at www.denise hildrethjones.com.

The employees of Thorndike Press hope you have enjoyed this Large Print book. All our Thorndike, Wheeler, and Kennebec Large Print titles are designed for easy reading, and all our books are made to last. Other Thorndike Press Large Print books are available at your library, through selected bookstores, or directly from us.

For information about titles, please call:
(800) 223-1244

or visit our Web site at:
http://gale.cengage.com/thorndike

To share your comments, please write:
Publisher
Thorndike Press
10 Water St., Suite 310
Waterville, ME 04901

DISCARD